The Antaran Codex

Also by Stephen Renneberg

THE MAPPED SPACE UNIVERSE

The Mothersea
The Mothership

In Earth's Service
The Riven Stars

SF/TECHNOLOGICAL THRILLERS

The Siren Project
The Kremlin Phoenix

The Antaran Codex

Stephen Renneberg

This novel is a work of fiction. Names and characters are the product of the author's imagination, and any resemblance to actual persons, living or dead, is coincidental.

Author website
www.StephenRenneberg.com

ISBN: 978-0-9874347-9-1

Illustration © Tom Edwards
TomEdwardsDesign.com

For Elenor with love.

Mapped Space Chronology

3.4 Million Years Ago to 6000 BC

Earth's Stone Age (GCC 0).

6000 BC to 1750 AD

Pre-Industrial Civilization (GCC 1).

1750 - 2130

The rise of Planetary Industrial Civilization (GCC 2).

The First Intruder War – unknown to mankind.

The Mothership

Start of the Blockade.

The Mothersea

2130 - 2643

The spread of Interplanetary Civilization (GCC 3) throughout the Solar System.

2629

Marineris Institute of Mars (MIM) perfects the first stable Spacetime Distortion Field (the superluminal bubble).

The MIM discovery leads to the dawn of Inceptive Interstellar Civilization (GCC 4).

2615

The Solar Constitution ratified, establishing Earth Council (15 June 2615).

2644

First human ship reaches Proxima Centauri and is met by a Tau Cetin Observer.

2645

Earth Council signs the Access Treaty with the Galactic Forum.

First Probationary Period begins.

Tau Cetins provide astrographic data out to 1,200 light years from Earth (*Mapped Space*) and 100 kilograms of novarium (Nv, Element 147) to power human starships.

2646 - 3020

Human Civilization expands rapidly throughout Mapped Space.

Continual Access Treaty infringements delay mankind's acceptance into the Galactic Forum.

3021

Dr. Anton Krenholtz discovers Spacetime Field Modulation.

Krenholtz Breakthrough enables transition to Incipient Interstellar Civilization (GCC 5).

3021 - 3154

Mass migration dramatically increases human colonial populations.

3154

Human religious fanatics, opposed to interstellar expansion, attack the Mataron Homeworld.

Tau Cetin Observers prevent the Mataron Fleet from destroying Earth.

3155

Galactic Forum suspends human interstellar access rights for 1,000 years (the Embargo).

3155 - 3158

Tau Cetin ships convert human supplies of novarium held in Earth stockpiles and within ship energy plants to inert matter (as human ships landed at habitable planets).

3155 - 4155

Human contact with other interstellar civilizations ends.

Many human outposts beyond the Solar System collapse.

4126

Earth Navy established by the Democratic Union to police mankind when Embargo is lifted.

Earth Council assumes control of Earth Navy.

4138

Earth Intelligence Service (EIS) established by the Earth Council.

4155

The Embargo ends.

The Access Treaty is reactivated, permitting human interstellar travel to resume.

The second 500 year Probationary Period begins.

4155 - 4267

Earth re-establishes contact with its surviving colonies.

4281

Earth Council issues Sanctioned Worlds Decree, protecting collapsed human societies.

4310

The Beneficial Society of Traders established to manage interstellar trade.

4498

Quantum Instability Neutralization discovered (much earlier than galactic powers expected).

Mankind becomes Emergent Civilization (GCC 6).

The golden age of human interstellar trade begins.

4605

The Vintari Incident.

The Antaran Codex

4606

The Battle of Tresik Prime.

End of the Blockade.

In Earth's Service

4607

The Nan Chen Disaster.

The Xil Asseveration.

The Riven Stars

Notes:

GCC: Galactic Civilization Classification system.

Asseveration: A solemn or emphatic declaration.

Chapter One : Vulpecula NP-28697

Navigation Point
Non System Space
Outer Vulpecula Region
1,068 light years from Sol
Autonomous Beacons

"*Silver Lining*, power down your engines and prepare to be boarded!" A stern Democratic Union voice ordered the moment we unbubbled and began maneuvering for the final run to Macaulay Station. "Do not attempt to re-engage your star drive, or you will be fired upon!"

It was the one thing every freighter pilot dreaded, being jumped after stopping for a course correction. While we were bubbled and travelling faster than the speed of light, we were blind, but safe. Once we dropped to flat space however, with sensors retracted and the autonav crunching numbers for the next leg, we were a sitting duck. Sensors were always stowed inside the hull during superluminal flight to protect them from bubble heat, giving a well positioned raider the opportunity for a knockout blow while their victim was still blind.

"Are they showing a transponder?" I asked,

knowing we only had seconds to decide whether to run or fight.

Jase Logan, my twenty six year old copilot, watched the curved display in front of his acceleration couch anxiously, waiting for our sensors to deploy through the *Lining's* windowless hull. At times like these, Jase was all business. He was blonde, brash, quick to anger, yet he had the makings of a fine pilot in spite of an oversized reckless streak. He'd been born on Oresund and, like most Ories, had been well on his way to becoming a mercenary before I knocked some sense into him a few years back and put him to work. When the automated transponder signal appeared on his display, he relaxed. "It's the *Nassau*!"

This was Raven space and transponders could be faked, although I'd never heard of the local Pirate Brotherhood pretending to be Earth Navy. That would have elevated them up the navy's kill-on-sight list, something most Raven commanders wouldn't risk.

"Does the energy signature match?"

Jase watched his display intently as we scanned the approaching ship. Ravens had many tricks, but faking E-plant emissions wasn't one of them. "It's definitely her. She's eight thousand clicks out and closing, weapons hot."

Our optical sensors locked into place and began feeding real time imagery to the flight deck's wrap around view screen. A dull gray frigate appeared, dead ahead and coming in fast. Her hull bristled with sensors and shield emitters, while spaced along her topside were four heavy guns in armored turrets. The ENS *Nassau* was the long, unforgiving arm of Earth law with enough firepower to blast any human ship or outpost that threatened to violate the galaxy spanning Access Treaty -– ensuring none did.

"What's she doing out here?" I wondered aloud.

The navy regularly inspected ships for contraband, although the trek to Macaulay Station was no prime trade route. Human ships passed this way once every three or four weeks, hardly justifying sending such an expensive piece of hardware out snooping around boonies space. If they knew we were smuggling, it would take an inspection team equipped with nanometric scanners to find our shielded compartment, equipment frigates didn't carry. Even so, we were only carrying pleasure-grams for the miners on Macaulay. Nothing too kinky or weird, just enough to help lonely isolated men relieve their boredom. The p-grams were borderline illegal, not enough to get the *Lining* impounded, just slapped with a hefty fine that would make this run a loss maker.

I flicked on the ship-to-ship communicator. "Hi *Nassau*. Glad to see you're out here keeping the space lanes safe. *Silver Lining* standing to." The spit-and-polish navy types would be irritated by my sloppy comms discipline, but I wanted them thinking I had nothing to hide and no understanding of navy protocols.

The frigate rolled crisply, bow over stern, aimed its four maneuvering engines towards us and began decelerating. The navy weren't exactly a welcome sight, but they were better than Ravens who would have stolen our cargo and left us dead in space without a second thought. Nevertheless, the navy made all traders nervous, mostly because every one of us smuggled a little, just to make ends meet.

"She's heading for the port lock," Jase said as he tracked the *Nassau's* trajectory. "You want me to meet them, Skipper?"

"No, I'll do it."

"You better warn Izin."

Izin was my engineer and a tamph – a terrestrial amphibian. Physically incapable of human speech, he relied on a vocalizer to produce human sounds. A small number of his kind had been marooned on Earth in the twenty first century – over two and a half thousand years ago – shipwrecked survivors of the Intruder War, a conflict that had raged across a third of the galaxy long before mankind was ever aware of such things. Izin's ancestors had started the war, but fortunately for us – and everyone else – they'd been defeated. The cluster of stars they called home had been under close blockade ever since by a fleet millions of years more advanced than any Earth Navy ship. Quite simply, the Galactic Forum – the nearest thing the Milky Way had to a governing body – considered the Intruder Civilization too dangerous ever to be let loose on the universe again.

The only tamphs not under blockade lived on Earth, now uncomfortably a part of Human Civilization where, limited to mankind's relatively rudimentary level of technology, they posed no risk to the rest of the galaxy. They stood far ahead of us on the evolutionary ladder and could have become the apex species on Earth if they'd arrived a century earlier. Instead, the descendants of the shipwrecked survivors had formed a small, remote enclave north of Australia known as Tamph City, technically an autonomous region within the Democratic Union. Tamphs were tolerated, but viewed with suspicion due to their reputation for a kind of mild mannered violence few humans understood. They could slit your throat before you even knew they were there, but if they gave you their word, they'd honor it to the grave. At least, the males would. The females were treacherous to a degree impossible for humans to understand.

Most humans didn't realize that in the highly matriarchical tamph culture it was the females who wielded the power and started the wars, not the males. That's why the females lived secluded, powerless lives in Tamph City, doing little more than breeding within agreed population limits, and why they were never allowed to leave Earth – at the polite insistence of the Tau Cetins. The TCs were the leading Orion Arm civilization and the only Forum Observer species in our part of the galaxy. Observers weren't exactly the law, but over millions of years they'd earned the respect and trust of other Forum members and now held a privileged position interpreting Galactic Law and advising the Forum membership. Observer species also possessed the most advanced technology and wielded the greatest military power in the galaxy, which for humanity meant we ignored their counsel at our peril.

Fortunately, Izin was male and we had an understanding. He served aboard my ship with complete freedom, providing he carried out his duty diligently and didn't kill anyone without my permission. So far, he'd never given me cause to doubt him.

I tapped the intercom. "Izin, you there?"

"Yes, Captain."

"The navy's coming aboard. Stay out of sight until they're gone."

"As you wish, Captain," he replied. Because his voice was synthesized, it was always difficult to tell how he felt, although sometimes his choice of words hinted at his emotional state.

"Plot the course to Macaulay," I said to Jase as I slipped off my acceleration couch. "I want to get out of here as soon as the navy lets us go."

"You got it, Skipper."

By the time I reached the port hatch, the *Nassau* had mated airlocks and was equalizing pressure. Presently, the inner hatch swung open and a hulking Union Regular Army Colonel wearing a dress dark blue uniform with an abundance of gold braid stepped through, ducking his square head under the hatch rim.

"Are you Kade?" he asked brusquely. "Sirius Kade?"

"Yeah," I replied, glancing into the airlock, looking for the scanning team. "Are you doing this alone?"

"This is no inspection. You're to come aboard the *Nassau*."

"Says who?" Inspections were one thing – I was bound to submit to those by law or the *Nassau* could legitimately blast us into our constituent atoms – but being taken aboard a navy ship without charge was illegal, not that legal niceties counted for much out here.

"I'm not at liberty to say." He motioned towards the airlock and waited. "I'm authorized to use force if you resist."

He was physically larger than me, obviously modded for strength. I knew from experience the genetic engineering they subjected URA troopers too included an unhealthy dose of brute courage, but I was ultra-reflexed, not that he would have any idea what that meant. My enhanced speed could turn this mountain of muscle into an unconscious lump of meat faster than he could blink, but then I'd soon have ten assault troopers pounding me into the bulkheads in retaliation. After I regained consciousness, I'd have to explain how I took out a URA Colonel unarmed – not something I could do.

"Seeing as you asked so nicely," I said, stepping into the airlock, followed by the Colonel. "You want to tell me what this is about?"

"Nope," the Colonel replied, staring straight ahead.

"Have I got a docking ticket outstanding? Owe some back taxes?" I persisted, but the demeanor of the URA officer remained impenetrable.

A pair of dark blue uniformed troopers saluted the Colonel as we stepped out of the airlock, then subjected me to the usual probing and scanning civilians endured before being allowed to enter a navy ship. I expected the standard retinal, alpha wave and DNA scans, but they made me strip, then subjected me to a full biomap – something I hadn't had to endure in eight years.

That's when I knew something serious was up.

There were ways of faking identities, of modifying appearances, even of tricking all the common signature scans, but there was no known way to fabricate a perfect copy of a human, although we could never rule out the possibility alien-tech could do it. A biomap was the only truly, incorruptible means of verifying an identify, which was why b-maps were so carefully guarded and so rarely used. Before I'd stepped aboard the *Nassau,* I'd have sworn the only validated version of my b-map was locked away in a high security facility over a thousand light years away on Earth.

So how did these muscle bound storm troopers get a copy?

The troopers finished their body scan and motioned for me to dress while they ran a full pattern check. By the time I was pulling on my dark brown flight jacket, my face appeared on a display beside their equipment: unkempt brown hair, green eyes, sharp cheek bones and a slightly bent nose. The nose used to be straight, but some lab rat on Earth had decided more than twenty years ago that giving it a slight twist would help disguise the radical genetic engineering I'd been subjected to. By the time I no longer needed a disguise, I'd grown used to the crooked nose and decided to keep it.

"It's him," one of the troopers said.

The Colonel nodded for me to follow him through cramped metal corridors to a briefing room which I knew from experience adjoined the ship's Tactical Warfare Center. Without a word, the Colonel left me alone listening to the hum of the ship. Presently, a hatch opened giving me a glimpse of the crowded TWC beyond. It was just as I remembered, filled with screens displaying every detectable object within reach of the ship's sophisticated sensors and manned by officers wearing interactive suits that networked them into the ship's real time data stream.

The view of the TWC was suddenly blocked by a statuesque woman with dark brown skin, finely sculpted features and penetrating eyes. Lena Voss wore a dark, well tailored civilian suit with a colorful scarf around her neck and small diamond earrings, although no wedding ring. I hadn't seen her in a long time, not since I'd left the service. Not surprisingly, she'd hardly aged a day, but then neither had I. My chronological age was forty six, while she was closer to seventy, yet neither of us looked a day over thirty. Longevity was a side effect of the genetic reengineering we'd both been subjected to, and though the EIS would never admit it, keeping us alive longer gave them a better return on their investment.

"You're late," Lena said, motioning me to a seat at the metallic conference table.

"I didn't know we had an appointment."

"Your flight plan out of Indrax said you'd be hopping this navpoint two days ago."

"If you'd told me we were meeting, I'd have got here sooner."

"If I'd told you, you wouldn't have come."

"Now you'll never know."

I'd lodged that flight plan before Jase had ended up in jail after a drunken bar fight. It was an unfortunate case of a gas miner's wife not being completely truthful about her marital status with my oversexed copilot. Jase had spent two days on ice while I bribed various officials to get him released. The bribe was coming out of his cut, of course, as were the miner's medical bills. For Lena to have known my intentions, her people must have been watching me and used a fast ship to report my flight plan.

She slipped into a chair while I remained defiantly standing. "Sit down, Sirius."

Whatever she was after was important enough to commandeer a navy frigate to meet me where no one would know I'd had contact with her or the navy. Giving me a choice was clearly not part of her plan, so I took my seat. She leaned forward slowly, giving me her spooky psionic-prober look and reached into the depths of my mind, assessing if I was still up to it. It wasn't a natural ability, it was engineered, but you needed genuine aptitude for the modding – something very few humans had.

I stared into her large brown eyes, feeling nothing,

keeping my emotions calm to make her job easier and get the psychic dissection over with as fast as possible. While we were both genetically modified, it was in our specialties that we differed. She'd gone mega-psi, a very rare choice that involved getting your brain rewired for transcendent mental powers. Most people went eye-hand and became weapons experts and field agents. A few – like me – went ultra-reflex, ideal for deep cover work because even without weapons, you were always armed and deadly.

If your modding took and you were top one percent, you were threaded – implanted from head to toe with bionetic filaments. The catch was you had to volunteer without knowing what you were volunteering for. It had to be that way to preserve the secrecy. You were given a spiel about joining an elite program, about doing your duty and serving in a way very few humans ever could, but you never really knew what you were getting into. After the implant surgery, months of physical rehabilitation followed, during which time they trained your mind to blend with the threading, to use its sensory inputs and to allow it to guide you instantly and without hesitation.

While I was purpose built for deep cover work, the mega-psi types like Lena became probers, able to extract secrets telepathically. A few probers became subverters, gaining the ability to persuade people to work for the Earth Intelligence Service – even against their will – while the really high functioning evolutionary freaks became breakers. Supposedly, a breaker could shatter a target's sanity with a thought, but they were rare – exceedingly rare. The rumor was there were only four, but you never knew who they were. Lena claimed to be a subverter not a breaker, although I had my suspicions. Her EIS security clearance was inexplicably high, but it was not something we ever discussed.

Presently, she drew a deep breath and relaxed, giving me an approving look. I guessed that meant I'd passed.

"Does the navy know who you are?" I asked.

"They know I'm in charge. That's all they need to know."

The entire crew would be speculating that an Earth Intelligence Service officer was aboard. The EIS were the only people who could give the navy orders and EIS officers were always civilians, which made it easy for navy crews to identify them, although such whispers were never discussed outside the ship. It had been drilled into the military relentlessly that their highest duty was the preservation of secrecy, even before the safety of the ship.

It was an essential, mutually beneficial partnership. The EIS investigated, infiltrated, sometimes eliminated, and if necessary, called in the Earth Navy to enforce. Mercy was never a factor.

"Do they know who I am, or why I'm here?"

"The crew knows nothing, not even the captain."

I nodded towards the Tactical Warfare Center beyond the hatch. "They've seen my ship."

"There'll be no record of the *Nassau* intercepting your vessel, or even coming to this location, and the officers who scanned your ship will say nothing."

No leaks? That could mean only one thing. "It's an all Union crew?"

Lena nodded.

That explained a lot. The navy might have been under the control of Earth Council, which represented the four distinct Earth civilizations, but the reality was the Democratic Union, who paid most of the costs, didn't fully trust its three 'allies'. When the EIS or the Union wanted something done without their three partners knowing about it, they used one of the few ships secretly crewed by only Union citizens. For Lena to have commandeered one of those ships meant her mission was top tier.

"That explains the URA's presence." The

Democratic Union's Regular Army provided combat forces when required, but the navy normally handled its own security. The only reason Lena had brought URA troopers with her was because their genetic engineering made them almost unbreakable.

"I couldn't trust your biomap to anyone else. The colonel is the only person who knows your name, and no one will ever get anything out of him. Only I know you used to be EIS."

Everyone sworn to secrecy, just like old times. "Are you going to subvert me, to force me back in?"

"No. You're going to volunteer."

"Am I?" I laughed. "Do I look crazy to you?" I'd had fourteen years of sneaking around in the shadows, of hunting down and eradicating mankind's maddest. That was enough. I'd left the service for the freedom I'd had growing up on my father's ship, when my brother and I had learnt from the best, before we'd gone our very different ways. I'd come out here hoping for a chance to find my brother, before the navy killed him, but that had become a forlorn hope. No one knew where he was, not even the EIS. I may have lost him, but I'd found my way, and I liked it. "I've got a life now, a real life."

"That's why you're so valuable to us. To me. You may not be on the payroll any more, Sirius, but I just confirmed you're as committed as ever."

"Maybe your spooky radar's a little off, Lena, because I don't feel like I belong to you or the service anymore."

"It's not about the service. If you found someone about to violate the Access Treaty and put at risk our entire civilization, would you allow it? Or would you eliminate the risk?"

"That sounds like a subverter question."

"Not at all."

"You forget, I've seen you work."

"I forget nothing, ever," she said meaningfully, reminding me that eidetic memory was an integral part of mega-psi reengineering. "And I'm not subverting you. Just answer the question honestly."

"I'm a creature of habit," I said, avoiding and answering the question at the same time.

She smiled, already certain from her probing that I wouldn't hesitate. "You don't get recruited unless that's true."

"So why me? You have lots of people out here. Good people."

"We do, but none like you. You're known out here as a trader, a businessman, maybe even a smuggler. Sirius Kade, captain of the *Silver Lining*, and a man with a foot on both sides of the law. You have a reputation and access to people we can't approach without raising suspicion. Your father was a trader. You and your brother grew up on his ship. You're one of them, one of the people out here – even though we both know you're not."

"They hate my brother. That's got to count against me." I hadn't seen him in twenty years, didn't even know if he was alive or dead, but I knew people wondered if we were the same.

"They fear your brother, but he's part of your cover. One very bad brother, one . . . not so bad brother, and a father many respected before he was killed. Your 'real life', as you call it, is the best kind of cover for a deep cover agent."

"And there's the problem. What you do, what we did, that's the past. There's no room in my life for that anymore."

"Consider it a contract – a well paying contract. We really don't mind treating you like a mercenary. We only care about results. You know that."

"And of course, money is no object."

She grinned. "Pick a number, as high as you like."

Damn, she really was desperate. "It's that serious?"

"That's why we need you. We need someone who is believable and who can do what's required."

If the Earth Intelligence Service was writing blank checks, then it was the real deal – an Access Treaty violation. The whole purpose for the existence of the EIS and the navy was to ensure there were no more Treaty violations, ensuring nothing would stop Human Civilization's second attempt to gain Forum membership – what amounted to Galactic Citizenship. It was a near impossible job with the scum of mankind scattered across several thousand light years, far from the watchful eyes of the four Earth collective-governments. They had formed out of the old nation states of Earth along cultural and philosophical grounds and still wielded most of humanity's economic and military power. Individually, they were each larger than most off world colonies combined and, as the Earth Council, they spoke for Human Civilization. Even though billions of humans had spread through Mapped Space, the vast majority of mankind still lived on Earth. It was why our ancient homeworld continued to call the shots and would do so for a long time to come.

The navy and the EIS – both created by the Earth Council – were the only truly unified expressions of mankind's will, of Earth's will. Both organizations were dominated by the Democratic Union, the largest of Earth's great power blocs spanning Europe, the Americas, Australasia and parts of east Asia. I was born in Mawson City, Antarctica, which made me a Union citizen even though I'd spent less than three years of my life on Earth. That birthright put me on the most trusted list, while Lena's psionic powers elevated me to the top.

She waited for my answer, fixing me with a perceptive gaze that made me feel as if she was boring into my soul.

I sighed. "OK." Simple as that. There were no contracts to sign, no hedging my bets, no way out. She was desperate and I was back in, for one last mission.

A hint of relief appeared on her face, revealing she hadn't been as confident that I'd help her as she'd seemed.

"My crew can't know?"

"Absolutely not," she said, leaning towards me. "Neither can the girl."

There was no female member of my crew, but I knew who she meant. "She knows nothing about my past."

"You never used to have a weakness, Sirius," Lena said. "You do now."

"Did your probing tell you that?"

She nodded. "She's all over your psyche like a flashing light."

"She's not my only weakness. I also can't swim," I added lightly.

"Good thing there's no swimming on this mission," Lena said. "Suppose she gets in the way?"

"Marie's over a hundred light years away. She won't be a factor." Marie Dulon had taken her ship to the Kazaris Belt to extract as many credits as she could from a bunch of hard working miners. She wouldn't be back for weeks.

"I hope you're right," Lena said doubtfully.

"What about my threading?" The bionetic technology implanted throughout my body had been deactivated the day I left the service. They couldn't reverse the genetic engineering, because the human body can only stand so much modding, but the implanted tech was different. They switched it off and locked it down the day I left. I'd missed it at first, but as the years passed, I'd almost forgotten what I'd lost.

"You'll need it."

"So how do we do this?"

Lena held out her hand.

"That simple?"

She nodded.

For a moment, I wondered if I really wanted my senses to be boosted again, to have my mind flooded with a situational awareness as far beyond the norm as sight was from blindness. It had taken me a long time to get used to not having it, and now I'd have it back – at least for a while. When the mission was over, I'd have to readjust to losing it all over again, but it was already too late to pull out, so I took her hand. A mere touch was enough to connect our nerve endings and allow her active tech to talk to my long dormant threading. In the blink of an eye, she passed a code through my nervous system into the bionetic threads running through every bone in my body, filaments that because of their biological nature were undetectable to any known human science. Suddenly, signals I'd not seen in eight years appeared in my mind, jarring me back into a long lost sensory reality, telling me about my environment – what was in it, who was in it – information I'd never have noticed without the threading.

I'd barely begun to process the new awareness when a flood of information poured from Lena's threading to mine. When I left the service, my bionetic memory had been wiped clean. Now she gave it all back to me, updated for the years I'd been away; DNA patterns for every known human criminal and for thousands of alien species; EIS and navy authorization codes; technical specs on all kinds of useful and nasty devices; contact and informant lists; recognition signals for every EIS agent and station; and diplomatic codes all the way to ambassadorial level for hailing alien ships and even Galactic Forum Observers.

Threading was one of mankind's most closely guarded secrets, designed to be indistinguishable from normal human DNA so even alien-tech scanners couldn't detect it. I could wipe it clean with a single thought and if I died, automatic safeguards would purge my bionetic memory before its data could ever be read. Even the Matarons, our one truly committed adversary, seemed unaware of our bionetics. They were so far ahead of us, they could break through any tech defense we had – and frequently did – but they were also complacent in their superiority. The EIS had waged a covert war against them for centuries, adopting unconventional methods to hide our innermost secrets. Of course, the Matarons might know everything and were just letting us think we had secrets. There really was no way to know.

When the data transfer finished, Lena let my hand go and studied me with genuine concern. “Are you OK?”

I breathed slowly, taking time to integrate my thoughts with the swirling array of threaded inputs assaulting my mind. “Yeah, just like bouncing off bulkheads in zero gravity. You never forget how.”

“Are you ready for the mission briefing?”

I felt oddly exhilarated at the threading input flowing seamlessly through my mind. It was something I thought I’d never experience again, something I’d convinced myself I never wanted, but now that I was active again, I felt strangely whole.

“I’m ready.”

Chapter Two : Hades City

Subterranean Habitat
Star HAT-P-5
Outer Lyra Region
0.91 Earth Normal Gravity
1,105 light years from Sol
1.2 million inhabitants

After we dropped the p-grams and supplies at Macaulay Station, we backtracked to Indrax – a small Indian Republic trade hub – and picked up deliveries for Hades City. The completion bonuses barely covered the cost of the flight, but they gave me a reason to go to Hades where Lena's fish was waiting to be hooked.

Hades moon was the largest of seven natural satellites and was tidally locked to a hot Jupiter, a gas giant orbiting close and fast to its star. The approach was tricky, requiring a fast descent into the giant planet's shadow to avoid getting fried by the star's plasma wind, while timing our run to intercept the moon as it orbited around to the giant planet's dark side. Scary anytime, but with the *Lining's* military grade bleeder shield, we were better protected than most.

There were three ships ahead of us when we arrived, orbiting a safe distance out from the star. Two made it down first time, while the third had to go around for a second attempt. When our turn came, I rolled the *Silver Lining* into the guide beam and throttled up. Our flight deck's curved view screen wrapped around us on three sides, giving the impression we floated in space above the star's boiling surface. With no windows anywhere in the hull, the optical sensors were our eyes, automatically filtering the star's blinding light down to tolerable levels. A digital overlay across the center of the screen showed our position in the guide beam and updated critical parameters as we dived towards the star.

Below us, drifting like a tiny dot above an ocean of superheated plasma was the gas giant. It appeared as an insignificant blue fleck against the star's immensity, growing rapidly in size as we followed the guide beam down and our shield's temperature soared. It was a race to reach cover before solar heat overloaded the shield, exposing our hull to the star's full ferocity.

"The shield's bleeding at sixty-two percent," Jase reported tensely, clearly more worried about the approach than I was. He was usually full of bravado and humor, but with the big G-type so close, he was unusually on edge. "It sure is hot out there!"

"Nervous?" I asked, letting him know I enjoyed seeing him squirm.

Jase stiffened. "Only of your flying!"

I grinned. "You're smarter than you look!"

He didn't know this wasn't my first landing at Hades and I wasn't about to spoil the fun by telling him. I'd spent the last few days feeding him horror stories – all true – of catastrophic landing attempts on the hot Jupiter's moon, neglecting to mention they were all before Earth engineers had installed new landing control systems. The canyon floor beyond the city doors was littered with wrecks, all hundreds of years old, testimony to poor judgment and even poorer conditions.

Soon, the gas giant began to fill our screen, hiding us in its shadow and allowing the *Lining's* shield temperature to stabilize. Several tiny black marbles floated above the planet, the largest of which was the near-Earth sized Hades Moon. It quickly swelled to a spherical airless world strewn with jagged mountains, ancient craters and deeply shadowed valleys, all seared black by the star's fiery breath.

When we entered the moon's gravity, the autonav rolled the ship and slammed on the brakes while I gently feathered the engines to imply they were overdue a maintenance cycle or two. We could have gone in faster but it never paid to advertise, especially as Raven spotters were everywhere. If they targeted us, I didn't want them knowing what the *Lining* was capable of until our lives depended on it.

Soon the glow of our engines lit up the blackened landscape, casting sharp shadows across the surface, then we thrust vectored hard into the long, straight canyon that led to the city's entrance.

"I'm reading closed doors," Jase announced.

"I was afraid of that," I said, feigning apprehension. "The door guy's a known stim-head."

"There's a door guy?" Jase asked, wondering why the city's outer doors were manually operated. "And he's a stim-head?"

"He must be psycho-dreaming again. I hope he doesn't forget to push the button."

"What button?"

When I saw the stunned look on his face, I chuckled, knowing the doors would snap open automatically moments before we were pulled down into the vertical docking shaft.

"Very funny," Jase said, realizing I was joking.

Hades City had been doing this for over fifteen hundred years. A thousand of those years had been during the Embargo, when mankind had lost its interstellar access rights, and Hades handled only their own local interplanetary craft. Like every other human settlement, Hades City had been forced to survive for ten centuries, cut off and alone, because a group of thirty-second century religious fanatics – opposed to contact with non-humans – had attacked the xenophobic Matarons. At a stroke, the fanatics not only created a formidable enemy who would accept no apology, but they set our civilization back a millennium.

The Galactic Forum had had no choice but to impose the Embargo. The Access Treaty was the basis of Galactic Law and we couldn't avoid its first and most important principle, the Responsibility Principle: *that every species is responsible for the acts of all its members*.

Responsibility was not just for law abiding citizens, but for every member of the species – no exceptions, no excuses.

For most species it wasn't a problem. For mankind it was a nightmare, because we had a special genius for producing crazies who thought they knew better than the rest of us. The Embargo had been intended to give us time to learn to govern ourselves, while also placating the enraged Matarons. Now that we had only fifty years to run on our second five hundred year probation, no-one – not even pirates and criminals who obeyed no other law – dared risk a second violation, because the next Embargo would be ten times longer than the first.

No sane human dared contemplate what ten thousand years of isolation would mean, yet there were still a few lunatics who desired nothing more than a second, vastly longer Embargo. It was why no mercy was shown to any who might put at risk mankind's interstellar freedom.

When we were ten clicks out, we reached the charcoal black graded flyway with its single line of lights leading to the city doors. Ragged cliffs raced past on either side as we skimmed fifty meters above the ground on thrusters and momentum alone.

"*Silver Lining*, your approach is within safe operating limits," Hades Control informed us reassuringly.

"That's what he thinks!" Jase said, irritated by my feathering of the engines.

"At least they're not waving us off," I replied lightly, knowing my flying had been deliberately borderline incompetent. If prying eyes were watching, they'd underestimate me as much as my ship.

The autonav threw a sensor read of the catcher's mitt onto the screen. It was a circular net of magnetic fields strung between the canyon's cliff walls. With the mitt looming large ahead of us, I let the ship have its way. At the last moment, the *Lining* rolled until our maneuvering engines were pointing at the magnetic field, then she threw hard G's at our inertial field, killing our velocity. For a moment we hung motionless, almost dead center of the mitt's sweet spot above two massive horizontal slabs of bleached white armor set into the canyon's burnt floor. The enormous doors shielded an entrance wide enough to accommodate the largest ships and made the *Silver Lining* look like an insect by comparison.

The City's docking system snatched us out of the vacuum and hurled us at the doors like a feather. The white armor slabs raced toward us, then a moment before we struck, they snapped apart just enough to let us in. We plunged down into a deep vertical shaft hundreds of meters across as the doors crashed together above us with enough force to cut a ship in half. Protected from the star's heat, our shield cooled rapidly as a conveyor of docking fields carried us down past rock walls illuminated by two opposing rows of white lights. The autonav sensed the magnetic fields now enveloping the ship and cut power to the engines and thrusters, automatically passing responsibility for ship safety to the spaceport's docking system.

"*Silver Lining* to Hades Control," I said, "we are

engine stopped and mag-locked. She's all yours."

"Hades Control to *Silver Lining*, confirmed. We have maneuvering responsibility."

Verbal confirmations hadn't been needed since the trickle of new Earth-tech had become a flood after contact had been restored centuries ago, but old habits die hard, especially those drummed into you from age four by a hard headed old man determined to turn his sons into first class pilots. Even though I trusted the tech, I still felt uncomfortable unless I heard the controller's confirmation.

Five kilometers beneath the surface was the spaceport's central cavern. It was connected to four large subterranean hangars by horizontal tunnels equally spaced like spokes on a wheel. The docking fields carried us into one of the spokes, past black rock walls punctuated by horizontal windows, to a well lit cavern and a berth that could have accommodated a much larger ship. Our landing struts lowered automatically, then the docking field dissipated and a tubular pressure bridge extended from the cavern wall, sealing itself over our starboard airlock.

I had to admit, the Hades moon moles had done a good job from the moment they'd plucked us out of the sky above their doors until they'd tucked us into our berth. Not bad for a free city over eleven hundred light years from Earth.

"Hades Control to *Silver Lining*, you are locked and docked."

"Thanks Hades Control," I said with just the right amount of relief.

"Log your manifest with the Port Authority before disembarking. Payment of docking fees and taxes is required before transferring personnel or cargo. Failure to make all payments in full will result in your cargo and ship being impounded until all debts are paid. Acknowledge this contract."

Being trapped for a thousand years in one of the

least hospitable systems humans inhabited had made the Hadians good at their job, but somewhat lacking in the social graces. "Contract acknowledged."

"Hades City is a lawful enterprise complying with all Earth Council directives. As such, infringements of the Access Treaty are punishable by death," the Controller added in a bored monotone, obviously a message he repeated to every arriving ship. It was a warning I'd heard many times in many systems – and they all meant it. The Hadians took their Treaty obligations seriously because, in spite of their miserable location, they were prospering.

After the Embargo had been lifted four hundred and fifty years ago, it had taken nearly one hundred and twenty years for Earth to discover Hades City had survived. Many similar outposts had not. Once Hades was back on the map, trade resumed and a trickle of new Earth-tech began to reach them. Within a decade, the navy sent engineers out to set up a repair base for new-gen starships, turning Hades City into a key logistical center at the outer edge of human settlement. Hades remained a free city, but a welcoming port to Earth Navy ships operating far from home. Once the navy came to stay, the money flowed – lots of money. Little wonder they executed anyone who threatened their lifeline to the rest of humanity.

Mankind had learned the hard way that access to interstellar space was a privilege not a right, a privilege that could be revoked in the blink of an eye.

I cut power to the shield, causing it to collapse rather than gradually de-energize. Anyone watching would believe the *Lining's* shield had barely survived the extreme heat outside, concluding we were equipped with an ablative shield, rather than the much tougher bleeder type.

Jase threw me a sideways glance. "You'll upset Izin doing that."

I smiled mischievously as Izin's voice sounded

through the intercom.

"Captain, I remind you there are maintenance protocols for shield deactivation."

"Thanks Izin, must have slipped my mind." He was a smart little tamph and would know I was lying.

"I know you like playing games, Skipper," Jase said, "but I think you're a little paranoid."

"Paranoid . . . cautious – no difference. I'm still alive. That's what counts."

Out here, low life informants made a healthy living selling out traders to anyone with a few credits and an armed ship. In the Outer Lyra region, it was to the Ravens, although there were other Brotherhoods, each with their own territory, all loosely affiliated. I preferred making their job as hard as possible, which was why I kept my aces hidden and my weapons ready.

A sultry, over-sexed female voice sounded over the intercom. "Hello Captain. I'm pleased to inform you that engine shut down is now complete. You'll also be delighted to know, the energy plant will be dormant in seven minutes."

"What was that?" Jase asked incredulously.

"Tamph humor?" I suggested before activating the intercom. "Thanks Izin. Ah . . . not sure about the new vocalizer settings."

Again, the ridiculously sexy female voice sounded on the flight deck. "My research indicated you boys would find this tonal combination stimulating, even arousing."

I shut off the intercom a moment. "I swear, he's trying to get even with me for crashing the shield." The voice might have been stimulating coming from a female *Homo sapien*, but as we knew it was coming from a one point two meter high amphibian with an oversized head, large bulbous eyes and small triangular teeth, it was simply unnerving. "We liked your voice the way it was, thanks."

"As you wish, Captain," Izin replied in his standard

male voice.

"Log the cargo," I said to Jase as I climbed out of my couch. We were carrying data dumps to synchronize the city's update level and one of the vacuum-radiation-sealed containers we were towing was full of supplies for Hades. "I'm going into the city to see what contracts are open."

"No problem, Skipper," he said without looking up. He was hurrying through his post-flight check list with a degree of concentration that told me he was keen to go moonside for a little recreation.

"And try not to get arrested this time."

Jase gave me a wounded look. "Who me?"

"Any fines come out of your cut."

Jase raised his hands innocently, "Only wine, women and song, I promise. No fights this time."

"That's what you said last time!" Doubting his sincerity, I headed for the airlock.

It was a short walk through the pressure bridge to our berth's gate. It DNA scanned my hand before letting me into the spaceport, where to my surprise, I found the air didn't have the stale metallic smell I remembered – a sure sign they'd upgraded their environmental systems since my last visit. Powered walkways carried many human and a few non-human passengers between the terminal and the ships, giving me an opportunity to practice using my threading's sensors.

The bionetic filaments read and amplified impulses passing through my nervous system that normally went unnoticed by the human brain. The threading then selected and displayed information it decided I needed to know, or in answer to my queries. The sensory amplification was augmented by microscopic, biological machines designed to be indistinguishable from human bio-matter. The most useful of these was my DNA sniffer. Providing I had line of sight, the sniffer could sense DNA sequences at short range, enough to identify a contact in a large room or on the street.

The sniffer scanned every person I passed, checking their DNA codes against a database of the Orion Arm's most wanted. Not surprisingly, I got a hit every few minutes. Hades City's distance from Earth made it an ideal hiding place for humans on the run. To most alien law enforcement agencies, it was an obscure human backwater, which was why there was also a disproportionately high number of unsavory non-humans in the city.

Little did they know how easily they could be discovered, irrespective of disguises or appearance altering surgery. The hits ranged from petty criminals, escaped prisoners and missing persons to a few hard cases that the local Unified Police Force detachment would have locked away in their deepest, darkest dungeon – if they'd known they were here. The non-human criminals were all known Orion Arm species whose DNA codes had been passed to UniPol by their representative governments. Handing fleeing criminals to our neighbors was a good way to build trust, but keeping bionetic technology a secret was more important than making friends, so I let the Orion Arm's mad and bad walk free.

The terminal was lined with screens listing every ship docked and their current status. There were personal data nodes everywhere for travelers to make enquiries or reservations, or contact ships directly. UniPol was supposed to watch all such communications on every world, but Hades City suffered from profound blindness where money making activities were concerned. It was a common trait among remote outposts.

It was why a precondition of renewing contact with Earth had been the merging of local police forces into UniPol. Integrating civil law enforcement into a single collective effort was officially intended to ensure local criminals didn't commit Treaty violations and unofficially designed to ensure Earth's enlightened interpretation of law was spread to every corner of

Human Civilization. Local governments retained nominal influence over their police forces, but the direct link to Earth – and to the EIS – quickly became more important. Joining UniPol was a sign of commitment to working within the Access Treaty, bringing with it huge benefits, while refusal meant continued isolation from the rest of humanity. Very few refused. In time, every major center became committed to UniPol. Only at the most remote stations, far from oversight, was there an opportunity to bend the rules, and Hades City was about as remote as it got.

Outside the spaceport, I hopped a silver commuter tube to the central commercial cavern, the largest in the city. It was a well lit expanse filled with a mix of historic carved stone and shining metal and glass spires surrounded by genuine Earth transplanted trees and flowers. Hades had started out as an uninhabited robot mining base eighteen hundred years ago, but centuries of digging had created abundant empty space which the Hadians had turned into a surprisingly comfortable habitat. The curved ceiling several hundred meters above was covered by simulated blue sky and drifting white clouds, creating an illusion so real I almost forget I was deep underground.

The surface might have been a charred cinder, but the excavated interior was remarkably amenable for human life. Out of necessity, mankind had made constructing such habitats an art form because the galaxy's prime real estate had been snapped up long before we entered the market. Interstellar civilizations had been emerging throughout the Milky Way for hundreds of millions of years, colonizing the garden worlds, leaving the late comers like us with a selection of barely habitable rocks no one else wanted.

It was the unavoidable fate of being the youngest interstellar civilization in a very old galaxy.

* * * *

The Bazaar was a rectangular cavern several kilometers long, south of the main business complex. The ceiling was smooth rock, not simulated sky, and the air was more like I remembered, breathable but metallic. Tailors, miners, workshops, hot food vendors and merchants galore were packed tightly together, all eager to sell me everything I didn't want. I hadn't been there in two years, but it had changed little. Aggressive peddlers still swarmed after me like insects, trying to shake my hand so they could get my attention and my credits, while a few shadowy types watched me pass, wondering if they could take me. Fortunately for them, none tried.

Emporium Zadim was right where I remembered it. Hideous outside and in, it was a gaudy place drenched in gold paint and heavy red drapes with a glowing sign out front flashing its name at every passerby. Two swarthy, muscle modded Berbers with uninviting demeanors and dressed in bright silks stood either side of the entrance. Judging by the indiscreet weapon bulges in their clothes, they were obviously guards, not doormen. When I passed them, their eyes followed me suspiciously, but they made no move to stop me.

The emporium's walls were hung with elaborate tapestries depicting the history of the vast expanse of land encompassing parts of Asia and all of Africa. The theological empire known as the Second Caliphate was the weakest of Earth's four great collective-governments, known for trade and conservative values rather than the technology and pluralism that characterized the immensely rich and diverse Democratic Union. Not surprisingly, there were no tapestries recalling the terrorist attack on the Mataron homeworld in 3154, almost fifteen hundred years ago. Even after all these centuries, the Calies still tried to forget the disaster a few of their number had inflicted upon mankind. Ironically, that history now made them the least likely to violate the Access Treaty, so great were their own social taboos against causing such a calamity again. In front of the tableaus were polished sim-wood tables laden with glittering gilded garbage. The real merchandise would be hidden, out of sight of UniPol investigators and robbers alike.

"Sirius Kade! My dear friend, I thought you were dead!" A basso, accented voice boomed across the room. He said it with such conviction, yet I knew his spies would have reported the arrival of the *Silver Lining* before we'd even berthed.

Ameen Zadim was a Caliphate merchant; corpulent, bearded, black bushy eye-brows and a hideous purple sash that held in his stomach and concealed the small, but highly effective stinger he always carried. Cali merchants like Zadim were found in most Union affiliated settlements, mostly because the Caliphate had established few colonies of its own, preferring instead to take advantage of the Union's openness and tremendous expansionist energy.

He advanced towards me, arms wide and embraced me warmly. Naturally, I kept one hand on my credit stick, so he couldn't steal it. "Ameen," I said returning the embrace with less enthusiasm, "You son of a camel thief, you've lost weight!"

Zadim stepped back, laughing, patting his expanding girth. "Yes, it's true, my wives feed me too well." He nodded reassuringly to the Berber muscle-jobs at the door. They hadn't taken their eyes off me for a second, but once Zadim vouched for me, they returned their malevolent gaze to the street outside.

"Come! I have coffee – not that terrible synth-bean poison the Chinese are selling! This is the real thing, all the way from Lam Dong Habitat, premium grade Viet beans. You should buy some. I know where you could double your money, only a week from here in your fine ship."

"Really? And what do you know of my fine ship, considering you thought I was dead?"

Zadim laughed, unconcerned that his little white lie

had been unmasked. "It is only good business to know what my competition is doing, or which traders are looking for cargo. You wouldn't be looking for cargo by any chance? I could use a ship as fast as yours." His eyes narrowed shrewdly. "Would you consider selling her?"

"You'll be the first to know, Ameen." I promised, lowering my voice, "Is there somewhere we can talk?"

Zadim's eyes suddenly glowed as he sensed opportunity. "Certainly my friend, this way." He led me deep into his emporium, stopping at a dark red drape which he pulled aside, revealing a room decorated as a Bedouin tent. A hookah stood smoking in one corner, an urn boiled in another and silk cushions lined the floor. Zadim poured us each a strong coffee, then we took up positions within reach of the hookah. He sucked on a pipe, then exhaled a toxic cloud that hung in the air like a cloud of gray poison.

I took one polite puff, then didn't touch it again.

"Now tell me, my dear Sirius, how may I help you?"

"I'm looking for a man, a Republic broker by the name of Mukul Sarat. Ever heard of him?"

He scowled dismissively. "If you're looking for cargo, I have some particularly interesting opportunities for a man like you."

"Not this time. I'm looking for Sarat. Do you know him?"

Zadim shrugged. "I know of him. A little rat among weasels. There is no profit in dealing with his kind. Why do you want him?"

According to Lena, the Indian Republic broker had arrived in Hades City almost a month ago. Two EIS agents had tried to make contact with him. Both were now dead.

"It's a personal matter."

Zadim studied me thoughtfully. "Ah! He has knowledge you seek. There is always opportunity in knowing the unknown. What is this information?"

"Nothing I can share."

Zadim looked crestfallen. "You do not trust me, Sirius? Me, your oldest and dearest friend?"

"You sold me a cargo of Iridian Spice that was rotten before I even took delivery–"

"Let us not trifle on the past, old friend!" He said quickly, then poured himself another coffee. "This Sarat, he pretends to be a man of taste, but he is a nasty little thief. He is not like us. He thinks he is above all of us . . . and he is a killer."

"You know that for a fact?"

"I know his kind." Zadim sobered. "You and I, we are brothers. We trade, sometimes we win, sometimes we lose, but we always have love and respect, even if we have an . . . occasional misunderstanding." He gave me a meaningful look which I took for an apology.

"Help me find Sarat and all is forgiven. The Iridian Spice deal, the time you stiffed me on payment for the Eden Jewel, even the Askari swindle."

Zadim looked profoundly wounded. "My dear Sirius, swindle is such a harsh word!" He appeared about to shed a tear, then gave me a sideways look. "You say, *all* is forgiven?"

"Help me find Sarat, and it'll be like you never cheated me, not even once."

"And you will run cargoes for me again?"

"Let's not get ahead of ourselves."

Zadim took a deep breath. "It will be like old times! I will send my little ferrets out among the weasels to find your Republic ratman, and you will not have to pay me even a single credit because we are family – again!"

"Distant relatives," I said, offering him a toast with my coffee cup.

Zadim smiled with delight. "Blood is blood!" Maybe it was genuine, maybe it was part of his act, even threaded I couldn't tell. He leaned forward, "You remember the Oniedyn belly dancers? Hmm? What a night!"

My head hurt just thinking of that feast. "I remember. You disgracefully over-tipped the tall one, with the big . . ." I gestured meaningfully.

He laughed. "Ha! I more than tipped her, my friend. She became my third wife!"

* * * *

I left Zadim's, hoping my new best friend would discover Sarat's location, and took the tube to the shipping district. It was a huge square cavern adjoining the spaceport, lined with warehouses full of cargo brought out by long haul transports from the Core Systems, the expanse of space within two hundred and fifty light years of Earth containing mankind's largest colonies. Once offloaded, the cargo was carried by local freighters to systems up to several hundred light years away. In the center of the cavern was a cluster of modern buildings, where shipping companies were headquartered, and a grand stone structure stood containing the Exchange. Every outpost and settlement had an Exchange, although this was one of the largest outside Core System space. The Exchanges were run by the Beneficial Society of Traders, the organization to which all traders belonged and which underwrote every contract, ensured every deal was honored and kept the wheels of interstellar commerce turning – for a slice off the top.

The trading floor was filled with people, gathered around dozens of free standing data nodes, small cylindrical stands arranged in neat rows. Large rectangular displays lined each wall, constantly scrolling through the list of open contracts, their destinations and completion bonuses. I found a spare node, signed for payment on the cargoes I'd just delivered, saw my digital-vault balance increase slightly, then started skimming data dumps Hades City wanted sent to regional outposts. With ships being the only way to get information from one system to another, data runs were a monotonous staple of the trade. Whether it was news, entertainment, statistics on everything from crop yields to hydrogen production, or simply a message to a distant family member, someone wanted to transfer it somewhere. It was dull subsistence work, but it paid the bills.

I searched for contracts under twenty light years with a low threat rating. Taking contracts to high threat systems paid well, but the risks were great and I wasn't looking for a fight. I'd marked six possible contracts when I spotted a familiar pair of beautiful dark eyes looking my way. They belonged to a petite woman with an elfin face framed by straight black shoulder length hair. While she appeared to be in her late twenties, I knew she'd had gene work done, enough to shave a decade off with no side effects. It wasn't as radical as what I'd been through, but it was good for civilian cosmetics.

Marie Dulon, captain of the *Heureux*, gave me a genuinely warm smile, but the look in her eyes told me she was as surprised to see me as I was to see her. For a moment, I wondered if that look meant she was with someone else and having me on the scene was an unexpected problem. Only one way to find out. I cancelled out of the data node, retrieved my skipper's tag – a slender encoded slip of metal which allowed me to enter into lawful, Society sponsored contracts – and approached her.

"Hello, Marie. I thought you'd be a hundred light years from here by now."

We'd planned to meet up in a few months, when our schedules crossed again. Neither of us had told the other they were going to Hades City, me because I hadn't planned to go there, but why was she here?

"Hello Sirius," she said in her Gascon accented voice. To my knowledge she'd never set foot on Earth, let alone visited Bordeaux, but her family had stubbornly retained their ancestral heritage. "If I didn't know it was impossible for you to track me through interstellar space, I'd think you were following me."

"Would you be disappointed if I were?"

"No, but I'd want to steal your technology so I could sell it to the highest bidder," she replied playfully.

I hadn't given it much thought, but she was right. If anyone ever figured out how to see through a spacetime distortion bubble, they'd become the richest human who ever lived. As far as we knew, none of the Orion Arm Local Powers – our interstellar neighbors – had that technology, perhaps not even the Tau Cetins, so the chance of mankind inventing it in the next hundred thousand years was zero.

"If I had that technology, I'd sell it myself."

"Then I'd have to marry you, but only because you were the richest man in the galaxy!"

"If I were the richest man in the galaxy, I wouldn't need to marry you. I'd just make you my concubine."

"If you had that many credits, I'd gladly settle for concubine."

We exchanged a long look, for a moment enjoying just being in each other's company again, then I asked, "So what are you doing here?"

"Looking for work," she said innocently, although the way she avoided my eyes told me she was lying through her teeth. "And you?"

"The same, looking for work." Now we knew we were both lying. "What happened to those oxy runs you were doing out to the Kazaris Belt?"

"The miners started haggling, trying to drive the price down."

"So you threatened to cut off their oxygen supply if they didn't pay up?"

She shrugged helplessly. "What's a girl to do?"

I glanced at her screen, seeing the contracts she was considering. Data dumps, protein packs, fishing and mining equipment, all going to the same place: a frozen hell hole I'd been to once before and never wanted to return to. "Planning on doing some skiing?"

"No, just killing time." She switched off her screen and retrieved her skipper's tag a little too quickly.

"Why do I get the feeling you're hiding something from me?"

She gave me a sultry look. "As if I have anything you haven't already seen."

Marie always used sex like a weapon, but I enjoyed her games so I didn't care. "Seeing you naked and knowing what you're thinking are not the same thing."

"No, but they're close," she said and kissed me on the cheek. "Got to run, Sirius. I'll see you soon."

Not giving me a chance to ask where she had to run to, she hurried out, giving me a wave at the exit before vanishing. I stared after her a moment, smiling to myself, then realized I'd forgotten to DNA lock her! Stalking my lover wasn't what threading was meant to be used for, but where Marie was concerned, I needed all the help I could get. Forgetting to lock her made me realize how out of practice I was with the technological wonder hidden throughout my body. On the chance she was a known criminal, I checked the list of Humanity's most wanted, but Marie wasn't listed. I'd have been surprised if she was. She'd cross the line if the reward was worth it, but she was way too smart to get caught.

I recalled Lena's warning about Marie being my weakness and wondered if she'd been aware Marie was heading for Hades City. Surely Lena would have told me if she'd known, so I figured her comments were simply the result of the mind probe, not intel on Marie's movements.

My sniffer scanned the data node she'd been using, found dozens of DNA traces, although none of the female signatures were Marie's. She hadn't worn gloves, so there should have been traces where she'd touched the data node console, but there was nothing. Marie must have been wearing skin seals to mask her DNA, which made no sense. Simply docking her ship revealed her identity to the entire city.

I logged into her data node and scanned the register of ships in port, but the *Heureux* wasn't listed. Either she was on someone else's ship or she was using a fake registry, which was against Society rules. Marie smuggled a little – we all did – but using a dummy registry in a port as big as Hades City was risky. She'd need a good reason for taking such a risk, which for her would be nothing less than a mountain of credits.

Wondering what she was up to, I took the walkway back to the spaceport. As mole-ports go, Spaceport Hades was a busy place: berths for hundreds of ships, all with pressure bridges connecting each ship to the spaceport; six well equipped maintenance docks, one large enough to take Core System super transports; and a secure zone set aside for the Earth Navy's exclusive use. There was nothing like it in human hands for five hundred light years, although some of the Local Powers had heavily populated worlds nearby, all of which were off limits to probationary mankind.

Near the *Lining's* gate was a viewport overlooking the berth. I stopped to check her paintwork, wondering if heat seeping through her shield had done any damage, but she looked as clean as a whistle. The *Silver Lining* was a Penguin class light freighter, small and fast, two and a quarter times wider than she was long. Her leading edge was crescent shaped, giving her the appearance of a flying wing, with two large maneuvering engines at the tips and three magclamps, each with their own support gantries, between the engines for towing vacuum-radiation-sealed cargo containers. The rectangular VRS containers quadrupled her interior cargo capacity and gave us the option of dumping cargo fast if we needed to run.

The two oversized engines were complemented by a series of thrusters discreetly hidden around her hull, making the *Silver Lining* one of the most agile ships not in military service. When towing three full VRS containers, she handled like an underpowered barge – sluggish and with terrible inertial drift. Without them, she was as fast in flat space as a system racer. Beneath her skin were the sixty spacetime distorters that generated the bubble for superluminal flight, while a dozen gentle bulges hid the emitters for our mil-spec bleeder shield. The single particle cannon mounted off center on top of her hull was deceptively impressive. Apart from being one of the most ineffective weapons a small ship could mount, it took forever to charge because its capacitor lost more juice than it stored – which was why I'd fitted it. And it was dirt cheap. Anyone scanning us from long range would see it charging up and assume the energy bleed came from a beast of a weapon, making them think twice about tackling us. That was the theory anyway. The *Lining* did have one real weapon hidden in a forward compartment, but it was only detectable when the outer doors were opened – which they never were, because the navy would impound her if they knew what she carried.

She stood on three landing struts, with her large underside cargo door open forming a rectangular ramp down to the rock floor. Two cargobots were unloading the hold while an eight-wheel flatbed hauler backed up under one of the VRS containers. When in position, its elevated platform rose to take the weight of the container, then Jase released the hull and gantry magclamps.

I was about to turn away when I noticed one of Izin's hull crawlers creeping over the starboard engine housing on an inspection tour. It was a six legged spider-like bot fitted with retractable arms and various sensors that enabled it to conduct hull scans and perform emergency repairs. We'd been docked only a few hours and Izin already had a full inspection cycle underway. He wasn't wasting any time, but he didn't have much else to do. Most humans were wary of tamphs, so in crowded ports he worked on the ship and stayed out of sight.

Izin was why the *Lining* was in such good shape. I'd get the gear, often from the black market, and he made it work. Sometimes he tinkered with it, improving the design. I could have patented some of his modifications and sold them back to the original manufacturer – or the navy – but then everyone would have what I had and where's the profit in that?

I headed for the gate, which read my DNA before letting me through into the pressure bridge. Jase was hurrying towards me from the ship's airlock, looking sharp in clothes that told me in a day or two, I'd either be bailing him out of jail or finding him dead drunk and broke in a back street. So I did the only responsible thing and had my sniffer DNA lock him. At least he'd be easier to find this time.

"Skipper, I've heard of this great place. You should come–"

"No, not tonight."

"Hot and cold running women! Every kind of drink you can imagine! Sixty four different games of chance and for a few extra credits, psychedelics even Earth Navy hasn't outlawed yet – only because they were just invented!"

"You're going to get arrested. You know that, right?"

"Not this time, Skipper. I have a plan!" He gave me a knowing look, then declared proudly, "I'm going to pace myself!"

"That's your plan?"

He laughed. "It's better than no plan! So, what do you say?"

"No, I . . . might have something else to do."

"Like what? It's Hades City, the hottest night spot in two hundred light years!"

"I know, but . . . she's here."

"Who?" Jase asked, then his eyes widened as he

realized who I meant. “Oh no! Skipper, she’s bad news. Forget her, come with me. We’ll show this city how to party!”

With a slight shake of my head, he knew there was no changing my mind.

He gave me a resigned look. “You don’t know what you’re missing,” he said before stepping through the gate.

While Jase went in search of a good time, I went to my stateroom for a shower, wondering what Marie was doing in Hades City. We’d discussed spending a few days together in the hot springs on Taralis, but not a word about Hades, even though she must have known she was coming here. So why keep it a secret? She’d obviously been surprised to see me and would rather I wasn’t here, which normally meant she was working on a deal and didn’t want competition.

I hoped that was all it was.

* * * *

A message arrived next morning, ship’s time – early evening Hades time:

Charon’s in the Slot has a rat problem. AZ

It was Zadim’s way of telling me his spies had picked up Sarat’s trail. I dressed quickly, grabbed a ration pack from the galley and stopped by engineering to find Izin watching his toys crawling over the *Lining’s* hull.

Izin Nilva Kren had been born on Earth at the Timor Sea Hatchery north of Australia more than a century ago. At one point two meters tall, the dark skinned amphibian was not physically imposing, but his icy persona and penetrating alien stare unnerved all who met him. Everything about tamphs seemed disproportionate to the human eye: the hips and shoulders were too broad; the bulbous, blue-green flecked eyes too far apart; the smooth, elongated head too large by far. He was small and streamlined for underwater speed, while the bulge on his forehead housed biological sonar that gave him sonic vision in darkness and long distance echo location underwater. His kind were ambush predators, different to man, but formidable on any world, in any galaxy. More importantly, Izin was an outstanding engineer and perhaps even a friend – if tamphs and humans ever really could be friends.

He sat in the middle of six large screens that wrapped two thirds of the way around him. I would have had to turn my head to see them all, but Izin, with his much greater field of vision, could watch them all simultaneously while impersonating a statue.

He slipped his vocalizer on over his narrow mouth and said, "The hull scan is now seventy eight percent complete, Captain. We sustained no damage during approach."

I expected nothing less from Izin's shield enhancements. "I want you to check all the ships in port. I'm looking for a Caravel D class medium freighter."

Izin didn't move, blink or even glance sideways at me, yet he knew immediately what was on my mind. "You think Captain Dulon is here?"

"I saw her yesterday in the city, but her ship isn't registered. I'm wondering why?"

"It would be best if you had as little contact with her as possible, Captain."

Not him too! "I just want to know how she got here. It's important."

"I understand."

I'm not sure he did. Tamphs were a matriarchal species, incapable of forming the one-to-one bonds humans did. I doubted tamphs even understood what human love was, although the overpowering pheromones the females exuded gave them an evolutionary power that ensured their will prevailed over the males, without question.

"Also, ramp up security."

"All security systems are fully operational, Captain."

"I know. I mean keep your eyes open. Watch out for anyone getting too close to the ship or trying to get inside."

"Do we have enemies here, Captain?"

Two of Lena's agents were dead. I didn't want to join their number once I contacted Sarat. "Maybe."

"Rest assured Captain, I will eliminate anyone who attempts to force entry into the ship."

That's why his kind had been under total blockade by hundreds of interstellar civilizations for thousands of years. "No killing. Just be on the lookout for anyone acting strangely." A tamph killing humans would be hard to explain to the port authorities.

"Am I permitted to use non-lethal force?"

"Absolutely! You can knock them senseless, just make sure they're still breathing."

"Very well, Captain. I will incapacitate anyone who seeks unauthorized entry to the ship. Does that include Captain Marie Dulon?"

I doubted Marie would try to board the ship, but if she did, I didn't want Izin blasting her. "Standing order: never hurt her. Ever. You can detain her, but don't hurt her."

"Understood, Captain. She is your matriarch. I will treat her as such."

It was as close as Izin would ever come to understanding our relationship. To him, a matriarch was higher than a queen, definitely not a friend or partner. Tamph males outnumbered females thousands to one, so there was little opportunity for them to ever form close personal bonds with a female of their species.

Pitying anyone who tried to break into the ship, I headed for the airlock. Like many pressurized habitats, Hades City prohibited personal weapons and took precautions to prevent them entering the city. So, I left my gun in its locker and took the tube down to the Slot, a long narrow cavern housing the city's red light district. Two broad avenues ran its length: the Grand Boulevard which blazed with lights, casinos and nightclubs; and Miner's Road, a dark street lined with brothels, psychedelic dealers and implant parlors. The dealers peddled chemicals designed to distort human perception while the implanters sold an impressive range of metal devices to enhance human abilities – not biotech like my threading, but as good as you'd get off-Earth without access to classified hardware.

My threading projected a map of the cavern onto my optic nerves as I moved through the Slot's frenetic atmosphere, avoiding the attentions of mammary modded ladies of the night and sidestepping an obstacle course of overdressed stim dealers. Two thirds of the way down the Grand Boulevard, I slipped across into Miner's Road and entered Charon's Bar & Grill, as dark and smoky a dive as I'd seen anywhere in Mapped Space. The music was deafening, accompanied by strobes flashing to a tribal beat, forcing patrons to shout into each other's ears as they drank and stimmed themselves into oblivion. Booths with small tables crammed with people lined one wall, a bar backed by mirrors and glowing lights the other, while a sea of intoxicated humanity thronged between the two. Working girls and stim dealers plied their complementary trades, while customers mingled in the kind of sexually charged atmosphere only chemical stimulants, loneliness and desperation at the edge of nowhere can induce.

I pushed through the crowd towards a large fat bartender and ordered a Hades Hellfire. The label said it was distilled from hydroponic plums, but my threading told me it was twenty percent alcohol and three percent chemicals guaranteed to give me mild toxic shock if I swallowed two shots. I swiped my credit stick over the bartender's scanner and leaned towards him.

"I'm looking for someone," I shouted over the chaotic music. "A Republic merchant named Sarat. Seen him around?"

He ran his eye over me skeptically. "Don't know him."

"Sure you do. Dark hair, moustache, tall. Has a couple of military clones for protection." At least that's what Lena's mission briefing had said. I could have rattled off Sarat's DNA sequence, but that would have unnerved the bartender, killing the conversation before it started. "Where is he?"

"Who wants to know?" he growled. He was blubber on muscle, with an intimidating demeanor suggesting he doubled as the bar's enforcer.

"Sirius Kade."

"You look like a bounty hunter," he leaned forward and sniffed, one hand vanishing below the counter, "but you smell like UniPol."

"And you smell like a sewerage outlet, but I won't hold that against you."

The bartender's hand whipped up from behind the counter holding a short black metal rod and swung it down at my head. If I was dead drunk, he might have connected. As it was, he moved in slow motion. I turned just enough to let the metal rod strike the counter, then I slammed his face down into the bar and drove my elbow onto his hand in one lightning fast motion. I caught the metal rod as it fell from his crushed fingers and released his head. He lifted his face, blood oozing from his broken nose, watching apprehensively as I examined his weapon. It was a simple metal club, but it could crack skulls in the hands of a big man. I turned it over once, gave him a reproachful look, then put it back on the counter in front of him, daring him to grab it again.

Once he realized going for the crude head cracker was a bad idea, I said. "Now that we understand each other . . ." I turned, pretending to look around the bar while my threading area-scanned the room. Behind me, the bartender eyed his metal club, wondering if he could take me while I was looking away, but wisely decided not to risk it. In my mind's eye, flashing red squares appeared around the faces of nine men and two women, indicating they were wanted criminals, while my sniffer picked up a DNA positive smear on a booth near the door. "Sarat sat over there, in that booth."

The bartender pressed a bar towel against his bleeding nose, wondering how I knew where the black market broker had been sitting, considering I'd never set foot in his seedy establishment before.

"So what'll it be, club or stick?" I said, holding up my credit stick and glancing at his metal club.

He gave me another puzzled look, wondering why I'd offer him money after just having broken his nose. "Stick."

I swiped my credit stick over his personal scanner. "Remember him now?" Tip or a bribe, it had the desired effect.

The bartender leaned towards me, speaking for my ears alone. "He's been here three times a week for about a month. Tipped big. Didn't drink much. Said he was waiting for a rich guy who never showed."

"What rich guy?"

He shrugged. I offered my credit stick again, but he shook his head. "Save your credits. I don't know who."

"How do you know he was rich?"

"Sarat asked if I'd seen a guy wearing diamond rings, fancy clothes and a pointy beard. No one wears diamonds down here, not if they want to walk out alive."

"Why does Sarat want to meet him?"

"He didn't say."

"If he comes in again, tell him Sirius Kade is interested."

"In what?"

"Just tell him that. Docking bay E-71."

Lena's people didn't know what Sarat was selling,

only that he was attracting a lot of interest from all the wrong people. They'd tried bugging him, but their highly sophisticated eavesdropping equipment had repeatedly and inexplicably failed. That was the biggest red flag of all. It almost certainly meant we were facing alien-tech we didn't understand and couldn't match.

"If he comes in, I'll tell him," the bartender said grudgingly.

Maybe he would, maybe not, but I swiped his personal scanner again for extra encouragement. "Get yourself a new nose," I said, and headed for the door.

Outside, I summoned the city's schematics from my bionetic memory and looked for somewhere off the snooper grid where I could tap the city datanet in private. I soon discovered a place a few blocks away. Ivan's was a dingy restaurant with several groups of stocky men sitting around tables drinking vodka and playing cards. No one was eating and the one waitress leaning against a counter didn't bother approaching me when I entered.

The men nearest the door glanced at me suspiciously, then one approached me with a bored look. "We're closed."

It was early evening, peak time for a restaurant. My threading told me they were small time gangsters who ran the local rackets. The EIS knew all about them, but left the local UniPol forces to deal with minor criminals.

"Anatoly told me the kalduny was good here," I said, hoping the EIS intelligence wasn't out of date. I'd never met Anatoly and according to my threading, kalduny was a type of stuffed dumpling that sounded inedible.

The gangster grunted and motioned me towards a vertical screen standing to one side. My threading immediately detected an aging body scanner, the kind that used to protect secret installations on Earth more than a century ago. It was low grade restricted tech – not classified – even so, it should have been out of reach of a bunch of second rate vodka swilling gangsters.

I stepped behind the screen and waited while Jolly Ivan studied an image of my skeleton and the few metal objects I carried. He rotated his index finger slowly, instructing me to turn in front of the scanner while he watched with a concentration that told me he knew what he was doing. Ivan recognized the synthetic bone replacements in my left shoulder, right shin and three ribs. It was the kind of high quality reconstructive surgery only the military or the very wealthy had access to.

"You got a lot of new bones," he growled in a heavy slavic accent.

"I survived an orbiter crash, years ago." It was a lie of course. A detailed bone scan would have shown the wounds were sustained at different times, but that was beyond the capabilities of Ivan's antique scanner. If he told me to strip naked, he'd find no scars. The EIS' skin regeneration therapy was flawless. Fortunately, the last thing Ivan wanted to see was me naked.

Finding no weapons, listening devices or any trace of the organic network threading my body, he nodded towards the rear and returned to his card game. I walked through to the back door and knocked. Presently, a door panel dilated revealing a face that could have belonged to Jolly Ivan's twin. The doorman received a bored nod from Ivan, then let me into a large, dimly lit room suffocating under a pall of smoke. Men and women gathered around small tables talking, drinking, shooting stims and occasionally laughing, all the time watching wall screens full of numbers, spinning wheels and a few games of chance even I didn't recognize. The surface of every table was fitted with info panels for placing bets, reading the latest odds, and conducting whatever business they were in while they waited for the next game to run its course.

I found an empty table, ordered an expensive drink and placed several large bets, then used the screen to access the city's datanet. According to my threading,

Ivan's gambling den was renowned for protecting the privacy of its high rolling patrons, including not tracking their online activity. It was why the clientele preferred Ivan's to the licensed casinos.

Thanks to Lena, I had a high level authorization code giving me access to the city's most secure areas which I used to run a series of searches starting with Sarat. He'd been a frequent visitor to the city over the past few years, although the details of the ship he used and his present location were blocked. Apparently Lena's authorization code wasn't quite high enough to pry into Sarat's personal affairs.

My second search found there were more than a hundred Orion Arm non-humans in the city, mostly Ascellans, Minkarans and Carolians, but thankfully not a single Mataron. Hades City had no record of any Matarons ever having visited the city, which was either reassuring if true, or an indication the Matarons had hacked the city's datanet.

Next, I checked Ameen Zadim's status. Not surprisingly, he was being investigated by UniPol for a variety of nefarious activities. Considering he was more use to me out of jail than in, I wiped his file. Zadim would never know I'd made his problems go away, because being the inquisitive little scoundrel he was, he'd not rest until he figured out how I'd accessed the city's inner sanctum.

Finally, I ran a search on Marie. There was no record of her, yet I'd seen her using her Trader ID at the Exchange. Those tags were issued by the Beneficial Society with encryption so complex, only the EIS could crack it. It had to be that way. The consequences for interstellar trade of not knowing who you were dealing with would be catastrophic because no contracts could be enforced, no trader could be trusted. Could she possibly be using someone else's ID? That was not only illegal, it would get her blacklisted by the Society – which was far worse.

“I hope you know what you’re doing, Marie,” I whispered to myself.

I waited until my two bets were complete, losing on both, then caught the tube back to the spaceport. At Gate E-71, I touched the door sensor. While it was confirming my identify, my sniffer spotted two contacts moving towards me. It quickly matched their engineered DNA, warning that they were augmented muscle-jobs, tough as they come with at least twice my physical strength. Their bulky bio-engineered muscle would make them slow, but if they got one hand on me, I’d never get free.

The gate unlocked as I stepped sideways a moment before a metal dart struck the bulkhead with a dull thud and fell to the floor. There was a wet spot where the dart’s tip had hit, telling me it was an injector, not an electro-paralytic. If I hadn’t moved, it would have taken me straight between the shoulders.

Turning towards my attackers for a first look, my sniffer illuminated them in my mind’s eye with red threat indicators. I was two meters tall, yet they both towered over me with upper body muscle that threatened to burst out of their tight fitting, elasticized black shirts. If it was a uniform, it wasn’t one I recognized. They had no insignia, no markings of rank. One had a shaved head and a faded scar over his left eye; the other a buzz cut and a massive, protruding jaw. Above the threat indicators, my sniffer flashed a tiny green marker indicating neither were on the mad-and-bad list.

I DNA locked them both and rolled sideways as Scarface fired a second sleep-dart, narrowly missing my shoulder. He might have been a lumbering beefcake, but he had good aim and I was unarmed. I guessed they were off a ship inside the spaceport, as they couldn’t have got the dart gun into the berthing area through port security.

Scarface slipped a silver dart into his little pistol, while Jawbones stomped towards me, being careful not to block his companion’s line of sight. His move told me they were a team, contract muscle used to working together. Not being on any wanted list meant they were either nobodies, or smarter than they looked.

I edged sideways, keeping Jawbones between me and his companion's dart gun. He clenched his fist and took a deep breath while still three steps away, telegraphing what was coming. He charged forward like an angry rhino, completely confident of his physical superiority and completely ignorant what ultra-reflexed modding could do.

I froze, feigning fear, raising my hands as if to protect my face while offering him my head on a plate. He took the bait, throwing the punch with enough force to crush bone if it connected. Halfway through delivering his slow motion pile driver, I darted forward, slipped effortlessly under his trunk-like arm and drove a hard, precise punch into his lower abdomen. My blow had half the power of Jawbones' haymaker, but I hit my target precisely while his bulging arm flailed uselessly through the air.

Jawbones coughed, unable to breath, then ignoring the pain, stepped forward and swung his other arm wildly at me. He might have been a lumbering elephant, but he was tough. Most opponents would have been on their knees, gasping for air, not coming back for more. He pivoted off his trailing foot as his fist chased me, so I kicked his advancing leg just enough to throw him off balance and send his second pile driver sailing over my head. Before he knew what was happening, I spun and snap-kicked him in the groin with the same foot that had taken out his leg. Jawbones doubled over, his forehead begging for an elbow strike that would have finished him, but my sniffer was flashing a warning that Scarface had shifted position and was now behind me.

Ignoring Jawbones' gift *coup de grace*, I rolled away from the crippled muscle-job, expecting to see a dart flash over my head, but Scarface was marginally smarter than his bonehead partner. He held fire, anticipating my roll, firing only as I came to my feet.

For a muscle-job, his timing was almost perfect.

The dart caught me below the collar bone. I ripped it out fast, but my left shoulder and arm were already useless. Whatever the dart was loaded with, it was strong stuff – and fast acting! I glanced at the open gate leading to the *Silver Lining*, already certain I wouldn't make it.

Suddenly, my head swam and my legs turned to jelly. Genetically resequenced balance or not, I stumbled and was out before I hit the floor.

* * * *

I awoke in an office, lavishly decorated in an ancient nautical theme. Pictures of old sailing ships adorned the walls above intricately detailed models of Spanish galleons in transparent vacuum cases. A marlin was mounted on one wall behind a polished mahogany desk and, even though they'd been extinct for eighteen hundred years, it looked real. Most impressive of all was the wall sized mural to my right, depicting an ancient sea battle that was more a chaotic melee than a fleet action. From the way light reflected off the brush strokes, it appeared to be an actual painting rather than a projection.

"It's an original," a smooth, Hispanic voice said behind me.

Pressure fields secured my wrists and ankles to a brown leather chair, telling me this wasn't the first time guests had been entertained in this way. "Looks stolen."

A well dressed man in his early fifties strolled into my line of sight. He had slick black hair, a neatly groomed triangular beard and wore a single sparkling diamond in his left ear. Even more ostentatious diamonds adorned his fingers.

"It's called the *Battle of the Albrolhos*," he said. "The Spanish and Portuguese defeated the Dutch off the coast of Brazil in 1631. An ancestor of mine commanded a ship there." He approached the mural, studying it closely before pointing. "I believe it was that one. Later, he become a Captain-General in the Spanish Empire."

"Impressive," I said, blinking away the drumbeat in my head.

"Not really. Phillip IV later executed him for treason." The man shrugged. "Every great family has a black sheep."

He was obviously the wealthy individual Sarat had been waiting for. He looked like a cross between a synth-dealer and an aristocratic art collector. I scanned and locked him immediately, but his DNA didn't show up on the Orion Arm's most wanted list. My sniffer told me there were two more signatures behind me, the same two who'd tagged me outside the *Silver Lining's* berth, while my threading's listener picked up the hollow click of footsteps on deck plating outside the room.

My host poured a dark red liquid into a wine glass. "Forgive the impolite manner in which my associates brought you to this meeting, Captain Kade, however, I wasn't sure you'd come willingly."

"Next time, try asking."

"I would, but I so dislike being disappointed." He sipped his drink. "And from what I've heard, you're not a particularly agreeable individual."

"You don't know me. I'm very agreeable, except when I'm jabbed in the neck with a sleep dart."

"Well, as you and I have no past disagreements, let us start as friends."

"This is how you treat your friends?" I glanced meaningfully at the glowing fields clamping me to the chair.

"Acquaintances then, or are we adversaries?" When I didn't respond, he said, "My name is Arturo Salbatore Vargis and I have the honor of being the captain of this ship, the *Soberano*."

"Never heard of you."

Vargis nodded understandingly. "I don't normally come out this far. This little rock may be fertile ground for men such as yourself, but I find there are few opportunities worthy of my interest."

Impressive, a boast and an insult in one. "And yet, here you are, among us low life bottom feeders."

"Yes, and we both know why."

"Do we?"

"Come Captain, I know you asked Ameen Zadim to find Sarat for you."

"Who?"

"Zadim's people have been scouring the city, asking questions, prying where they shouldn't. Did you really think no one would notice?"

Zadim was sneaky enough to ensure his people wouldn't draw attention to themselves. The only way Vargis had picked up my trail was if someone working for Zadim had sold us both out.

"What people notice isn't my concern."

Vargis put his drink on the table. "Let me make this easy for you, Captain Kade. I have a proposition for you, one that does not involve Mukul Sarat."

"If you're talking money, you're talking my language."

"I knew we could come to an understanding," Vargis smiled as if the deal was already done. "There is a contract waiting for you at the Exchange. Two hundred and fifty thousand credits to deliver a confidential dispatch to Zen Tau Base. No detours, no delays and you leave immediately. Oh yes, and Zadim forgets all about Sarat."

Ten times the going rate to carry mail to a rundown Chinese outpost over three hundred light years away at the edge of nowhere? It would take three months to get there, fully bubbled with no stops.

Vargis leaned forward. "Once you make the delivery, keep going. You will not return to this region of space for . . . let's say a year after you reach Zen Tau."

"That's a generous offer," I said thoughtfully, as if

considering the deal, "except Zen Tau is Yiwu space and I don't speak Chinese." The Yiwu, the Obligation, had been the dominant Chinese organized crime syndicate since the early 45th century, and I was on less than friendly terms with them.

"The Yiwu will leave you alone once you make the delivery – and you can learn Mandarin on the way."

The Yiwu would leave me alone? Seriously? If true, Vargis was more than an overdressed snake oil salesman with irritatingly well-groomed facial hair. More likely the delivery would have the opposite effect. He was sending me three hundred light years to make it easy for the Chinese mafia to ensure I never came back.

"And if I don't take the contract?"

Vargis face hardened. "That would be most unfortunate. For you, for your crew, for your ship. Trust me, Captain Kade, I have only your best interests at heart." Vargis emptied his glass, "Take the contract and leave Mukul Sarat to me."

I felt a now familiar sting in the back of the neck and was out before I could reply. At least this time, I was sitting down when I lost consciousness.

* * * *

I came to on a bench seat in the spaceport terminal. It was some time before I had the strength to stagger onto the walkway back to the *Silver Lining* and fumble my way through the airlock. When I stepped into the darkened pressure-suit compartment, a short barreled shrapnel gun almost took out my eye.

"Easy!" I yelled, lurching clumsily away from the business end of Izin's street sweeper. "It's me!"

It had been several thousand years since the shotgun had been invented, but looking into the business end of its descendant was as intimidating as ever. Magnetic acceleration and exploding micro munitions might have replaced gunpowder and shot, but the effect on human flesh in a cramped passageway was just as gruesome.

"My apologies, Captain," Izin said, lowering the shrapgun and stepping back from the inner hatch, motioning towards a twenty centimeter long polished metal object lying on the deck. It was as thick as my fist in the middle, tapered at both ends, with a single neat hole blasted through its center.

"What is it?"

"A minidrone. It attempted to board the ship several hours ago." He tapped the small six millimeter shredder pistol at his hip, confirming where the tiny hole in its side had come from. With his tamph eyes and inhuman steadiness, Izin was a frighteningly deadly shot with any precision weapon.

My DNA sniffer gave the minidrone the once over, but it was clean. "Why the artillery?" I asked, nodding at the shrapgun.

"Hull sensors covering the pressure bridge have been deactivated. I don't know how or by who." Izin was a walking Earth-tech encyclopedia. If he didn't know how it was done, it meant alien-tech had been used against us. "I considered it to be an attack on the ship, so I selected the optimal weapon for fighting in confined spaces." He lifted the shrapgun meaningfully. "Only the hull sensors aspecting the pressure bridge have been disabled, so this was clearly the point of attack."

"Only one came through?"

"Yes, Captain. I have a hull crawler outside inspecting the damage now."

My bionetic memory didn't recognize the minidrone, so if it was Earth-tech, it was custom made. "Take it apart. Tell me anything you can about it – highest priority."

Izin picked up the minidrone. "Is there something I should know, Captain?"

"I'm working on a deal and we have some unfriendly competition."

"Is the order prohibiting lethal force revoked?"

Tough question. If I let Izin off the leash, I could end up with problems with the port authorities and if I didn't, the next attempt to get inside the ship might succeed. I decided to play it safe, for now. "Not while we're in port, unless they start shooting first."

"As you wish," Izin said.

He led the way back to engineering, setting the shrapgun and minidrone down, then took in his six screens with a glance. "The hull crawler reports five hull sensors were destroyed by a highly concentrated thermal effect with an active area of nine microns."

"That's kind of small, isn't it?"

"Nine millionths of a meter," Izin said. "Earth technology is incapable of producing a thermal weapon with that level of precision."

"Can you calculate where the weapon was fired from?"

"Perhaps."

"There's a ship called the *Soberano*. Find out if they could hit us."

Izin tapped into the spaceport's datanet and quickly scanned the ship registry. "The *Soberano* is a Mammoth class super transport less than three years old, owned by Pan Core Shipping."

"A mammoth?" I whistled softly. "She'd make us look like an Kunarian buzzfly."

Mammoths were over two hundred thousand metric tons – fifty times the size of the *Silver Lining* – and they rarely left Core System space. No wonder Vargis' office was so spacious.

"The *Soberano* arrived a few days ago."

"What's she carrying?" Ten years of supplies for Hades City?

"Her manifest says she's empty."

"No cargo?"

"Confirmed by customs inspectors."

Pan Core Shipping was one of the largest shipping companies in Mapped Space. Why would they send such an expensive ship out here empty when they had thousands of smaller, faster vessels in their fleet? "What was her embarkation point?"

"Shinagawa Station."

"That's a long way to come for no trade profit."

The big Japanese orbital shipyard complex was over nine hundred light years away in Inner Cygnus, well inside Core System space. No wonder Vargis wanted no competition. I'd be nervous too, if I'd spent months staring at well decorated bulkheads for nothing. Whatever Sarat was up to, it had been in the planning for a long time, long enough to hook Pan Core and get them to bankroll sending one of their biggest ships to the edge of Mapped Space.

"The *Soberano*'s maintenance history indicates she spent seven weeks refitting at Shinagawa before departure," Izin said.

"Makes sense. Give her a refit before a long haul."

"She'd undergone a major maintenance cycle two months before that. A second refit in such a short period of time should have been unnecessary."

Shinagawa Station was one of the few major shipyards outside the Solar System, used by shipping companies and Earth Navy alike. The station was famous not just for its robot dockyards, but its vast stores of equipment, including naval ordnance. Suddenly, I realized why the *Soberano* had docked a second time. "They put naval weapons in her cargo holds!" It would explain why she was empty – she had no room for cargo!

Whatever Vargis was after, he intended to protect it.

"If Earth Navy found out," Izin said, "Pan Core would be in serious trouble."

"Can we see the *Soberano* from here?"

"No, she's in the southern cavern, docked across berths S-36 to S-45."

She was so big, she took up ten births!

Izin called up her registry holo, displaying it on one of his six screens. She looked like two stretched spheres joined by a long oblong. The stern sphere held her twin energy plants and sixteen maneuvering engines in four rows of four, while the bow sphere held command, control and crew sections. Ten large rectangular doors were spaced along each side of the hull, marking the location of her twenty cavernous cargo holds. She was certainly large enough to have been transformed into a veritable battleship, although with her cargo doors sealed, there'd be no visible evidence of it. Whatever Sarat was selling, no pirate would ever get their hands on it, once Vargis got it aboard the *Soberano*.

Neither would I.

"How many crew?" I asked.

"Minimum complement of twelve, life support for thirty."

I'd assume he had thirty aboard; crew plus more like Jawbones and Scarface. The *Soberano* would be slower than the *Lining* bubbled and would wallow like a whale in flat space, but if I was right about the refit, she'd hit like the devil.

I started to leave, but Izin touched a control and the image of another ship appeared. "This is the only Caravel D class ship docked. Berthed at W-4."

I took one look at the old girl and recognized her immediately. If the *Silver Lining* was a tow boat, the *Heureux* was a barge. Her hull configuration was simple: three box-like cargo holds ahead of a lopsided superstructure mounting a single large maneuvering engine astern. Spaced along the top of the cargo holds were clamps for a dozen VRS containers, although I'd rarely seen Marie use them. Like most work boats, it was a simple, utilitarian design. The paint job was subtly different and her registry number had changed, but the modified vector housings on her well worn engine were unmistakable. No wonder Marie was nervous to see me. She knew I'd recognize the *Heureux* anywhere, no matter what disguise she was wearing.

"That's her." The *Heureux* had been in Marie's

family for three generations. She was almost eighty years old, but thanks to tender care and regular maintenance, she was still a reliable, if elderly, workhorse.

"According to the port register, that ship is the *Vandray's Promise*. The Captain is Esmin Vandray."

"Esmin? . . . Good work, Izin."

I'd known Marie to pull a few reckless stunts, but I'd never seen her risk her license before. Using a fake ship registry and borrowed skipper's tags seemed crazy, even for her. I sure hoped whatever she was up to, was worth it.

I would have liked to figure out what that was, but knew I had to find Sarat soon, before Vargis sidelined me, permanently.

* * * *

I tried sleeping off the effects of being drugged twice, but after what seemed to be only minutes, I became aware of a pungent aroma. At first I thought I was dreaming, but the scent of incense grew stronger, eventually jarring me awake. My stateroom's wall screen was set to simulate a window with the shades drawn, creating an illusion that it was more than a metal box. The feeble light penetrating the 'shades' illuminated a thin pall of gray smoke floating in the air. I heard a man inhale, then saw the end of a fume-stick glow revealing a swarthy face amidst the darkness.

Ignoring the throbbing in my head, I sat up and stared into the shadows to the right of the window sim where a dark form sat. Blue smoke wafted from his slender fume-stick, slowly filling my stateroom with an intoxicating haze that would take the atmo scrubbers days to clear.

Somehow he'd gotten inside the ship, bypassed Izin's elaborate security system and then made himself comfortable in my stateroom without triggering my threading's proximity sensors. Such a feat should have been impossible. I tried DNA locking him, but as far as my threading was concerned, he didn't exist. Not even a thermal trace. My olfactory analyzer told me the smoke came from an expensive Pashtun narco-leaf that heightened well being without distorting perceptual thinking. Inexplicably, it was unable to identify the physical source of the smoke, even though I was staring straight at the fume-stick.

"Being a light sleeper is a good thing for people in your line of work, Captain Kade."

My visitor spoke in a cultured Republic accent, which my listener identified as coming from Kerala or Tamil Nadu in southern India – a good fit to Lena's briefing profile.

"Mukul Sarat, I presume?" My listener had been able to analyze his accent, telling me the entire room wasn't suppressed, just a highly localized area around him. The EIS had been trying to produce a personal dampening field for years with no success, yet my guest was clearly protected by just such a device, leaving me in no doubt he was geared up with alien-tech.

Sarat nodded, showing no surprise that I'd guessed his identity. He was tall and bald, with a gaunt face and dark sunken eyes. "I understand you wish to bid at my auction?"

"That's right."

"Perhaps you were unaware that this is an invitation only gathering, and frankly, a man such as yourself lacks the financial resources to participate."

"And yet you broke into my ship, beat my security, and are stinking up my room with that weed you're smoking."

"I'm a curious man."

"Curious enough to destroy my hull sensors so you could sneak aboard."

"Consider it a demonstration," Sarat said, "of my . . . connections."

"You better hope my engineer doesn't find you aboard," I said, "or the only thing you'll be connected to is the wrong end of a shredder."

"Ah yes, I heard you had a pet tamph. I never cared for them myself – too hard to control."

"Only if you can't earn their respect."

"I prefer fee for service. Which brings me to the reason for my visit. I've done some checking on you, Kade. You're notorious for making rash decisions and acquiring enemies."

"I'm just misunderstood."

"It's why I believe your interest is genuine, but my little gathering is full."

"No it isn't, or you wouldn't be here."

"Or I might just want to know how you heard about my auction?"

"Jie Kang Li hired me to represent him. He didn't tell me how he knew or what I was buying, he just told me to win."

When you lie, lie big. Jie Kang Li was the supreme head of the Yiwu, the largest and most powerful Chinese crime syndicate in Mapped Space. That made him one of the ten richest humans alive and the only one not an Earth resident. Li was also the People's Federation of Asia's most wanted criminal, and considering how long he'd evaded them, their biggest embarrassment. Even the Earth Intelligence Service couldn't find him, which meant he was either a ghost or a genius – probably both.

"You don't know what the merchandise is?" Sarat asked.

"Not a clue," I said, hoping Sarat would volunteer the information.

Sarat reflected on my lies briefly. "Li is at least a thousand light years from here, which makes your story impossible to check."

That's why Lena had picked Jie Kang Li as my cover story. "I can prove it."

"How?"

Lena had given me an Earth Bank digital-vault with sufficient funds to play the game. It was DNA coded for my personal use and was as good as cash anywhere in Mapped Space. Digital-vaults were the only way to transfer funds between star systems that had no way of accessing a central data repository on Earth. Global banking systems may have been highly centralized in the days before interstellar travel, when distances were negligible, but interstellar banking was exactly the opposite. Distance and time dictated it. It had made Earth Bank as much an idea as an institution, and had created the most splintered, decentralized use of data in human history. Billions of digital-vaults scattered across thousands of light years – each a tiny piece of the Bank's central repository – allowed anyone access to their funds no matter how many months or years they were away from Earth. You didn't contact the bank – you couldn't! – you carried it with you, wherever you went.

I retrieved the small rectangular device from the ship's safe and swept it over my desk scanner. The credit stick checked my DNA before revealing the balance to the ship's processing core, which then replaced my view screen's window sim with an obscenely large number. If I was inclined to steal from the EIS, I could have taken the money and lived like a potentate for the rest of my life. Fortunately for Lena, the *Silver Lining* was enough for me.

Sarat took one look at the king's ransom locked inside my credit stick and sat back, convinced. Money really does talk, in any system, in any century, particularly to men like Sarat.

"Why would Jie Kang Li trust you with so much money? Why not send one of his own people?" Sarat asked.

"Maybe he trusts me more than his own people. Or maybe he doesn't want them knowing what he's doing."

Sarat sucked on his putrid fume-stick thoughtfully. "I've heard your word is good, Kade."

"So is Jie Kang Li's money."

"You really don't know what you're bidding on?"

As soon as he said it, I knew he was hooked! "I'm just a hired gun with a fast ship. I get the stuff. I take it to him. He pays me a huge commission and we are done. That's all I care about."

"You could steal his money. It's more than all the commissions you'll ever earn."

"Where would I go with it? I'm already at the ass end of Mapped Space. If I stole from Jie Kang Li, I'd be dead within a year. This way, I'm rich and alive."

"A most desirable combination," Sarat mused as he blew smoke across the room, his mind made up. "Welcome to the deal of the millennium, Captain Kade." He stood and dropped a data chip on my desk. "We meet in ten days. This is the location. Be on time."

He walked to the hatch, "Remember, if you bring the authorities with you, it won't just be me you'll have to deal with. The other bidders represent the richest and most powerful organizations known to man. If you expose them to unnecessary risk, being hunted by Jie Kang Li will be nothing compared to what they will do to you."

"I'm sure Jie Kang Li feels the same. That's why he hired me. I'm discreet."

"Then we understand each other." Sarat turned to leave.

"Do you want to tell me what I'm bidding on?"

"Ask Jie Kang Li," Sarat said slyly before slipping out into the corridor.

I hurried after him, thinking I should escort him down to the airlock in case Izin ambushed him, but found the passageway was empty. There were Earth-tech stealth suits, shadow suits and chameleon suits, all devised to make a man harder to see. I know, I'd worn them all, but the one thing we still hadn't mastered was perfect invisibility.

It was simply more proof that Sarat was using alien-tech – a lot of it – although whose it was and how he got it was a mystery.

* * * *

Izin's large blue-green eyes slid back and forth, scanning horizontally. He did that when he was irritated, as if he was constantly searching his surrounds for the source of his annoyance. It was one of the few tamph mannerisms I'd learned to read on his otherwise impenetrable amphibian face.

"Jase accessed the airlock last night at two-oh-five, ship's time," Izin said as he studied the security logs in engineering. "He then left the ship at two-fifty."

"It wasn't Jase," I said.

"The pressure bridge's gate and our own airlock sensor both scanned his DNA before opening, although the hull sensors near the airlock were still being repaired."

"It was a man called Mukul Sarat, using alien-tech."

"Which tech?" Izin's synthesized voice was typically calm, but the way he fixed his gaze on me made me feel uncomfortably like prey.

"I don't know, but I intend to find out."

The alien-tech could have come from any of the Orion Arm Local Powers, or even one of the more distant civilizations we had sporadic contact with. They all had the technology to pick our pockets, starting with the Ascellans who were a mere ten thousand years ahead of us. They were the nearest in development to mankind, but there were thousands of others, all far more advanced than the humble Ascellans. The Matarons had the motivation to scheme against us, but they were so extremely xenophobic they didn't trust anyone, especially not human defectors. Or was Sarat a dupe rather than a defector?

"Did you get anything from the minidrone you blasted near the airlock?" I asked.

"No, Captain. It didn't conform to any known human device, although its technology was within human limits."

"What about its components?"

"They were all constructed of Earth sourced materials."

"All of them?" I asked suspiciously.

"My metallurgical analysis was very thorough, Captain."

"Doesn't that strike you as strange?" After three thousand years of industrialization, Earth's industries were now increasingly dependent on off world resources.

Izin hesitated, surprised at his oversight. "It is statistically improbable that every component would be constructed from Earth sourced minerals."

Someone had gone to a great deal of trouble to hide who they were, down to obtaining raw materials from Earth itself to use in manufacturing the equipment they'd given Sarat.

"Slice into the city's surveillance system. Find Jase." If Sarat was using alien-tech to fool the airlock's DNA scanner, the one thing he couldn't know was my copilot's DNA code. He could have only gotten that from the source, which meant he'd gone after Jase.

"It will take time, if you don't want them to know what I've done."

I had no doubt Izin could sneak in without being detected, but if Jase was in trouble, I didn't have time for him to go tiptoeing around. I summoned the access key to the city's surveillance system from Lena's download and wrote it down. "Use that."

"How did you get this security code, Captain?"

"Everything's for sale in Hades City."

He didn't believed me, but he put the code to use immediately. In less than two minutes, he found Jase and I was on my way back to the Slot.

* * * *

The Cerberus Hotel in the middle of the Slot's well lit Grand Boulevard was the third largest casino complex in Hades City. It was filled with gambling machines and beautiful woman, both adept at separating a man from his credits with ruthless efficiency. It was exactly the kind of place Jase couldn't resist. His room was on the thirtieth floor, a suite with all the trimmings; views of the Slot's bright lights, a spa, richly upholstered lounges, red carpets and mirrors everywhere.

When I arrived, the door was closed, the 'do not disturb' indicator was glowing and a pin sized hole in the door surrounded by black scoring revealed the locking mechanism had been melted. I slipped quietly inside, finding the room lit only by light spilling in from the street below. It was almost five AM local time and Jase could have been making up for lonely weeks in space with female company in another suite, but as I started towards the bedroom, my threading picked up a thermal signature and a kaleidoscope of chemical residues.

I found two attractive young woman lying either side of Jase on an enormous bed. All three were naked, although only Jase was showing anything like normal thermal readings. I reached down to move one of the girls aside. As soon as my hand touched her skin, my threading got a detailed read on her vitals, instantly informing me that she was almost room temperature and had been dead at least five hours.

My threading analyzed the oil and sweat on my hand from her skin, warning me that a toxic mix of Blue Dream and Screamer had been pumped into her in doses that would have killed an Askeeri thunderbeast. The first was an hallucinogenic, the second a notorious sex drug, but together in those doses, they were poison.

I didn't bother checking the other girl. One look told me she was also dead.

"Jase!" I shouted, slapping his face. He moaned incomprehensibly, but his eyelids barely moved. I shook him roughly. "Jase! Can you hear me?"

"Skipper?" he slurred as his head rolled sideways without opening his eyes.

My threading used my eyes to optically scan his naked body, looking for unnatural marks, but found nothing. It wasn't until I examined the soles of his feet that a target indicator appeared in my mind, highlighting a tiny circular abrasion two millimeters across. That was where Sarat had lifted Jase's DNA code. Whatever tech he was using to beat the spaceport locking systems, it still needed a tissue sample to work. My sniffer could take a proximity scan of a suspect's code without contact, but it couldn't use it to trick DNA locking systems, just track the signature.

Like the dead girl, his skin was secreting Screamer, although at a much lower rate. Fortunately, he was sweating only a hint of Blue Dream. They'd given him enough to knock him out, but not kill him. I guess Sarat knew killing Jase would have made it personal, obliging me to seek revenge, whereas linking him to the deaths of two girls would just get him locked up long enough that I'd have to leave him behind.

I dragged Jase into the shower and turned the cold water on full. He shuddered from the shock of freezing water, partially opening his eyes.

"Snap out of it!" I yelled, "we have to get out of here."

"What . . . are you . . . doing here?"

"You were drugged. Blood stims."

His face contorted in confusion. "No stims . . . I . . . paced . . . myself."

"I know. Get dressed!"

"The . . . girls . . . ?"

"They're dead."

"What?"

"It's not your fault." It was my fault, for letting him out. I hadn't realized Sarat would go after him to weaken me.

Jase rolled sideways and vomited while I returned

to the bedroom and placed the first girl close to her companion, making it appear they were together. I put Jase's key in one of their purses and filled their hand bags with casino chips as if he'd paid them to wait for him in his suite. There were Blue Dream and Screamer stim tabs in Jase's bags, enough to make him look like a dealer. I transferred several shots to the girl's handbags and flushed the rest. If we were lucky, they were hookers and UniPol would assume it was self inflicted. His biotraces were everywhere, but if we left his bag and spare clothes in the room, UniPol might think he was coming back.

Jase staggered into the bedroom, clumsily toweling himself off. I helped him dress, then guided him to the door, leaving the 'do not disturb' indicator on, hoping we had at least ten hours before cleaners entered the room. By the time the local authorities started looking for Jase, I planned to be far outside the system.

When we reached the ground floor, I took his weight, then we stumbled between the gambling tables to the front entrance. Several security guards glanced at us, but thinking we were a pair of drunks on our way home, made no move to stop us. Once outside, I carried Jase to the tube back to the spaceport, hoping there wouldn't be a long wait for a launch window. We weren't scheduled to depart, so if the traffic was heavy we could be stuck waiting for clearance for hours – enough time for the city authorities to stop us leaving. I wondered how much it would take to bribe the port controller to bump us up the list, but figured once word got out there were two dead girls in the Slot, the bribe wouldn't stick. Unfortunately, the city's blast doors were strong enough to withstand a small asteroid impact, making it impossible for us to shoot our way out.

Hades City might have been a molehill, but if we didn't get moving, it would soon become a rat trap.

* * * *

Back aboard the *Lining*, I poured Jase into his bunk to let him sleep it off, requested the first available launch window from port control, then went to my stateroom to find out where we were going. Before I read Sarat's data chip, I called Zadim.

"Sirius, did you find your little ratman?" Zadim's voice asked as his plump face appeared in my holo display, blinking back sleep.

"He found me, but that's not why I called. Someone working for you doesn't know how to keep a secret."

"How do you know this?" Zadim asked suspiciously.

"A competitor found out about my interest in Sarat." It was the only way Vargis could have known I was trying to buy into the game. "Now that we're blood brothers again, Ameen, I thought you should know."

"I will attend to it at once," Zadim said with a heavy tone. "It is most regrettable when one cannot trust one's own relatives. Safe voyage, my friend. I look forward to your return, and our future ventures together."

Zadim's face disappeared from the space above my desk, then I scanned Sarat's disk and watched as an Earth-sized world appeared in its place. Astrographic data floated either side of the planet's image, giving me its vital statistics at a glance. The northern and southern hemispheres were almost identical, covered in white sheets of snow and ice. A thin band of blue ocean separated the two frozen hemispheres, marking an equatorial zone seven hundred kilometers wide, where temperatures remained barely above freezing year round. The equatorial ocean was filled with icebergs and a few island chains, while in the western hemisphere, a thousand kilometer long strip of green marked the northern tip of the only continental land mass not entirely buried beneath ancient glaciers.

I could scarcely believe my eyes. It was the same planet Marie had been searching for contracts to at the Exchange. Now I knew why she was in Hades City. She was either a bidder in Sarat's auction, or she was going to steal whatever he was selling!

I stabbed the intercom. "Izin!" I yelled in a rage, wishing just this once, she'd trusted me enough to tell me what she was doing.

"Yes, Captain?" Izin replied as calm as ever. If he could tell I was angry, his artificial voice showed no sign of it.

"Has *Vandray's Promise* left port?"

There was a moment's silence as he checked if Marie's disguised ship was still docked. "Yes, Captain. She undocked three hours ago."

"Where's she headed?"

Another brief silence as Izin processed my inquiry. "Her flight plan indicates she's headed towards the Arkina Nebula."

"The hell she is!" There was nothing in the Arkina but H-miners and Ravens. "Any word on our launch window?"

"We're eighth on the departure list," Izin replied. "Launch is scheduled to occur in one hundred and forty three minutes."

I switched off the intercom and stared at the bleak world floating in front of me. It resembled a spinning top of snow and ice, where the richest scum in Mapped Space were gathering for a black market auction that put at risk mankind's future as an interstellar civilization.

It was a world known throughout Mapped Space as Icetop.

Chapter Three : Icetop

Marginally Habitable World
Creshan System
Outer Lyra Region
1.03 Earth Normal Gravity
1,204 light years from Sol
42,000 inhabitants

The voyage to Icetop was one of the riskiest a human ship could undertake. It was located four light years beyond the astrographic data gifted to mankind by the Tau Cetins over two thousand years ago, data covering half of one percent of the galaxy. The TC navigational charts enabled human ships to travel safely out to twelve hundred light years from Earth, giving us a freedom we could never have achieved alone. Approximately a quarter of all mass in the universe was dark matter, slow moving and practically undetectable by Earth-tech, yet with enough gravitational influence to catastrophically collapse fragile spacetime bubbles. The faster a ship travelled beyond the speed of light, the more extreme was the curvature of space caused by its bubble and the greater the risk of gravitational collapse. At the *Silver*

Lining's top speed of one thousand three hundred and fifty times the speed of light, ambient spacetime curvature caused by local gravity would collapse the bubble in an instant. It was why dark matter posed a constant threat to navigation, which the Tau Cetin charts solved by identifying the locations of billions of dark matter hazards with infallible precision.

Those same navigational hazards had disrupted the expansion of the very earliest interstellar civilizations eons ago, trapping them in small, isolated pockets for hundreds of thousands of years. Initially there were few spacefaring species, but slowly their numbers grew, each exploring their immediate parts of the galaxy, often at great cost in terms of lives and ships, all the time improving their technology. When the early civilizations eventually encountered each other there were occasional conflicts, but in time they learnt to coexist and eventually to share their knowledge, completing the great collective work of mapping the galaxy and founding a true Galactic Civilization.

It was not an empire ruled by one, but an immensely heterogeneous association open to all. The members were often vastly unequal in achievement and markedly different in character, yet all were equally protected by Galactic Law. As probationary members of the Access Treaty, mankind was entitled to half a percent – no more, no less. It was a promise of what full membership would bring and while it sounded tiny, it gave humanity access to millions of star systems – provided we played by the rules.

That was our biggest challenge.

In fifty years, when our second attempt to qualify for membership ended, we'd get a major increase in status by gaining a permanent seat on the Galactic Forum, alongside tens of thousands of other, older civilizations. It was just the first step in gaining access to a little more of the galaxy and having a voice – albeit a very small voice – where it mattered most. There were many levels of sharing, each one had to be earned, but for now our focus was simply to qualify for that first, most junior level of galactic citizenship. Unlimited sharing was a very long way off. By the time mankind was a senior member of the Forum, our civilization would have vastly transformed and our species would have moved on to the next stage of evolution beyond *Homo sapiens*, so immense were the time scales involved. They were time scales set by those who'd already trodden the path and knew the extraordinary length of the journey – a journey without short cuts.

For a species who'd been using stone tools a mere twenty thousand years ago – less than the blink of an eye in cosmic terms – the enormous time scales were daunting, but it was also a fair, rules based system, where every advance was earned and no one could deny what was rightfully due. Its fairness was why the great panoply of civilizations throughout the galaxy, from young to old, from primitive to incomprehensibly advanced, all supported it and why they united against any who threatened it.

The Tau Ceti gift had been an inducement, not a prison – proof that the benefits of joining the system and playing by its rules far outweighed opting out. We could send our ships beyond the limits of the TC charts if we wished, but the risks became unacceptably high the further out we went. Consequently, Mapped Space defined the physical extent of Human Interstellar Civilization, growing as we explored.

Icetop was four light years outside the TC charts, further than was generally practical to go given the navigational hazards, and the limits of our technology, but we'd explored it ourselves, making it one of the few human contributions to Mapped Space. We'd only gone to Icetop because the promise had seemed so great. Astronomical observations had detected a planet in the Creshan System of approximately the right size in roughly the right orbit for a human habitable planet. It orbited a G-type star of about the right age, offering the hope of a new Earth. We could have reached it in relative safety using a bubble at sub light velocity, but even at half the speed of light, the journey would have taken eight years. We needed to get there fast to make it assessable, so over a hundred and fifty years ago a navy survey team had been given the job of finding a way there. It took seven attempts with robotic probes before they finally succeeded. The first six probes were destroyed by dark matter gravitational effects that each subsequent probe avoided, so through trial and error, a path was found to the Creshan System. Once the navy knew where the dark matter was, a painstaking study of each hazard's gravitational effect allowed the navy to predict its trajectory. The danger was there were other dark matter anomalies wandering slowly out there that the navy hadn't detected, and which would inevitably drift into the charted space lane. It hadn't happened since the path to Icetop had been opened, but one day it would, with disastrous consequences.

It was why every flight to Icetop was a gamble.

When the navy finally surveyed the hoped for new Earth, they found a planet fourth from its star, in an orbit skirting the outer edge of the zone where liquid water could exist. More than seventy active volcanoes dotted the frozen wastes of Icetop, adding enough greenhouse gas to keep the equatorial region marginally habitable, but not to roll back the ice covering the four southern continents or to expose the vast northern ocean. Abundant oceanic life had generated a breathable atmosphere while the strip of exposed land at the equator permitted subarctic agriculture. It was, however, the iceberg filled oceans, offering fishing grounds potentially as rich as any seen on Earth, where Icetop's future wealth lay. Those frigid waters had attracted sizeable Core System investment to fund seeding the ocean and building the infrastructure required for commercial fishing.

It was precisely because Icetop was a spinning ice cube that it had escaped colonization by other civilizations – a lucky break for us. If we ever decided to warm it up, it might still become a new Earth, but that was a long way off. Earth Council habitually baulked at the cost and risk of terraforming any planet, especially one outside Mapped Space. Even so, they'd placed a small settlement on Icetop to establish our ownership rights. After all, it may have been a cold windswept hell hole, but it was lawfully ours.

Landing on Icetop was a simple insertion. With no traffic or orbital debris to dodge, we jumped onto their Landing Control's guide beam and simply dropped into the freezing atmosphere. The vacant lot that passed for a spaceport normally received less than a ship a month, although we soon discovered we were the seventh ship to land in less than forty eight hours. Minutes after engine shut down, a transmission arrived from Mukul Sarat with directions to the meeting place.

When the dust cleared, our external optics gave us a clear view of the other six ships already parked on the paved landing ground. The massive *Soberano* took up the entire southern end of the apron, four clicks away, while Marie's *Heureux* was only a few hundred meters east of us. The other ships were all strung out to the north. The closest was a small, disk shaped yacht that reeked of money. Further north, a utilitarian PFA container carrier, that was little more than a cube shaped skeleton with rectangular compartments for crew and propulsion, stood alongside a small intersystem ferry. At the northern end of the spaceport, parked as far away from the other ships as possible, was a rugged looking half cylinder with suspicious black scars along its sides.

"The yacht is from the Core Systems," Izin said as he joined Jase and I on the flight deck. As usual, he'd digested the port registry in the horizontal blink of his amphibian eyes. "She's the *Ariel*, owner's name withheld. The freighter is from Chengdu Xin. It claims to be carrying machine parts, although it's unloaded no cargo since landing. The ferry belongs to Mukul Sarat and that last ship is supposedly a bulk ore carrier called the *Cypress Vale*."

Izin's amphibian face never revealed his emotions but his words describing the last ship revealed his skepticism. The 'ore carrier' was obviously an old Earth Navy Vigilant class cutter. It had to be at least two hundred years old and looked as if it hadn't received hull maintenance for decades. The Vigilants used to carry a single heavy weapon and a respectable shield, although the navy would have stripped her down before selling her. Even so, whoever rescued her from the scrapyard could have refitted her with black market gear.

"Who's is it?" I asked.

"The port registry has no other data," Izin replied.

"I don't suppose the port authorities have questioned its class designation?"

"No."

Either they were grossly incompetent and couldn't tell a bulk ore carrier from a garbage scow, or they'd been paid to look the other way.

"It's got to be a Raven," Jase said. "Look at those hull scars!" It had taken Jase half the flight out from Hades City to recover from the stim bomb Sarat had pumped into him, and the second half for me to convince him not to go looking for payback.

"When it's dark, send a hull crawler over there. Find out what she's armed with." I glanced at the other ships curiously. "Check them all."

"I'll prepare a crawler this afternoon," Izin said.

I switched on the autonav's holo emitter and fed in Sarat's coordinates to see where we were going. All Jase and Izin knew was that we were here to acquire an illegal item I had a buyer for. Any profit would be split three ways after expenses, as usual. "Jase is coming with me. Izin, you'll stay aboard. This is no place for you."

"I would need a heavily insulated thermal suit to

survive out there," Izin agreed. Tamphs found cold climates unpleasant and exposure to freezing temperatures fatal.

A glowing marker on the western edge of Fjordheim, the only continent not buried under ice, highlighted where we were. A high mountain range cut across the middle of the land mass, spawning deep river valleys that fed fiords along both coasts. The *Silver Lining* had landed outside Tundratown, the only sizeable settlement, which served as both spaceport and seaport. A small village had also been established at an anchorage on the eastern side of Fjordheim for emergency repairs and crew swaps. The band of exposed ocean linking the two coasts was dotted with islands, mostly uninhabited although some were used by the fishing fleet as distant support bases. A third of the way around the equator from Tundratown was a string of dots marking the only archipelago on Icetop in the equatorial ring.

"That's where we're headed," I said, pointing to the tiny island chain. Sarat's message had given the latitude and longitude, and the *Lining's* astrographics data base revealed their name: the Dragon's Teeth.

Jase peered at the hologram curiously and shrugged. "Why come all the way out here and then fly a third of the way around this iceball to do this deal?"

"Because there are no eyes out there," I said.

Icetop had only three aging communications satellites in equatorial orbit and a tiny UniPol station in Tundratown with no global surveillance capability. Considering the navigational hazards, no Earth Navy frigate would risk coming out here unless they were going to bombard the planet. If enforcement was required, the navy was more likely to send expendable grunts out in a freighter. Several times a year, a naval liaison officer came out with the regular supply ship for an inspection, but that was the extent of Earth's reach. Icetop was as remote a place as a man could go and still find a trace of human civilization.

Whatever Sarat was selling, he was taking no chances with the law.

* * * *

Sarat had reserved a seat for me on a transport flying out to the fishing fleet's base in the Dragon's Teeth Archipelago. A fisherman, who suddenly developed an acute affinity for my credits, vacated his seat for Jase while a small gratuity to the pilot ensured no objections from the flight crew.

The aircraft was one of a small fleet of sub-orbital scramjets that shuttled supplies and replacement crews out to a network of isolated bases supporting Icetop's fishing fleet. Like the spaceport and Tundratown, the transport smelled of fish, not surprising considering sea creatures were the lifeblood of the colony. One hundred and thirty five years ago, seed populations of phytoplankton and Atlantic Cod had been released into the ocean. Both were naturally adapted to arctic waters, but some genetic reengineering on Earth had perfectly aligned that adaptation to Icetop's biochemistry. Within a few decades, the oceans had filled with the Earth transplanted life forms and commercial fishing had begun. The only effect on the indigenous aquatic species was to see their numbers increase dramatically as they acquired a taste for Earth-plankton. In particular, a large, slow moving creature that floated with the planet's ocean currents had begun to multiply to the point where it was constantly caught in the cod nets. The fishermen called them drift-whales, although they were neither air breathers nor mammals. Fortunately for Icetop's economy, their body chemistry allowed them to be processed into a thick oil suitable for combustion heating, although their meat was inedible.

The scramjet seated thirty and was fitted with small windows allowing us to see the ragged ice sheet to the south and the large icebergs that had broken free and were drifting towards the equatorial current. Occasionally the wakes of large factory ships could be seen dragging nets which scoured the oceans for cod and drift-whales. After several hours, the vast ice sheet to the south gave way to snow capped mountains and the dark plume of a distant volcano belching gas into the atmosphere.

Soon after the volcanic cloud fell behind us, the transport nosed down and began gliding on short delta wings towards a chain of jagged rock spires that rose from the cold, choppy seas like widely separated black spears. Watching the icy dark blue water below, I realized how underdressed Jase and I were in our thermal suits. The fishermen were all clad in yellow self-sealing flotation suits, enough to keep them alive even if they were swept into the sea. By contrast, our suits could withstand the arctic winds, but if we hit the freezing water, we'd be dead in thirty seconds.

The transport leveled off and flew along the scattered line of black needles. Waves crashed against their bases, throwing up clouds of white foam that were instantly whipped away by the wind, while their tips were lost in low hanging cloud hundreds of meters above the ocean. Most spires had landing platforms high above sea level, protruding from caverns carved out of the rock. After we'd passed more than twenty spires, the transport banked sharply, lowered its landing gear and threw itself recklessly onto a landing platform. The magnetized platform grabbed the scramjet's landing skis before the wind could hurl us into the sea, then a series of slender metal poles rose from the edge of the platform and began generating an invisible pressure wall around the landing pad, shielding the scramjet from the worst of the wind.

When the hatch cracked open, freezing sea air flooded into the cabin as the fishermen quickly filed out. We followed them across the partially exposed platform towards the shelter of the hangar inside the rock, surprised by the severity of the wind whipping over the top of the pressure wall.

Jase peered out at the rolling sea, dotted with icebergs and wind driven white caps. "Why would anyone want to live here?" he yelled over the whine of the wind.

"Do you know how much real cod sells for on Earth these days?" I yelled back, eager to get inside. Protected by the pressure wall, the wind wasn't strong enough to blow me into the sea, nevertheless my aversion to water made me feel uncomfortably exposed.

Jase gave me that sharp, hungry look he always got when he smelled money. "How much?"

"Enough to make good people sign five year contracts." When interest momentarily flashed across his face, I asked, "Thinking of changing careers?"

He glanced at the bleak, windswept sea and shook his head. "Not a chance!"

At the hangar's entrance we passed through another pressure field, this time into warm air where the scream of the wind was muted to a distant howl. A large metal door hung suspended above us, ready to roll down to shield the chamber if the winds grew too strong for the pressure field. Parked inside the hangar were three small utility aircraft used to ferry replacement crews and supplies out to the factory ships and link the isolated spire communities together. The hangar wasn't large enough to bring the heavy scramjet inside, which was already receiving passengers for the return trip to the mainland. The outbound men and women had completed their three month tours at sea and were returning to Tundratown for some hard earned rest.

Below the hangar, the spire was honeycombed with storage facilities, workshops, a small hospital and accommodation for the hundred people who operated the base. Due to the ferocity of the rolling seas surrounding the Devil's Teeth, there were no docking facilities for the fishing fleet. Everything and everyone had to be moved by air.

Mukul Sarat emerged from the back of the hangar wearing a more expensive version of the flotation suits the fishermen wore, suggesting he was a regular visitor to this barely habitable planet. "Captain Kade," Sarat said as he approached, "welcome to Icetop."

We shook hands, but our gloves prevented my threading getting direct physical contact for a DNA scan. Just as when he'd visited me in my stateroom, my threading registered nothing about him. Whatever he was carrying completely neutralized my bionetics, but for him only. I was still getting hits on everyone else in sight. Hiding my irritation at being out-teched, I said, "This is Jase Logan, my copilot."

Sarat gave Jase a surprised look, confirming my suspicion he'd expected me to leave Jase in Hades City. Accepting the unavoidable, Sarat extended his hand. "Welcome."

"We've met," Jase said, refusing to accept Sarat's outstretched hand. "Don't you remember?"

Sarat withdrew his hand slowly, glancing warily at me. "Do we have a problem, Captain Kade?"

I threw Jase a warning look. "No, no problem."

Sarat studied Jase uncertainly, then motioned to the elevator. "This way."

The lift took us up through the center of the spire to a surprisingly spacious penthouse. We stepped out into a large lounge area flanked by three floor-to-ceiling windows shielded by pressure fields and equipped with deployable metal shutters. The sprawling room was decorated with replica tribal ornaments and deeply padded chairs covered in tanned drift-whale hide, while the view out over the iceberg strewn ocean was hazy, but spectacular.

"This penthouse belongs to the owner of one of the largest fishing fleets on Icetop," Sarat explained as we took in the view. "I've rented it from him for this occasion."

"I guess fishing does pay," Jase observed as a solid looking individual with a military style haircut approached us with a portable scanner.

The guard quickly found our weapons, but we declined to hand them over.

"Your weapons will be returned to you, when you leave," Sarat assured us. "My guards will ensure you are quite safe."

"As safe as I was in Hades City?" Jase asked sharply.

Sarat eyed Jase suspiciously. For a moment, I thought he was going to have his guard throw Jase out, then Sarat relaxed. "You are my guest here. In Hades City, you were a potential threat. You may accept my hospitality, or you may leave."

"We accept," I said, handing over my bulky MAK P-50. When Jase refused to budge, I gave him a sharp look. I knew he'd rather shoot Sarat than accept his hospitality, but he kept his anger in check and passed his twin fraggers to the guard.

Everyone relaxed, then Sarat led us towards one of the corridors that led off from the central lounge. "We're only ten meters below the peak of the spire. There's a lookout up there, but I wouldn't recommend it. The winds are strong and very cold at this altitude, particularly this time of year."

Sarat showed us into a well appointed apartment with a single large bed and a drift-whale upholstered sofa. My threading picked up more than a dozen tiny thermal signatures placed around the room, devices designed to ensure we had no secrets from our host.

"Unfortunately," Sarat said, indicating the solitary bed, "I was expecting only one of you."

"We're not planning on staying long," I said.

"You'll be here for two days. It will take that long to complete the bidding process."

I gave him a puzzled look. "Seems a long process

for an auction."

"It's the seller's custom."

"You're not the seller?"

"I'm just the middle man."

"Who's the seller?"

"You'll meet him soon enough," Sarat said as he stepped towards the door. "Introductions and the first round will commence after lunch."

Sarat withdrew, closing the door behind him. Jase immediately turned to me, "Skipper, before you say anything, that bastard murdered two girls! My friends! And drugged the hell out of me!"

"I know."

"I'm going to frag him into little pieces!"

"No, you're not! We're here to get whatever he's selling, and leave. Forget your vendetta now or I'll put you on the first transport back to the spaceport myself."

Jase's jaw tightened as he fought to contain his anger. He wasn't to know my words were for the listening devices eavesdropping on our conversation, and to reassure Sarat, who was almost certainly watching us.

"Promise me, you'll let me at him," Jase demanded, "when this is over."

"No. I have a deal with Sarat and you're going to honor it." Right up until I put a slug in Sarat's head myself, not just for the two girls, but also for the two EIS agents he'd killed.

"Damn, what's got into you, Skipper?"

"This is a big deal for us," I said, speaking to Sarat's snoopers again. "If you want to be in on it, you play by my rules and by Sarat's rules."

Jase was ready to explode, but he started to believe I actually meant it. Slowly he cooled. "OK, Skipper."

"Good. Be on your best behavior and we'll get out of here and collect the biggest payoff of our lives," I said, silently increasing my fee to Lena, purely for Jase's sake.

Sarat would now believe he understood me, that I

was all about the money and therefore predictable. Revenge was a luxury this mission couldn't afford, although in time, I intended to complete both, then Jase would understand.

* * * *

We had cod for lunch, served in our room, then a burly guard in a dinner jacket led us to a rectangular audience chamber with a long pressure field covered window running the length of one wall. A factory ship was visible two clicks out, holding position as small aircraft took turns delivering fresh crew and supplies. The other walls were polished rock, decorated with images of frozen landscapes and drift-whale bones, while the rock floor had been carved to appear as if it was covered in slate tiles – a useless but expensive embellishment. At the far end of the room, circular metal plates lay flush to the floor and ceiling, emitters for a high fidelity holo communicator.

Sarat was waiting in the meeting hall with Marie, Vargis and three others I didn't recognize. Marie was surprised to see me, while Vargis barely acknowledged my existence. I gave Marie a sly smile, leaving her in no doubt I'd expected to see her here. It was our little game, who could outsmart who, and I might as well let her think I'd known what she was up to all along. It had been that way ever since we'd met two years ago on Galis, when she'd sweet talked a hydroponics dealer into cancelling my contract and giving it to her. I don't think she really cared about the contract, just beating me, which was more about personal chemistry than interstellar trade.

The three others with Sarat gave me appraising looks, assessing how big a threat I posed. I DNA locked them all, but only one, a tall cutthroat of east African descent named Gwandoya was wanted. He wore brightly colored silks, tightly braided shoulder length hair and a full beard threaded with colored jewels. He was in mankind's top one hundred most wanted, criminal royalty with a bloodthirsty record that would normally have obliged me to ensure he didn't leave here alive. The other two were clean skins; a small Chinese man and a tall Union business type. Both wore tailored suits and looked as if they belonged in board rooms rather than in the company of cold blooded killers like Gwandoya.

We exchanged polite nods then I caught Vargis' eye. "Did you find someone to do that Zen Tau run?"

Vargis looked dismissively down his nose at me. "You'll wish you'd taken my offer by the time this is over."

"Yeah, that was the chance of a lifetime," I replied sourly, then turned to Marie. "I really couldn't let you go skiing all by yourself," I said, reminding her I'd seen her looking for Icetop contracts at the Hades City Exchange.

"What are you doing here, Sirius?" she asked.

"The same thing you are. Well, not the losing part – I expect to win."

"The will to win is the key to personal excellence," the small Chinese man said.

I suspected he was quoting something, but had no idea what. "It's certainly better than losing."

"Sometimes winning is fatal," Gwandoya said, fixing me with a stony stare, "for those who lack the strength to keep what they win."

"I've never had that problem," I said, holding his gaze, offering him an unspoken challenge. Perhaps I could goad him into starting something that would allow me to deal with him in a way that wouldn't draw suspicion.

"Let me remind you all," Sarat said, trying to ease the tension, "that everyone here is my guest, and that no unpleasantness of any kind will be tolerated." He stared pointedly at me and Gwandoya, then took up position beside the holo communicator plates and waved for his muscle-bound butlers to hand out refreshments. "Thank you for coming to this secluded location," Sarat continued. "I'm sure you all agree, being out of reach of the authorities makes the effort worthwhile, particularly for the successful bidder. Now then, to the introductions." He motioned to the Chinese man first. "Bo Qiang, a lawyer bidding on behalf of a collector of rare alien artifacts from Earth. Beside him, we have Mr Gwandoya, representing . . . a large and successful cooperative."

Sarat was referring to the Pirate Brotherhood, whose only cooperation was in working together to pillage remote trade routes. Gwandoya was not just a notorious murderer and thief, he was the local kingpin, head of the Ravens, the Brotherhood's local chapter whose reach extended throughout the Outer Lyra region and beyond. The old navy cutter at the spaceport was undoubtedly his, making it a priority that we got back to the *Lining* with the goods and took off before he did.

"Next we have Mr Breckinridge, head of a major mining conglomerate and the lovely Captain Dulon, who will be bidding on behalf of the Beneficial Society of Traders."

I hid my surprise at hearing the Society was involved in something this shady. They were normally painfully careful to be seen to stay on the right side of the law, if for no other reason than their dependence on Earth Navy for protection and for landing rights at navy controlled spaceports across Mapped Space. Now I understood where Marie's fake Captain's tags and ship registry had came from. They weren't fakes. The Society had issued them to her. I leaned towards Marie and whispered, "You must know people in high places, *Esmin*. Did you choose that name? I could really see you as an *Esmin*."

She scowled, whispering back, "You'll pay for that."

"Whatever the price, *Esmin*, it was worth it!" I said with a wry smile.

"Next we have Senor Arturo Salbatore Vargis, representing the Chairman." Sarat gave Vargis a respectful, welcoming nod. For a moment, I wondered if Sarat showed a hint of favoritism towards Vargis, or was it simply deference to the Chairman, the shadowy mastermind behind the Consortium. The Consortium's existence was sometimes considered a myth, but the EIS knew there really was a secret alliance of powerful companies who manipulated economies of entire worlds for their own ends.

"And finally," Sarat continued, "the last member of our group, Captain Sirius Kade, who will be bidding on behalf of the most venerable Jie Kang Li."

Marie gave me an astonished look. Bidding for the Beneficial Society was one thing, that was a legitimate business, but bidding on behalf of one of the largest organized crime syndicates known to man genuinely shocked her.

"You're kidding?" She whispered. "The Yiwu?"

"I owed Li a favor," I lied, knowing she was disappointed and that no matter what happened, I could never tell her the truth.

Jase was also giving me a strange look. "That's who we're working for?"

Marie glanced at Jase, then back at me even more puzzled. "You mean even he doesn't know?"

I shrugged helplessly. "It's just a pick-up and delivery."

Jase looked uncomfortable, but he'd go along with it if I said so.

"The auction will be conducted according to Irzaen tradition," Sarat continued. "This means there will be three rounds of blind bidding. None of you will know what the other bids are, only the winning order. Two bidders will be eliminated after each of the first two rounds, with the winner being decided in the third round."

I'd heard of the Irzaens, but humanity had almost no

contact with them. They weren't an Orion Local Power and had no ambassadorial links with Earth. The Irzaen homeworld was supposed to be in the Scutum-Centaurus Arm, tens of thousands of light years away. They had a reputation for being shrewd, but honest traders, with links spanning the entire galaxy. That put them so far ahead of mankind, we assumed we had nothing of interest to offer them. So why were they now selling us alien-tech? And how could we even pay for it?

"Allow me to introduce Ani-Hata-Ga," Sarat said, pronouncing the name very quickly, with a slight guttural accent. "He is the Irzaen trade representative offering the merchandise you are here to bid on."

The metal floor and ceiling plates glowed to life as a holographic image of a quadrupoid appeared beside Sarat. There was a moment of unease, as humans accustomed to alien life forms that were mostly bipedal, viewed a species from an entirely different evolutionary path. The Irzaen had an ovoidal torso with four muscular arms and a slightly flattened spherical head containing a pair of evenly spaced, slat-like eyes. His arms were dexterous, each sprouting three stubby manipulators suitable for operating technology and strong enough to allow the Irzaen to walk on them like four legs. There was no way to judge his size, considering the image was a hologram without a point of reference, although he wore a complex series of belt-like straps across his double-shoulders, supporting metal objects of unknown purpose, which suggested he was somewhat larger than a human.

"Greetings good customers," an artificially synthesized basso voice said as one of the four arm-feet lifted and made a horizontal sweeping gesture of greeting. "We meet to determine who is most worthy of our gift of exchange."

Gift? Was that quadrupoid humor? If Lena's credit-vault was anything to go by, whatever he was selling was going for more than the net worth of most human worlds.

Sarat signaled to his butler-guards, who carried a small table into the meeting hall and placed it beside the Irzaen hologram. Sitting on the table was a silver dome a meter across. When the butler-guards withdrew, Ani-Hata-Ga motioned with one of his four arm-legs and the dome vanished, leaving only its thin metal base visible beneath a black metal octagon. A single gold metallic thread ran around the octagon's sides, while inscribed on its upper surface was a grid like pattern of angular characters. My threading searched through every known human and alien character set, but was unable to find a match.

"Be here the Antaran Codex for which our interaction exists," the Irzaen hologram said. "You have the Irzaen Promise of its authenticity."

The Irzaen Promise might have been the gold standard of guarantees from one end of the galaxy to the other, but it was wasted on a bunch of cynical, distrustful humans about to be separated from a mountain of their credits.

"That's all very well, Mr . . . Ga," Henry Breckinridge said in a politely suspicion tone, "but shouldn't we be given a demonstration?"

It was exactly what I wanted, but I dared not ask in case it signaled to the others I had no idea what I was bidding on.

"A demonstration will be provided when the bidding process is complete," Sarat said, "prior to the winner making payment and taking delivery, of course. Until that time, the Antaran Codex will remain encased in a protective field. And for those of you unfamiliar with the Irzaen Promise, let me assure you, it is worth far more than any demonstration or scan, both of which can be faked. If that is insufficient, I'll arrange for a transport to take you back to the spaceport immediately."

There was uncomfortable shifting amongst the bidders. No one wanted to withdraw or be cheated by an alien they knew nothing about.

"Is the technology stolen?" Bo Qiang, the Chinese lawyer asked.

"No," Sarat replied, "why do you ask?"

"Antares is a restricted system," Bo said. "No one is allowed to enter it."

"Esteemed customer," Ani-Hata-Ga said, "the provenance of the Antaran Codex is not in doubt. As you surmise, it was obtained from the dying star system you call Antares, although it did not originate from there. It is a region you are not yet entitled to enter, although the Irzae face no such restriction."

I queried my bionetic memory for Antares. It was a red supergiant in Scorpius, twelve million years old and ten times larger than Earth's sun. Because of its immense size, its life was short. Within a million years, it would become a supernova and at only five hundred and fifty light years from Earth, would become the brightest star ever seen in Earth's sky. And Bo Qiang was right, it was on the Access Treaty's restricted list, those star systems that no human ship could enter without triggering a treaty violation. Restricted systems were rare. Some were inhabited by advanced civilizations who chose not to be disturbed by unwelcome visitors; others contained primitive species not permitted contact with low level interstellar civilizations like ours; and then there were systems restricted without explanation. They were the rarest of all. Antares was one of those.

"Why is Antares restricted to us?" I asked.

"It is a graveyard," Ani-Hata-Ga replied, "and the rights of the dead are respected by all and enforced by the Forum."

"What kind of graveyard?" Breckenridge asked.

"Of ships. Many wrecks are adrift in the Antares System, awaiting their final end. They are all that remains of a great battle that took place long ago. Much life was lost, many ships destroyed, no gainful exchange for anyone."

"A battle?" I said surprised. The only interstellar war I'd ever heard of had been with the Intruders, and they'd come from outside the great spiral of the galaxy. "I thought the Forum prevented war."

"It does, between civilizations," the Irzaen trade representative confirmed. "Civil wars are a different matter, governed by the Great Fourth Principle."

The Development Principle allowed each civilization to progress in its own way, according to its own laws and customs, without interference, providing it did not adversely impact others. I hadn't realized that extended to allowing interstellar civil wars.

"A race known as the Kireen came close to exterminating themselves," Ani-Hata-Ga continued. "The wrecks in the Antares system were left as a permanent monument to the dead, one that has stood for over seven million years."

"Are you saying the Codex is over seven *million* years old?" Vargis demanded.

"Ridiculous!" Gwandoya snapped. "How can it still be working?"

"The passing of time affects it not," Ani-Hata-Ga replied, "for the Codex is the most durable of all devices ever constructed. It has always been this way, for without it, trapped are we all."

"Can it be traced back to Antares?" Marie asked warily.

"An Observer would have the skill to determine the origin of the merchandise, however, possessing it is not the same as removing it."

"Can it be traced back to you?" I asked, wondering if we could blame the Irzaens.

"We merely dispose of the merchandise. We did not salvage it."

"Who did?" I asked.

"Those who sell to us, do so with the knowledge the Irzae never betray a trust." He made another hand gesture of unknown meaning. "But I perceive your concerns. I give you the Promise of Irzae, those who ever watch the graveyard of Antares know no human has ever entered there. That is your protection."

"But if you sell it to us, does that get you into trouble?" I persisted.

"There are conventions and prohibitions," the Irzaen said carefully. "In truth, esteemed customer, such a sale breaks convention, but is not explicitly prohibited."

So this quadrupoid was peddling a seven million year old piece of alien-tech, looted from a graveyard mankind was barred from entering, by a grave robber we couldn't identify and sold to us by a hologram who was bending, but not breaking interstellar law. And even though the Tau Cetins would take one look at it and know where it came from, there was supposedly no risk to us. I was finding it hard to swallow. So were the others, yet no-one was leaving.

"Are you ready to begin, bidding the first?" Ani-Hata-Ga asked.

There were cautious nods and murmurs of agreement.

"You shall each make a confidential opening bid," Sarat said, "which will be collected in secret and revealed this evening after dinner."

"Why the wait?" Gwandoya demanded impatiently.

"After the bidding closes," Sarat replied, "we will fully authenticate your digital-vault balances to ensure each bid is valid."

Digital-vaults had layers of authentication. Most transactions were executed quickly with the lowest level security, but full validation took time to process encryption keys through complex multivariate analyses. It was what enabled each vault-key to effectively be a tiny piece of Earth Bank itself.

"You will enter your bids into this console," Sarat said, motioning to a small Earth Bank auctioneer held by one of his butler-guards. The sturdy, rectangular machine was coated in black, poly-dense armor, with an unbroken Earth Bank molecular seal at the only access point, proof the machine's internal systems had not been tampered with in any way. Such machines were rare outside the Core Systems, not only because of their cost, but because Earth Bank rarely let them out of their sight. Its verdict would be final and unequivocal and it would ensure the appropriate digital-vault keys were updated. "Shall we set the floor price at one thousand tera-credits?"

Sarat watched us all, assessing if this astronomical figure was within our reach. I didn't know if he'd picked that number because it was the price the Irzaen had instructed him to begin with, or because I'd shown him my bankroll – which in hindsight was a mistake. Either way, none of the other bidders seemed perturbed by the number, so I guess they all thought the Antaran Codex – whatever it was – was worth it.

"Only one thousand tera-credits?" Breckinridge joked as he stepped forward, having decided to bid first as a show of confidence. The mining magnate inserted his vault key into the auctioneer and entered his bid, watched intently by Bo Qiang. I exchanged looks with Marie, seeing uncertainty in her eyes.

"So Esmin, who's going to win?" I whispered.

"The best woman of course!" she said with more confidence than she felt. "And if you call me that name again, I'll share your innermost secrets with . . . Jase!"

I feigned a frown. "You wouldn't?"

She smiled, daring me to keep taunting her.

When Breckinridge completed his bid, Vargis went next. When he was finished, I motioned for Bo to go next, but he declined.

"I prefer to bid last, Captain Kade, if you don't mind. It is an ancient Chinese tradition."

"I didn't know that," I said, approaching the machine and sliding Lena's vault-key into the Earth Bank auctioneer, then waited while it verified my identify.

There must have been a strategy to this kind of bidding, but I had no idea what it was. All I knew for sure was if I went too low, I'd be eliminated in the first round. I began to realize why the Irzaens had a reputation for shrewdness. This process was designed to panic buyers into paying as much as they could afford. I decided not to go all out in round one, but didn't want to low ball myself, so I bet three quarters of the balance in the vault and hoped I'd still be in the game tomorrow.

Marie followed me, then Bo Qiang went last.

With round one bidding concluded, we retired to the lounge for cocktails and small talk. While I sipped my drink, I wondered what kind of alien-tech would attract a mining magnate, a pirate king, a white collar criminal genius, the Beneficial Society and a Chinese alien artifact collector? Whatever it was, even though Lena had given me an obscenely large bucket of credits to play with, I had a feeling it wouldn't be enough.

* * * *

An impressive table was set for dinner in a banquet hall with panoramic views of the iceberg strewn sea. Before the first course arrived, a darkness descended over the ocean outside, broken only by the distant lights of a solitary factory ship.

By unspoken agreement Marie and I sat together, while the inscrutable Bo Qiang sat on my other side. The other three bidders sat opposite, with Jase at one end of the table and Sarat, smoking one of his foul smelling fume-sticks, at the other. Sarat's butler-guards moved around the table serving food and drinks efficiently, but without courtesy. To my surprise, dinner was not seafood, but included meat and vegetables, obviously prepared by a gourmet chef with imported ingredients.

Presently, Vargis turned to Sarat and asked, "Why should we trust these Irzaens? For all we know this could be an elaborate swindle."

"Trust is their business, Senor Vargis. If they cheated you, other more important customers would hear about it."

"But why would anyone care if the Irzaens cheated us?" Breckinridge asked.

"The Irzaens are an ancient and distinguished civilization," Sarat replied. "Cheating the newest interstellar civilization in the entire galaxy would harm their reputation. That's what they care about, not us."

"Even if they don't cheat us," I said, "what possible use are our credits to them?"

Sarat took a long slow pull on his fume-stick, before exhaling. "They have no interest in our technology, our art or our culture, but they have discovered one thing we have that they want. You see they're herbivores, which partly explains why they are one of the least aggressive species in the galaxy. Recently, they became aware of an Earth plant, called *convallaria majalis*, more commonly known as the 'lily of the valley'. It's an extremely aromatic plant, especially to Irzaen senses, and one they find particularly appetizing."

"Are you saying they want to buy flowers from us?" Gwandoya growled contemptuously.

"No," Sarat replied, "They want to buy food from us. A lot of food. Once they have the credits from this deal, they'll establish diplomatic relations with Earth. They will then place a large ongoing order for that plant triggering a great new agricultural industry for mankind, one that will allow us to trade with one of the more advanced civilizations in the galaxy. They get – what is to them – a rare and exotic delicacy and we get rich. Everyone wins."

It made such good sense I began to wonder whether there really was an impending Access Treaty violation. If the Irzaens were the reputable traders Sarat claimed and the deal was ultimately about food, then the only risk was related to the Antaran Codex itself, and I wouldn't know what that was until after the bidding. Even if the Codex really was harmless, I had to win the auction in case it wasn't.

The next course came and the conversation splintered. Presently, I whispered to Marie, "So Esmin, how long have you been fronting for the Society?"

She held up her knife, admiring its sharp edge in the light. "Are you sure you want to keep calling me that name?"

"Well, since you put it like that . . ."

She lowered the knife to her plate. "My family has lived and breathed the Society for generations. I don't front for them, I am them."

It had never occurred to me before, that there were inner layers to the Beneficial Society of Traders which were hidden from some members, even second generation members like me. Perhaps it was more of a secret society than I realized. "I'm surprised they're interested in an old alien-tech relic."

She gave me a puzzled look. "Really? How could they not be? It's everything they ever wanted?"

I was burning to know why the Society wanted it so badly, but once she realized I was in the dark, she'd play me. Irrespective of what we were in the bedroom, in this game we were competitors – and that's how we both liked it.

"Buying stolen or illegal alien-tech might upset the navy," I said, "maybe even the Earth Council."

"The risk is worth it. You of all people should see that," she said without looking up. "So how did you get mixed up with Jie Kang Li?"

"Oh, we go way back." When I'd been a serving EIS agent, I'd taken down a high ranking Yiwu crime lord and his gang on Shengtai, which was why I avoided PFA systems these days. There were still plenty of Yiwu agents out there who might recognize me. "Li introduced me to kung pao chicken. It's a little hot for my taste, but he insisted I'd get used to it. I never did."

She looked bemused, unsure if I was joking or not. "What will the Yiwu do with the Codex, if you win?"

"Jie Kang Li didn't tell me."

She sliced through the beef on her plate, adding absently. "It's not something I thought they could use."

"That's what I said when Li offered me the job."

She turned towards me with a knowing look and whispered, "You have absolutely no idea what it is, do you?"

As usual, she'd seen right through me. "Nope, not a clue. Care to throw me a bone?"

"If only you hadn't called me Esmin so many times!" She drained her glass of imported wine, patted me on the shoulder with mock sympathy and excused herself for the ladies' room.

When she was out of earshot, Bo Qiang leaned towards me and said in a low voice, "The Yiwu Alliance would find many uses for the Codex."

"I wouldn't know."

"Oh yes," he continued slowly. "They would pay a great deal for this kind of opportunity and would be very disappointed not to win. One might say, even angry with anyone who got in their way."

I realized Marie's presence had distracted me, preventing me from noticing how carefully Bo had been listening to our conversation. I realized he'd shadowed me to the table, choosing his seat only after Marie and I had chosen ours, ensuring he sat beside me where he could listen to my every word.

"You say that like a man with knowledge of such things," I said.

Bo inclined his head evasively. "I am a simple lawyer. I revere my ancestors. I care for my family. And I work tirelessly for my client."

"Right," I said warily, sensing there was something else going on with Bo that I didn't understand. "Your client is a collector?"

"Most assuredly, Captain Kade. He is a man of

great discretion, diverse interests and . . . sadly, an unforgiving nature."

There was no mistaking his implied threat, although I wasn't sure why this seemingly innocuous little man would want to threaten me. "I guess you'll be in trouble if you don't win."

"There is one thing my client does not collect, Captain Kade."

"And what would that be?"

"Enemies," Bo said quietly.

"Everyone has enemies."

"An enemy is only an enemy until he is dead, and then he is just a corpse," Bo said with quiet menace.

For the first time, I realized there was a cold ruthless streak in little Bo. He'd hidden it well, but for some reason he'd decided to reveal it to me. "Right, he has no enemies because he's unforgiving."

"Precisely."

I had a terrible feeling I knew what Bo was trying to tell me and it wasn't simply that the enemies of his client ended up dead. "This client of yours, this unforgiving collector, his name would be . . . ?"

"Jie Kang Li," Bo whispered so no-one else would hear.

"Of course it is," I said knowing my cover was blown.

I wondered if I could kill Bo without drawing attention to the act. The others were talking quietly among themselves. The butler-guards were hovering nearby, but no one was paying us any particular attention. I knew when Marie returned, all male eyes would be drawn to her beauty, if only for a moment. With ultra-reflexed muscles, I could kill Bo with a single, lightning fast blow to the temple, or break his neck, but could I do it fast enough not to be seen? "It seems Jie Kang Li is bidding against himself."

Bo sipped his green tea, replacing the cup slowly. "I think not, Captain Kade."

"Then one of us is not who he says he is."

Bo pursed his lips thoughtfully. "Apparently not."

Marie returned to the room and for a moment all eyes turned towards her as expected. I tensed, thinking I could drive a knuckle into Bo's temple in under a second, then pretend he was choking and jump to my feet to help him, masking the blow.

"The cautious seldom err," Bo said quickly.

I hesitated. "What?"

"The cautious seldom err," he repeated. "Confucius said it four and half thousand years ago. Wise then, wiser today."

"I guess so."

"Attempting to strike me down would not be cautious, Captain Kade. Indeed, it would be a grievous error."

He'd read my body language? I'd tensed ever so slightly, preparing to strike in a way that should have been impossible to read.

Bo saw the confusion on my face. "In martial arts, one studies the eyes, not the form, to anticipate an opponent's move. For a grand master, a look is an eternity."

I'd telegraphed my intention with my eyes? It seemed impossible but Bo was telling me he was a grand master – and he'd been right! Even if he wasn't re-sequenced, a grand master might just be fast enough to deflect an ultra-reflexed blow. It was something I'd never put to the test and decided with no chance of surprise, this wasn't the time or place to try. I visibly relaxed, leaned toward him and whispered, "You're not really a lawyer, are you?"

"I know where the law begins, where it ends and all that lies beyond."

I took that as a yes, giving Marie a welcoming smile as she returned to her seat. While she refilled her wine glass, I whispered to Bo, "Do we have a problem?"

"Not tonight. Tomorrow perhaps."

I lifted my glass and toasted him. "Until tomorrow then and . . . to caution."

Bo inclined his head, returning my toast with his cup of green tea, throwing me another piece of Confucian wisdom, "Silence is a true friend who never betrays."

"To silence," I said, wondering if I could make a deal with Bo as he seemed in no hurry to expose me.

At the end of the table, Mukul Sarat tapped his wine glass several times for quiet, then said, "I'm pleased to inform you that the Earth Bank auctioneer has validated all bids, making this an extremely prosperous group."

Everyone had their poker faces on, revealing nothing, except for Gwandoya who appeared increasingly irritated by the process. Clearly, he was used to taking what he wanted and killing anyone in his way.

Sarat motioned to the polished rock wall behind him, which dissolved into a blue screen. "The qualifying bids will be displayed on this screen. If your name does not appear, you will not be participating in the second round. The entire process is automated and controlled by the Earth Bank auctioneer to the extent that even I do not know the results."

We all focused our attention on the screen to see Arturo Vargis' name appear first.

"Congratulations Senor," Sarat said, "Your bid was the highest."

There was a round of polite congratulations from everyone except Gwandoya. Vargis nodded curtly with no sign of surprise or relief. From his demeanor, it was obvious he expected to win, and now he had the tactical advantage of knowing the highest bid. A moment later, Bo Qiang's name appeared on the screen.

"Congratulations Mr Bo," Sarat said, "your bid was the second highest."

Again Gwandoya was the only bidder not to acknowledge the qualifying bidder. Bo's face was impassive, but for a moment I saw a flicker of anger and surprise in his expression. He took a breath, burying whatever had incensed him and accepted the congratulations humbly. Bo then fell into a brooding silence, although he gave no hint as to why.

When my name appeared next, Sarat said, "Congratulations Captain Kade, your bid has qualified you for the second round."

"Way to go, Skipper!" Jase said enthusiastically, holding up a glass of Sarat's finest wine and throwing it back in one gulp.

I acknowledged the other's congratulations, seeing the tension on the faces of the three contenders now competing for the final place. Marie was worried while Breckinridge's courteous joviality was replaced by a nervous intensity. Gwandoya looked like he was about to explode, making me glad that Sarat had disarmed him.

Finally, the last name appeared, bringing a smile to Sarat's lips. "Congratulations Mademoiselle Dulon, you are the fourth bidder."

Marie's tension was instantly replaced by a gracious smile. "Thank you."

"At least you'll be joining us for breakfast," I whispered.

"It's a pity you won't be here for lunch," she said through her smile.

Gwandoya stood up angrily, stared at the screen with bulging eyes and a clenched jaw, then smashed his glass onto the floor and stormed out.

"Not a good loser," I said.

"Hopefully you will take your defeat tomorrow in a better spirit," Vargis said.

"I'm not a good loser either."

"He really isn't," Marie said in a confiding tone, "although he should be, because I beat him all the time."

"I only let you win to give you a false sense of security."

"Sure you do," Marie said patronizingly.

Sarat turned to the mining magnate. "Thank you, Mr Breckinridge, for coming all this way. I'm sorry it hasn't turned out better for you."

Breckinridge shrugged. "Thank you for the invitation."

Sarat stood slowly. "That concludes tonight's proceedings. Breakfast will be at eight, bidding at ten. The bar will remain open as late as you like." Sarat excused himself and disappeared down a corridor leaving us in the care of his humorless butler-guards.

"Open bar! My kind of place!" Jase declared, motioning to one of the butler-guards to bring him another bottle.

Marie and I exchanged inquisitive looks, then by mutual agreement – with the contest still in the balance – decided not to retire to the same room.

"See you in the morning," she whispered to me in a way that promised another night, then she headed off down the corridor to her apartment.

Jase took the fresh bottle from the butler-guard, then we headed back to our room. He took a swig, then said in a low voice, "For a moment there, Skipper, I thought I was sleeping in the hall."

"For a moment, you almost were."

* * * *

An alarm shrieked out of the darkness, snapping me instantly awake. Jase sat up on the sofa blinking in protest when I switched on the lights. It was three AM and the warbling siren was coming from outside our room. We dressed quickly and hurried towards the siren emanating from the meeting hall. Several guards stood over Henry Breckinridge, lying in a pool of blood in front of the Antaran Codex. His body had been neatly cut in half through the chest.

"Oh man," Jase said, wincing at the gruesome sight.

Sarat rushed in wearing only a robe, cursing under

his breath when he saw Breckinridge's bloody corpse. "Get this cleaned up immediately!" He yelled at the guards.

Several of his men hurried off down a corridor as Marie, Bo Qiang and Vargis arrived.

Sarat turned to us with an apologetic look. "I didn't expect anyone in this group to try to steal the Codex." He motioned to the flat metal disk upon which it sat. "There are no guards in here for a reason. They're not needed. As you can see, the Codex is well protected."

"You should have warned us," Vargis snapped. "Suppose I'd tried to examine it?"

"Then we would have one less person to bid against," Bo observed dryly.

"I told you it was shielded," Sarat said. "That should have been enough."

If I'd lost the first round, that would have been me lying on the floor in pieces instead of Breckinridge. I took a closer look at what I'd assumed was simply a polished metal container used to transport the Codex. My threading detected no thermal or electromagnetic signature, yet it had generated enough energy to cut Breckinridge apart and to do so without scarring the wall behind him.

"The base is alien-tech, isn't it." I said. "Is it Irzaen?"

"They used this device to deliver the Codex to me," Sarat admitted.

"So it's a vehicle and a weapon?" I asked, surprised at the incredible miniaturization that had gone into the transport device. We had no accurate information on how far ahead of us the Irzaens were, but it was far enough to ensure my threaded senses couldn't detect their technology.

"It's a secure means of transport until the winning bid is decided," Sarat said. "When we have concluded our business, it will release the Codex and return to the Irzaens."

"Why are they not here in person?" Bo asked.

"They prefer to work through intermediaries," Sarat replied, "although I assume they have a ship in this system."

"Have you ever met them, face to face?" Marie asked.

"We communicate via holograms."

"Holograms are easily faked," Vargis snapped. "I demand we meet this Irzaen in person. I want to know who I'm dealing with!"

Vargis might have been a supercilious slime ball, but he knew a dodgy deal when he saw one. No wonder the Chairman had sent him out here to represent the Consortium.

"That won't be possible," Sarat said. "Their atmospheric requirements are somewhat different to ours, but let me assure you, I've been dealing with them for more than two years and they've never given me cause to doubt them. If you play by the Irzaen rules, there will be no more surprises. The only reason Mr Breckinridge is dead is because he tried to steal the Codex."

I noticed we were short one other member. "Where's Gwandoya?"

"On his way back to the mainland," Sarat replied. "Once he was disqualified, he insisted on leaving immediately."

"You should have kept him here until the winner was safely off planet," I said, certain Gwandoya would be waiting in orbit for whoever won the Codex.

"I must agree with Captain Kade," Bo said. "It was unwise to allow Gwandoya to leave."

"What's the matter, gentlemen," Vargis said, "Afraid of a bunch of rag tag pirates?"

I wanted to say that not all of us were flying battleships, but instead, refrained from letting Vargis know I'd investigated his ship's movements. "Some of us prefer to err on the side of caution. Right Mr Bo?"

Bo Qiang nodded. "Indeed."

The guards came and covered Breckinridge's body, then we started back to our respective apartments as the clean up began.

When we were out of earshot, Marie whispered to me and Jase. "Gwandoya's not going to let the winner just fly away."

"Maybe we should let Vargis win," Jase said, "So they kill each other."

"Then we'll split the salvage," Marie agreed.

"You can have the salvage," I said, "I want the Codex."

* * * *

Early next morning, I went up to the lookout at the top of the rock spire. It was a low walled square cut into the spire's apex with no protection from the icy wind. A skeletal tower in one corner housed a communications relay and the local weather station, while heating elements embedded in the rock prevented ice forming on the floor. The lookout had panoramic views of the distant rock spires spread in a line from the north west to the south east, and of the endless white capped sea dotted with icebergs surrounding them.

I activated the small communicator Izin had fitted with a powerful encryptor and, using my body to shield it from the wind, said, "Izin, are you there?"

His response came through with surprising clarity. "Yes, Captain. My hull crawler was unable to complete the activities you requested. It was destroyed before it got within range of the cutter."

"If that ship takes off, track it. We'll need to know where it is when we leave."

"It launched early this morning, Captain. I lost contact with it when it moved to the far side of the planet."

Gwandoya was clearly going to make getting away

from Icetop in one piece tricky. Perhaps he'd never intended to win, just to know where and when the auction was to be held, so he could pick off the winner. "Do you have access to our location?"

"No, Captain. The system defenses there are extremely sophisticated."

"I can't win without help." I'd already bid three quarters of Lena's EIS money and placed only third with two rounds to go. With Vargis representing the Consortium, his pockets were sure to be deeper than mine.

"You'll need to give me access from your side."

The elevator door opened and two of Sarat's butler-guards emerged with assault weapons leveled at me. "Got to go," I said quickly, raising my hands in surrender.

One of the guards snatched the communicator out of my hand. "No unauthorized communications!"

"Authorized by who?"

The guard ignored my question, holding the communicator in front of my face. "Who were you talking to?"

"My ship. I was checking on how our maintenance was proceeding."

"Why was the signal encrypted?"

So they had been listening in, even up here. "I use it to discuss commercially sensitive information. I have this thing about nosy people with assault weapons knowing my business."

The guard gave me a stare colder than the wind tearing at my face. "Why wasn't this communicator detected when you arrived?"

"Your people scanned me, ask them." I neglected to mention the communicator had been sealed inside my left boot, insulated from all but the most advanced detection equipment.

The guard pocketed the communicator. "You'll get it back when you leave. Do you have any other communication devices?"

"Not that I can think of, but I have a notoriously bad memory."

Under other circumstances he would have clubbed me with his weapon, but as I was Sarat's guest, he restrained his more brutal impulses. "Breakfast is in ten minutes," the guard snapped, then he and his companion returned to the elevator.

If I couldn't find a way to contact Izin, my instincts told me there was little hope of stopping Vargis winning. I watched the iceberg filled sea for a while, gathering my thoughts before going down to breakfast.

* * * *

"It is such a pity you have all come so far, for nothing," Vargis said as he sipped a strong black coffee. There was no smile, no play at humor, just an unabashed show of confidence designed to unsettle his competition.

"It was worth coming," Marie said, "just to sample Mr Sarat's excellent food and wine."

Sarat nodded appreciatively. "Our Irzaen host commissioned me to ensure your comfort. He was most generous. Lavishing attention on high net worth customers is part of the Irzaen culture."

"If we're dealing with Irzaens," Vargis said suspiciously.

"If this is the first time the Irzaens have traded with humans," Bo asked astutely, "how did they pay for all of this?"

Sarat lit a fume-stick. "They gave me a small quantity of precious gems, which I sold for currency."

"Did you pick Icetop?" Marie asked.

"No. Ani-Hata-Ga selected the planet, although I found this specific location." Sarat replied.

"So they know enough about us to know the navy doesn't come here," I guessed, and to choose Sarat as their middle man. "That would make this a good place to hide a ship in-system without being detected, for as long as they like."

"I wouldn't know," Sarat said evasively.

"They could even have a base here," Marie suggested. "From what I've seen, the locals would never detect an alien presence on this planet."

"Anything is possible," Sarat conceded, showing a remarkable lack of curiosity. Clearly, he was being well paid not to ask questions.

The Irzaens had chosen their middle man and their location well, which for a species with almost no contact with Earth showed a remarkable level of understanding. Watching Sarat puffing on his fume-stick, I wondered if he realized he was useful to a point, but one wrong move and he could quickly find himself expendable.

"If they do have a base here on Icetop, they won't need it once the Codex transaction is complete," Sarat added. "They will open a permanent embassy on Earth and negotiate a trade treaty."

"Why do you call it a Codex?" I asked. "It's an archaic word for a book, isn't it?"

Vargis gave me a surprised look, wondering how much I really knew, but said nothing.

"There is no exact equivalent description of this device in our language," Sarat said, "So the Irzaens chose a word that carried the qualities of the device. It's highly compact, easy to access and virtually indestructible."

"Nothing is indestructible," Bo said.

"It would require a fusion explosion to penetrate its structure, and as such weapons are banned there is little chance it will ever be destroyed."

"Why does it need to be indestructible?" I asked.

"Ani-Hata-Ga told you that without the Codex, we are trapped," Sarat replied, toying with me. Whatever his meaning, it was obvious the others understood it. "The ancient Romans invented the first Codex because they needed something more durable than scrolls. I'd say a device able to survive drifting in space for eons is highly durable. Wouldn't you?"

A book meant knowledge, but what kind of knowledge? Alien science was virtually useless to mankind because we lacked the industrial base to put it to work and the theoretical background to understand it. Yet, Vargis, Bo and Marie were all convinced of the Codex's value.

"I assume the Irzaens have equivalent devices," Vargis said. "Why not just sell us one of theirs?"

"Because an Observer would immediately recognize their technology. The Irzaens would find that embarrassing. Selling old relics is simply business, but gifting their own technology is a political decision."

"What you mean is if the deal goes bad, Ani-Hata-Ga takes the fall," Vargis said, "Instead of the Irzaen government."

"Exactly."

"But the Irzaens are a galactic species," Marie said. "Wouldn't that make them Observers?"

Sarat shook his head. "They're nowhere near that level. Few are. Ani-Hata-Ga believes an Observer would consider it possible we found the Codex drifting in space – because it's almost true. Selling it in secret, with no way to trace it back to the Irzaens, avoids both embarrassment for them and censure for us."

Almost true was still a lie and it was Earth Council policy never to risk lying to an Observer. There were few Observer species for a reason. They were the oldest, most advanced and impartial civilizations in the galaxy. An Observer representation to the Forum was treated as fact, which was why the membership supported their recommendations. They were never wrong, never asserted anything they couldn't prove beyond doubt and only ever recommended a decision that was fully within the letter and spirit of the law. From a human perspective, we assumed the Tau Cetins – the only Observer civilization Earth had ever had contact with –

could use their magic to see right through any lie. We might omit mentioning secrets like bionetics, but if they asked us a straight question, we always gave them a straight answer, no matter how difficult. Fortunately, providing we played by their rules, they rarely ever asked us any questions.

"When you return the silver machine the Codex came in," Jase said, "you could track it. Find out where the Irzaens are hiding?"

Sarat looked thoughtful for a moment, considering the odds, then shook his head. "Ani-Hata-Ga would detect any probe I launched to track the device. That might jeopardize my future dealings with the Irzaens." Sarat chose his words carefully, revealing he would cheat the Irzaens in a heartbeat, but only if he could get away with it.

Our host finally stubbed out the remains of his fume-stick and stood. "It is time for the next round."

* * * *

Soon after we had gathered in the meeting hall, the holographic image of the Irzaen trade representative appeared. "Greetings, good customers," Ani-Hata-Ga began formally, "and appreciation to those who sought exchange, but whose desire was insufficient to settle."

With one of the eliminated bidders dead and the other waiting in orbit to kill the winner, Ani-Hata-Ga was thanking no-one present. It made me wonder if he was broadcasting from a location so remote that he was unaware of what had been happening.

The Irzaen made a sweeping gesture. "Let us begin bidding the second."

Sarat motioned us to the Earth Bank auctioneer, which would again record our bids. Following Irzaen tradition, Marie, having been the lowest bidder in the first round, logged her bid first. I went next. Having decided playing games would get me eliminated early, I bid the entire balance on Lena's digital-vault. Bo followed me, showing no sign of anxiety, then Vargis as winner of the first round bid last.

Once the formalities were concluded, we gathered together in the lounge for synth-bean coffee and idle time watching the ocean outside being whipped up by strengthening winds. The conversation was muted as we awaited the Earth Bank auctioneer's decision on who qualified for the final round. Marie looked apprehensive, while Bo remained impenetrable and Vargis stood by himself, impatient to collect his prize and start the long voyage back to the Core Systems.

Eventually we were summoned to lunch after which Sarat announced, "The auctioneer has now validated the second round bids. If your name does not appear on the screen, you have been eliminated."

He turned towards the screen in the rock wall. Marie clenched her fists nervously while Vargis tried to appear calmer than he was. Only Bo sat back impassively, strangely relaxed as if he had nothing riding on the outcome. When I caught his eye, he shook his head slightly, telling me something was wrong. It was a look he might have given a confidant, leaving me with the sense that he no longer considered blowing my cover. There was something more important on his mind, although he made no attempt to explain what it was.

Outside, the sky was turning dark gray as a broad storm front came rolling down from the northern hemisphere ice plains. The pressure fields shielding the windows had automatically ramped up, blurring the view and muting the hollow howl of the wind.

Behind Sarat, the wall screen turned blue as everyone held their breath and the second highest bidder's name appeared.

Sarat turned to me. "Congratulations, Captain Kade."

"Yeah!" Jase declared enthusiastically. "That's what we're here for!"

I accepted Sarat's congratulations gracefully, feigning happiness, knowing I'd lost the auction. I'd bet my limit and still only placed second, making the final round a mere formality.

"Well played," Marie said tensely, but her eyes told me she hated losing.

"Thanks," I said mildly, wondering if she'd have to pay penalties to the Beneficial Society for not delivering on her contract.

A moment later, my final round opponent's name appeared.

"Congratulations Senor Vargis," Sarat said. "Once again, you are the highest bidder."

Vargis relaxed, regaining his confidence with his second triumph. "I hope Jie Kang Li doesn't put a price on your head for coming second, Captain Kade."

"I could say the same to you about the Chairman, or will he just demote you to janitor when you return empty handed?" I glanced at Bo. "Better luck next time, Bo."

Bo was staring at Sarat, deep in thought, then he offered me his hand and another piece of Confucian wisdom. "Our greatest glory is not in never failing, but in rising every time we fall."

"That's the spirit," I said, shaking hands.

"I would like to make you an offer, Captain Kade," Bo said. "I propose to pool my vault with yours on the understanding that we share the Codex, should you win."

Was that why he hadn't betrayed me to Sarat? He'd decided he couldn't beat Vargis alone and was keeping me as his insurance policy. "When you say share," I said, "who gets to hold the Codex?"

"If you bid without my help, you do. If you bid with my help, I do, but you may accompany me on my ship."

It was the old rule, the last money to the deal called the shots. "I'll think about it," I said turning to Sarat, aware Vargis was now watching me intently. "Is there a problem if Bo, Marie and I combine our–"

"Since when did I agree to share?" Marie

demanded.

"Since you got eliminated and your only chance of getting a slice of the action is to pool your resources with Mr Bo and me." I turned to Bo. "Right?"

Bo Qiang nodded. "I am willing to share with Captain Dulon, on the same terms."

"Is a collective bid acceptable?" I asked.

"All Ani-Hata-Ga cares about is the final price," Sarat said. "Side deals are not his concern."

"That was not part of the arrangement!" Vargis snapped.

"Syndicates are not explicitly prohibited," Sarat said. "You yourself represent the Consortium, which is a very large syndicate."

"But they have been eliminated already!" Vargis said, glancing at Marie and Bo Qiang.

"Captain Kade makes the bid. How he comes by his funds is not my concern." Sarat sucked on his fume-stick thoughtfully. "From what I know of the Irzaens, they're not a sentimental people. They'll welcome the highest possible bid." Vargis fell silent, scowling, then Sarat continued, "The final round will commence in thirty minutes."

I gave Jase a look, inviting him to follow me away from the others. When we were out of earshot, I said, "We need to find a way to contact Izin – fast."

"Why, you're doing great!"

"I'm about to get my butt kicked, unless Izin can find a way to fix the result."

Jase sobered. "Sarat's guards aren't going to let us anywhere near their comm system."

"I know. Think you could take one, unarmed?"

Jase grinned. "Hell yeah! Two of them – three if I was drunk!"

Probably not, but I liked his eagerness. "Try to avoid getting yourself killed or letting Sarat know what you're doing, but if we don't find a way to rig this game soon, we won't even make shuttle fare off this ice cube."

* * * *

When we met in the meeting hall for the final round, I took Bo and Marie aside to give them the bad news. “Much as I appreciate the offer Bo, I’m going it alone.” Bo simply nodded agreeably, barely disappointed. “Do we have a problem?” I asked, code for was he going to blow my cover?

“No, we would have lost anyway,” Bo replied fatalistically.

“If you felt that way, why make the offer?”

“I’m a curious man, Captain Kade. I wondered if the Irzaens really want the highest bid.”

“You don’t think they do?” Marie asked, surprised.

Bo glanced uncertainly at Sarat. “I do not know, but this game is not what it appears.”

“If we had to share it,” Marie said when I turned to her, “we’d just fight over it. I’ll tell the Society they didn’t give me a big enough bankroll.”

“I’ll vouch for that.”

“As if the Society trusts you!”

We turned to the end of the hall as the floor and ceiling holo plates glowed and the Irzaen trade representative appeared beside Sarat.

“Greetings good customers,” Ani-Hata-Ga began formally, “welcome to the rewarding stage of decision. Let us begin bidding the final.”

With all eyes upon Vargis and me, no one noticed Jase’s absence. Outside the gray clouds had turned black and the howling wind was driving snow horizontally past the long window, threatening to overpower its pressure field. Before we started bidding, the guards lowered the large rectangular metal shutter over the window, sealing us off from the outside world.

Sarat motioned to the Earth Bank auctioneer. “Captain Kade, you have the honor of bidding first.”

I stepped up to the Earth Bank device, slid Lena’s digital-vault key into the slot and bid one credit. There was no point betting the limit, because I already knew that wasn't enough, so I decided to test whether the entire process really was machine controlled. The auctioneer accepted the bid without any judgment on the amount, then I rejoined Marie and Bo.

"Finally, we can get this over with," Vargis said irritably when it was his turn to bid.

"Don't pay too much," I said, knowing that if he won, I could tell him if he bid more than two credits, he'd overpaid.

* * * *

"All systems are controlled from a room on the west side of this level," Jase said when we met beside a shuttered window in the lounge after bidding was complete. "One guard out front, maybe more inside."

Taking those guards head-on would be difficult. If it turned into a bloodbath, it would be impossible to get the Codex out quietly. "Where are they getting their power from?"

"It comes up through a switching room behind the elevator, from the fishing fleet's support base below. It's locked, but unguarded."

"Could you break in?"

"Shouldn't be too difficult."

"OK. Cut the power for five minutes only at exactly six o'clock this evening. If the power doesn't go out at that time, I'll assume it's not going down."

"What are you going to do?"

"Find out how well Sarat's guards see in the dark."

* * * *

The lights went out right on schedule. With the storm shutters closed, the entire penthouse was immersed in darkness, temporarily blinding everyone except me. My DNA sniffer painted the usual identifiers over the heads of the guards, telling me who they were, while the bionetic filaments in my optic nerves detected enough thermal traces to paint infra red ghosts in my mind's eye, showing me where they were. Those I couldn't see, I heard blundering around in the darkness, stumbling and yelling to each other.

It wasn't perfect but in the land of the blind the threaded EIS agent is king.

I slipped past red ethereal images of guards feeling their way helplessly along the walls until I reached the control room. The guard outside was better trained than most. He was as blind as the others, but he remained in position in front of the door waiting for the lights to come back on. I approached him silently, knocking him off balance with a leg sweep and drove his head hard against the wall. There was a sickening thud of skull bone on rock, then I caught his body and lowered him to the floor before feeling for the control room door. Being in constant use and guarded, it wasn't locked, but when my hand passed over the door sensor, nothing happened. No power to the lights meant no power to the doors, so I had to slide it open with both palms pressed flat against it.

My threading detected two guards inside, one seated, the other feeling his way along the wall towards the entrance. I took a step towards the standing guard's red ghost and kicked him more or less in the kidneys. There was a grunt as he doubled over in pain and surprise, then I finished him by slamming his head down into my rapidly ascending knee. I let the second guard fall to the ground as I turned to take out the seated guard, but he was already on his feet and moving towards me.

"Ritter, what is it?" he demanded warily. He'd heard the door open and his companion hit the floor, and was smart enough to realize there was someone else in the room.

I darted towards him, driving a punch for his throat, but he stepped sideways so I only brushed his neck. The guard instinctively lunged into the darkness, catching me with a glancing blow – not enough to slow me down, but the contact told him where I was. He swung his other hand in a roundhouse punch that struck the side of my head. It was a lucky hit, giving me no chance to block. I was airborne before I even realized what had happened, then I crashed onto the rock floor. Momentarily dazed, whirling stars danced with threading symbols before my eyes. Disoriented, I rolled away, making far too much noise but buying a few seconds to clear my head.

The guard's red ghost moved to the left, trying to flank me, knowing I was down. He launched a balanced kick into the darkness, narrowly missing my face. I knew from the way he snapped his leg back, without losing his balance, that he was well trained. My threading gave me the advantage of limited vision, but he'd got in the first blow and I had no time to recover. There were only seconds left before Jase restored the power. Once the lights came back on and the guard could identify me, I'd have no choice but to kill him – not something I wanted to do.

I slapped the floor loudly with my right hand and rolled silently away to the left, climbing to my feet. The guard immediately fired at my hand slap, illuminating his position with the electromagnetic muzzle spark of his gun.

I kicked towards his wrist, with my balance still off from his lucky punch. The kick wasn't perfect, but the force was enough to break his arm and send the gun spinning away into the darkness. The guard didn't utter a sound, but immediately swung his good arm at my head. I caught his wrist and turned, pulling him towards me and catching his ankle with my foot, throwing him face first to the floor. Before he could move, my knee crashed into his back, paralyzing him as the lights came back on. The guard tried to turn, but my elbow struck the back of his head like a hammer, driving his face into the rock floor with a sharp crack. Thankfully, his body went limp, saving me from having to break his neck.

I exhaled slowly, patting the back of the unconscious guard's head. "That might of hurt, but it was better than the alternative."

I climbed to my feet, still a little groggy, and felt the bulge on the side of my head. Luckily, it was hidden beneath my hair. If it had been on my face, my cover would have been in tatters.

I dragged the guard lying in the corridor inside and closed the door, then studied my surroundings. The control room was filled with communications and weather monitoring equipment, as well as screens viewing every room, including our sleeping quarters. Ignoring the surveillance system, I activated the direct comlink to Tundratown and selected the channel I knew Izin would be monitoring.

"I'm receiving you," Izin replied, careful to avoid words that would identify either of us, should anyone be listening. "Your signal isn't encrypted."

"I know. I haven't much time. They're using an Earth Bank auctioneer to manage the bidding. You need to make sure I win."

"It's impossible to break Earth Bank encryption, even if I had access to your location."

The penthouse's control system was manually isolated from the maintenance facility below as a precaution during the auction. With the flick of a switch, I reconnected the penthouse to the local datanet, giving Izin a backdoor. "How's that?"

"I can see their systems now, but they will see me connect."

"No one will see you, but me. Do it now." A moment later, the screen in front of the communications console illuminated with an external request for secure access, which I immediately accepted. "How's that?"

"I have full access."

"Good. Now hide yourself. You're on your own."

I quickly deleted all recorded vision from the

security system for the last hundred hours and switched off the surveillance system. Satisfied no one would see me leave, I stepped through the door and hurried back to my quarters, where I was soon soaking the swelling on the side of my head in freezing cold water.

Getting Izin through the back door was the easy part. If he couldn't find a way into the most secure financial device man had ever invented by the end of dinner, Vargis would have the Codex. A few hours later, it would be safely inside the battleship *Soberano*.

Getting my hands on it then would be virtually impossible.

* * * *

Sarat apologized for the power failure at dinner, making no mention of my visit to the control room, although security became noticeably tighter. The butler-guards no longer tried to conceal the weapon bulges beneath their jackets, and the guards at the elevator now openly carried assault weapons. Under this pall of armed security, we gathered to wait for the Earth Bank auctioneer to finish its validations and discuss the one thing on our minds, the Codex.

"Considering it's alien-tech," I said, "how do we use it?"

"There is no 'we', Captain Kade," Vargis said. "I won't be sharing it with you."

"One cannot share what one does not yet possess," Bo observed dryly.

"Thank you," I said, turning to Bo. "Confucius?"

"No, Bo Qiang."

I toasted Bo with my glass. "To the great Bo Qiang, sage of the galaxy!" Bo inclined his head, accepting the compliment, then I turned back to Sarat. "Assuming the issue is undecided . . .?"

"The Codex has a universally adaptive interface which allows it to communicate with any computing technology," Sarat said. "All it requires is conductive contact and access to data storage. It will do the rest."

"Smart little box of tricks," Jase said from his position between Vargis and Bo. His absence during the blackout had gone unnoticed because he'd made it back to our room before the surveillance system had been reactivated.

"I take it the Codex was constructed by the people who built the ships now wrecked in the Antares System?" I said.

"Yes, the Kireen. According to Ani-Hata-Ga, they were an ancient civilization from the Norma Arm of the galaxy. Highly advanced, but dangerously divided. They were frequently in conflict with themselves. The graveyard monument in the Antares System is the only one of its kind in human Mapped Space, although I understand there are others scattered throughout the galaxy."

"Considering how old the Codex is," Marie said, "won't the Kireen want their property back?"

"Sadly no," Sarat replied. "Their civilization collapsed millions of years ago. They're not extinct, but the worlds the survivors live on are insufficient to allow them to reestablish themselves."

"They destroyed their own homeworld?" Bo asked.

"The word Ani-Hata-Ga used was 'exhausted'. Their homeworld survived entirely on resources brought from off world. When it lost access to those resources, its industrial civilization could not sustain itself and their off world colonies could not survive alone. Imagine Earth in a few thousand years when its minerals are fully depleted and it's entirely dependent on off world resources."

"Earth wouldn't survive without the Core Systems now," Vargis said a little pompously, "but we'd survive without Earth. We did it before, we could do it again."

"Much of our technology and industrial production still comes from Earth," Sarat countered. "Without

Earth, we'd be crippled."

"That's what Earth wants you to believe," Vargis said. "There are some in the Core Worlds who'd like to see an end to Earth Council meddling in our affairs."

"And they're the people who'd get the whole human race in trouble," I said sharply.

"Why doesn't someone trade with the Kireen?" Marie asked. "Without the novarium the Tau Cetins gave Earth to power our starships, we wouldn't be where we are."

"The Forum made a Fifth Principle ruling against the Kireen."

The Extinction Principle requires Treaty members to take any action within their power to prevent another species from becoming extinct, irrespective of the wishes of the species or its rulers. The preservation of life was quite simply more important than any other consideration because it allowed future generations the opportunity to progress beyond the mistakes of their ancestors. When a species became extinct, there were no second chances.

"So to stop the Kireen wiping themselves out," I said, "no one in the galaxy is allowed to trade with them?"

"Exactly. The Forum decided that giving the Kireen what they needed to rebuild their civilization would only hasten their extinction – not something they could permit."

"Because genocide is the worst possible Treaty violation," I said. "Lucky they didn't block mankind on that basis."

"They nearly did," Sarat said. "Fortunately, there were centuries of peace after the Tactical World War, so the Forum gave us the benefit of the doubt."

"It's a twisted legal argument," Vargis said with obvious distaste, "isolating an entire species so it doesn't destroy itself."

Sarat shrugged. "Perhaps, but the Kireen are not

extinct. They still make war on each other, only instead of using fleets of starships they now use stone tipped weapons. I guess some evolutionary lines become dead ends, even among interstellar civilizations. So you see, the creators of the Antaran Codex will not come asking for their property back. It really is just a piece of salvaged alien-tech for sale. Speaking of which," Sarat said rising, "shall we conclude our business?"

"You said there would be a demonstration?" Vargis asked.

For once we were thinking alike, although for different reasons. He wanted to confirm he was buying the genuine article and I wanted to know what that article was.

Sarat nodded, "Of course, Senor. This way."

We assembled in the hall, now filled by the muted scream of the wind outside the metal shutters, then Ani-Hata-Ga's three dimensional image appeared.

"Greetings good customers," the Irzaen said. "Welcome to the joyous moment of transaction, to which all our efforts have been focused."

"Esteemed Principal," Sarat said, addressing the Irzaen formally, "a demonstration has been requested."

"Fitting indeed is it to confirm the faith we have all shown," Ani-Hata-Ga said, then vanished.

"Where'd he go" Vargis demanded, suspecting he'd been cheated.

Sarat motioned for calm. "The holographic projectors Ani-Hata-Ga has been using are required for the demonstration."

The circular base of the transport device supporting the Codex glowed, then it floated from the table, down to the holo projector's floor plate. When conductive contact had been established between the Codex and the holo emitter, a three dimensional image of the Local Group of galaxies appeared. More than fifty smaller galaxies orbited the two great formations at the center, the immense spiral of Andromeda and the smaller barred spiral of our own Milky Way Galaxy. Together, the Local Group formed a sparkling gathering of a trillion stars spanning a sphere ten million light years across.

"Here be the scope of the Antaran Codex," Ani-Hata-Ga's voice sounded from the ether. "To prove its worth, let us investigate what is known to you as the Galaxy Triangulum, three million light years distant." The image zoomed into the local group, sending galaxies flying off the sides as the focus shifted towards the third largest of the local galaxies. "To cross the plane of Triangulum from the point closest to this galaxy to that most opposite, shown is the path to be followed." A bright red line zig zagged through the spiral galaxy's forty billion stars, depicting the course a ship would follow for the fastest possible transit from one side to the other.

Suddenly, I got it!

The Antaran Codex was like Mapped Space. It identified every atom of dark matter lurking in the endless void of space, but instead of covering a mere half of one percent of our galaxy, it spanned ten million light years! It's why the Codex had to be virtually indestructible, why the Irzaen had said without it we were trapped – because we'd be unable to navigate between the stars without it. It was the keys to the kingdom! Not just our kingdom, but to dozens of kingdoms, even those currently far beyond the reach of our technology.

"It includes maps of all the galaxies in the Local Group?" I asked.

"Such is its extent, unparalleled in accuracy," the Irzaen responded.

"And all the space between the galaxies," Sarat added.

"How did the Kireen get all this information?" I asked, astounded by the sheer size of its coverage.

"The same way this spiral arm, or our entire galaxy, was mapped," Ani-Hata-Ga replied. "Many thousands of civilizations over millions of years shared their individual knowledge to gain access to the whole. No one civilization could achieve this, only collectively could it be done."

"The Tau Cetins never told us sharing existed on such scale," Marie said.

It had been taken for granted cooperation was limited to those civilizations inhabiting the Milky Way Galaxy. No one had ever considered the senior Forum members were in partnership with civilizations in other galaxies, or even had contact with them! The distances were so vast, it seemed impossible that the true cooperative civilization we were seeking to join was intergalactic in scope.

"What purpose would it serve for you to know?" Ani-Hata-Ga asked. "Much time will pass before you could use such knowledge."

He was right. I did a quick calculation, discovering it would take the *Silver Lining* more than two thousand two hundred years to reach Triangulum.

"If the Codex device is seven million years old," Bo asked, "is the data not out of date?"

"How could it be?" Ani-Hata-Ga asked.

"In all that time, everything has moved. Old stars have died, new stars have been born."

"Valued customer," Ani-Hata-Ga replied, "What is once known is known for all time."

"But that would mean the Codex can predict the evolution of the physical universe itself!" I said.

"Your description of the merchandise is correct, although this particular product's usefulness is constrained to the extent you have seen. A larger device is required for detailed astrographic mappings of the entire universe. We have no such product for sale, although they do exist. With regret, the Irzae are not permitted such devices."

"Do the TCs have them?" Marie asked.

"We do not know what the Tau Cetins have access

to," Ani-Hata-Ga replied, "although it is known they sent ships deep into what you call the Virgo Supercluster during the Intruder War. This demonstrates knowledge far greater than the expanse of this Codex. We Irzae have no such capability."

As the Irzaen's words sank in, the shocked look on the faces of the others told me none of them had fully understood what the Antaran Codex really was. It knew where every element of the visible and non-visible universe was hidden and used that knowledge to produce detailed mappings across ten million light years. It could compensate for every gravitational variation, every collision, every explosion, and predict any variable that would impact the Local Group into the distant future. The variables to be calculated were almost infinite and demonstrated complete mastery of the physical sciences.

"None of us are going to Triangulum in the foreseeable future," Vargis said. "The proof I seek is for our galaxy."

"As you wish," Ani-Hata-Ga replied.

The image of Triangulum was instantly replaced by the Milky Way, and a dozen courses were plotted from a point a third of the way out from the galactic center to various points in the outer rim. "Here the Codex reveals multiple pathways from your Earth to the edge of this galaxy."

Vargis nodded, convinced. With the Codex in their possession, the Consortium could send ships across the Milky Way in search of business opportunities. If the others had won, it would have allowed the Beneficial Society to monopolize travel beyond our current Mapped Space and build a trade empire rivaling even the Irzaens, or enabled Bo and Gwandoya to move their criminal operations far beyond the reach of Earth Navy.

"Does it know where habitable planets and resources are?" I asked.

"They are all computed outcomes from known data," the Irzaen trade representative replied.

That explained Breckinridge's interest. With it, his mining conglomerate could have exploited distant, untapped mineral resources.

Now that I understood what the Irzaens were selling, I knew whatever the price, the Antaran Codex was worth it.

"That concludes the demonstration," Sarat said. "Are there any other questions?"

No one spoke as the Irzaen transport device lifted off the floor and carried the Codex back to its display table. The image of the Milky Way vanished the moment it lost contact with the floor plate, replaced by Ani-Hata-Ga's cumbersome quadrupoidal form.

"Pleased we are that the moment of decision has arrived," Ani-Hata-Ga said.

Sarat turned towards the plain rock wall behind them. A screen, identical to the one in the main dining area, glowed blue as the Earth Bank auctioneer advised it who the successful bidder was. Now that Vargis had seen what the Codex could do, he was already calculating how the Consortium would exploit its vast potential. That desire triggered a moment of uncertainty as he faced the prospect of losing. We watched the screen waiting for the winner's name to appear. Instead, it flickered from blue to white noise and back several times.

Was Izin blocking the result?

Sarat glanced at one of his butler-guards. "What's wrong?"

The guard shrugged, turning to the Earth Bank auctioneer and examining its settings. "Nothing, it's working perfectly."

Behind Sarat, the screen flashed back to life and my name appeared on it. The characters were a different size and shape to what we'd seen before, but the result was visible for all to see. And its meaning clear: Izin had broken the unbreakable.

"Yeah!" Jase declared with a fist pump. "Good

work, Skipper!"

Sarat turned towards me. "Congratulations, Captain Kade. I'm sure Jie Kang Li will be very pleased with his acquisition."

"That's impossible!" Vargis exploded, glaring at me. "There is no way the Yiwu could have topped my bid!"

"You underestimate Jie Kang Li," I said. "Many people make that mistake." I glanced at Bo who seemed genuinely surprised I'd won.

"The Promise has been fulfilled," Ani-Hata-Ga said officially, "completing the activity for which we have gathered here this day. Humble thanks." His image vanished, signaling the end of the auction.

Bo stepped forward to shake hands. "Well done, Captain Kade." He leaned forward, adding in a low voice. "It appears someone underestimated you." He glanced meaningfully at Vargas.

"Thanks Bo," I said, following his gaze, wondering what he meant. "No hard feelings?"

Bo gave me a philosophical look. "One cannot be angry over failing to obtain the unobtainable."

Marie gave me a grudging smile. "I thought he had you." She leaned close and whispered, "How'd you do it?" She said, telling me she knew I'd cheated.

"I paid what it was worth," I whispered back.

She kissed my cheek, then with her lips close to my ear, said, "Now I know you're lying."

Sarat motioned for me to approach. "The auctioneer will automatically update your vault-key."

I wondered how long I had before Sarat discovered the Earth Bank auctioneer had deducted only one credit from my balance. I realized I'd made a foolish mistake, bidding only one credit. As soon as Sarat saw the transfer, he'd know the result had been fixed. I needed to grab the Codex and get out of here fast, before he set the guards on me.

Sarat retrieved the Codex from the invisible

protective field encasing it, and offered it to me. "This is now yours, Captain Kade. I'm sure your benefactor will put it to good use."

I hesitated. "You're sure it's not going to cut me in half, like it did Breckinridge?"

"The protective field is keyed to my bio signature," Sarat explained. "Only I can remove it safely from the Irzaen transporter, but now that I have, it's quite safe."

I took it, testing its weight. "It's lighter than I expected."

"And infinitely stronger than the hardest polysteel," Sarat assured me.

My palms tingled as the device began to interact with the bionetic filaments in my hands. Shocked, I realized it sensed my threading and thought I was a system it could link with! I tried blocking it, erecting a neural barrier in my wrists, but it had no effect. Whatever was coming out of the Codex passed through my defenses as if they didn't exist.

"The auctioneer will take care of my commission," Sarat continued, "and the transfer to our Irzaen host's representatives on Earth."

I turned to Jase, nodding for him to take the Codex, trying not to look alarmed by the alien-tech assault on my threading. The tingling sensation was halfway up my arm by the time Jase took hold of the alien device, breaking the nascent link that had almost turned me into a human terminal. While Jase ran his eyes curiously over the Codex, I clenched my fists, relaxing as the tingling sensation passed.

"Guard it with your life," I said.

"Absolutely," Jase replied, turning to Sarat. "Now that we're done, where are my guns?"

Sarat hesitated, wondering if Jase was about to take his revenge for Hades City.

"Purely to guard the Codex," I said quickly. "Right Jase?" More a command than a question.

"Yeah," Jase said reluctantly, "If you say so,

Skipper."

I gave Sarat a reassuring nod, then he motioned to a nearby guard, who hurried away.

"The shuttle is waiting on the landing pad below," Sarat said, "to take you back to the spaceport."

"This'll be a fun flight back," Marie said, "with Vargis ready to skin you alive."

"We'll make sure it's where he can see it," I said, "But no touching." Especially not by me!

Two guards approached carrying an engineering diagnostic scanner similar to what Izin used to examine sealed components during maintenance cycles. They set the rectangular machine down in front of Sarat who picked up the Irzaen transport device that had guarded the Codex and placed it in the scan compartment. The guards locked the scanner, then initiated a full diagnostic cycle.

"Your Irzaen friends may not take kindly to you stealing their technology," I said.

"They'll never know," Sarat said. "This maintenance scanner isn't designed to reverse engineer alien-tech, but you'd be surprised what some companies will pay for even partial scans of non-human technology."

A guard appeared carrying a large tray displaying an assortment of weapons and my confiscated communicator. Marie pocketed her two small, but lethal, needle guns and a close range bolt-stunner, then Jase and I retrieved our sidearms.

"You're carrying three guns now?" I asked, surprised as I pocketed my communicator.

"I always did," She replied, amused that it had taken me this long to penetrate one of her many little secrets. "And you're still lugging around that hand cannon. Isn't it time you got something a little less . . . brutish?"

"I like brutish!" I said, feigning defensiveness as I tested the weight of the Magnetically Accelerated

Kinetic Precision-50. The hard hitting heavy pistol fired the full range of smart hypersonic projectiles, making it a versatile problem solver. My top of the line P-50 was bulkier than the standard MAKs, but its range and accuracy enhancements ideally suited my ultra-reflexed senses.

"Or you might just have an issue with the size of your . . . gun?" She taunted.

Jase chuckled. She looked meaningfully at his identical pair of frag-guns. "Why are you laughing, blondie? His weapon's obviously bigger than yours! Is that why you need two to compensate?"

Jase winced at her sharp tongue. He rested his free hand on one of the short range, gunfighter weapons now secure in its hip holster. "I thought a woman like you would know using both hands requires more skill."

"Really? Did you learn that all by yourself, late at night?"

I grinned as Jase realized he should quit while he was behind. "I'm not saving you," I said as I holstered my P-50.

One of the guards approached and whispered to Sarat briefly, who then turned to us. "Unfortunately, the storm has grounded the shuttle. You'll have to stay here one more night."

"Can't it fly above the storm?" Jase asked.

"Yes, but it can't land or take off in this wind. The moment it left the pad, it would be pushed into the cliff. It's happened before. The shuttle pilots won't fly in these conditions."

"I'll fly it," Jase said. "I'll show them how it's done."

"They won't allow that. The storm will ease by morning. You can fly back to Tundratown then."

That gave Sarat time to discover I'd cheated the auction, but unless Jase and I hijacked the shuttle, we had no choice but to stay.

"In that case, I hope you've still got some of that

Merayan red left," Marie said, giving me a look promising a long and eventful night.

"I'm sure we do," Sarat replied, "courtesy of the Irzaen trade mission."

* * * *

Jase positioned the Codex on the table in front of him like a trophy during dinner, toasting it occasionally and resting his glass on it in a way that clearly irritated Vargis. Bo sipped his green tea impassively hiding his amusement at Vargis' irritation, while Marie and I made a heroic effort to empty our Irzaen's host's wine stocks. The meal had barely finished when Vargis rose and without a word withdrew to his room to escape Jase's exuberant celebrations. Eventually Bo and Sarat departed, while we finished the last bottle.

"You'll be a rich man once Jie Kang Li rewards you for swindling the Consortium out of the Codex," Marie said.

"Here's to Jie Kang Li," I said toasting my cover story. I emptied the glass and poured another, thinking once Bo told his criminal master I'd pretended to represent him, there'd be a price on my head.

"To Mukul Sarat, may he rot in hell!" Jase said venomously. He drank directly from the bottle, then slapped it down heavily on the Codex and flopped into his chair, staring blankly ahead. "I don't even remember their names," he said bitterly, recalling the two girls Sarat had had killed in Hades City.

Marie watched Jase, shaking her head. "The key to untold riches, and he's resting his drink on it!"

"It survived seven million years adrift in space," I said, "and can withstand a fusion explosion. I think it's safe to assume it's waterproof."

We emptied our glasses, then I whispered to Marie, "Another bottle or . . . ?"

"Or?" she asked, feigning innocence. We

exchanged unspoken thoughts, then she smiled and stood up, helping Jase to his feet. "OK hot shot, time for bed."

While Jase stumbled to his feet, I scooped the Codex up one handed, forgetting in my intoxicated state my earlier encounter with it. Marie gave Jase a gentle nudge towards the hall leading to our quarters, then we followed arm in arm.

"So, will you trust me enough next time to tell me what you're up to?" I asked.

"I trust you, Sirius, just not with my money."

I became vaguely aware of a tingling in my hand. I realized it was the Codex, trying to link with me again. The alcohol dulled my instincts, letting me wonder if my earlier wariness had been unwarranted. I decided to watch the Codex as it worked its way up my arm's bionetic filaments towards my shoulder. When it found one of my scapula storage nodes, it began downloading masses of data, as much as it could push through my threading. It seemed to be simply a benign data transfer, then something else shot through the bionetic filaments in my arm. It passed the data storage area in my shoulder blade and rapidly spread through my body. By the time we reached the hallway, the download had consumed fourteen percent of my threaded memory capacity and the searching presence had begun to tap my sensory core. My vision blurred, the sound of the wind outside distorted and I began to lose my balance. A threading security alert flashed into my mind, warning that the autonomous command center in my collar bone was under attack. The threaded inputs in my mind's eye went haywire, distorting into scrambled gibberish, as whatever the Codex had spawned into me shattered my threading's innermost defenses.

Adrenalin suddenly overpowered the numbing alcohol, giving me momentary clarity. I triggered the one thought psionicly embedded into the consciousness of every threaded EIS agent. It was the one safeguard that ensured if we were ever captured, if alien-tech ever tore us open the way the Codex was ripping me apart, we would reveal none of the secrets we carried.

EMERGENCY PURGE AND WIPE! I thought, unlocking the last ditch rescue protocol, the threaded equivalent of a bullet to my bionetic brain.

"Here! Hold the key to riches," I said, pushing the Codex into Marie's hands.

"You know I love riches!" she said with a smile, taking the Codex.

White spots flashed before my eyes as the emergency protocol erased everything my threading knew – everything Lena had uploaded into me – and tried to crush whatever the Codex had infected me with. My ears were assaulted by high pitched tones, a thousand unknown odors battered my sense of smell, bitter and sweet flavors tormented my sense of taste, all of it imagined. I stumbled and fell, no longer in control of my arms and legs, unable to breathe.

Marie tried to grab me, but I was too heavy and it happened so fast. I crumpled to the rock floor, limp as a fresh corpse, heart no longer beating. When threading failed, it took the entire nervous system with it. It was bionetic technology's Achilles heel.

"Sirius, are you OK?" Marie asked, kneeling beside me confused and concerned.

It wasn't the first time I'd initiated a purge and wipe – I'd done it in training, but never in the field. And never like this! It took longer than in the simulator, because the protocol sensed an alien influence and scrubbed me clean with ruthless precision. To the emergency protocol, whether I lived or died was irrelevant. All that mattered was the destruction of the alien force and the deletion of everything stored in my artificial memory. When it came to bionetics, agent survival was secondary to secrecy.

A simple thought appeared in my fading mind: CLEAR.

The rescue protocol released control of my body,

giving me one chance to revive before physical death.

RESET BIONETICS, I thought, ordering a full system restart.

Sensation returned to my body. My heart began beating again and with a gasp, my lungs filled with air. I took several quick breaths while Marie leaned over me, unaware how close to death I'd been. My threading's sensory capabilities came flooding back, but my bionetic memory was empty, wiped clean. All the security codes and clearances that allowed me to identify myself to other EIS agents, to the navy, to every human and many local alien governments were gone. If I needed help now, I couldn't call for it. I was completely on my own.

"You OK, Skipper?" Jase asked, as he turned on wobbly legs and looked back towards me.

I gave him a reassuring nod. "Just too much Merayan wine, I guess," I mumbled as I sat up, no longer inebriated. The purge had wiped all trace of alcohol from my system, reading it as a poison to be destroyed. I relaxed, feigning mild drunkenness.

Marie relaxed and whispered meaningfully, "Not too much, I hope. Your night is far from over!"

I gave her an appreciative look, knowing with the alcohol gone from my system, she would be surprised how unimpaired my performance would be!

When we reached my door, Jase eyed us both curiously.

Before I could say anything, Marie said, "My room is second on the left."

Jase nodded, resigned to his banishment. "I know."

"And don't go through my things," she added. "I'll know if you do."

Jase gave her a wounded look, then headed towards her room to sleep while I let us into my quarters.

"Where should I put this?" she asked, holding up the Codex.

"On the dresser." I had decided I couldn't risk touching it again. Whatever its universally adaptive interface was, it was a menace to my threading.

She placed the alien device on the table, then approached me slowly, in that feline predatory way of hers that I adored. We locked arms, then lips, then I forgot all about the Antaran Codex for a few hours.

* * * *

An explosion shattered the night, then the sporadic crackle of magnetic accelerated gunfire reverberated through the darkness with increasing intensity. I sat up, listening to the cacophony of battle and the confused shouts of men echoing through stone walled corridors.

"What's going on?" Marie asked sleepily.

"Sounds like war's been declared." I jumped out of bed, dressed quickly and was just strapping on my P-50 when Jase burst into the room, one fragger in hand, the other holstered.

"There's something out there!" he declared. "It's tearing Sarat's guards apart."

"What do you mean 'it'?" Marie asked, pulling the covers up to conceal her nakedness.

"I saw a blur in the dark!" Jase said. "It's big! And fast!"

I switched on my P-50. It was loaded with anti-personnel slugs; nasty against flesh, weak against armor. "Stay here."

"No way, Skipper!"

"Guard that!" I said pointing at the Codex sitting on the dresser. When I passed him, I added in a lower voice, "And Marie."

"I don't need guarding!" she declared, throwing off the sheets and running naked to where her clothes were. Instead of dressing, she checked her guns.

"Fine! You guard him!" They could look after each other, but only I was threaded and ultra-reflexed, giving me an edge neither of them could match. I turned to Jase. "Whoever's out there is after the Codex. Make sure they don't get it!"

"Damn it Skipper, you have all the fun!"

I took that as agreement. "When you get your own ship, then you can have all the fun." I exchanged a silent farewell look with Marie, who had finally started pulling on her clothes, and slipped out into the corridor.

The penthouse lights were out. Red and orange tracer streaked past the end of the corridor amid a diffuse red glow spilling across the central lounge area from the windows. The storm was raging outside and the metal shutters should have been covering the windows, so where was that light coming from?

Another explosion shook the spire, followed by the sound of a rock wall collapsing. Sarat's guards yelled over the gunfire, their voices heavy with fear and confusion.

"It's over there!"

"On the left."

"I'm hit! I'm hit."

"It's behind you!"

"Damn it's fast!"

A man screamed in terror and was abruptly silenced.

"He's dead," another yelled in panic.

"It's behind us! Shoot it! Shoot it!"

Sarat's guards were all hard ex-military types, but whatever they were fighting was getting on top of them. I cranked my threaded optics to maximum and crept towards the end of the corridor.

Two guards lay dead on the floor to the right, outlined by the red glow from the windows. Their bodies radiated ghostly thermals with hot spots marking where blood welled from shrapnel wounds caused by anti-personnel slugs. Their weapons lay nearby, still glowing infra-red hot from having recently been fired. One guard was missing an arm, cleanly severed from his body. It wasn't a blast wound. It looked like his arm had been surgically sliced off.

To my left, the shadowy forms of five guards fired at the source of the red glow as they fell back towards the meeting hall. They were working together, afraid but not panicking, covering each other's retreat like pros and yelling sightings of their adversary. A dark slender blur, half again taller than a man, flashed past the end of the corridor trying to flank them. It vanished to my left, then a muzzle flash lit up the five guards, hitting one in the chest and hurling him against the wall. The attacker's gun sounded like the suppressed sonic boom of a Union Regular Army Forger, a heavy assault weapon that could punch through any Earth-tech body armor. Yet the attacker was clearly non-human!

So why would an alien be using Earth-tech weaponry against humans?

Sarat appeared in the meeting hall's doorway on the far side of the lounge, yelling for the guards to fall back. He withdrew inside as the four surviving guards retreated after him, firing as they went. Suddenly, a new stream of tracer flashed across the room from the right as another guard appeared, running alongside the windows towards the meeting hall, firing wildly.

The alien blur swept past me again, leaping back across the room, too fast for the guards to hit. An eye-hand modded EIS sniper might have got it, but toughness modded grunts had no chance. It fired while in the air, momentarily silhouetting itself with the muzzle flash, revealing a willowy reptilian torso, slender triangular head, long lean arms and legs and a whip-like tail which flicked through the air for balance. The alien held the Forger in one hand and a long knife-like weapon with glowing edges in the other. The URA assault gun was too heavy for a man to hold one handed, but the alien wielded it as easily as it did the blade. In a flash, the attacker swept past the guard running for the meeting hall, raising the knife, then slicing him apart from shoulder to hip. The alien-tech blade passed effortlessly through the guard's body as if it encountered no resistance, then the man's corpse collapsed in two pieces.

Weapons fire from the remaining guards flashed around the agile reptilian silhouette, but it was too fast. At the door, one of the guards took a blast in the shoulder, and was knocked to the floor. As the wounded guard tried to rise, the reptilian raced forward and decapitated him with a single stroke of its blade. Without slowing, it darted into the meeting hall, firing and slashing with the speed and precision of a highly trained, fearlessly aggressive assassin.

I crept into the lounge where my sniffer got line of sight on five dead and two wounded guards. One of the rectangular metal window shutters had been smashed in and now lay on the floor, partly covering a dead guard. A dull gray hull floated outside the window, surrounded by a soft red light which repelled the snowstorm's icy blast. The dark opening of a hatch in the hull was aligned to the open window, marking where the reptilian had entered the penthouse.

A stun grenade detonated inside the meeting hall as weapon flashes, shouts and screams filled the air. Knowing it was almost over, I raced across the lounge area. When I was halfway across, the wall exploded. The blast threw me sideways, hurling me onto the hard stone floor and sending me sliding into the side wall. For a moment, I lay stunned as the thunder of gunfire and the screams of dying men were drowned out by the ringing in my ears.

My vision blurred, making the threading's markers over the dead and dying guards in my mind's eye unreadable. In the meeting hall the gunfire ceased, signaling the last of the defenders were dead. A moment later, the tall reptilian emerged carrying a rectangular box. I didn't recognize it at first, then as I started to regain my senses, I realized it was the diagnostic scanner Sarat had put the Codex's transport device in the day before. I squinted, trying to clear my vision as I realized the reptilian wasn't after the Codex at all. It wanted the transport device and the scans Sarat had made of it!

While it strode towards the shattered window and the craft beyond, I pulled myself across the stone floor towards my P-50 lying nearby. I got my hand on it, then clumsily sighted on the reptilian. My arm rocked unsteadily, sending the first shot high into the rock ceiling. Instinctively, the reptilian dodged sideways while I weakly tried following its movement, firing again and again, missing several times until a white impact ring flashed at its shoulder. The reptilian stumbled from the impact, then straightened unhurt. The slug had been deflected by its dark, skin tight suit – not body armor but a skin hugging defensive shield.

No wonder the guards hadn't been able to hurt it!

Rather than shoot me with the URA Forger, it dropped the diagnostic scanner and reached across its chest to a scabbard sewn into its ornately layered black body suit. It drew its knife, fitted with a blade almost as long as my forearm and inlaid with intricate serpentine carvings. The ritual assassin's weapon came to life as an electric shimmer glowed along the sharp edges on both sides of the blade from point to hilt, while on the flat of the blade, the lines of serpentine carvings glowed starkly white. I'd heard of these weapons, but never seen one first hand. It wasn't really a knife, but a quantum weapon able to sever atomic binding forces on contact. With new found purpose, it started towards me.

I held down the P-50's trigger, going to full auto, burping slugs three times a second. Flashes burst across the reptilian's chest as its skin shield deflected my hypersonic slugs. The reptilian staggered from each impact, taking a step backwards, then my P-50 clicked empty and the room fell silent.

Realizing I was out of ammo, it started towards me with its knife angled down, ready to inflict a decapitating death blow. It crouched, about to leap at me, when a familiar crackling sound broke the silence. Two streams of fragmentation slugs caught the tall alien in the side of the chest, shattering on contact and knocking it off its feet. Surprised, it rolled away, turning in confusion towards the twin streams of gunfire tracking its movement.

Behind the flashes of the twin fraggers burping on full auto, blonde hair appeared from the shadows of the hallway. Jase walked toward the reptilian, eyes locked on his target, blasting with both guns held at arm's length. The reptilian's skin shield erupted in overlapping impact rings as slugs peppered it, then its torso rippled with electric force lines as its shield began to overload.

The reptilian darted sideways as a siren began to wail throughout the penthouse. Thinking it would soon be facing many more guards, the alien retreated, powering off the blade and sliding it into its chest scabbard as it ran. It scooped the diagnostic scanner off the floor without slowing, then leapt through the shattered window into the craft floating outside. Dull gray metal irised shut, sealing the hatch, then the craft shot straight up away from the spire exposing the lounge to the full force of the icy wind outside.

Jase bounded toward me, holstering his guns. "Skipper? Are you OK?"

I sat up slowly, nodding. "I told you to stay with the Codex."

"I did – until I heard your MAK singing," Jase said, referring to the distinctive high pitched sound of the P-50's magnetic accelerator. "I knew you were up to your eyeballs in trouble!"

I climbed slowly to my feet. "Get back there and keep an eye on it."

Jase gave me a hurt look. "You're welcome – for saving your life." He started back towards the room.

"Jase." When he stopped and looked back, I said, "Thanks, you did good."

He gave me a cocky grin and hurried back to our quarters while I tried to make sense of what had happened. Wind and snow blasted in through the open window, illuminated by the floodlit landing platform several hundred meters below. The two wounded guards were now both dead, their body temps plummeting in the freezing arctic air. In the meeting hall, all of the guards were dead, some with limbs or heads severed by the reptilian's killing blade. Sarat lay near the back wall, breathing in short, sharp gasps, close to death. His lower abdomen was soaked in blood and his right leg was missing from above the knee.

I knelt beside him. "Who are you working for?"

His terrified eyes focused on me as he made a gurgling sound. "Ani- . . . Hata- . . ."

"No, you weren't. I'm not even sure he exists."

Confusion spread across his face. "Irzae . . ."

"The Irzae had nothing to do with this. The alien that attacked, have you ever dealt with its kind before?"

"No." Sarat coughed blood and made a gurgling sound. "Holo . . . gram . . . only."

He'd been deceived all along, never suspecting who he'd really been dealing with.

"Why?" he wheezed.

"Because they hate us," I whispered.

The look on Sarat's face told me he didn't understand, then his eyes glazed over and his head rolled lifelessly forward.

I gave my sniffer a chance to scan the room, but it found only human DNA. When I returned to the lounge, it was the same story – human traces everywhere, but nothing I could use as evidence to prove what I already knew to be true. The lounge was freezing now with snow blasting in over the remains of dead guards and wrecked furniture. I retraced the movements of the reptilian, searching for any bio-trace, finishing at the wrecked floor-to-ceiling window. The shutter had not been blown in by an explosion, because that would have left an energy trace that could have been used as evidence. Instead, the window had been pushed in as if the alien craft had simply rammed it. Wary of the slippery, snow covered rock floor and the treacherous wind, I was about to give up when my sniffer indicated a possible trace.

I dropped to my stomach and crawled through the snow to the edge, feeling the full force of the arctic wind on my face. Certain that whatever was out there would soon be gone under the press of the storm, I eased my head out over the edge to give my sniffer line of sight. The sheer rock face fell away to the landing platform far below where the floodlit scramjet shuttle was lashed down by cables and magnetic clamps and whipped by blasting snow. Below the landing platform, enormous sea swells crashed against the black rock spire, throwing spray high into the air.

Immediately below the floor, my sniffer searched the slick rock face for biological traces. A targeting reticule suddenly flashed into my mind, highlighting a point on the rock less than a meter away. Jase must have winged the reptilian as its skin shield failed because there was a droplet of blood on the rock face. One tiny drop! The wind was rapidly tearing away what little genetic material was left, but as I leaned closer, the sniffer got a positive read on the sample. My bionetic memory had been wiped, but some things were hard coded into the filaments themselves so no matter what happened, I could never lose them. This was one of those! The DNA sniffer matched its read to the hard coded data structure triggering a threaded alarm inside my head. It was a warning I'd only ever received in training, a warning I never expected to encounter in the field, but based on what I'd seen, it was a warning I expected.

The blood trace reeked of Mataron DNA!

I'd recognized the reptilian form and the assassin's quantum blade, but machines can be built to take any form. This tiny blood trace proved there was a Mataron on Icetop, who'd butchered Sarat and his men and stolen the alien-tech device that had delivered the Codex into human hands. I knew now the Matarons wanted us to have the Codex, but without anyone knowing they gave it to us – only they hadn't counted on Sarat's greed. He'd sabotaged their plan by scanning their transport device, forcing them to expose themselves. There must have been something in that scan linking the Matarons to the Codex.

Or maybe they feared the scans would be enough for the Tau Cetins to smell a rat, a reptilian rat. The Matarons didn't fear much, but they feared the Tau Cetins. Our reptilian enemy was seven hundred thousand years ahead of us, but the TCs were millions of years ahead of them. That kind of inferiority left the Matarons with no way of knowing what TC technology could do, and not knowing made them paranoid.

Ever since human fanatics had landed on Kif-atah, the Mataron homeworld, and detonated their ship's energy core in 3154, we'd faced an implacable enemy who would accept no apology, consider no reparation. The human fanatics, opposed to alien contact, had chosen well. They gave the militaristic and highly xenophobic Matarons someone to focus their hatred upon, someone who could never hope to match them militarily, yet whom the Forum would never allow them to harm. They'd tried to destroy Earth after the terrorist attack, only to be humiliated when their fleet had been disabled at the edge of the Solar System by a single Tau Ceti ship sent to find out what all the fuss was about.

Months of Forum level discussions had followed, resulting in Earth's stockpiles of novarium – the element needed to generate the immense quantities of energy required for interstellar travel – being rendered inert by the Tau Cetins. Every human ship in Mapped Space had suffered the same fate. Even now, almost fifteen hundred years later, we still didn't know how they'd done it.

At the time, hardly anyone on Earth even knew what was happening until a TC ambassador explained it to us. It didn't matter that the rest of mankind condemned the terrorist attack and executed everyone associated with it in the most uncompromising retribution ever seen in human history – in the eyes of the galaxy we were responsible. It was the first, most basic principle of the Access Treaty, the Responsibility Principle. Our collective-governments were responsible for the actions of all our people, no matter how crazy, and we'd failed to take that responsibility seriously.

One tiny group of crazies had ruined it for the rest of us.

For the next ten centuries, the Forum imposed Embargo prevented novarium from entering human hands, giving us time to sort out how we governed ourselves and stranding mankind in the Solar System and on the colonies and outposts we'd taken centuries to establish. Many outposts survived, although some withered on the vine with frightening consequences for the last survivors.

That's what happens when you break the Access Treaty. They don't exterminate you, they isolate you. It's more civilized than genocide.

When the Embargo ended a thousand years later – much to the ire of the Matarons who'd sworn never to let us back out – the TCs arrived with a new supply of novarium and we started a second five hundred year road to Forum membership, only this time if we screwed up the resulting Embargo would be ten times longer. It was why the Earth Navy and the EIS had been founded, to make sure we didn't get it wrong a second time. It was a tough job, made more difficult by the Matarons constantly plotting against us.

The Mataron hatred of mankind was fueled by the exponential growth of Human Civilization. While the Matarons had the technology to traverse the galaxy, their innate xenophobia had limited them largely to their own system and a few tiny outposts, whereas human willingness to be locked inside flimsy ships for months or years on end had seen mankind spread to the limits of

Mapped Space at a speed that utterly infuriated the vengeful Matarons. Even the Tau Cetins were surprised at how quickly we'd expanded. They'd thought it would take us five thousand years – we did it in less than five hundred. The difference was the Tau Cetins didn't care how far we went, or what we did, providing we obeyed the law.

Fortunately, the law was just and the Tau Cetins argued that Mataron protests lacked any factual basis, and so were dismissed. The fact the Matarons had remained neutral during the Intruder War, refusing to help the other Local Powers even when they were fighting for their very lives, had left the Mataron Supremacy with few genuine friends. Of course if we screwed up again, the TCs would have no choice but to side with the Matarons because Observer Civilizations had a duty to impartially interpret and, when necessary, enforce galactic law.

Considering how badly the Matarons wanted us back in the bottle, I wondered why they'd go to so much trouble to give us exactly what we desired most, the ability to explore and colonize as far as we wanted without restriction. We lacked the technology to even get out of the relatively small, ten thousand light year long Orion Arm, let alone cross the vast Milky Way or reach other galaxies, yet the mere promise of such freedom was always going to be irresistible to mankind.

It was that allure that made the Antaran Codex bait, but for what kind of trap? Whatever it was, the Matarons were actively fabricating an Access Treaty violation, and we'd walked right into it.

The realization chilled me more than the freezing winds wiping away the last trace of Mataron DNA from the slick black rock. I was filled with a desire to destroy the Codex, but as it was virtually indestructible, that would be impossible. I considered handing it over to the Tau Cetins, but would possessing it be enough to trigger an Access Treaty violation?

I crawled back into the lounge, then hurried towards my quarters while my mind raced through endless possibilities. The lights were still out, but there was enough light reflecting in from the lounge area to let me see by threaded optics alone.

The door to my quarters was ajar. Inside, Jase and Marie lay unconscious on the floor. My threading told me they were stunned, not dead, their weapons lying close to them. One look at the dresser told me the Codex was gone!

In a blur of rage, I was sure Vargis had stunned them both and stolen the Codex while I'd been distracted by the Mataron agent. I tried shaking Jase awake, then I heard footsteps in the corridor. A man appeared in the doorway, flashing a small hand light in my face, momentarily blinding me, but my threading told me it was Vargis.

I leapt at him, dragging him into the room and jamming my empty P-50 in his face. "Where is it?" I yelled, knowing this was no longer just about a piece of alien technology, but about mankind's destiny as an interstellar civilization.

He tried to wrestle me off, swinging the light at my head like a club, but I blocked it and hit him in the face with the butt of my gun, knocking him to the ground.

"What did you do with it?" I yelled.

"What are you talking about?" Vargis demanded as a trickle of blood ran from his forehead.

"The Codex! Where is it?"

"It wasn't him," Marie said groggily as she tried to throw off the stun effect.

"He's got it! I know he has!" I declared, ready to beat him senseless with my bare hands. Vargis was the sleezeball who'd tried to cut me out of this deal from the beginning. He represented the big money, the people who stood to make the most from the Codex. I knew he'd do anything to get it.

"No," she held her head as she sat up slowly. "It

was Bo."

Bo? How could it be congenial, unassuming, intelligent Bo, who'd not blown my cover when he'd had the chance? I actually liked him, even his Confucian quotes. It couldn't be Bo.

"It's true," she said. "Bo stunned me. He's got the Codex."

Vargis pushed me away angrily, adjusting his clothes. "You let an insignificant, paper shuffling lawyer steal the Codex out from under your nose! You're a bigger fool than I thought!"

Jase stirred, wincing as he rubbed his head. "What hit me?"

"The shuttle's the only way off this rock and it's grounded," I said, releasing Vargis and racing back out through the lounge to the elevator. To my relief, it was still working. By the time the door opened, Jase staggered out to join me.

"Sorry Skipper," he said on the way down. "He must have been in your quarters when I came back. I never even saw him."

We took the elevator down to the hangar.

"Sarat's dead," I said after the doors closed.

Jase gave me a surprised look. "Did you do it?"

"No, it was the Mataron."

Jase nodded grimly. "Saved me the trouble."

When the doors opened, we started towards the office as the elevator began climbing back up to the penthouse. The rectangular storm shutters were down, sealing off the hangar, but the shuttle was visible through a window in one of the door segments, still securely anchored to the landing platform outside.

We found Bo lounging in a chair in front of the duty officer's table. He looked up, surprised to find my P-50 aimed at his head.

"Where's the Codex?" I demanded, sensing from the confusion on his face that something was wrong, something I didn't understand.

"You don't have it?" Bo asked. He had nothing with him which he could use to hide the Codex and he obviously had no idea what I was talking about.

"No! It's gone," I said.

Realization appeared on his face. "Stolen?"

Oh no! I thought, beginning to suspect what had happened. "You didn't take it?"

"No." Bo glanced at the duty officer. "How long have I been here?"

"Since the shift change," the duty officer said, eyeing my gun warily. "We've been studying weather patterns, figuring out when the shuttle can fly."

An alarm began beeping from the airspace console beside the duty officer. He turned towards it with growing unease.

"What is it?" I asked.

"Some fool's coming in to land!"

"Is it the same vehicle as before?"

The duty officer gave me a puzzled look. "As before?"

"There was a vehicle hovering outside the penthouse windows. Fifteen minutes ago!"

"No sir," the duty officer replied, motioning to the airspace display. "There ain't been nothing out there since the storm hit – until now."

"It was bigger than your shuttle. You couldn't miss it from the landing platform."

The duty officer scowled. "No one goes out there in this wind! Not unless they want to go swimming!" He activated his communicator. "Dragon Base Three to incoming aircraft, identify yourself." When there was no response, he said. "I don't care who you are, the pad is closed. Do not attempt to land. Acknowledge."

He waited, but the approaching craft continued to ignore his hail.

"What type is it?" I asked, craning my neck to see his display, now showing a contact marker approaching the spire.

The duty officer shrugged. "Don't know, but its trajectory's sub-orbital." He leaned towards his display, eyes widening. "Damn fool! He ain't going for the pad! He's landing on top."

"Of the spire?" I asked. "At the lookout?"

"He's going to kill himself!" the duty officer declared, shaking his head in disbelief.

The airspace display showed high, but constant winds. A good pilot with the right machine could land there. Apart from me, there was one other flyer on Icetop who could do it. "It's Ugo! Has to be!"

Jase gave me a stunned look. "Gadron Ugo?"

"Come on!"

We raced back to the elevator. The indicator showed it was up at the lookout. I called it down, counting the seconds.

"Ugo's on the other side of the planet, Skipper," Jase said, scarcely able to believe what I was thinking.

"He's up there," I said, glancing skywards, "Right now! About to land!"

When the doors opened, we stepped inside finding a sprinkling of snow scattered across the floor.

"If Ugo's here Skipper, that means . . ." Jase said warily as the elevator carried us up through the spire.

"Yeah," I said dismally.

The lift doors opened, blasting Jase and I with freezing winds so powerful we had to grab the safety rails to prevent being blown off our feet. Embedded in the rock outside the elevator entrance was a grappling harpoon, fired from an off-white cargo lighter hovering fifteen meters away, nosing into the wind. Its side cargo door was open and a cable ran from the lighter's interior to the harpoon embedded in the rock. Marie stood just below the small cargo transport, wearing a harness attached to the cable that prevented her from being blown off the spire. She carried the Codex in one hand and reached up with the other to one of the *Heureux's* crewmen who stood tethered inside the lighter's cargo door.

"She's got it!" I said, scarcely able to believe she'd pull a stunt like this, after the night we'd just shared.

"Damn! She stunned me! In the back!" Jase shook his head in disbelief, then took a step towards the door to go after her.

I pushed him back. "No!" I yelled over the screaming winds. "You'll get blown off!"

The *Heureux's* crewman hauled Marie up into the lighter and quickly snapped a safety line onto her belt before freeing her from the harpoon's cable.

She turned back towards the lift, giving me a smile and yelling over the screaming wind, "I'm sorry my love, it's just business!"

"Marie!" I called back desperately. "Come back! You don't understand!"

She blew me a kiss, then stepped inside. A moment later, the cable whipped free of the lighter and the hatch closed.

Looking down at us through the lighter's cockpit window, a big, bald man sat grinning as he expertly wrestled the controls. Gadron Ugo was Marie's pilot-navigator. He'd served her father for more than twenty years and now that she'd inherited the *Heureux*, he was her pilot too. Ugo mocked me with a salute, then the stubby winged transport nosed up as he fed power to the engines. It climbed on a tail of white light, picking up speed quickly before vanishing into the low clouds racing above us.

"Oh man," Jase said, "I knew we couldn't trust her!"

"She doesn't know what she's got herself into!" I said, certain Marie thought she was still playing our competitive little game and this was just a chance to go one up on me.

Jase's eyes widened, adding in an even more astonished tone, "I can't believe she stole it from you!"

"Yeah, she's a piece of work all right!" And she's

in danger!

"What are we going do now?" Jase asked miserably, thinking he'd lost his share of the commission.

"The only thing we can do," I said as snow swirled around our legs. "Go after her and get it back!"

* * * *

There was no UniPol station in the Dragon's Teeth island chain, only fishing company executives and support staff, none of whom wanted to take responsibility for investigating the slaughter that had taken place in Sarat's penthouse. The tiny UniPol unit operating out of Tundratown agreed to send an investigator on the next shuttle, but all they'd find would be corpses mutilated by shrapnel and knife wounds. The bodies would be frozen until the naval liaison officer made his regular visit in a few months, but he'd have no more success in discovering what had happened than UniPol.

To avoid waiting for the local investigator, Jase and I assured the maintenance base manager we saw nothing, then caught the first shuttle out, along with Vargis and Bo. Before leaving, we all promised to visit the UniPol headquarters in Tundratown for questioning, although none of us had any intention of talking to the law. As expected the *Heureux* was long gone by the time we landed at the spaceport, giving Marie almost a day's head start. Outside the shuttle, a skimmer was waiting to carry Vargis across the landing ground to the *Soberano*, which was already warming up its engines. He climbed aboard the small ground vehicle without a word and raced away.

"Sore loser!" Jase muttered as he started towards the *Lining* to prep her for launch.

I shook hands with Bo at the foot of the stairs wheeled up against the shuttle. Even though he'd lost the auction and seen the business end of my P-50, he remained remarkably courteous.

"You're going after her?" Bo asked as we shook hands.

"Oh yeah."

"Before you embark on a journey of revenge," Bo said, dipping into his endless supply of Confucian quotes, "dig two graves."

"I'm not after revenge Bo, just what's rightfully mine." He didn't realize I was as worried about Marie's safety as I was about the alien-tech device she'd stolen from me.

Bo gave me a knowing look. "Rightful ownership is open to interpretation, Captain Kade, considering you . . . modified the rules in order to win."

Damn, he knew! "I evened the odds."

Bo nodded appreciatively. "I don't know how you did it, but cheating was the only way you could win. You would never have beaten Vargis otherwise – none of us could."

"If you thought Vargis had so much money, why bother coming?"

"I didn't know Senor Vargis was going to win until after I arrived."

I gave Bo a curious look. "What do you mean?"

Bo raised his hand to his left eye, peeled back his eyelid and popped his eye into his palm, leaving his eye socket empty. He held up the prosthetic eye for me to see. "Why do you think I went last in the first round? It was so I could see your bids with this, and out bid you all. Then I would have had the commanding position of always bidding last and of always knowing what you bid."

I glanced at his cybernetic spying eye, puzzled. "But you lost the first round!"

"Yes, even though my bid was the highest." he said, waiting for the implications to sink in.

"The auction was rigged?"

"From the very beginning."

So we were simply window dressing, hiding the auction's real purpose. "That's why you didn't blow my cover?"

"There was nothing to gain. Senor Vargis was meant to win no matter what any of us did. You outbid him in the second round, yet he still won."

"But you offered to pool your resources with me."

"Your second bid was impressive, proving you represent someone of substance. Call it a hunch, but you didn't strike me as the kind of man who would surrender easily." He shrugged. "I was correct, although perhaps I should have offered Captain Dulon a deal instead." He gave me a rueful look. "We all have our weaknesses."

"So someone cracked Earth Bank security just to get the Codex to Vargis," I said thoughtfully.

"To the right people," Bo said, "knowing how to defeat Earth Bank encryption would be worth even more than the Codex itself."

I couldn't tell him it was the Matarons who'd cracked it. Earth Bank security was so fiendishly complex, it defied any human attempts to penetrate it. Even the EIS, who'd tried for years to break into it, had been unsuccessful. Only superior alien-tech could have done it. If I could have gotten the auctioneer to the EIS, they might have been able to reverse engineer what the Matarons had done. I began to wonder what had happened to the Earth Bank device after the Mataron attack. It may have been buried under the rubble of a collapsed wall or hidden in the darkness – I couldn't be sure – then my eyes fell to the large case Bo was carrying. His knuckles were white from the weight, even though his face showed no strain.

"I'll be damned!" I said. "You stole the auctioneer!"

"This trip has not been a complete waste," Bo conceded.

My threading flashed an alert into my mind, warning that a tiny particle stream was painting my chest. It took only a moment for the threading to determine Bo's ship had me targeted. They must have been listening in on our conversation.

"Any chance of sharing?" I asked for the benefit of whoever had me in their cross hairs.

"I think not, Captain Kade." Bo slipped his robotic eye back into its socket.

In the distance, Vargis' skimmer rode up into one of the *Soberano's* cavernous cargo holds, then a large rectangular door lifted up and sealed shut behind him.

"Well Bo, I guess Mr Li won't be too disappointed in you after all."

Bo smiled, almost embarrassed. "My friends call me . . . Jie." He gave me an amused look as understanding appeared on my face. An organization as secretive as the Obligation would never send a lackey to gamble all they were worth on a piece of unproven alien-tech. Only one man could make such a decision and that was the inimitable Jie Kang Li himself. "Perhaps one day Sirius Kade, you really will work for me. I could use a man like you. Then you can tell me how you beat the perfidious Mr Sarat. Until then, please do not pretend to work for me again. I would not like to have you killed."

"Deal."

Jie Kang Li hesitated, then smiled. "One credit!" He tapped his prosthetic eye meaningfully, telling me with a gesture how he knew my final bid for the Codex. "An intriguing choice!" he said, before heading towards his deceptively decrepit container ship.

With a growing sense of urgency, I hurried towards the *Lining*. Jie Kang Li's ship lifted off as I reached the airlock, rising like a point of brilliant white light towards the low hanging clouds with an acceleration belying its antiquated appearance. Once inside, I went straight to the flight deck where Jase was finishing his pre-flight checks.

"All I need is a destination for the autonav," he said with a quizzical look as I climbed onto my acceleration couch.

"Marie's got an open contract with the Beneficial Society," I said. "She'll want to collect on it before I can stop her."

Jase made a face. "Oh no!"

"I'm afraid so. We're going to Axon."

Axon Way Station was home to the closest Society Headquarters. It was a haven for traders and smugglers alike, a place where cargoes were swapped and profits made without fear of surprise inspections by nosy Earth Navy officers. Unfortunately, the local crime bosses had posted a kill bounty on my head, thanks to a little disagreement a few years back.

"Have we got a launch window?" I asked as our wrap around view screen revealed a light dusting of snow was beginning to fall across the spaceport.

"There's no schedule," Jase said. "Control requested we broadcast when we're ready. If anyone else broadcasts, we have to give them two minutes head start before going ourselves."

I guess it made sense, considering they normally only saw one ship a month. I activated the communicator, setting it to all bands and announced, "*Silver Lining* declaring launch."

Jase released the autonav. Our landing thrusters lifted us off the apron, tilted our nose skyward, then our two big maneuvering engines came to life, sending us racing up into the clouds at twenty gravities. The autonav expertly balanced the ship's inertial field, uniformly accelerating every atom in our bodies at nineteen gravities, ensuring we felt only one gravity inside the ship. Tundratown's cluster of prefab buildings, strung out along the sprawling harbor shore, quickly disappeared beneath the clouds. For a few moments, dense gray water vapor surrounded the ship, then we broke out into clear air and climbed rapidly up through the thinning atmosphere.

Icetop's curvature quickly appeared as blue sky

faded to black, then a contact indicator illuminated on the screen. It was above us and to port, showing no transponder signal and approaching from high orbit on an intercept course. It was over twenty thousand clicks away, thrusting hard towards a firing position that would catch us soon after we cleared the atmosphere. They had to have been watching the spaceport from orbit and begun maneuvering the moment we lifted off.

"Its energy levels are eight times ours," Jase said, eyes locked on the neutrino detector's display. That much power meant big engines or hungry weapons, probably both. He ran the neutrino profile through the system. "It's Gwandoya!"

Izin had recorded the profile of Gwandoya's old navy cutter when it had lifted off, adding it to the recognition database as a matter of routine.

I switched on the intercom. "Izin, we're going to need power to the shield. Expect weapons fire."

"What kind of weapons fire, Captain?" Izin asked in his synthesized voice as calmly as if I'd requested a wash and a wax.

"Assume the shield's going to bleed hard to stay up."

"Understood," Izin said, focusing his attention on ensuring the energy plant would be ready to give us everything it could.

"You're not planning on fighting that thing are you?" Jase asked apprehensively. We both knew the *Lining* was no match for a navy cutter – even an old one.

"Not a chance!" Our single particle cannon could do little more than tickle the cutter's reinforced hull, while the little nasty hidden in our bow was strictly a one shot gamble. If we missed this close, Gwandoya would have no choice but to blast us to bits to prevent us firing again. "I'm going to run like a Valurian jackrabbit with my tail on fire."

"Glad to hear it, Skipper. Not that I object to fighting, just dying."

The autonav indicated we needed nine minutes to reach the minimum safe distance for superluminal flight. The trick would be staying alive long enough to show Gwandoya a clean pair of heels.

"We've cleared the mesosphere," Jase reported as we emerged into the deep blackness of space.

I reset the autonav, kicking our maneuvering engines up to thirty five gravities, our maximum, inertially shielded acceleration. The engines could have pushed the *Silver Lining* higher, but that would have exposed us to unshielded acceleration, pinning us to our couches barely able to breathe.

"I've got another contact," Jase announced. "It's coming up from the planet." It took a moment for the third contact's transponder to register. "It's the *Soberano*!"

She was exactly two minutes behind us on a similar trajectory. If the *Soberano* was even half the ship I thought she was, Gwandoya's old cutter would have little chance against her advanced weaponry.

"Heave to and surrender the Codex!" Gwandoya's voice blared from the flight deck's comm system.

I felt momentary relief that he didn't know Marie had the Codex, reassuring me that she'd gotten away clean.

"We don't have it," I replied casually.

The cutter's higher orbit and greater velocity gave her the initiative and there was nothing I could do about it. It was as great an advantage for the hunter as diving out of the sun from high altitude was during the old days of aerial combat. If we didn't do exactly as Gwandoya ordered, he could come in fast, cripple us as he passed, then decelerate and come back to loot us at his leisure. If we surrendered, he could keep us targeted as he decelerated down onto us, blasting us if we so much as blinked.

"You're lying!" Gwandoya said. "I paid one of Sarat's guards to tell me who won."

“Sarat and his guards are dead. They were killed before the Codex was stolen.”

“Cut your engines now,” Gwandoya said in a more threatening tone, “Or I will destroy them.”

“He’s not bluffing, Skipper,” Jase said anxiously. “There’s a hot spot on his starboard side!”

Jase threw the infra red sensor feed up onto the view screen as an overlay. A glowing red bloom appeared halfway along the cutter’s hull where a large weapon was charging, perfectly positioned to fire. Gwandoya was clearly an expert at this kind of fighting – dropping in fast on a defenseless trader – and he was too smart to let me talk him in circles, buying time while we raced out to bubble.

“Cut the engines,” I said to Jase, then transmitted to Gwandoya, “*Silver Lining* powering down. Send a boarding party. You’ll see we don’t have it.”

“A wise decision, Kade,” Gwandoya growled.

The cutter immediately tumbled one hundred and eighty degrees, showing us its stern, and began decelerating hard to match us. All the time, the red heat bloom of the cutter’s charged weapon remained expertly angled at us, Gwandoya’s way of telling us he never took his finger off the trigger.

Jase gave me a confused look. “You’re going to let him board us?”

“If I let Gwandoya board this ship, I’ll never get it back.” Even if he searched the *Silver Lining* from top to bottom and found nothing, he’d keep her as a prize and space us for his trouble. “Izin, how fast can you get the shield up? No safeties, just throw it out there.”

“Nine seconds,” Izin said. He’d been listening to everything said on the flight deck since I’d warned him I’d need the shield.

“How long before they see it?”

“I can hide the activation for the first few seconds.”

“OK, you have shield control,” I said as my mind raced trying to figure out how I could distract Gwandoya long enough to get the shield up. At that range, he only needed a second to knock us out.

"How many crew do you think he has?" Jase asked, wondering if we could fight it out at the airlock.

"A hundred, maybe a hundred and fifty." Too many for a gun fight.

The *Soberano's* contact marker was growing in size now that we'd cut our engines. I rotated the optics, bringing the super transport into view as she came roaring up from the planet's surface.

"Give me a tight link to Vargis," I said. When Jase indicated we were beam-locked, I hailed the super transport. "*Silver Lining* to *Soberano*. Request immediate assistance. We are about to be boarded by pirates." I had no doubt Vargis had been watching the exchange between us and Gwandoya and knew exactly what was happening.

Vargis reply came back immediately using an omnidirectional transmission, ensuring Gwandoya heard his reply. His face appeared in the center of our screen with the *Soberano's* expansive control room visible behind him. "Captain Kade, I have to say I'm not entirely sure who the pirate is, you or Gwandoya."

"Listen Vargis, you don't have to like me, but you know what's going to happen if Gwandoya's men get aboard this ship. I know you can stop it."

Vargis feigned confusion. "I have no idea what you mean. The *Soberano* is a defenseless freighter. Considering she's worth at least . . . ten thousand times what your little garbage scow is worth, I really can't get involved. I'm sure you understand." Vargis' face vanished from the screen.

"That scumbag cut us off!" Jase exploded.

I swung our optical feed back towards Gwandoya's cutter. She was close now, almost on top of us. Her square stern, dominated by one large circular engine surrounded by four small boosters, glowed blue with ionized light. She would be monitoring our every move, but Gwandoya's desire to take the *Silver Lining* intact would make him reluctant to wreck us until he was sure we were running. I was gambling that his greed would buy us a few valuable seconds when his cutter was most vulnerable.

Our interior cargo hold was empty, but we still had one external VRS container clamped to maglock two, the center of the three towing positions between our engines. The container was full of scrap metal destined for Tanos, junk yard of the Outer Lyra region – nothing we couldn't afford to lose.

Jase furrowed his brow in confusion when he saw me studying the cargo manifest. "Even a pirate wouldn't want any of that garbage."

"Oh, he wants it," I said with conviction. "He just doesn't know it yet."

"*Silver Lining* preparing for docking," I said, then slowly turned our bow towards the cutter as if we were a lumbering freighter offering our starboard airlock for docking. Gwandoya's sensors would tell him our particle cannon was stone cold and, if he knew about our hidden bow compartment, he'd see the outer doors were closed. "Get ready."

"For what?" Jase asked apprehensively.

When our bow was aimed across the cutter's deceleration path, I said, "Izin, power the shield . . . now!"

Izin started shield activation while I pushed the engines to thirty five G's, sending the *Lining* shooting forward as if she'd been fired out of a cannon. Before Gwandoya could attack, we were beneath him, directly astern of his engines and outside his big gun's firing arc. I immediately nosed up toward the cutter and accelerated into its engine blast, filling our screen with the glow of her engines.

Jase tensed. "Skipper! Don't ram him!"

I chuckled, without taking my eyes off the screen, amused Jase thought I was that crazy.

A thermal warning appeared on the main screen as the cutter's engine blast began to heat our hull – nothing the *Lining* couldn't handle while the shield was activating. Our collision alert sounded, then I released maglock two, dropping the external VRS container and rolling hard away. We narrowly missed one of the cutter's boosters before flying out from behind her stern on the side opposite to her main gun. I barrel rolled again, keeping the cutter's bulk between us and their big stick, then sent the *Lining* racing up alongside the cutter's scarred black and gray hull.

By now Gwandoya knew we were running, but his collision alert would be wailing in his ears as our container full of scrap metal hurtled towards his main engine. The cutter began to thrust sideways and spin on its axis, trying to bring its big gun to bear as it dodged the container. Good ship handling for a pirate, but the cutter was too big and slow for that kind of maneuver.

If there were weapons on the blind side of the cutter, they weren't ready, because we passed along her hull without a single shot being fired. I swung the optical feed to view astern as we passed the cutter's bow, keeping it center screen while we climbed away. A bright flash erupted from the cutter's stern as the VRS container struck Gwandoya's main engine, then a massive fireball engulfed her aft section. It blasted away from the cutter in all directions, forming a rapidly expanding orange ring of superheated plasma with the raider at its center.

At that moment, our battle shield came to life, momentarily dimming our view of Gwandoya's ship. By the time our optics compensated, the blast ring encircling the crippled pirate vessel had expanded to reveal its stern had been blown off and was now drifting away from the rest of the cutter. Amidships, the infra red bloom was coming into view as the cutter's hull spun, bringing its main weapon around to bear on us. Its engines may have been destroyed, but the energy plant in the center of the ship was still able to power its weapons. A beam of searing yellow lashed out from the infra red bloom and began eating into the *Lining's* shield.

"Damn!" Jase wheezed. "He's got a can opener!"

It was slang for a fusion beam, a short range naval weapon that could slice open lightly armored hulls like tin foil. They required enormous capacitors to charge, which is why Earth Navy fitted them to much larger ships than cutters. Gwandoya must have gutted the interior of his ship to mount it, but how did a rabid murderer like Gwandoya get his hands on such a weapon?

"Captain," Izin called over the intercom, "the shield is bleeding at four hundred and thirty percent." His artificial voice sounded calm, but I knew he was worried. "Failure is imminent."

"Just a few more seconds," I said, knowing we were piling on the distance between us.

The fusion beam stayed locked onto us as we pulled away, testament to the accuracy of Gwandoya's targeting system. Below our stern, a brilliant white disk formed and began to grow as the *Lining's* shield struggled to radiate away the incoming energy pouring into us. The shield thinned, but the distance between the two ships grew until the glow softened and began to slowly shrink. Soon the fusion beam's intensity fell away, diffused by distance.

"The shield has stabilized, Captain," Izin reported.

Far behind us, the cutter's stern had begun to tumble and was no longer aligned with the rest of the ship. The blast ring had expanded into a large circular cloud that was slowly cooling, while secondary explosions rippled along the cutter's hull from the wrecked stern. After each explosion, a slender plume of atmosphere vented hundreds of meters out into space as another section of hull decompressed.

"She's had it!" Jase said incredulously. "I can't believe you smoked it with a trash can."

"It's a first for me."

The fusion beam ceased firing as a gray lifeboat shot away from the cutter, propelled by a low power thruster. We waited expectantly, but no more lifeboats launched. Even overloaded, that one lifeboat couldn't have carried more than forty. A cutter that size should have had at least four such escape craft, but Gwandoya must have removed the others to make room for his oversized can opener.

"Do you think Gwandoya made it out?" Jase wondered aloud.

"People like him always do." They were usually the first to jump ship and thought nothing of leaving others behind. I watched the cutter for a moment, noting the atmospheric plumes were thinning as Gwandoya's ship died. It might take weeks or years, but eventually Icetop's gravity would pull it down to a fiery end in the planet's atmosphere. I climbed off my acceleration couch with a melancholy feeling. I knew Gwandoya and his crew had been responsible for many deaths over the years, but no one who lived in space ever liked to see another ship destroyed. "When we reach minimum safe distance, bubble for Axon."

"I don't suppose I could convince you to head for Breega instead?" Jase asked. "I need some sun after all that ice."

Breega was an arid world, so hot that the human settlements were all located below ground or in high mountains.

"Why there? You can only step on the surface at night?"

"Yeah, but the only ice they have is in their drinks."

"Next time," I promised, then headed to engineering where Izin was still meticulously watching our shield levels. "You can drop the shield, Izin. Did we take any damage?"

"Nothing I can't repair in the next few days."

I watched Izin de-energize the shield, then said.

"Good work back there on Icetop. How did you manage to crack the auctioneer?" It was something even the EIS would find useful.

"I didn't. I told you, Captain, I could not break its security. I found the auctioneer passed the results to a softbot, which displayed the message. All I did was subvert the softbot, replacing Captain Vargis' name with yours."

"Oh," I said thoughtfully. "So the auctioneer thinks Vargis won?"

"Yes Captain, not that it matters now."

"It will to Vargis."

"Why is that, Captain?"

"Because it would have transferred the money from his vault-key, even though he got nothing for it," I grinned thoughtfully. "I wonder if that double dealing slime ball knows?"

"He will the next time he examines his vault balance."

"Good thing he didn't check it before takeoff," I said amused. "Rather than leave us to Gwandoya, he might have blasted us himself!"

Chapter Four : Axon Way Station

Free Station
The Shroud Dark Nebula
Outer Lyra Region
Artificial Gravity
1,082 light years from Sol
18,000 inhabitants

It took three weeks to make the seventy-eight light year voyage to Axon Way Station, a sprawling ramshackle structure that had grown haphazardly over the centuries into one of the largest free floating habitats outside Core System space. It was gravitationally anchored to the edge of the Shroud, a vast dark nebula of dust and ionized gas which in a few million years would begin spawning new stars, turning the cold dark nebula into a glowing spectacle of light and color. The station had originally been a hydrogen refinery established by the Axon Corporation over three centuries ago. Being located halfway between Hades City and the Outer Cygnus colonies, it quickly became a favored rest stop for trade ships. Once the traders came, the merchants and smugglers followed.

Axon was a free station, a self governing commercial enterprise under corporate rather than political control. It was on friendly terms with the four Earth collective-governments, but was carefully independent of them all. That autonomy and its location fuelled the illicit trade which transformed Axon into the black market capital of the Outer Lyra region. There was a small UniPol outfit there providing a semblance of law and order to the more civilized inhabitants, while the local EIS cell operated in secret who, thanks to my purge and wipe, I had no way of contacting. The station's location, freedom and thriving trade made it a natural choice for the Beneficial Society's regional headquarters, which said volumes about how close the Society was to the black market. The next nearest Society HQ was months away, which was why I was betting Marie was headed to Axon.

The Outer Lyra run was always hazardous because the Shroud created natural bottlenecks marked by navpoint beacons where ships unbubbled to make course corrections. Ravens were known to lurk around the edges of these natural choke points, occasionally picking off easy prey and running the moment a navy frigate appeared. Everyone knew there was a Raven base inside the Shroud, although no one outside the Brotherhood knew where it was. Even inside the Brotherhood, it was a closely guarded secret, known only to a handful of senior navigators, all of whom would die fighting rather than be captured by the navy.

This time around, we had a clean run all the way to the second last navpoint, where we picked up a signature drifting at the extreme edge of sensor range.

"Can't tell what it is," Jase said. "No transponder, no energy emissions. I can't even tell if it's human."

It was human. No one else used our navpoints. "Any emergency beacons?"

"Nothing. No active scanning either. If it's alive, it's just listening."

It could have been anything from a derelict to a Raven ambush. I studied the signature warily, well aware of the tricks the Brotherhood used to lure well meaning fools to their deaths. There was no mayday signal and its reactor was stone cold, indicating it was a lifeless wreck. Even so, I hated leaving a ship adrift in case there were survivors – then I remembered my brother. He was out here somewhere, maybe in the Shroud, maybe in a place like it. Whenever I saw anything that looked like an ambush or was tempted to do something stupid, I thought of him, imagined how dangerous it would be if he were laying the trap and then I bubbled the hell out of there fast.

"We'll report it when we get to Axon," I said, not that they'd do anything about it. The Shroud might have been a shortcut, but it was also a place of death, where the only favor the living could do for the dead was not join them.

We had our course corrections down to a fine art and were soon on our way towards Axon. A few hours later, we unbubbled a hundred thousand clicks out, leaving our transponder off while we checked what ships were docked. We were outside the range of the station's heavy weapons, which would be targeting us as a matter of course, waiting for us to identify ourselves. In the Shroud, taking a first look from long range with no transponder signal was a sensible precaution, although entering weapon's range without revealing who you were was a fatal mistake.

There were more than twenty ships docked, but the *Heureux* was not among them. Either we'd passed her in flight or I'd guessed wrong and she was heading for a more distant Society base, probably Xantis in towards the Core Systems.

"Show them who we are," I said, lighting up our maneuvering engines while Jase activated the transponder.

I booked a berth with Axon Control as we

approached the sprawling black structure. It was lined with thousands of points of light, marking its many viewports, although there were fewer active lights near the abandoned refinery at the center where the lowlife types fought each other for scraps. The station was constructed of dozens of vertically aligned cylindrical habitats of different lengths and thicknesses, some with their sides pressed together, others separated by connecting tubes. The ends of the cylinders mostly bristled with aerials and towers, although a few contained transparent domes covering parks and housing for the obscenely rich. Robot workers and human engineers floated like insects around several skeletal sections under construction, while dull metal gun emplacements ringed the station and a dozen orbiting weapon platforms showed Axon took its defense seriously. No Raven ship had approached within weapon's range for more than a century, although they occasionally performed long distance scans of the docking zones to see who was in port.

"Are you staying on board, Skipper?" Jase asked warily.

"No. You are."

He winced. "There'll be trouble if the Krieger brothers hear you're on the station."

There used to be three brothers, famous drunks, gamblers and bullies who ran one of the local crime gangs. Thanks to a shakedown gone wrong, there were now only two, and both had sworn to kill me for dealing with their murderous brother. It wasn't their station of course, they just acted like it was.

"By the time they find out I'm here, we'll be long gone," I reassured him, certain the Krieger brother's informants would be lining up to give them the good news if they got a sniff of my arrival.

Jase looked doubtful. "I'll be ready if you need help."

"No matter what happens, don't leave the ship," I

said, certain that if Jase so much as set foot on the station, they'd grab him and offer to trade him for me, then slit both our throats. They were predictable that way.

Jase gave me a frustrated look, but knew my mind was made up. He had no history with the Krieger brothers, and I wanted to keep it that way – for his sake.

"Prepare docking clamps," I said as the *Silver Lining* settled into the guide beam leading to our mooring position, secretly hoping the Krieger brothers' eyes weren't everywhere.

I didn't have time for games, not this trip.

* * * *

Dock security was non-existent at Axon. In high threat space everyone was openly armed and would fight rather than surrender their personal protection, so I was able to wear my P-50 holstered when I boarded the station.

If Hades City was a honeycomb of well lit caverns, Axon Way Station was a labyrinth of mostly dark and grimy corridors, straining life support systems and gang controlled no-go areas. The exceptions were the white zones, at the extreme upper and lower ends of the station, where the rich lived. They were protected by private armies, were supplied with ample power, clean air and good food and lived in sprawling homes with panoramic views of the Shroud. They could have been a million light years from the lawless center of the station.

The black zone was located in the oldest, most dilapidated part of the station, around the old refinery, where local stim-heads called 'fynies' would put a slug between your eyes for your boots – let alone the mountain of credits I was carrying. The fynie dominated black zone survived on minimal power and choked on air fouled by a leaking network of disused pipes and rusting gas tanks.

Between the two white zones and the decaying

black zone were the grey zones, home to illegitimate businesses and well armed vigilantes who kept the worst of the fynies sealed in their rotting slum. Elevators and walkways connected the gray and white zones and a hull skimming ferry service ran between the two wealthy ends of the station, but there was no functioning transport link into or through the black zone.

The gray zone's stim labs were the center of Outer Lyra's drug trade, and its workshops manufactured every kind of weapon known to man. Scattered between the stim and weapon manufacturers was a vast array of medlabs offering an impressive selection of bizarre body mods and implants. Most infamous of all was the Cauldron in Upper Gray, the reddest red light district in five hundred light years. Everyone knew what Axon was, even the navy, but it provided a protected stopover that the navy didn't have to pay for, so they let it stay in business.

After paying our mooring fees at the gate, I passed through into the station without even a retinal scan, proof Axon didn't care how many systems a man was wanted in, so long as they got paid. I took an elevator to Upper White Commercial, to visit Shipping Control to confirm the *Heureux* hadn't put in at the station in the last month. Marie's old freighter was slower than the *Lining*, so I held on to the slim hope I'd passed her and she'd dock in the next day or two.

Hoping I might have better luck with the Society, I headed for their Outer Lyra regional headquarters. It was on the far side of Upper White's retail district, a spider's web of broad corridors lined with shops overflowing with merchandise of every description, most of it stolen. Many of the smugglers feeding Axon had Raven links, and made healthy livings out of disposing of the Brotherhood's booty in ways UniPol found difficult to trace. The smugglers would pick-up the loot from prearranged drop zones in the Shroud and sell it in Axon, or some other black market center, before passing the funds to Raven vault-men, minus their cut of course. It was an efficient operation, where everybody got rich. Very rich.

It was why Earth Navy couldn't stamp out the Brotherhood, and why the Society's regional headquarters was a well appointed fortress that forced me to hand over my P-50 before letting me in. Like all traders, I had no choice but to be a member of the Society because running cargo was their game. They owned it. The further out from Earth you went, the truer that was. They protected the vendors by underwriting every contract – for a healthy three percent skim off the top – and they ran the Exchange, which only Society members could access. It was a racket and it was legal, but we got discounts from Society endorsed dealers which eased the pain a little. Technically, the Society didn't get a cut of smuggling money, but their skim was inflated to take a piece of that action too, although no one ever discussed it.

After settling up the commissions I owed the Society, I requested a heads up if the *Heureux* docked. Members could always contact each other through the Society, with no questions asked, no records kept. I then checked which of Axon's merchants were Society authorized vendors, and as such, required to offer me discounts. The run in with Gwandoya had left me feeling the *Lining* was underdressed, especially now that I was doing double duty for the EIS. As luck would have it, Armin's Armaments was still on the list. Everybody bought from him, because his gear was premium grade and came with permits – probably forged – but good enough to pass Earth Navy inspection.

I retrieved my gun on the way out and took the elevator down to Upper Gray, where the streets were crowded and the air was a kaleidoscope of fragrances, not all of them pleasant. Everyone down there was carrying, except for a few well dressed richies who were escorted by heavily armed guards in body armor. Stim-dealers worked the street corners and a few grubby looking fynies skulked in back alleys, but generally everyone was well mannered.

Politeness tends to accompany a plethora of guns on hips.

A bunch of under nourished idlers lounged outside Armin's. Not fynies, but bottom feeders nevertheless. One was barely conscious, pressing a dark colored stim tube into his neck, pumping toxins into his blood stream at a steady pace. Another wore a brain wave modulator with the visor down and was using his hands to simulate firing a weapon as he lived through the helmet's scripted gun-fantasy. A third sat on a low, graffiti laden wall staring at a small device in his hand. When I reached the entrance, he aimed the device at me. Too late I realized it was an alpha wave scanner, recording the identities of everyone who passed within range. He looked up at me, eyes wide, thinking of all the credits he was about to make, then jumped to his feet and ran. I considered shooting him, but DNA locked him instead before he fled into an alley.

The idler poisoning his blood supply with the stim tube turned his glazed eyes in my direction, pointing his fingers at me like a gun and mimed shooting me. Thanks for the warning. I considered removing his larynx with the stim tube, but he was so toxxed, he probably would have enjoyed it. The smart thing to do would have been to get back to the ship, but I really needed to sharpen the *Lining's* teeth, so I went inside expecting a reception committee when I came back out.

Armin's Armaments was a warehouse covering three levels with armed guards at every door and autoturrets in every ceiling. I didn't have to hand in my gun as I entered – there was no need. Signs everywhere warned customers not to touch their weapons, otherwise the autoturrets would open fire. For my personal safety, they would immediately kill anyone who acted unsafely – including me. Very comforting! It was hardly surprising Armin's had a reputation for being the most peaceful place in either gray zone. A pity there was only one way in or out.

Being careful to keep my hands where the autoturrets could see them, I wandered through ordered galleries displaying everything from tiny pinhole stunners small enough to fit inside a woman's purse to holographic displays of ship based heavy weapons that would have been at home on an Earth Navy battle cruiser. For several hours, automated vending machines explained in excruciating detail the technical specs of dozens of ship borne weapons small enough to replace the *Lining's* feeble particle cannon.

Eventually I found a vending machine talking my language.

"The Celestial Dynamics KD-496 Proton Burst Cannon may be optionally fitted with a fully insulated, multi-phase capacitor guaranteed to limit thermal emissions to less than one point eight percent during charge cycles."

In other words, a stealth cannon – exactly what I was looking for. The price was obscene and the cycle time slow, but the sneaky charge capacitor allowed the burster to power up undetected by Earth-tech sensors. The Tau Cetins would know in a nanosecond if the weapon was active, but as I was never going to do anything as stupid as shoot at them, that hardly mattered. The burster hit like a weapon three times its size at a respectable range, which made it a good match for the *Silver Lining*'s main defenses: her speed and her shield.

Kicking an adversary in the pants and running like hell was my kind of fighting.

It made no sense to put such an expensive piece of kit on a ship as small as the *Lining*, which is why no potential foe would expect it. Fortunately, Lena could afford it, and I figured she owed me. After receiving Armin's rock solid guarantee the weapon would be delivered to the *Lining's* cargo hold within the hour, I made a significant dent in the EIS vault-key's balance, then went downstairs to the urban warfare section and bought an apple.

I expected the idler with the alpha wave scanner to be outside with his friends, so I needed something to keep them away. The small spherical device was just large enough to fit inside my hand without being noticed and its effective radius was small enough not to turn half the station against me.

"How many G-Max Sensory Assault Grenades do you require, sir?" the silver, multi-armed vending machine asked, holding up the demonstration model for me to inspect.

"Just one."

"They come in a box of twelve, sir. I am not permitted to split packs."

"OK, I'll take a box."

"Would you like them delivered to your ship with your other purchases?" the vending machine asked politely. It was perfect for dispensing information and taking orders, but lacked any real intelligence.

"I'll take one with me, deliver the rest."

"Very well sir. The activation code will be automatically loaded into the device as you leave the store. Internal guard systems have been advised the weapon is currently inactive."

"Thanks," I said, relieved to know the autoturrets wouldn't shoot my arm off the moment I touched the grenade.

"We offer a full range of intensive urban assault courses, sir. These courses are recommended if you require training in deployment techniques for your high quality, money back guaranteed munitions in a manner designed to achieve maximum effect."

"Thanks. I've got it covered."

"As you wish, sir," the vending machine said, then one of its flexible arms handed me a G-Max SAG. I hadn't used a weapon like it in years, but they were relatively simple to activate, and for the ultra-reflexed, easy to throw accurately. "Do you require any other assistance, sir? We have a special on TNK Body Armor. Today only. All sizes. Would you like to try a set on, sir?"

"Some other time," I said, heading for the exit with the grenade hidden in the palm of my hand.

The moment I stepped through the door, my threading drew a red targeting reticule around the face of the idler I'd DNA locked earlier. He stood across the street with a group of shaven headed thugs, each with a pair of thunderbolts tattooed on their foreheads in a "V" formation. They carried metal pipes with handles – electro-shock clubs – nasty thug weapons capable of inflicting excruciating pain, but not fatal wounds. Several had handguns, still holstered, telling me they were here to take me alive. The tallest and heaviest of the group had his back to me. At the promptings of his companions, he turned towards me. Like the others, Heiko Krieger had the same distinctive V-shaped gang insignia tattooed on his forehead and additional matching thunderbolts striking down from his dark eye sockets.

We locked eyes on each other, then he said, "That's him!"

I sensed movement behind me. An electro-shock club jabbed me in the back, sending a neuroelectric charge coursing into my spine and hurling me onto the street. I lost muscle control and collapsed onto the metal floor. My threading detected the attack and kept my fingers locked around the grenade by overriding my nervous system. By the time my body started to respond, Heiko and his gaggle of muscle-modded sycophants were all around me. He kicked me in the stomach with metal tipped boots, spinning me around onto my back. A threading status message flashed before my eyes, informing me my ribs were bruised, but not broken. Half a dozen shock clubs began pounding me, all set to low intensity so they wouldn't stop my heart. My threading, sensing the assault, blocked my pain receptors sending my body numb while my keeping my fingers clamped on the small metal sphere in the palm of my hand.

When they finally stopped jabbing me with their torture sticks, Heiko leaned down towards my face. "I've been waiting for you, Kade!"

I tried to open my mouth to compliment him on his dental work, but all I could manage was an indignant gurgling sound.

"My brother and I are going to keep you alive for a long, long time." Heiko and Kord were kings of the local protection racket. I hadn't intended to kill Niklaus, their uglier older brother, but he'd left me no choice. "But you won't be lonely. You're going to make a lot of friends where you're going, the kind who like raw . . . red . . . meat."

Heiko grinned viciously, stroking my cheek with his shock club. I could feel my skin pinching from the neuroelectric shock, but my threading's pain blockers spared me the worst of it. A puzzled look slowly appeared on his face as he began to realize something was wrong.

ENABLE SPEECH, I thought. When my threading gave me vocal control, I said, "Lower . . . and to the left . . . Hmm, better!"

Heiko scowled and removed the shock club from my face, grabbing my jaw with his free hand. "You toxxed out, Kade?"

"Yeah, by your smell!" I sniffed experimentally. "Don't you ever get to wash down here?"

Heiko gave me an astonished look. "You are one dumb, smart mouthed freak! You're going to spend the rest of your life in a tiny little cage, Kade! Except when we bring you out to play." He jabbed me again with his shock club, twisting it spitefully as my body convulsed.

I opened my mouth, feigning an inability to speak.

Heiko withdrew and shock club and leaned closer.

"What?"

ENABLE FULL MOTOR CONTROL, I thought, overriding my threading, then when his face was close, I said, "I . . . don't . . . like . . . cages," and smashed my forehead into his nose.

Heiko fell back, hand over his snout as blood began seeping through his fingers.

SUPPRESS OPTICAL, THREE SECONDS! I thought, pressing the grenade's detonator and letting it roll free of my hand.

My threading shut off the optical feed from my eyes, giving me nothing but blackness, while the grenade jetted up off the ground to eye height and emitted a blinding white pulse. It was longer than a simple flash and intensely white, yet completely silent.

My vision returned as the grenade clattered to the ground, its power supply exhausted. Everyone in the street was doubled over, hands on eyes, some groaning, some screaming, all blind – temporarily. I staggered to my feet while Heiko and his little band of torturers stumbled around me stunned. All had dropped their electro-shock clubs in their rush to press their hands to their eyes.

I picked up Heiko's inactive club, tripped his ankle with it and sent him face first onto the deck. While he lay there holding his eyes, I tapped him lightly on the back of the head with the club. "Heiko, watch your step!"

"I'm going to kill you, Kade!"

"Not today you're not." I flipped him over with my boot, turned the electro-shock club on and ramped the power to maximum, then slid it under his back.

Heiko's body began to shake uncontrollably as neuroelectric pulses twitched his muscles so fast, he couldn't roll away from the club. He'd be stuck bouncing like that until one of his girlfriends could see well enough to switch it off.

I leaned towards him. "This was fun, Heiko, but

let's not do it again."

I straightened, stretching shock-stressed muscles and walked stiffly towards the elevator. Once Kord found out his brother had been stomped on, they'd both come looking for me with their assorted friends. I'd have to put Izin on guard duty at the airlock, just in case they tried to get aboard ship. He'd like that.

Izin was, after all, an ambush predator extraordinaire.

* * * *

There was a message waiting for me from the Beneficial Society when I got back to the *Silver Lining*. A report had been logged with Axon Control that a Caravel D class medium freighter had been sighted adrift near navpoint two along the Outer Lyra passage. It hadn't been showing a transponder and was close to where we'd detected the unknown contact on our way in. Now that I knew the contact was the same class as Marie's ship, there was no doubt in my mind we'd detected the *Heureux* without realizing it!

I contacted Axon Control and asked if they'd sent a rescue ship, but they informed me they had none to send. When I offered to investigate, they gladly gave me the sighting report. That's when I smelled a rat. The report had been logged by the *Soberano* a few hours before we arrived at Axon! They hadn't docked, just done a flyby, calling it in from distance. That's why it had taken so long for the Society to hear about it.

It was unlikely the Ravens would have caught Marie napping, but if they had, the *Heureux* wasn't equipped to fight. The old freighter was a rugged workhorse, lightly armed, but no match for a combat ship. Like most freighters, she was equipped to fast bubble, to escape before being forced to fight. So why hadn't she used it? Had a Raven been waiting inside the navpoint safe zone? They normally prowled out near the edges to avoid navy patrols and collisions with incoming ships.

Or had the *Soberano* attacked the *Heureux?* It was possible, but I doubted even Vargis would shoot up a defenseless freighter, and if he had, why risk retribution from the navy by calling in the sighting? After detecting the *Heureux*, he may have decided not to risk his ship, knowing the Ravens would see the *Soberano* as the catch of a lifetime.

Anxious to get back out there, I met Izin and Jase in engineering to show them the message.

"Izin, I want you to install the new burster while we're underway." It had been loaded aboard only minutes before my return, yet in that time Izin had already examined the parts and read the technical manuals. He was a quick study.

"The hull crawlers can work in shifts," Izin said, "to limit their exposure to bubble heat."

"Good. How long will it take?"

"Six weeks."

After all the time I'd spent picking the perfect weapon, studying every stat, calculating every possible tactical use, the one thing I hadn't considered was how long it would take my tamph engineer to install it. "You've got two hours." That's how long it would take us to get back to the navpoint where the *Heureux* was adrift.

"Captain, the capacitor is too large for the weapons bay. I'll have to install it in the cargo hold and upgrade the arterials from the energy plant. The weapon will then need to be tested and the targeting system recalibrated. It's a major overhaul."

Clearly, I'd underestimated the effort required to sharpen the *Lining's* teeth. "OK, leave the old cannon in place for now. It's better than nothing."

"Barely!" Jase said.

"But get started on any upgrades that won't take the old gun offline."

"Yes, Captain."

"Jase, dig out the log records on that contact we spotted on the way in, and calculate its drift vector. Once we get back out there, I want to spend as little time as possible searching for it."

"Suppose it drifted into the cloud?" Jase asked apprehensively.

"Then we go in after it." The gas and dust would reduce our sensor range, but it would also make it tougher for Ravens to find us.

"That's bandit country, Skipper."

"I know." Ravens had made a fine art out of hiding in nebulas, but they used the same sensor tech we did. Even so, it was only a matter of time before they spotted the *Heureux*, then they'd have not only the ship and Marie, but the Codex as well.

I could ransom Marie, but if the Ravens got their hands on the Codex, I'd never get it back.

* * * *

We unbubbled at the center of the navpoint where we'd previously sighted the derelict ship. I kept our transponder off and our power levels low to conceal our presence while we listened for any sign of the *Heureux*.

"I've got a faint energy source fifty million clicks out," Jase said. "It's inside the Shroud – definitely not the *Heureux*."

Faint energy readings meant it was sneaking, like us, keeping its energy plant reacting as low as possible to limit the release of tell tale neutrinos. "Have they seen us?"

"If they have, they don't know what to make of us."

"Let's not give them time to figure it out."

I selected the autonav's best guess of the *Heureux's* drift vector, retracted sensors and performed a sub-second micro-bubble into the Shroud. When we could see again, we were more than a million kilometers inside the thin mistiness at the edge of the dark nebula and now just ten million clicks from the stealthy contact. The Shroud's sensor clutter blinded us to their position and, I hoped, hid us from them, making the Raven scout believe we'd bubbled out.

The optics sensed a shadow forty thousand clicks away. The computer automatically oriented the view screen image towards the shadow and drew a thin outline of its silhouette. A display square appeared beside the outline, then dozens of hull configurations flashed through the square as the computer tried to match the profile. Suddenly, one hull configuration stuck, then rotated and spun to match the outline. The library hologram flashed to confirm a match and a neat inscription appeared below the outline.

Caravel D class medium freighter
12,500 metric tons
Registry unknown

"Jackpot!" Jase declared as the display square vanished from the screen.

"Let's hope our sneaky friend isn't looking this way," I said, feeding power to the maneuvering engines and sending the *Lining* surging through the dust and hydrogen vapor towards the hulk. Our sudden spike in energy output lit us up like a Christmas tree, while the heat blasting from our engines turned the cold cloud into a growing infra red source, signaling our presence. Even with interference from the Shroud, it wouldn't be long before we had company.

"She's stone cold," Jase said as the neutrino detector found no sign of a reacting energy source inside the *Heureux*, signaling she was a dead ship.

So where were the crew? Where was Marie?

Slowly the shadow grew in size, becoming a silhouette, until the three rectangular holds and its stern superstructure were visible. The *Heureux* drifted bow first through the nebula, showing no running lights.

"I don't see any damage," I said as we came alongside, satisfying myself that there were no holes or energy burns anywhere along its length.

"It looks like she just lost power," Jase said, "and kept on going."

I rolled the *Lining* over and matched velocities as we came alongside the *Heureux's* stern superstructure. If anyone was alive, that's where they'd be. While I mated airlocks, Jase kept his eyes on the sensors.

"A ship just unbubbled at the edge of the Shroud," Jase said. "We've got active scanners lighting us up."

"Let them look." The gas we'd heated up on the way in would be messing with their sensors, buying us a little time.

A point marker appeared on the wrap around view screen showing where the snooper was. We couldn't tell what kind of ship it was, but I assumed it was the same contact we'd picked up prowling the edge of the Shroud when we first arrived.

"There are two more contacts, very faint, a long way off," Jase said. "No transponders on either of them, but they must be big for us to be reading them from here."

"They're all Ravens." It was a tactic long favored by the Brotherhood. The nearby contact was the eyes and ears, the two distant prowlers were the teeth. The scanning ship would be small, fast and expendable, while the larger, more valuable combat ships were far enough out that they had time to run if it turned out they were stalking a navy warship. "How close is the scout?"

"Eight hundred thousand clicks, and coming in real slow."

The pirate commander would be on the scanning ship. His two attack dogs would be charging weapons, getting ready to bubble in on top of us once they received the order, but they'd only come once they knew how weak we were. Considering they could micro-bubble to us in under a second, we were a sitting duck locked up to the *Heureux*.

I searched for an old log entry. When I found it, I deleted the *Lining's* name from it, then passed it to Jase. "Send that on all channels. It should buy us some time."

Jase glanced at my selection and grinned. "I hope the Shroud's screwing with their sensors or they're going to die laughing, right before they blow our brains out."

"I'm betting this close to the *Heureux*, they can't see what we are. Send it."

Jase began broadcasting the log entry we'd recorded on our way into Macaulay Station, a hail from an Earth Navy officer accompanied by the ENS *Nassau's* frigate transponder signal. Both were genuine, they just weren't ours. "Power down your engines and prepare to be boarded! Do not attempt to re-engage your star drive, or you will be fired upon!"

Moments later, the snooper's neutrino levels spiked as it turned and began accelerating hard away from us.

"That got their attention!" Jase said. "The two distant contacts have slammed on the brakes."

"We spooked them, that's all."

A distant fuzzy blue light appeared on the view screen as the Shroud's dust and gas diffused the glow of the scout's engines. He was holding his nerve, running obliquely away from us so his sensors weren't blocked by his own engines, trying to confirm if we really were the ENS *Nassau.* If he'd fully bought our ruse, he'd be superluminal already and our Raven problem would be solved.

"Keep a close eye on them," I said. "Once they see there's no frigate charging after them, it won't take them long to figure out they've been conned."

"I've got heat!" Jase exclaimed, then his brow furrowed. "From the *Heureux*! It's too small to be her energy plant."

"Where?"

"Starboard side of the superstructure."

I'd been on board Marie's ship often enough to know its layout reasonably well. "It's their lifeboat. It must still be racked." If their lifeboat had heat, it had power, and there was a chance Marie and her crew were still alive! I climbed out of my acceleration couch. "Let me know the moment that scout starts back towards us."

"You're going over there alone?"

"One of us has to stay aboard and fly the *Lining* out of here if those Ravens come back." I started for the hatch as Jase realized I would order him to leave me on the *Heureux*, rather than risk losing the ship. He opened his mouth to protest, but I cut him off. "And kill that navy transponder, they got the message."

* * * *

I slipped into my pressure-suit, cycled through the airlock into the *Heureux* and found myself floating in zero gravity. Main power and life support were off and my head-up display told me there was vacuum outside my suit. A few feeble emergency lights threw a faint red glow into the corridor, which my helmet lamp drilled with a brilliant white beam. Ahead, a magnetic boot and a coffee cup hung motionless in the otherwise deserted corridor.

"The *Heureux*'s decompressed," I said over the short range communicator. "Izin, feed some power into her and run a diagnostic. Find out what happened to their life support."

"You'll need to activate the umbilical link, Captain," Izin replied.

I pulled myself to the control panel beside the inner hatch and turned the release that gave the *Lining* access to the *Heureux's* systems. "Umbilical enabled."

I brought my feet up, preparing to push gently away from the bulkhead when Izin's mechanical vocalizer sounded in my ears again, this time in emergency mode, louder and faster than normal.

"Captain! Disconnect umbilical immediately!"

Izin almost never used emergency mode. Knowing something was up, I spun back to the control panel and severed the connection. "It's done. What's wrong?"

"Something tried to access our ship's systems," Izin replied, now using his vocalizer's normal mode again. "Standby."

Curbing my impatience to get to the lifeboat, I floated beside the airlock's inner door while Izin implemented some technical trickery. Minutes passed and he still hadn't given me clearance to proceed.

"Izin, I'm waiting."

Presently, Izin said, "There's something controlling the *Heureux*. It tried to spawn itself into the *Silver Lining* via the umbilical. I've isolated its embryo within our system, but it will take time to remove. Now that I know how it propagates, I can block it spawning again."

"OK. Get rid of it," I said, recalling the strange probing I'd felt when I'd touched the Codex. Was that what had crippled the *Heureux*? "Jase, any sign of the Ravens?"

"I've lost the two distant contacts, and the scout's still moving away. It's cut its engines and is just drifting, listening."

"He wants us to chase him," I said, "so he can get a good look at us."

"You may reactivate the umbilical, Captain," Izin said.

I threw the release again and waited while my tamph engineer ensured that whatever was in the *Heureux* didn't spread to the *Silver Lining*.

"It lay dormant in *Heureux*'s airlock emergency system," Izin explained, "waiting for an umbilical connection. I've now purged it from the *Heureux*'s airlock."

"OK. Get life support and gravity back online. I'm heading for the emergency bay now."

I pushed off from the airlock and began gliding

through eerily lit corridors. The *Heureux* was three times the size of the *Lining* by tonnage, although her interior volume was considerably greater. It made getting to the lifeboat rack from the airlock quite a long float in zero gravity.

"Captain," Izin said after several minutes, "You need to sever the connection between the *Heureux*'s processing core and the rest of the ship."

"Why?"

"Whatever's controlling the *Heureux* is in her processing core. It's blocking me from accessing any of the ship's systems."

"Can't you kill it from where you are?"

"No Captain. It's highly adaptive. I've never seen anything like it. The processing core will have to be physically isolated – not something I can do remotely."

If Marie and her crew were in the lifeboat, a few more minutes would make no difference. "Understood," I said, immediately performing a zero-G roll and kicking off a bulkhead to send myself gliding down another corridor towards system control.

After several minutes of floating through corridors and dodging drifting debris, Izin said, "The aggressor embryo in the *Silver Lining* has been destroyed, Captain."

I wondered if a human engineer could have dealt with the threat as effectively as Izin. Tamphs weren't just smarter than humans, their minds were faster because their segmented brains allowed them to think in multiple simultaneous streams – a little trick evolution had so far denied *Homo sapiens*.

When I reached the *Heureux's* processing core, in the dim red light it seemed even more spacious than I remembered. Although larger than the *Lining's* compact equivalent, it was less sophisticated. Marie's old freighter was equipped with the bare minimum of what it needed to get the job done and almost every system was overdue for replacement. By contrast, my EIS background had given me a taste for sophisticated tech, which was why the *Silver Lining* was a technological treasure trove with a tinkering tamph engineer constantly making improvements.

My helmet beam revealed the central processor's access panels had been removed and were now adrift in the compartment. The loose panels weren't the result of sloppy maintenance, but an attempt by the crew to stop whatever had commandeered their ship's processing core. Considering the state of the *Heureux*, they'd clearly failed.

I glided into the compartment towards the octagonal control console in the center of the room. As I neared it, the form of a man floating face down, close to the deck came into view. He wore a pressure-suit and his head and arms were wedged inside the back of the console where he'd been working when he died. A magnetic shifter, a long wrench-like tool to remove panels, floated close to his body. I pulled myself down to him, then eased him away from the panel, turning him so I could see his transparent faceplate. His skin was swollen and purple from decompression and trickles of freeze-dried blood had crystallized around his nose and eyes.

"I'm in the processing core," I reported. "Marie's engineer's here. He's dead."

He'd been trying to do exactly what Izin had asked me to do, sever the central computer's connection to the rest of the ship. I checked his suit, finding a tear in the right leg below the knee. It wasn't the ragged tear symptomatic of accidentally snagging the suit, but a straight line, blackened at the edges as if a cutting torch had sliced it open. Inside the tear, the engineer's leg was burnt, seared to the bone.

Decompression may have killed him, but it was no accident.

I grabbed the magnetic shifter out of the air and kicked away from the processing core, spinning in mid flight to angle my boots towards the wall, cursing myself for not having brought my P-50. While I drifted towards the bulkhead, I swept the compartment with my helmet light. An eight legged hull crawler was creeping across the ceiling towards me like a predatory spider stalking its prey. It had been almost overhead when I'd kicked away from the central console. The crawler was an older model than the type Izin used, but just as impervious to hard vacuum. It carried a plasma torch in one of its leading arms which suddenly glowed to life, adding a harsh, flickering yellow tint to the compartment's dim red emergency light.

I switched on my boot's magnetic clamps moments before they touched the bulkhead and stuck fast. Holding the mag shifter like a club, I was acutely aware that as a weapon, it was greatly inferior to a burning plasma torch.

"Ah . . . Izin, how good are hull crawlers at zero-G combat?"

"Hull crawlers are not designed to operate unanchored to fixed surfaces, Captain," Izin replied, "however, they are programmed with basic Newtonian physics in case they become separated from an anchoring surface."

The crawler picked its way carefully across the ceiling towards me. It seemed to be sizing me up, preparing to attack. But that was stupid! Hull crawlers were dumb maintenance machines, not tactically aware battle bots.

"Could a hull crawler beat a human in zero-G combat?"

"Of course, Captain, with the proper programming."

How about an ultra-reflexed human with a mag shifter?

"Humans are not well adapted to zero gravity," Izin continued, "whereas hull crawlers are able to coordinate their extremities with a precision impossible for biological entities. Why do you ask?"

"I'm facing an octo with a hot plasma torch!" I

replied. "It killed Marie's engineer and I'm next."

"I'll be right there, Skipper!" Jase yelled.

"Stay on the sensors, Jase. If those Ravens come back, take the *Lining* and get out of here fast!"

"But I can get there in–"

"No! If the *Lining's* destroyed, we're all dead."

Jase fell silent, then Izin said, "I will come, Captain. I can restore the *Heureux's* systems faster over there."

It would take Izin at least five to six minutes to suit up and reach me, but I didn't have that long.

"OK Izin, you come," I said, watching the meter long machine creep towards me.

I switched off my boot magnetics and kicked off, gliding away from the crawler. Seeing I was about to escape, it scurried across the ceiling and down the wall, slashing at me with the torch, scalding the metal base of my boots. It could have caught me if it had jumped, but it chose not to lose contact with the wall. The crawler might have had better zero-G moves than me, but it clearly didn't like to use them. Having failed to cut open my pressure-suit, it ran down to the floor and scuttled after me as I glided away.

I tumbled, then using my legs like springs, bounced off the bulkhead and glided diagonally across the room away from the octo. It ran up onto the central console and stabbed after me with the glowing torch. I rolled again, this time activating my boots long enough to clamp onto the bulkhead and swing towards the entrance.

The octo anticipated my move and tried to cut me off as I launched myself at the hatchway. It reared up on its back four legs, lunging at me with the torch, but I swatted it away with the mag shifter, sending myself spinning out of control. My helmet crashed into the ceiling, then I reverse tucked to offset the spin and caught the edge of the hatchway with my free hand. My body slammed clumsily into the wall, almost knocking the air out of my lungs, then I pushed off with my knees, pivoted around my hand and flew backwards through the hatch. The eight legged killer-bot rushed after me as I floundered across the corridor until a toe of one boot caught the ceiling. I pushed sideways, out of the crawler's sight, then walked across the ceiling to the wall near the hatch.

The octo scuttled into the corridor, lifting a leg to climb the wall as I swung the shifter down onto its fragile sensor dome. The transparent hemisphere and the fragile optics within shattered, blinding the murderous bot. I pushed off the wall, tumbling clear as the crawler swept the torch wildly over its head, then performed a fast, zero-G somersault followed by a rebound off the opposite wall that sent me hurtling back at the crawler. I crushed its body with a ferocious, two handed hammer blow that sent me careening away, leaving the octo shorting out behind me. By the time I got a magnetized boot to a metal surface, the octo was drifting lifelessly in the corridor, eerily lit by its burning torch.

It hadn't been pretty, but I still remembered enough of my zero-G training to be dangerous. I made a mental note to start practicing again, as soon as possible.

"So much for Newtonian physics," I said. "The crawler's dead."

"Good job, Skipper!" Jase exclaimed with relief.

"I'm entering the airlock now, Captain," Izin informed me.

I floated to the lifeless octo, switched off the torch, then returned to the systems control console. It didn't take long to find the dead engineer had been close to disconnecting the processing core from the rest of the ship. Whatever had infected the *Heureux* must have summoned the crawler to protect it. I quickly finished what the engineer had started, then as I floated up from the control console, I saw a second crawler standing in the corridor, watching me through the hatchway. It lifted one of its legs to reveal an electro welder, which burst to life.

"Not another one," I muttered.

I lifted the mag shifter like a club, ready to do battle, then the crawler's central torso exploded. Legs and bits of its body casing drifted apart. One leg tumbled end over end into the compartment past my helmet. Presently, Izin appeared carrying his six millimeter shredder. It looked like a toy pistol with a disproportionately long barrel, but in his inhumanly steady hands, it was a weapon of lethal accuracy.

Izin floated into the compartment carrying a small tool box and my P-50 slung over his shoulder. He holstered his gun and threw mine to me.

"Thanks," I said, strapping it on, glad to be rid of the shifter.

"There are other hull crawlers inside the ship, Captain. I destroyed one near the airlock and another in the corridor." He turned towards the central computer. "I'll clean their computer's hardware, then reinitialize the system. It'll get them to Axon, but they'll need to do a full rebuild later."

"Getting atmo back is the priority." I'd feel better once the ship was pressurized again and the crawlers couldn't kill me just by puncturing my p-suit.

I left Izin to clean house and started towards the lifeboat bay. I saw no more crawlers as I glided through gloomy corridors, then as I approached the lifeboat compartment, Izin announced he'd scrubbed the *Heureux's* processing core back to clean metal, and was beginning the emergency rebuild.

The large hatch to the lifeboat compartment was open, but the space door was still closed. It could be chemically blown from the hull in an emergency, but either the crew hadn't wanted to leave, or hadn't been able to.

The *Heureux's* lifeboat was a rugged, stretched egg-shaped craft with no capacity for superluminal flight and enough supplies and power for months adrift in space. It was equipped with a small cockpit window for the pilot to eyeball surrounding space, although the underpowered thrusters were only useful for docking. Highly sensor reflective material coated its thin hull, complementing two long range emergency beacons, although the chances of rescue if no one was looking for you were virtually zero.

Light from the small cockpit window spilled into the bare metal compartment. I was about to push myself towards it when a spindly shadow charged out of the darkness. I fired once, shattering the hull crawler into a dozen pieces and discovering Izin had loaded my gun with explosive slugs. I caught one of the crawler's legs as it tumbled past, examining it for a moment, then floated towards the front of the lifeboat.

My heart was beating as I approached the window, worried at what I might find inside. Or not find. At the window, I relaxed when I saw Marie floating inside, talking with her barrel chested copilot, Gadron Ugo, and several other men and one woman wearing crew suits.

I holstered my gun and rapped on the window.

Marie and her crewmen looked up surprised, then she kicked off a chair and came gliding towards me with a fearful look. She started motioning with her fingers, miming spider movements, warning me about homicidal hull crawlers and pointing frantically into the darkness behind me.

I was delighted to see she was genuinely worried about me, so I played dumb. I smiled and pretended I thought her spider miming was a wave, so I waved back, grinning like a Cheshire cat. She shook her head and gestured even more frantically into the dark, growing rapidly alarmed and frustrated that I didn't understand I was about to be torn apart by a murderous hull crawler.

Finally, I held up the leg of the destroyed hull crawler. Surprise flashed across her face, then I showed her my P-50 with a knowing look.

She relaxed, giving me a relieved smile and blew me a kiss.

* * * *

By the time Izin had restored life to the *Heureux*, the Raven scout had begun edging back towards us, probing the Shroud with powerful long range scanners making me anxious to get underway. Finally atmosphere returned, allowing me to remove my helmet and the lifeboat's hatch to be cracked open.

"I knew you'd find us!" Marie said as she jumped out, wrapping her arms around my neck and kissing me with gusto.

When I came up for air, I said, "Just business my love?"

She smiled coyly. "You know how it is Sirius, a girl's got to make a living!"

"So where'd you hide the Codex after you stunned Jase back on Icetop?"

"Under the bed." The same bed we'd put to more pleasurable pursuits only hours before! She saw the look on my face, adding apologetically. "I didn't have time for anything else! I was going to tell you Vargis stole it, but when he walked in, I had to blame Bo."

"Anything to get me out of the way!"

She shrugged helplessly. "Ugo was waiting. He'd been circling since midnight."

"Nice stunt. It nearly got you killed."

She looked surprised. "What do you mean?"

"What do you think crippled your ship?"

"Mannie said it was a system problem."

"He was . . . wrong."

She sobered. "You've seen him?"

I nodded somberly, telling her with a look that he was dead.

Tears clouded her eyes. "We knew his air supply must have run out, but I hoped –."

"It wasn't his air supply." When she gave me a puzzled look, I added, "It was a crawler."

"Another one?" she said puzzled, thinking only the

crawler in the emergency bay had malfunctioned.

"They were all taken over by whatever crippled the *Heureux*."

Gadron Ugo, the bald headed man mountain who doubled as Marie's de facto guardian, stepped forward and put a big arm comfortingly around her shoulders. "I'll take care of Mannie." He gave me a nod, the nearest I'd get to a 'thank you', then left with the surviving crew members.

"So what happened?" I asked.

"The helm just stopped responding and our engines shut down. Mannie cooled the energy plant as a safety precaution, then we decompressed for no reason. After we got to the lifeboat, he went off to do repairs. That was the last we saw of him. A few hours later, a hull crawler tried to force open the hatch. It nearly killed us, but we managed to lock it out."

"When did the *Soberano* show up?"

She gave me a puzzled look. "The *Soberano*? I haven't seen Vargis since Icetop."

I couldn't believe he'd simply run, even if the Ravens were nearby. "Where's the Codex?"

"In system control. Mannie tried analyzing it, but it was unresponsive. I thought we'd all been conned."

I activated my communicator. "Izin, is the Codex up there with you?" I hadn't seen it, but I'd been distracted by a deranged plasma torch wielding octo at the time.

"What is it?" Marie asked.

"Vargis knew you were here."

"And he left us to die?" she exclaimed incredulously.

"He reported your position to Axon Control. That's how I found you."

"Captain," Izin's voice sounded in my earpiece, "it's not here."

"Damn! Vargis boarded your ship and took the Codex!" He must have made the same guess I had, that Marie was heading to the Society's regional headquarters at Axon.

"That thieving bastard!" Marie said.

"Well, you stole it first." I realized that wasn't quite true. "Actually, I stole it first, you stole it second, he stole it third!"

She gave me a canny look. "I knew you cheated!"

"I improvised."

The crawler in the processing core must have seen Vargis take the Codex, so why weren't there bits of destroyed crawler and dead *Soberano* crewman littering the system control compartment? Then I remembered Bo believed Sarat's auction had been rigged to ensure Vargis won. Could the homicidal crawlers have simply let him take the Codex, because whatever controlled them knew he was supposed to have it – that the Matarons wanted him to have it?

I activated my communicator. "Jase, what's the status on those Ravens?"

Marie looked alarmed. "Ravens?"

"The scout's back to the edge of the Shroud," Jase said, "coming in slow. No sign of the other two."

I quickly recounted how we'd scared off the scout. Now that it was back, I didn't need to see the two Raven combat ships to know they were out there, waiting for the order to attack. "You need to get the *Heureux* out of here – fast."

"What are you going to do?"

"I've got to find Vargis. He doesn't know what he's dealing with."

"And you do?"

I couldn't tell her Vargis was the unwitting target of a Mataron scheme to wreck our civilization. "You'll have to trust me on that."

"Vargis knows one thing. He knows what it's worth," she said slowly, deep in thought, "and he's got a plan to exploit it." Realization appeared on her face, then she gave me a wily look. "You have no idea where he's gone, do you?"

"Not a clue. Do you?"

"Maybe."

"You didn't even know he boarded your ship! How could you possibly know where he's taken the Codex?"

"Women's intuition," she said evasively, "and he said something back on Icetop."

"We haven't got time for this, Marie. Where's he headed?"

She pressed her lips tightly together and crossed her arms defiantly.

So that was it! "You're not coming. Your ship will barely make it to Axon, even with Izin's help."

"There's room on your ship."

"For you?" I laughed.

"Ugo can get the *Heureux* to Axon while you, my dear Sirius, are in desperate need of . . . me."

"Not in a million years!"

"How about one in a million, because they're your odds of finding Vargis without my help."

"I know he didn't tell you where he was going."

"Not in so many words."

"So you're guessing?"

"I'm reading between the lines."

"Tell me what you know and if it pans out, you'll get your fair share."

She gave me an incredulous look. "It's not that I don't trust you, my love, it's just that daddy taught his little girl never to let other people handle her credits." She ran her finger across my shoulder teasingly. "You can handle my *other* assets, but not my credits!"

She was right about the odds. Vargis could be headed anywhere in Mapped Space. Finding him would be impossible without help.

I groaned, certain Jase and Izin would think I'd gone out of my mind, especially after the way she'd played me on Icetop. "If you're lying to me, I swear, I'll space you myself."

"As if you could possibly do that to me!" She gave me a sly look. "Partner."

* * * *

"The scout's started a high-G run into the Shroud," Jase's voice sounded urgently in my earpiece. "It's going to pass within ten thousand clicks of us."

There'd be no hiding what we were at that range, then the two combat ships would bubble in on top of us and make sure none of us went home alive.

"Understood," I said as I entered the *Heureux's* system control room. Izin was packing his equipment away, watched by Ugo, who by his disdain was clearly not a tamph lover. "Can they get underway?"

"Their autonav is going through pre-start now, Captain," Izin said. "They'll be able to bubble in fifteen minutes."

"The Ravens will be on us in ten," I said as Marie appeared in the hatchway carrying a small bag ready to board the *Lining*.

She wore a headset so she could listen in on communications between the two ships. "Can you buy Ugo some time?" she asked.

"We can try." I turned to Ugo. "If the combat ships jump in, we'll have to run."

"I know." His eyes flicked to Marie with the worry of an adoptive father. "Don't wait for us," he said, giving me free reign to do whatever was necessary to ensure Marie didn't fall into Raven hands.

"They won't catch us," I promised.

Marie hugged Ugo. "I'll meet you at Axon," she said, then we hurried to the airlock and cycled through into the *Lining*.

Once the airlock sealed, I called Jase. "We're in. Let's go."

"Where to?"

"Across the scout's trajectory, nice and slow. Make

it look like we're itching for a fight."

"OK, you're the boss," Jase said uncertainly.

High speed was the resort of the weak, slow the choice of the strong. If we raced out there with our hair on fire, the two ships would close upon each other so fast, they'd have only a few seconds to fire before their opposing velocities carried them out of weapons range. It would then take time for both ships to decelerate and come back for another pass, giving either an opportunity to escape. It's what the scout was banking on. It was coming in fast for a look, not a slugfest, intending to race away into the safety of the Shroud's sensor clutter while its two attack dogs did the fighting. By going out slow, I was telling the scout I wanted more time in weapons range. It was a message they'd relay to the two combat ships, making them hesitate until they knew how big a stick I carried.

A dull thud echoed through the hull as the *Lining* released the old freighter. Marie and I hurried to the flight deck while Izin disappeared towards engineering. By the time I was sliding onto my acceleration couch, Jase had us on a course to the closest point intersecting the scout's trajectory. Marie climbed onto the third couch placed centrally behind us, and slightly above the two piloting stations. Ideally, the *Lining* should have had a pilot, a sensor specialist and a navigator, who doubled as weapons operator in a crisis, but Jase and I juggled the duties between us, so the third seat was usually vacant.

"Any sign the scout's getting cold feet?" I asked.

"Yeah, he's pulling low forties," Jase replied, "but the two brawlers are powering weapons thirty million clicks out."

"OK. Let's see what he's made of," I said, activating the autonav. "Retract sensors."

Jase gave me an apprehensive look when he realized I was going to micro-bubble out to the intercept point. "You sure, Skipper? We'll be a sitting duck if that scout's packing any real firepower."

"I'm betting he isn't, but he sure as hell will think we are." It was an aggressive move, but it would keep the Ravens guessing and would buy Ugo a few more minutes. Unfortunately for the scout, it wasn't all bluff.

The screen went blank as we retracted sensors to protect them from bubble heat, then for a fraction of a second we stretched spacetime around us and moved out to the interception point. The moment the bubble dropped, Jase deployed our sensors, bringing the screen back to life. I rolled the *Lining* bow over stern, applied a short high-G blast from the engines to kill our velocity, then rolled again so we were facing the scout at almost a dead stop, giving us maximum time in weapons range.

The maneuver was not lost on the Raven scout.

"You're just going to sit here?" Marie asked.

She was a trader, born and bred. All her training was in how to avoid getting into a fight, not how to start one. "It's the best place to be if you want to slug it out."

"Isn't this tow boat a little small for that?" she asked skeptically.

"You might be surprised." I said as the scout yawed ninety degrees, still pulling high G's, but now sliding away from its previous trajectory. "That Raven's not taking any chances."

"That's because he has two killers to do his fighting for him," Marie said.

"Be ready to bubble when you see double!" I said absently as I programmed the autonav to run the moment our sensors detected the combat ships in two locations at once. The old escape mantra was the key to surviving this kind of fight. When the Raven combat ships attacked, they'd bubble in travelling faster than the speed of light for a fraction of a second. Because the signals our sensors read travelled at the speed of light, we'd pick up both the attacker's sensor ghost from their starting location and their actual presence nearby simultaneously – seeing double. That was the signal to run for our lives. We'd pull our sensors while they deployed theirs, and with luck we'd be superluminal before they could open fire.

For the navy, sensor ghosting was the signal to open fire, and the rationale for their battle saying – start trouble when you see double. They rarely got to use it because equally matched combat ships rarely bubbled into battle. They stalked each other with eyes open, careful not to give their opponent the chance for a knockout blow. In naval combat, it was decidedly better to receive than to give – to wait for the enemy to bubble blindly in to you than for you to bubble out to them with sensors stowed. It was simply the physics of space flight and it inherently favored the defensive, at least for the first few decisive seconds – unless one side had overwhelming superiority, in which case all bets were off. Weaker ships usually had the opportunity to escape before ever coming within weapons range. It was why the navy struggled to eliminate the Brotherhood, even when they had them cornered. The navy simply couldn't engage them quickly without placing their own ships at unacceptable risk.

It was different for the traders. The Brotherhood would pounce as soon as a trade ship appeared, knowing their prey lacked the firepower to hurt them. It came down to how alert the trader crew were and whether they were equipped to fast bubble away before the pirate could deploy sensors and open fire. It was the ultimate game of cat and mouse.

Only this time, we were a mouse impersonating a cat.

"Are you going to fry our sensors again?" Jase asked, wondering if I'd wait for the sensors to retract or go early and let the bubble burn our eyes out. "You know how irritated Izin gets when he has to replace them."

"No, we'll have time." I was normally prepared to cook our sensors if our lives depended on it, but I needed them to recover the Codex. The danger was if the Raven attack ships used a sensor feed from the scout, rather than wait for their own sensors to deploy, they could fire immediately. That would hurt. The only solution was to ensure the scout was in no shape to see for the combat ships.

"I'm reading a big shield," Jase said, eyes glued to his sensor display. "Ablation type. Class five or six. No weapons."

"Your little pop gun won't do more than tickle that shield," Marie said.

"Let's hope they're ticklish." I glanced at Jase. "Range?"

"Seventy thousand clicks and closing fast."

Marie leaned forward, wondering what I was waiting for. "Shouldn't you be charging your gun?"

"No point. You're right, it'd have no effect." In the few seconds we'd have to hit the scout as it streaked past, the particle cannon would do little more than excite a few ions in the Raven's shield, while charging it might encourage the combat ships to come in early. Better to keep them guessing, and with no active weapon signatures on the *Lining's* hull, the scout wouldn't appear to be in any immediate danger.

"Got another contact!" Jase exclaimed.

I glanced up at our view screen. A large marker dead ahead represented the scout racing towards us, while two smaller symbols to the upper right indicated where the two combat ships were waiting, but nothing else. "Where?"

"Behind us! It's in the Shroud, half a million clicks astern." Jase whistled slowly. "It's bright! It's damn near overloading our neutrino detector!"

I leaned toward his console. The contact's immense energy output alone told me what it wasn't – it wasn't one of ours! "What's it doing?"

"Nothing," Jase said. "It's just sitting there watching us."

"What's the spectral analysis?" Marie asked.

Jase furrowed his brow in confusion. "I got zero spectral!"

"That's impossible," Marie said in a tone indicating she thought he was reading it wrong. "Station keeping thrusters alone should be giving you something."

I reoriented the optical feed towards the unknown contact astern. The *Heureux* had shrunk to a tiny sliver almost lost in the dust and gas of the Shroud, while the bright energy contact appeared as a rounded black mass lurking in the misty darkness. Our recognition system couldn't get enough of an outline to attempt a silhouette match, but even if it had, I knew the prowling ship was a design unknown to our civilian catalogue. It didn't matter. I'd seen enough to know why Jase was getting no spectral readings.

"It's not using ion based technology."

Jase glanced at me, immediately grasping the implications. "Same guys from Icetop?"

"Wait a minute! There were aliens on Icetop?" Marie asked confused.

In her desire to get away with the Codex, she'd stunned Jase before he could tell her a Mataron had killed Sarat and his guards.

"At least one," I said. "Maybe more."

"Why's it following us?" she asked.

"Nosy aliens," I said evasively.

Alien ships from across the galaxy regularly shadowed human ships without making contact, mostly out of scientific curiosity. Studying ships using what they considered to be ancient technologies was a window back into their own antiquity as interstellar civilizations, not a reason for open contact. In two and half thousand years, we hadn't encountered a single civilization still using ion propulsion for sublight travel, although what they used remained a mystery. This time, however, I was certain our shadow was no curiosity seeker.

It was Mataron.

They knew the limits of our technology with

frightening precision, although it did them no good. They could avoid most of our sensors at will, but not even a civilization as advanced as theirs could mask neutrinos produced by their ship's energy plant. Out of all the thousands of civilizations we'd encountered, only the Tau Cetins could do that, and we suspected that was because they no longer used reactive energy sources.

I wondered if the Mataron who'd attacked Sarat's penthouse was on that ship, and whether he knew who I was. When dealing with alien civilizations, I assumed they could do anything I could think of – that way they never surprised me. I decided the Matarons knew I'd swiped the Codex out of the Consortium's hands, making me a threat to their plans. It was why I had their attention now.

They'd be hoping the Ravens finished me off, but dared not interfere in case the Tau Cetins detected the residual effects of their technology, or worse, were themselves out there now, watching unknown to any of us. Fear of giving the Tau Cetins a reason to intervene would force the Matarons to watch helplessly from the shadows, hoping one group of humans destroyed another, even though they could have vaporized all of us in a heartbeat.

A rules-based universe had its advantages, even for a technologically immature, expansionist species like mankind.

"Ignore them," I said, focusing the optics on the Raven scout again and switching my console's mode from piloting to weapons. "Opening outer doors."

The scout would detect the two meter circular opening appear in our bow. With luck, their nerve would break and they'd bubble away while they still could. Seconds passed and the Raven scout kept coming, sliding rapidly away to starboard. A flashing red targeting reticule appeared on the main screen framing the scout, signaling that it was still out of range.

"He's thirty thousand clicks out," Jase said. "Seven

degrees off line."

"The dynamics are still in our favor," I said, watching how the yaw acceleration of the scout was affecting our firing solution. The Raven would now pass us six hundred kilometers to starboard. Another micro-bubble would improve our chance of a kill shot, but we'd have to go blind for a few seconds, giving the wolves an opportunity to pounce – not a risk I was prepared to take a second time. "The warhead is set to arm three seconds after launch."

"What warhead?" Marie asked confused. "I thought you were bluffing!"

"This is how I bluff."

We had one bird in the launcher and three reloads. Not an arsenal by any means, but a nasty surprise for an opponent who wasn't expecting a hypervelocity anti-ship drone in the face. The ASD's warheads were conventional, not reactive – technically only marginally illegal. The drone fired a statically charged penetrator through the target's shield into its hull, delivering a high yield chemical explosive that wrecked fragile systems and triggered localized explosive decompression.

"Twenty thousand clicks," Jase said with intense concentration.

The drone was taking our sensor data now, constantly presenting me with a range of firing solutions. I selected a sixty five percent hit probability, then let the drone take charge. Soon the targeting reticule on screen turned green, indicating the Raven was in range, but the drone stayed put while the scout came hurtling towards us.

Jase gave me an impatient look. "Are we shooting, Skipper, or waving as they go by?"

"Any second now."

At last, the drone decided it was time to go to work. A point of brilliant white light shot away from the hull and curved away to starboard.

"Go baby!" Jase exclaimed.

Marie's eyes narrowed in surprise. "Is that a drone?"

"It's only a little drone," I said.

It flew towards a point well ahead of the scout, then when it reached the Raven's projected trajectory, it turned sharply to go head to head with its target.

"They'll be needing clean underwear about now!" Jase said.

"How'd you get that past the navy inspectors?" Marie asked.

"What inspectors?" I said lightly, glancing at Jase. "Does Izin know anything about inspectors?"

Jase shrugged, feigning ignorance.

We'd been checked many times by the navy, but the physical space the ASD launcher occupied was small and Izin had the compartment cleverly shielded. If the navy found such an obvious ship killer hiding in the *Lining's* bow, they'd have impounded her on suspicion of being a privateer. She wasn't the only trader to carry such a weapon, but she might have been the smallest.

Trade ships were allowed any shield and defensive weapon they could afford, but hull puncturing hypervelocity anti-ship drones were reserved for Earth Navy ships alone. Even the Brotherhood preferred disabling weapons to ship killers. After all, there was no profit in destroying their prey. They wanted to capture operational ships with their cargoes intact.

Marie watched the lightweight drone track towards the Raven scout. "You'll lose your ship if the navy ever finds out about that thing."

Before Lena hired me, that might have been true. Now I could probably get an upgrade, courtesy of the EIS. "I won't tell if you don't," I said as the glare of the drone began to fade into the Shroud's gas and dust.

"The Raven's overcharging his shield," Jase reported as the scout ship began dumping all available energy into its defensive field, not that it would do any good against the drone's meter long penetrator.

"They don't realize what it is," I said. They were acting like it was a simple torpedo that would detonate against their shields – a fatal miscalculation.

"Man, they're cooking their engines!" Jase said.

The scout's high velocity made it difficult to maneuver as our little robot-of-death closed on its target. The anti-ship drone's marker on our screen flashed as it entered its terminal phase and began charging its penetrator warhead. The Raven scout's sensors would have detected the sudden surge in energy from the drone, alerting them too late to the danger they were facing.

"They've stopped scanning us!" Jase said.

"They're pulling their sensors," I said, imagining the panic spreading on their bridge. "They're going to bubble."

"Is there time?" Marie asked.

"No," I said somberly. "Ravens aren't equipped to fast bubble." Their ships sacrificed fast spacetime distorters for extra weapons, or in the scout's case, more powerful sensors.

There was a flash as the drone hit the outer edge of the shield and fired its slender, electrostatically charged penetrator. Energy sparkled around the penetrator as it dived into the shield, then smashed through the hull. A tongue of orange flame burst from the scout's bow as the chemical warhead exploded and the forward section of the Raven ship explosively decompressed. If it had been a reactive warhead, the scout would have been vaporized, but there was no way even Izin could hide such weapons from the navy.

The scout's engines died and its shield collapsed as it lost main power. The scout's surviving crew would be weightless and trapped in airtight compartments as the crippled ship drifted deeper into the Shroud.

Jase whistled. "Eat that Raven boys!"

Marie winced as she watched the wreck hurtle past us, completely out of control. "There'll be survivors over there."

"Not our problem!" Jase declared belligerently, itching to blast the wreck just to finish them off.

Marie gave me a concerned look. They might have been Ravens, but now they were human beings in trouble, trapped in a doomed ship. All her life, she'd lived by the ethos that you always helped fellow spacefarers in trouble, no matter who they were. It was more than tradition, it was who she was.

It wasn't who I was.

"He's right," I said. "They'll need rescuing, but not by us." If the scout's energy plant had survived, they might regain control, but odds were the Raven scout would never fly again. I glanced at Jase. "What are the two prowlers doing?"

Jase suddenly remembered there were two very dangerous combat ships still watching us. "Their energy levels are spiking!"

They were going to bubble, but were they coming in for us, or running?

Ugo's ugly face appeared on screen, thrown up automatically when the incoming signal reached us. "We're leaving now. Good luck, Marie."

Before Marie could speak, a warning alarm sounded. Ugo's face vanished, replaced by images of two gray metal ships barely two hundred clicks ahead. One was a long rectangular ore transporter, bristling with weapons. The other a spherical intersystem tug with a single heavy naval gun mounted ahead of its four enormous maneuvering engines. Beyond the Raven combat ships, two markers showed where they'd been moments before. The autonav kept the ghost images on screen longer than they were actually there, so we understood what had happened. The Ravens immediately began extending sensors through their hulls, preparing to target us. Our screen went blank as the *Lining's* autonav pulled our sensors and fast charged our spacetime distorters. For a moment, the flight deck was filled with silence as we held our breaths, knowing it was a race between our automated escape system and their automated weapons.

Two hundred kilometers away the tug fired its one big energy weapon as the *Lining's* bubble formed. The Raven crews on the two combat ships saw a dead straight line of light flash away into the interstellar depths as their energy blast streaked through the space we'd occupied a fraction of a second before.

On the *Lining's* flight deck, we stared at the blank screen until it filled with numbers describing everything from bubble integrity to hull temperature. It was enough to tell us we were superluminal and safe.

"Be ready to bubble when you see double!" I said with a triumphant grin.

"I've heard it a hundred times," Marie said, "but that's the first time I've ever seen it done!"

"Done by the best!" Jase yelled with both fists in the air. "Yeah!"

"Did the *Heureux* make it?" Marie asked.

"I'm sure Ugo got her away," I said. He and I might not have been on the best of terms, but he was a first class pilot. He'd be long gone before the Ravens got anywhere near the *Heureux*. "So, where's Vargis headed?"

"He told me on Icetop he was going to scan the Codex down to its component atoms. He didn't just want what was in it, he wanted its technology too."

"That's your clue?"

"He didn't say he was taking it back to the Core Systems or to Earth, or even copying the data on it. He was very specific."

"How does that help me find him?"

"Do you know how to scan a piece of equipment like that, down to the atomic level?"

"Sure," I said. "How?"

"You need a picometric scanner. Do you know how many there are out here?"

"I'm guessing . . . six?"

"There's only one and it belongs to Biosphere Builders Incorporated. Heard of them?"

"Yeah, they genetically engineer indestructible Earth organisms to take over entire planets."

She nodded. "They have a research facility on a candidate world sixty light years from here. We did a delivery there once, when I was young."

"It's a long shot," I said, unconvinced.

"Do you know who owns BBI?" When I shrugged, she said, "The Consortium."

The Consortium was rumored to control many companies. It didn't mean it was true. Nevertheless, if she was right, it narrowed the odds considerably. "And the name of this biosphere the Consortium is building for all mankind?"

"Deadwood."

Chapter Five : Deadwood

Terraforming Candidate World
Riarnon System,
Outer Cygnus Region
0.994 Earth Normal Gravity
1,029 light years from Sol
15,400 inhabitants

Deadwood was a mega-flora planet that had suffered a cataclysmic mass extinction event four million years ago. A planetoid had passed close by, gravitationally triggering seismic shifts in the planet's tectonic plates causing more than six hundred volcanic eruptions. Billions of tons of dust and volcanic gas had spewed into the oxygen rich atmosphere, strangling most photosynthetic dependant life forms. Only a handful of species sheltering in caves and living off ecosystems built on fungal growth survived. The giant flora that had dominated the planet for over half a billion years did not. Buried under volcanic ash and starved of sunlight, the mega-trees died and slowly petrified. Its continents were now covered by massive stone forests that formed a woven monument to the great plants that had once ruled supreme and were no more. The planetoid itself – known to the colonists as the Tree Killer – had fallen into a stable orbit a third closer to the system's star than Deadwood. Geological analysis indicated the planetoid was not a native of that system, but a rogue world that had drifted in from interstellar space before wreaking destruction upon its hapless victim.

The catastrophe not only destroyed the planet's rich ecosystem, it deterred other interstellar civilizations from colonizing it – an unusual outcome for a world that had been well suited to oxygen breathing life forms. Over the next several million years the atmosphere cleared and the species that had survived emerged from their subterranean sanctuaries to repopulate the planet's surface. When mankind reached Deadwood, it was still a ghost of its earlier ecological diversity, although it retained the potential to become a rare jewel – if Earth was prepared to provide the polish. Most important of all, prior claims had long been abandoned.

According to the Tau Cetins, there were over fifty million habitable planets in the galaxy, an infinitesimally small number compared to the trillions of planets orbiting the galaxy's two hundred billion stars. Our problem was that most were off limits because they were already inhabited by some form of intelligent life, or were deemed close to spawning such life.

Deadwood was an exception.

It was a long haul from Earth and it needed a lot of work, but given a few centuries of planetary engineering and a name change, it might just become mankind's second home. Human Civilization consisted of hundreds of colonies on marginally habitable worlds and thousands of artificial habitats in economically useful locations, but there was no truly perfect Earth-like world. We were, after all, picking from the scraps left by a great many other civilizations over the last billion years.

Commissioned by the Earth Council, Biosphere Builders Incorporated had set up one of the most sophisticated terraforming assessment programs in mankind's history. Now they were determined to transform the once destroyed planet into a garden world and make the greatest profit ever recorded. They'd determined we had the technology and were now developing the planetary engineering plan that Earth would pay for. The one problem they faced was the tiny community of survivalists who'd beaten BBI to the planet by less than a century. They'd set up a back-to-nature home called Refuge among the petrified mega-trees and were now engaged in armed insurrection to keep the planet builders away.

Knowing BBI had spared no expense on their assessment facility, we unbubbled over the opposite side of the planet from their base. With our active sensors off and our transponder disabled, we were relatively stealthy, provided we flew on minimum power to keep our neutrino emissions low.

"I can hear two communications and one navigation satellite," Jase said as he listened with passive sensors only. "There's nothing actively scanning us."

A three dimensional image of the planet rotated slowly on our wrap around screen. It wasn't a real time optical feed, but a projection based on our relative aspect to the planet. It showed the BBI complex on the far side, located within a soft blue hemisphere that defined its tracking envelope, a vast volume covering a tenth of the planet's airspace out to geosynchronous orbit. If we stayed where we were, eventually the base would pick us up as the planet's rotation brought it over the horizon towards us.

Other than the main BBI facility, there were dozens of automated science stations scattered around the planet, but no sign of any independent settlements. It was as if the survivalists no longer existed.

"There's nothing down there," Jase said.

"Maybe they up and left?" I suggested.

"They'd never do that," Marie said emphatically

from her couch behind us. "Refuge is on the coast of the northern continent."

"So where's the beacon?" I asked.

The *Lining* should have been picking up Refuge's locator beacon and automatically placing it on the planet's image. Those beacons were fully autonomous and built to withstand any natural disaster so ships could always locate settlements from orbit, no matter what disaster might strike them.

"They don't use locator beacons and they have no approach control," Marie said.

"So how are we supposed to find them?" I asked as I started the *Lining* gliding towards the atmosphere.

"You're not," she said. "They don't like visitors."

I double checked our astrographics catalogue, the data base of human habitation meticulously maintained by Earth Navy. Surprisingly, there was no indication that the survivalist settlement had ever existed.

"If they've been here for ninety years," I said, "how come there's no record of them?"

"Their reference must have been deleted!" Marie said.

"Now who do you suppose could have done that?" I said bitterly, knowing only a substantial bribe could have wiped out all record of an entire colony.

The astrographics catalogue was automatically and constantly updated at every spaceport, with the latest changes carried by every ship and prioritized by entry date. It was an organic system that ensured all ships always had the most current information, although it normally took several years for an Earth sourced change to reach every ship and settlement in Mapped Space. Nevertheless, a deletion update could cause all record of a remote colony to eventually vanish, so no one would ever know it had ever existed, let alone that its inhabitants had a prior claim.

"All it takes is one corrupt officer in the right place to change the catalogue," Marie said, "and BBI would have this world all to themselves."

It seemed whenever I got near the Consortium, I smelled rats. It wasn't an odor I appreciated. "No wonder the survivalists shoot strangers on sight!"

"Let's hope they don't shoot us!" Jase said.

"They may not trust us," Marie said, "but they hate BBI."

"Think you can find them?" I asked as we nosed into the upper atmosphere.

"I remember a big harbor, like an inland sea," Marie said thoughtfully. "Cliffs on one side, a long peninsula on the other, and lots of giant stone trees."

"Stone trees? That narrows it down to eighty percent of the planet's land surface!" I zoomed Deadwood's image towards the small northern continent. On the southern coast was a curved expanse of water, trapped between a rocky peninsula and the mainland. "What do you think?"

"That's it!" Marie said.

While there were data gathering stations all over the planet, both on land and in the oceans, the number of stations decreased markedly near the inland sea. Either BBI had voluntarily chosen not to collect terraforming data near Refuge, or the survivalists had decided for them. Using minimum power to remain stealthy, I let the planet's gravity pull us down, applying just enough kick from the thrusters to carry us to fifteen degrees above the equator. While the *Lining* may have resembled a flying wing, she was incapable of generating aerodynamic lift. She needed help from the thrusters just to glide through the atmosphere with the grace of a falling rock.

Presently, the navigational image of the planet was replaced by real time optics as we approached the sprawling harbor. Ragged cliffs dominated the eastern shoreline while a low rock barrier paralleled the coast some distance away to the west. At the extreme southern end of the harbor, a narrow gap between the cliffs and the rocky peninsula provided access to the open sea beyond. When we cruised over the entrance, a white cable supported by bright orange floats became visible linking the opposing headlands.

"It's a net!" Jase said surprised.

It sealed the harbor entrance, turning the interior into a protected aquatic habitat. Further north, green smears appeared beneath the surface. Jase zoomed the optics towards one of the green patches, revealing a thick kelp bed where dark streamlined forms darted between giant underwater plants.

"I thought this planet was dead," Jase said.

"Some life forms survived," Marie said, "but not those. They're transplants from Earth."

A family of sea otters broke the surface, paying us scant attention as we passed overhead. I realized the net across the harbor entrance wasn't so much to protect the otters as to prevent them from swimming away into an empty ocean where they'd starve to death.

We flew on over the harbor's calm waters, past several small work boats harvesting kelp and otters. Some were fitted with masts and sails, others were oared. The crews stopped and watched as we passed, but ominously, none waved a greeting.

"They don't look happy to see us," I said.

We flew on towards a towering wall of stone trees with gigantic interlocking branches broad enough to land on, yet eerily absent of leaves. There was no soil exposed to direct sunlight, only a rocky shoreline where thousands of otters lay sunning themselves. With the petrified forest dominating the land, there was no sign of even subsistence agriculture, although the soil that had once supported such monolithic flora must have been rich and deep. Surprisingly, the dead forest was not the bleached white of death, but a sea of reds, browns and yellows from the iron oxides and manganese that had transformed wood to stone millions of years ago.

"Greenery, to starboard!" Marie declared, pointing to the right of the view screen as if she was looking through a window.

In a dead mineralized world, any greenery was a sign of life, so I banked gently in the direction Marie had indicated. Soon we were hovering above a thick cluster of branches wrapped in dark green vines that stretched down into the shadows below. Carved stone houses nestled among the greenery, most decorated with flower filled planter boxes. Drably dressed people emerged from the houses, shielding their eyes from the glare of our thrusters as we floated past the village. Beyond the houses, cows, sheep and pigs were corralled in stone enclosures alongside shallow strip fields growing crops on soil hauled up from the forest floor. A network of stairs had been carved into the branches leading to other houses and tree-farms scattered far across the forest canopy. South of the settlement, a small stone bridge led to an immense branch whose upper curve had been leveled to form a landing area. Several ancient aircraft were parked in front of a long stone building that, from the air, appeared to be a maintenance facility.

I gave the village a wide berth, ensuring it wasn't struck by the down blast of our thrusters, then landed near the antique aircraft. Armed men and women came running towards us from the village, although none started shooting.

"Why do I get the feeling they want to lynch us?" I said as I climbed out of my acceleration couch.

"Don't worry, Sirius," Marie said comfortingly. "They won't want to lynch you, until they get to know you."

"Izin and I will cover you from the cargo door," Jase said. "If they make any hostile moves, we'll blast them!"

"No shooting, no matter what happens. This is their home. We're the invaders."

"But Skipper, suppose–"

"No buts! No guns!" I turned to Marie. "I don't suppose you know anyone who might help us?"

She shook her head. “No, but I remember they’re kind of traditional. If we go down as a couple, that might confuse them long enough to start talking.”

We’d spent the last few weeks living as husband and wife on the flight here, although the survivalists wouldn’t know that. We could just as easily have been BBI representatives come to tell them they had twenty four hours to find another planet before we destroyed them from orbit.

When the airlock outer door began to cycle open, Marie grabbed me and we kissed for a long time. By the time we finished, the outer hatch was wide open and the lynch mob outside had lowered their guns and were watching us curiously.

“We have an audience,” I said.

“I knew they wouldn’t shoot a pair of unarmed lovers!”

“So the kiss was just to manipulate these poor country folk!”

“Maybe,” she said slyly.

“You’re the most scheming woman I’ve ever met.”

“You’ve only just worked that out?”

I sighed. “Shall we go meet them?”

“Let’s,” she said taking my arm as if we were simply going for an evening stroll.

We climbed down onto the petrified mega branch and walked slowly towards the welcoming committee.

“Good day folks,” I said. “Who’s in charge?”

* * * *

Julius Klasson was lanky and sun-tanned with rough stubble on his chin and an easy manner. He was also the nearest thing the survivalists had to a leader. He lived in a simple cottage made of petrified wood bricks quarried from the forest and decorated with furniture made of the same material, polished smooth to bring out their metallic colors.

"You're lucky to be alive," Klasson said as he motioned us to a stone bench seat fitted with hand sewn cushions. He took a large single stone chair, adding, "Some of our folks shoot strangers on sight."

Hospitality was clearly not required to survive on a post-mass extinction world.

"All strangers, or just those from BBI?" Marie asked pointedly.

"No difference. They all want to level our homes, and we ain't going to let them."

The dirt-poor farmers outside scratching in shallow trenches with hand tools couldn't have appeared less formidable. The impression was accentuated by Klasson's Spartan house and simple clothes.

"BBI's a big corporation with a lot of money," I said. "No offense, but you don't look like you're in any position to stop them."

"Looks can be deceiving flyboy." He glanced meaningfully at an ancient long barreled hunting rifle perched against the stone wall. "We've been shooting up their shiny little bits of junk for years."

"When they're ready, the Consortium will come in here with mercenaries packing state of the art firepower. You won't be able to stop them with a handful of antique guns."

"Watch me."

I liked his courage, but doubted his sanity.

"They want to terraform this planet," Marie said. "You've already started. Why not make a deal with them?"

"We ain't changin' the planet, we're adaptin' to it. Yeah, we brought kelp, and sea urchins to eat the kelp, and otters to eat the sea urchins, and we eat them all, but we didn't destroy the dinotrees to do it. We live with them."

Dinosaur trees? I glanced through the window at the gigantic stone mega-trees Refuge clung to. In a way, they were like dinosaurs, only bigger.

"This planet is nearly dead," I said.

"Not dead! Comin' back to life. The forest is full of small animals, insects, even our vines. We scattered seeds from the air about seventy years ago. Now the vines are all across this continent. In another hundred years, this continent will be green again." He glanced at the thickening, leafy vines snaking around the enormous limbs of the dinotrees thoughtfully. "They want to terraform the planet with high explosives, but we don't need to do that. We can live here just as it is."

It didn't matter whether Klasson was right or wrong, once BBI's plan was accepted by the Earth Council, large scale demolition would begin and there would be nothing he could do about it.

Klasson saw the skepticism in my eyes. "We were here first. They can go find their own damn planet."

"They've deleted all record of your existence," Marie said. "There's nothing left to support your claim."

"There's us. We're proof."

"Not if you're dead," I said. One minute's bombardment from orbit and all that'd be left of him or his bedraggled tree farmers would be a pile of ash.

"You sure you don't work for 'em?"

"I don't, but I intend to pay them a visit."

Klasson eyes narrowed. "Why would you want to do that?"

"They've got something of mine, something I intend to get back."

"What would that be?"

"An alien artifact," Marie said. "We're . . . collectors."

Klasson gave us a dubious look. "Hmph." He stood and retrieved a triangular metallic object from a stone shelf and threw it to me. "What's that worth to you?"

I turned the object over in my hand, noting it was marked with a script I'd never seen before. "What is it?"

"You tell me, Mr Collector. There used to be aliens here millions of years ago, before the Tree Killer ripped the guts out of the planet. They must have cleared out fast, because they left a lot of stuff behind."

"Alien tech?" Marie asked, smelling an opportunity.

"Relics. You just got to know where to look."

"Which aliens?"

Klasson shrugged. "Don't know. Never paid much attention to the ruins. Never met an alien."

I turned the artifact over in my hands curiously. Whatever it was, its power source had depleted long ago. I tossed it back to him. "Thanks, but I'm after something specific."

He returned the relic to its decorative position on the shelf. "So you're going to steal something from those BBI lab monkeys and you don't want them knowing you're coming. Right? And you figure I can help you."

I nodded. "Do you know a way in?"

Klasson grunted noncommittally. "It's a big base and it's well guarded."

"You've been there?"

"They kidnapped one of my people a few years back – for questioning. I went in with some of the boys and got him out." His leathery face slowly cracked a smile. "They don't kidnap our people no more."

Clearly there was more to that story, but I was already certain he was our man. "How'd you get in?"

"Walked in. Shot up the place. Walked out. Home in time for supper."

Klasson might have been nuts, fighting a war he could never win, but I was beginning to like him. "Feel like another walk?"

His face darkened. "They've increased their security since then. Got a lot of tech guarding the place now."

"What we're looking for will be with their picometric scanner," Marie said. "Ever heard of it?"

"Nope, but the lab's on the east side."

"Help us and we'll help you," Marie said.

"How you going to help me?"

"We'll bring you weapons," she said.

I gave Marie a surprised look. "We will?"

"You don't look like no gun runner," Klasson said.

"I'm not," Marie said putting her arm around my shoulders, "But Sirius here is one of the best smugglers not in jail." She turned towards me. "Aren't you?"

I'd smuggled contraband, just to make ends meet, but running guns was another matter. As far as the navy was concerned, that was a capital crime, punishable by death. "What do you need?"

"Better guns, smarter ammo and a few sat killers."

"How many guns?"

"A thousand."

Was this guy equipping an insurrection or an army? Even so, a few hundred hardened survivalists sneaking through Deadwood's petrified forests taking shots at terraformers with modern weapons could tie up BBI and the Consortium for years. I found the idea strangely appealing.

"Got any money?" I asked.

"Nope. Have you?"

I still had Lena's credit vault. Would she mind if I used it to pay for a small war on a dead planet? I knew Armin's Armaments had everything Klasson wanted, even satellite killers, but they were illegal and would draw the attention of navy spies. "I'll get you a hundred guns, spare parts and enough smart ammo to keep you in business for the next twenty years, but no sat killers."

Klasson considered the offer a moment. "If you get killed, I get nothing."

"If I get killed, I won't be dying alone."

His weathered face took on a calculating look as he wondered how many BBI goons I could take with me. He probably would have guided me to the base just to annoy BBI, treating any guns he got out of the deal as a bonus. "How many of you?"

"Both of us," I replied, "And my engineer . . . He's a tamph."

The survivalist arched his brow curiously. "Never met one. Heard of 'em. This planet would suit tamphs, down on the equator. Ain't much life in the oceans, not much for 'em to eat, but the climate's good. Throw a few fish out there and they'd be right at home."

"Izin could tell his friends on Earth. If they got here, BBI would never get rid of them."

"Hmm. I heard tamphs are good fighters."

"You have no idea." Because of their history, tamphs weren't allowed in the military or the EIS, and because of their inhuman abilities, they weren't allowed guns on Earth. Even so, legends persisted from the ancient past of what they were capable of. Having seen Izin fight, I knew the legends were true.

Klasson looked thoughtful, perhaps imagining tamphs swarming through the warm equatorial waters to the south, then he said, "For a hundred guns, parts and ammo, I'll get you to the base. After that you're on your own."

"You got a deal," I said.

Klasson picked up a plate of dried, spiced seaweed. "Hungry?"

* * * *

Julius Klasson's aircraft was an old sub-orbital ferry armed with a pair of modified laser mining drills. It could destroy undefended robotic science stations in a few passes, but its makeshift weapons barely qualified it as a combat vehicle. That didn't seem to bother the survivalist leader, who flew the rusting ferry like he was piloting a strike fighter.

"You'd do better trading for spare parts than guns," I yelled over the rattling ferry's noisy engines as we skimmed the ocean at mach four.

A tangled cliff of dinotrees slid up over the horizon ahead, marking the location of Deadwood's largest continent. It straddled the sub-tropics south of the equator, was dissected by snow capped mountains in the north and stretched to a slender spur of land in the south that almost reached to the pole.

"If you can find me parts, I'll take 'em," Klasson said, "But I still want them guns."

He nosed up, climbing high enough to pass over the top of the petrified forest before leveling off closer to the stone canopy than safety or common sense dictated. Occasionally, he dropped into valleys or skirted tall dinotrees, sometimes flying under massive branches or through openings that seemed barely large enough for his aircraft.

"When will we be in sensor range?"

"Soon," Klasson replied. "The base is in a caldera. We'll use the crater wall for cover. You'll have to make your own way down from there."

"Why'd they put it on top of a volcano?"

"A super volcano," Klasson corrected. "It's been dead a couple of million years. They went there because it's the largest open space on the planet, and has a lake in the middle. Cheaper than clearing land and building a dam."

I glanced back at Marie and Izin sitting behind us on cramped jump seats. Marie gave me an anxious look, unimpressed by Klasson's reckless flying.

Beside her, Izin had one of his large eyes close to a window, studying the petrified forest below. "What are the small flying animals called?" he asked.

"Where?" Marie said excitedly, turning towards a window.

"There," Izin said, pointing at spot in the forest at least ten kilometers away.

Marie squinted, unable to see what Izin's naturally telescopic vision had picked out.

"Tree gliders," Klasson said. "Aggressive little bastards. Won't attack a man by 'emselves, but a pack of them will eat you alive."

"There are carnivores here?" I said, surprised any

apex predators had survived the Tree Killer mass extinction.

"Hell yeah. They eat rock hoppers mostly, little rat-like critters that live off moss and fungus, but it's the saberwolfs you got to watch out for."

"Saberwolf?"

"That's what we call them," Klasson said. "Their teeth are sharp as hell and they're fast little buggers. Bigger than a dog, quiet as a cat, mean as the devil. They'll take your leg off before you even know they're there."

"Any in the crater?"

"Yeah, but they stick to the trees mostly. Nothing on this planet likes open spaces. Be tough for them if BBI destroys the forest."

"At least you wouldn't have to worry about them eating you," Marie said.

"I don't give it a thought," Klasson said. "And I don't want 'em wiped out. It's their planet. They got more right to be here than we do."

Izin leaned forward. "Can you eat them?"

Klasson glanced back at Izin curiously, unused to speaking with tamphs or to the sound of Izin's synthesized vocalizer. "Yeah, but by the time you cook 'em enough to kill the local bugs, the meat's no good. It's like eating boot leather. We prefer our Earth animals. Trouble is, so do they!"

"They're not affected by the organisms in your animals?" I asked.

"Ain't none. Everythin' our grandparents brung went through full decon. Even them! They didn't come here to poison this planet."

The petrified forest began to show signs of broken trunks and branches. Soon the entire forest lay on its side, felled millions of years ago by a devastating volcanic eruption triggered by the Tree Killer's passing gravity. Giant angular roots, torn from the ground, rose up sharply out of the lava plain. The petrified dinotrees all lay aligned away from the source of the ancient blast, now marked by a ragged cliff rising hundreds of meters into the air.

Klasson banked slowly as we approached the caldera's rocky rim wall, coming around to cruise just below the crest as we looked for a landing spot.

"That'll do," Klasson said at last as he rotated his ferry's two wing engines to the vertical, slowing to hover. He nosed over onto a narrow perch just large enough for the landing struts, leaving the tail of his aircraft jutting out over the cliff.

"How do we get down the other side?" I asked.

"You slide," he said with a grin, adding, "it's not as sheer as this side."

Klasson threw his shoulder against the squeaking side door, forcing it open, then we filed out after him. As soon as Izin was outside the aircraft, he moved as far from the cliff's edge as possible.

"What do you think of the view, Izin?" I asked, delighting in his fear of heights.

Klasson looked appreciatively out across the lava plain, over shattered stone trees to the vast petrified forest in the distance. "You can see better from over here."

"Here will do?" Izin replied with his back to the cliff.

"You can't see nothing there," Klasson said.

"I have acrophobia."

"You what?"

Izin slung his long thin bag over his shoulder, taking a firm hold of the nearest boulder. "I'm uncomfortable with heights."

"He's terrified of them," I added helpfully.

"No kidding?" Klasson said. "But you spend your life flying?"

"Travelling inside a starship is not the same as hanging from a cliff," Izin said. "My people prefer lowlands and water, not cliff tops. We're amphibians, not birds!"

"It's not just him," I said. "It's all of them, scared to death of heights!"

"And you would drown in a bathtub," Izin said before turning and starting towards the top of the cliff.

Marie and I exchanged amused looks at my engineer's embarrassment. His people were at least as smart as the Tau Cetins and far more ruthless as warriors. It was why the major galactic powers had blockaded the Intruder Civilization for more than two thousand years and showed no sign of letting them out. Who would have thought with all their fearsome reputation, they couldn't admit to having a weakness?

"He hasn't heard the last of this," I whispered mischievously.

"Don't make him angry," Marie warned.

"What'd he mean about the bathtub?" Klasson asked.

"Sirius can't swim," Marie explained.

"Is that a fact?" Klasson said.

"I had no need to learn." When Marie gave me an amused look, I added defensively, "There's no swimming in space!"

"One's afraid of heights and the other can't swim," Klasson said uncertainly. "I sure hope you fellas can fight!"

"That's what I'm here for," Marie said, patting me on the cheek with mock sympathy before climbing after Izin.

At the cliff top, we crouched behind a rocky parapet where we could observe the BBI base lying some distance from the foot of the caldera wall. It comprised a cluster of sparkling white prefab buildings containing research labs, maintenance and communications facilities, a large energy plant and accommodation for several thousand scientists, engineers and their families. Surrounding the base were sprawling green fields and terrestrial forests where genetically enhanced Earth flora was being tested prior to large scale transplantation to Deadwood. Machines worked the fields, supervised by technicians and supported by an intricate irrigation system distributing water from the deep lake in the center of the caldera. Between the fields were greenhouses containing plants being tested for both warmer and cooler latitudes and small enclosures where reengineered Earth animals had their tolerance to Deadwood's microbial life tested. East of the base was a small, well equipped spaceport where the *Soberano* lay across the landing apron, almost too big to be accommodated.

I glanced at Marie. "I guess they do have the only picometric scanner in this part of Mapped Space."

Klasson pointed to a lattice-like needle rising high above the crater floor. "That communications tower between the spaceport and the base has got sensors that'll see you once you're away from the cliff face."

I turned to Izin. "Can you take care of that?"

He unsealed his long bag and pulled out a military grade SN6 sniper rifle equipped with low power optics that complemented his naturally telescoping eyes.

When Klasson saw the rifle, his eyes bulged. Having been stuck on a backwater like Deadwood all his life, he'd never even heard of a SN6, but one look told him it was a thoroughbred. "Nice gun."

"It pulls to the left," Izin said, lifting the rifle and sighting on the distant communications tower. For several minutes, he patiently studied his target in minute detail, sighting with his head tilted slightly away from the barrel so his large bulbous eye could focus accurately. "The sensors are dependent on a power conduit running up through the center of the tower," he said eventually, sliding a twelve centimeter long round into the breach.

"No way you can make that shot," Klasson said. "It's twenty two kilometers! I've measured it."

"Twenty two thousand, three hundred and forty one

meters exactly," Izin corrected, reading the distance off the rifle's range finder. He took up his firing position, becoming as still as a statue. Tamphs were ambush predators, evolved to hide and wait for their prey to approach, then strike without warning. To camouflage themselves, they'd evolved the ability for absolute physical stillness, making them perhaps the most formidable snipers in the galaxy.

Izin seemed to take forever to fire. When he did, the only sign was a slight whisper as the magnetically accelerated projectile shot from the barrel without recoil or flash. He watched as the projectile's fins extended to stabilize its flight, keeping the low power scope sighted until he saw a spark as the cable was cut.

"It's done," Izin said, lowering the rifle.

"That's impossible!" Klasson declared, pulling out an ancient pair of binoculars from a worn case strapped to his belt. It took him a few seconds to find the severed end of the cable, then he whistled slowly. "Damn!" He turned to Izin, with a mix of admiration and confusion. "I thought you said it pulled to the left?"

"It does. One millimeter every twelve thousand meters. I compensated for it."

"Right," Klasson said slowly, then he turned to me. "I want a hundred of them guns, and whatever ammo he's using!" He leaned toward Izin. "Any more at home like you, son?"

"There were twenty thousand in my spawning," Izin replied. "All genetically identical to me."

Klasson blinked. "Can they all shoot like you?"

"Exactly like me."

The survivalist leader imagined twenty thousand tamphs armed with SN6's going to war. "Next time you're home, you tell your brothers to come on out here. Tell them to bring their guns. We could use their help."

"They would find the coastal regions appealing, although Earth Council would be apprehensive about a large scale migration of my kind from Earth, especially if they were armed."

"Not to mention the rest of the galaxy," I whispered under my breath to Marie.

Izin turned to me. "If a maintenance team attempts to repair the damage, am I authorized to stop them?"

"Absolutely," I said, letting Izin off the leash. "You're on overwatch. Don't let them fix the sensors or get in our way, but if they run let them go."

"As you wish," Izin said, sliding another round into the breach.

I turned to Klasson. "Are you heading back now?" When we finished, Jase would do the extraction from the edge of the base, freeing Klasson to return to Refuge.

"I might stick around a while! I want see this tamph shoot some more!"

"My name is Izin Nilva Kren."

"Didn't mean no offense . . . Izin." It was the first time Klasson had used his name, a sure sign my tamph engineer was no longer simply an alien oddity.

"You're welcome to stay," Izin said. "Would you like to test fire the weapon?"

"Hell yeah!" Klasson said, rapidly warming to Izin's matter of fact approach.

"I'll keep the channel open," I said, then Marie and I climbed over the crest and began scrambling down into the mouth of the ancient volcano.

* * * *

The full extent of the super volcano's one hundred and ten kilometer caldera could only be seen from space. The far side rim wall was hidden beyond the horizon as we scrambled down over weathered volcanic rocks into the vast cauldron. Once on the crater floor, we used broken rock formations and giant boulders to mask our approach to the base. It was almost three hours before we came in sight of the patchwork of test lots circling the BBI research facility. Between the outer test lot and our position was an open expanse of level ground cleared to ensure anyone approaching would be seen by the communications tower's sensors.

Marie started to move out from behind the boulder we used for cover, but I caught her arm and pulled her back. "Wait."

She gave me a puzzled look. "The tower sensors are down."

"I know." I said, pulling a short black tube from my pocket and placing it to my eye. I set the monoscope to visual wavelengths and swept the open area ahead, zooming in to every shadow and shape. It looked clear.

"Satisfied?" Marie asked.

"Almost." I switched the monoscope to infra-red with radiant surface heat suppressed and repeated the search. This time I noticed tiny heat points circling each other to our left. Below the heat points was a larger, faint thermal source a few degrees above ambient temperature. I switched back to visual to discover the point sources were insects circling low to the ground. They were the first indigenous life forms I'd seen since landing. Lying in the dirt below the swarming insects was a dog-sized animal with a dappled, gray hide and two short curved teeth pointing down from its jaw. The saberwolf's side was torn open, exposing purple flesh and dark blood that still glistened in the sunlight. The insects swarmed around the animal's intestines, while its hide bordering the wound still smoldered.

I handed the monoscope to Marie and pointed. "Over there."

"Izin, you watching?" I asked over the open channel.

"Yes, Captain."

I picked up a small rock and hurled it over the cleared ground towards the dead saberwolf. A cylindrical autoturret mounting a short barreled cannon popped up and blasted the rock. Before the fragments hit the ground, the autoturret had vanished back into its bunker.

"I thought Izin took out the sensors?" Marie said.

"It must have local targeting."

"It came from a circular metal plate to your left," Izin said. "There's another to your right, further away. They're close enough for their fields of fire to overlap."

"OK. The left one first." I picked up another rock. "Call it."

There was a moment's silence while Izin readied himself. "Throw."

I hurled the rock, then the autoturret immediately popped up and obliterated it, before vanishing back into its armor plated hideout. A moment later, Izin's slug flashed past and struck the ground a dozen meters beyond.

"He missed!" Marie said surprised.

"He's getting his timing right," I said, picking up another rock. "Ready."

Up on the ridge top, Izin slid another slug into the SN6's breach, adjusted his position and recalculated the travel time of his projectile to the autoturret. "Throw," he said, firing before the rock left my hand.

The autoturret popped up when Izin's projectile was already in flight. It destroyed the rock, then exploded as Izin's smart slug detonated inside its metal housing. Electrical short circuits flashed from the turret as the barrel shuddered and skewed towards the ground at an awkward angle.

"Now the other one," I said.

"Throw as far as you can," Izin said, "forty five degrees to your right. I will not fire the first time."

I tossed a rock as directed, then some distance away another autoturret appeared and fired. When Izin had readied himself, I hurled another decoy. The second autoturret popped up and was immediately torn apart by Izin's micro-munitions.

"One of those things failing is a malfunction, two is sabotage" I said. "Izin, is anyone coming out?"

We waited while Izin studied the base. "There's no

visible activity."

Considering the ever-present threat of Klasson's survivalists, I knew security couldn't be sleeping, so where were they? I waited a little longer, then said, "We're moving."

Marie and I stepped out from behind our boulder and jogged across open ground towards the first test lot. We were halfway across when Izin's voice sounded in our earpieces.

"An aircraft is lifting off from the center of the base. It's heading towards you."

We were in the open with no cover and no time to reach the nearest test lot. I drew my P-50, replaced the anti-personnel magazine with armor piercing slugs, and went down on one knee hoping the aircraft wasn't armed. Marie moved away a short distance and drew both her needle guns. They would do little damage against a large vehicle, but their flash might distract the pilot while I tried to bring the aircraft down. Once we had it on the ground, Izin could help us, but he was too far away to do anything while it was airborne.

My P-50 was still charging when a dull gray cargo lifter appeared above the base and flew towards us. It was rectangular, with four large tilt thrusters slowly vectoring from vertical to horizontal flight as it picked up speed and altitude. I followed it in my sights as it headed straight for us, then realized it was continuing to climb and pick up speed. The pilot looked down at me as he passed on our right, then the lifter raced away towards the crater wall, narrowly clearing the rim, before diving down the other side.

"It's moving away fast," Izin said, "at low altitude."

Marie and I ran towards the first test lot, assuming the pilot had reported our presence and expecting a welcoming committee to come charging out to greet us.

"There's another aircraft taking off," Izin said.

A white intercontinental research glider rose above the base, extended a pair of long gossamer-thin wings and moved off slowly to the south. When it passed over open ground, an autoturret popped up beneath it and fired, cutting the vehicle in half. The autoturret continued firing until the glider's single thruster hit the ground and burst into flames.

I holstered my P-50, exchanging puzzled looks with Marie. "Looks like they have more to worry about than us!"

Keeping watch on the base ahead, we crept into the first test lot filled with date palms and rubber trees. A silver and white column-shaped machine, twice the height of a man, stood in the center gathering data on each species' suitability to the climate and susceptibility to indigenous organisms, while also controlling the test lot's irrigation and nutrient dispersal system. Nearby test lots had similar monitoring systems, feeding data to the base's biolab.

Two small cropbots riding on metal treads, and equipped with flexible arms, tended the plants and ensured the equipment functioned perfectly. From the rim of the caldera, we'd seen white coated technicians in the fields as well, but now they had vanished.

We slipped across a dirt road into a corn field, turning into one of the narrow tracks that criss-crossed the test lot. A spherical machine with a circular red glowing eye-like sensor emerged from the corn and floated towards us. It stopped a meter from us as a thin red laser light flashed out from its eye, probing us.

Izin's voice sounded in my ear. "One step to the left please, Captain."

I did as instructed, then the sentry bot's eye shattered as Izin's slug drilled it perfectly. A small internal explosion shook the machine, sending it crashing to the ground.

"Cutting it a little close weren't you, Izin?" I said, glancing back up to the crest of the crater wall where my tamph engineer was perched.

"I could have shot sooner, Captain, but you might

have lost an ear."

Thankful I still had two ears, I said, "That's three of their watch dogs dead. Any guards coming out for a look?"

"No activity, Captain."

"What does Klasson think?"

We waited while Izin discussed the lack of security with the survivalist leader. "He believes the guards should have come out to investigate by now."

Increasingly apprehensive about why we were being ignored, we hurried through the corn field towards a long white, three story prefab building. As we reached it, a siren began wailing.

"Izin, what's happening?"

"People are running towards the eastern side of the base," he replied. "No one is approaching your position."

Whatever had triggered the siren, it wasn't us! We hurried to the corner and looked around the side. The prefab was a cropbot storage and repair facility. A paved road ran past it to other large white structures, all of which were open and deserted.

"Looks like we missed the party," I said, watching several men in the distance running away, oblivious to our presence. They ran hard, like their very lives depended on it. One tripped and fell. His companion abandoned him without even a look back.

"They're scared!" Marie said as the man who'd fallen jumped to his feet and started running again.

"Yeah, but of what?"

Beyond the warehouses were the accommodation blocks, laboratories and the energy plant. The spaceport's control tower rose in the distance, not far from the enormous upper works of the *Soberano* which were visible above the base's buildings.

"Izin, which way?" I asked

"Mr Klasson says the biolab is ahead of your position and to the right."

Marie and I hurried across the road, increasingly

certain no guards were going to stop us as we ran past a row of abandoned buildings. Three blocks along, an open topped six wheeled all terrain vehicle with a flatbed tray at the rear, sped past with two uniformed guards sitting in front. They paid us no attention as the ATV turned onto the main road out of the base and headed away at high speed.

"Even the guards don't care we're here!" I said.

"The base appears to be deserted, Captain," Izin reported.

Marie gave me a concerned look. "I'm getting the feeling coming here wasn't such a good idea."

"Me too," I said as we started running again.

At the next cross street, Marie pointed to a white four story prefab with darkly tinted windows and a sign depicting an atom over the main entrance. "That must be it!"

We ran to the entrance as a long silver arrowhead flew in over our heads from the direction of the spaceport. The sleek executive transport came in fast and quickly landed on top of the biolab, indicating whoever was on board was in a big hurry.

"Izin, who's on the roof?"

"Four men. Three are armed. I don't have a clear shot."

With the siren wailing relentlessly, we tried the biolab's front door, but it was electronically locked. I might have expected the building to be secured at night, but I couldn't understand why it was sealed shut in the early afternoon. I drew my P-50 and blasted the lock, then slid the door open and stepped inside. Two men and a woman wearing white head to foot anti-contamination suits ran towards us. I aimed my gun at them, thinking they were charging us, but they ran past us.

"There are more trapped upstairs!" one of the men yelled as he ran outside.

There were elevators near the entrance, stairs to the right and a floor map of the facility on the far side of the foyer. Pico scanning was on the third floor. Not wanting to risk being trapped in the elevator, we took the stairs. When we reached the third floor, we heard banging and muffled, frightened voices calling for help from a door labeled Genetics Lab 2.

"Get away from the door!" I yelled, then blasted the lock.

Two women wearing the same anti-contamination gear as the three on the ground floor rushed out. "Thanks! We thought we'd never get out."

"How long have you been in there?" Marie asked.

"Six hours," One of the lab technicians said as they started for the stairs.

"What's that alarm?" I called after them.

The lab tech glanced back, surprised I didn't recognize it. "The evacuation alert!" she said before disappearing down the stairs.

"We definitely shouldn't be here," I said, wondering what they were evacuating from.

I forced open two more doors in response to cries for help before we reached an entrance labeled 'Picometric Scanning'. I blasted the lock, then slid the door open to find a large laboratory with a brightly lit, arch shaped machine at its center. The arch supported a translucent circular projector which was emitting a high pitched whine and directing a tight blue beam down onto the Codex, which sat on a flat metallic scanning surface.

Vargis stood beside the Codex impatiently while my two old friends from Hades City – Scarface and Jawbones – threatened a white coated technician. None of them had heard me shoot the door lock over the siren and the deafening whine of the malfunctioning pico scanner.

"Shut it down!" Vargis yelled.

"I can't!" the technician replied helplessly. "It'll damage the Codex!"

"It's indestructible, you idiot!" Vargis shouted, turning to his two enforcers. "Shoot it!"

Scarface fired once into the top of the arch, shorting out the pico scanner with a flash, silencing the machine. The blue emitter beam shut off, allowing Vargis to grab the Codex.

I pushed the door wide open, raising my P-50. "I'll take that!"

Scarface pushed the technician aside and turned a nasty looking hammer gun towards me. I leapt back into the corridor as he fired. The hammer gun's slow moving slug popped a micro field moments before it hit the wall, punching a hole through it bigger than Izin's head. It was a short range, notoriously inaccurate weapon, but one hit would cut a man in half.

I dragged Marie back down the corridor as Scarface fired again, blasting a large hole through the white wall and spraying the corridor with debris. We kept running as sections of wall exploded behind us until we were safely past the neighboring lab. Once out of range we stopped to survey the corridor, now strewn with shattered white prefab fragments.

"Wow! They're not kidding!" Marie said.

Vargis' pet knuckle-draggers might have been slow, but they didn't need speed or accuracy with that kind of artillery. "Izin," I whispered, "We're on the third floor, half way along. Vargis is here. Can you see anything?"

"No Captain, the windows are too dark."

"Sirius Kade!" Vargis yelled from inside the pico lab, "you have an annoying habit of turning up uninvited."

"The Codex isn't what you think it is, Vargis."

"On the contrary, it's everything I expected!"

I had no choice but to tell him. "It's Mataron. They wanted you to have it. They're setting you up."

"The Matarons?" Vargis laughed. "If I told the Chairman that, he'd have my head. He's very unforgiving of incompetence."

"It sabotaged my ship!" Marie yelled. "It'll do the same to yours!"

“I brought it all the way here from the Shroud,” Vargis said, “in a specially insulated vault. My ship is fine.”

“Maybe it couldn’t link to his systems,” I said softly to Marie, then yelled, “The Codex linked to the base, didn’t it Vargis? Through the scanner. Now the base is being evacuated. Why?”

“You expect me to believe the Codex caused the evacuation?” Vargis yelled.

“That’s what it does. It attacks our technology!” I said creeping towards the nearest hole in the wall.

“Thanks for the warning, Kade. I’ll be sure to pass it on to our cyber-weapons group.”

I fired a single shot through the hole at the windows, then jumped back as both muscle-jobs blasted the wall, showering the corridor with white prefab chunks.

“I see a damaged window,” Izin’s artificial voice sounded in my ear. “How close are you?”

“We’re clear,” I said. “Let them have it!”

Moments later, one of Izin’s penetrator rounds smashed through the side of the building and detonated a cloud of micro munitions in the center of the lab. A dozen tiny explosions sent shrapnel splinters flying in all directions. I took a step forward, about to run towards the lab, when a disk-like mortar-drone flew out into the corridor. I turned and threw myself at Marie, knocking her though the open door of the last lab we’d unlocked. We hit the floor together as the mortar-drone’s upper surface popped up three centimeters, revealing ten small explosive shells lying side by side. The self propelled bombs launched together, detonating against nearby walls, tearing the third floor apart. One bomblet flew past the doorway behind us, through the corridor and detonated in the stairwell. I was vaguely aware of a lump of prefab wall glancing off my head, then after a while, a familiar artificial voice sounded from my earpiece.

“Captain, respond.”

I couldn't have been out for more than a few seconds, but I could barely hear Izin's voice over the deafening tone in my ears. Marie stirred beside me, dazed from the explosions. I climbed to my feet and staggered into the corridor. The entire third floor was in ruins and spot fires were taking hold everywhere. The pico lab's wall had collapsed. Scarface and the lab technician were both dead, shredded by Izin's shrapnel slug, and Vargis, Jawbones and the Codex were gone.

Marie emerged into the corridor clutching both her needle guns. Together we stepped into the lab, avoiding the two bloodied corpses on the floor. The picometric scanner was riddled with tiny holes, except for where the Codex's impenetrable alien-tech skin had absorbed Izin's shrapnel blast, leaving an undamaged footprint on the flat metallic scanning surface.

"The fool!" I whispered, knowing Vargis had left me no choice. Whatever he thought he was going to do with the Codex, I knew he was playing right into the hands of the Matarons. "Izin," I wheezed in a voice I barely recognized.

"Yes, Captain?"

"Vargis has the Codex! Don't let him leave!"

The view screens on the walls were cracked and pitted with shrapnel. Some were inactive, some hissed with static, while those that still functioned repeatedly flashed the same message:

EVACUATE! EVACUATE! EVACUATE!
ENERGY PLANT SUPERCRITICAL!

A timer was ticking over fast showing less than four minutes remaining.

Marie holstered her gun, staring at the screens. "That can't be good."

I stepped towards the nearest functioning display. Row after row of barely visible numbers ghosted behind the alert message, corrupting the base's control system.

Whatever those ghost numbers were, they didn't belong.

DIGITIZE OPTICS, I thought, triggering my threading to record everything I saw in perfect detail.

"Captain," Izin's voice sounded over the slowly receding ringing in my ears. "Vargis' vehicle was shielded. I could not destroy it."

"What's it doing now?"

"Heading for the spaceport. The *Soberano* is preparing to lift off."

"Is Klasson still with you?"

"Yes, Captain."

I closed the channel and turned to Marie. "If they come for us, there won't be time to clear the blast radius."

She nodded slowly. "I know."

"Izin, get aboard Klasson's crate and get as far away as you can," I glanced at the timer. "You have three minutes until the E-plant explodes."

"Captain?" Izin said uncertainly.

"Get out of here now, while you still can. I'm going to call out a series of numbers I want you to remember." If he could pass the number sequence to Lena Voss, the EIS might still have time to figure out what they meant. "Go to Hades City Spaceport. Ask for–"

"Be on the roof in one minute!" Klasson yelled at us through Izin's communicator.

"Klasson! The E-plant is supercritical. There isn't time!"

"Then haul ass, flyboy! I ain't letting you die 'til I get my guns!"

"You can't make minimum safe distance if you pick us up!" When he didn't answer, I swore under my breath. Marie and I ran through the door Vargis had used to escape, then up stairs to the roof.

"Klasson's ferry can do mach four," Marie said hopefully as we scaled the stairs.

"He needs ten times that to outrun the blast!"

Three men wearing the *Soberano's* crew uniform

lay dead near where the executive transport had landed. Izin had cut them down, but Vargis and Jawbones were not among them. The down blast from Klasson's ferry's engines swept the roof as it dropped out of the sky in front of us, landing hard. Its rear cargo door was already open, with Izin standing at the entry motioning for us to run to him.

Behind us, the *Soberano* lifted off. The super transport rose on more than forty thrusters, turning slowly in the air as one of her huge cargo doors opened outwards. When the door was horizontal, a tremendous energy blast flashed from the hold's dark interior, destroying a building on the far side of the base. The *Soberano's* cargo door immediately started to close as she nosed up and began climbing on her sixteen engines, forcing us to shield our eyes from the dazzling light radiating from her stern. As she became a receding star, twenty ejection pods streaked skywards from the eastern side of the base, each carrying a hundred people to the distant safety of orbit.

Marie and I ran to the ferry as the blast of its engines died, and charged up the ramp into the cargo compartment.

"Go!" I yelled

Izin began raising the rear door, filling the cargo compartment with the grinding metallic sound of rusting servos as the ferry's engines roared to life. It lurched into the air as I hurried forward to the cockpit. Klasson was flying one handed, remarkably relaxed as the ferry's engines rotated to the horizontal.

"Once you're over the crater wall, go low!" I yelled as I slid into the copilot's seat.

"Nah, the trees will block us," Klasson said as he put the ferry into a steep climb.

"The crater wall will absorb some of the EMP." Even if by a miracle, we could escape the blast wave, the electromagnetic pulse would fry the ferry's systems, sending us nose diving into the ground at four times the speed of sound.

"This old girl won't survive even a flicker of EMP."

"Going high won't help!" We'd be exposed to the full force of the blast when the E-plant went up.

"Don't be so sure!" Klasson said with a sly grin.

I thought he'd lost his mind, then Jase's voice sounded over the communicator. "Cut your power now!"

"Never flew a glider before," Klasson said as he silenced the old ferry's engines. "First time for everythin'!"

The roar of the engines was replaced by the whistle of wind over the hull as the ferry hurtled through the air. A large shadow passed over the cockpit, then the *Silver Lining* dropped down on top of us. Brilliant blue lights appeared either side of Klasson's ferry as the *Lining's* two engines, glowing on minimal power, dropped either side of us. The *Lining's* number two gantry's maglock glowed to life overhead, snatching the ferry out of the air as if she were an empty VRS container. The ferry slammed up hard against the gantry's maglock, knocking Izin and Marie off their feet as it was locked into place by powerful magnetic fields.

"I got you!" Jase's voice yelled from the cockpit's communicator. "Hold on."

"Oh no!" I muttered, realizing we were outside the *Lining's* inertial field, leaving us no protection from her acceleration. "Brace!" I yelled.

Marie and Izin rolled flat on the cargo deck as Klasson looked up curiously at the three towing gantries extending from the *Lining's* stern, seemingly unaware of what was coming. A moment later, the ferry filled with blue light as Jase fed a trickle of power to the ship's engines. The *Lining* stood on her tail and began streaking up through the atmosphere, crushing us under the enormous weight of acceleration many times greater than Klasson's rust bucket could ever have achieved. The old ferry had no chance of outrunning a reactive explosion, but the *Lining* could do it easily, providing the acceleration didn't kill us. We gasped for air as Jase piled on ten gravities – as much as he dared. I nearly blacked out as I sank into the hard copilot's seat which had never been designed for that kind of acceleration. Beside me, Klasson gritted his teeth, shocked by the force pressing down on him. After what seemed an eternity, Jase shed a few G's to let us breathe, although we still couldn't move.

Outside, a shimmer obscured the air as the *Lining's* battle shield went up.

We continued climbing, picking up speed and piling on distance between us and the doomed E-plant. Suddenly, the sky around us filled with a stark white light. I squeezed my eyes shut, facing down away from the blinding flash. Below us, the BBI base vaporized, turning the ancient caldera into a boiling lava crater. The blast wave expanded like a bubble, ionizing the atmosphere to the edge of space and dumping star-intensity heat on our shield. A sphere of orange and red glowed around the *Lining* and its captive ferry as the curvature of the planet appeared. For several seconds, we raced through the upper atmosphere as the air inside Klasson's poorly pressurized rust bucket began to thin, then the shield cooled and the acceleration eased, letting us move again. Soon we dived back towards the safety of the lower atmosphere, now half a continent away from the blast zone.

"That was close," I said, glancing at the ferry's blank control console.

The *Lining's* battle shield had protected us from the blast, but not the electromagnetic pulse. While the ship's hull was designed to reflect radiation, the old ferry's systems had been fried by the EMP. I did a quick status check of my own, finding my biological threading had been unaffected, although all of my mechanical equipment was dead. Only my P-50 had survived, because like most weapons, it was EMP-shielded.

"Your ferry's had it," I said.

"Yeah, she was a good old girl," Klasson said, glancing back through the cockpit window at the glowing dome rising beyond the horizon behind us. "It was worth it, to put an end to them terraformin' shenanigans!" He chuckled, then craned his neck as he watched twenty points of light angling for orbit high above us. "Looks like most of them dirt doctors got out alive."

I followed his gaze to the ejection pods. The light radiating from their engines was proof they'd escaped both the blast and the electromagnetic pulse intact. "Where will they go?"

"Refuge most likely, unless they got a deal with the smugglers."

"Will you accept them?"

"Yeah, but only 'cause the kelp beds needs a good cleaning." He grinned. "Might do them terraformers some good to get their hands dirty and their feet wet."

"They'll rebuild the base."

"No stopping it I guess, but by the time they do we'll have a hundred of them fancy rifles and a few of Izin's little sharpshooting cousins helping us out."

The way he said it, it sounded like fun. If the navy confiscated the *Lining* for smuggling his guns, I might even join him. "It'll take a year for word to get back to the Core Systems, then another year or two to get replacements out here."

"Yeah, and then they got to grow them test plants all over again." He gave me a crafty look. "Enough time for you to go get me an orbital gunship!"

I laughed. That was definitely impossible and he knew it, but I went along with his dreaming. "Anything else?"

Klasson sighed thoughtfully. "A case of Kentucky bourbon. I'm not talking 'bout that pisswater from New Bardron. I want the genuine article – from Earth."

"You've got more chance of getting an orbital gunship."

He sighed wistfully. "I figured you'd say that, but a man can dream, can't he?"

* * * *

The *Silver Lining* kept hold of Klasson's ferry until we landed in Refuge. Jase waited while we all climbed out, then released the maglock. The old ferry crashed onto the petrified branch with a clatter of loose metal, now a pile of scrap to be cannibalized and melted down. An hour later, all of the ejection pods had splashed down in the harbor and were being towed to shore by survivalist boats. They were virtual enemies in an undeclared war, yet the survivalists treated the people in the pods, more than half of whom were women and children, with compassion and care.

Marie and Jase accompanied Klasson to Refuge's tavern to celebrate the destruction of the BBI base while I returned to the *Lining* with Izin. I immediately transcribed the ghost numbers I'd seen in the picometric scanning lab for Izin to analyze. To my surprise, he found the going particularly tough.

After more than an hour staring at the ghost numbers and having made no progress, Izin said, "Considering the vagaries of human memory and the quantity of data involved, it's unlikely you have accurately recalled the data. These numbers are almost certainly meaningless."

Normally he'd be right, except I wasn't using human memory, I was using bionetic storage and I knew my transcription was perfect. Of course, I couldn't tell Izin that. "Trust me, they're the numbers and they mean something."

"Even if you have recalled the data correctly, the base's system suffered a major malfunction. The numbers themselves may be corrupt."

"Corrupt or not, I need to know what they mean."

Izin reluctantly returned to his analysis, sitting like

a statue amid his six screens, eyes darting back and forth as his focus constantly shifted. Occasionally he used the ship's processing core to run tests, but mostly he did it in his head. I left him alone, certain that if he could find no meaning in the numbers, Vargis had escaped and the Codex was now free to do whatever the Mataron's intended. I returned to my stateroom and drafted a report for Lena Voss, the first of its kind I'd written in years. The fact that I'd let the Codex slip through my fingers only made it harder to write.

"Captain?" Izin's voice sounded as I was reviewing the final draft hours later. "You were correct. These numbers have meaning."

"I'll be right there." I hurried across to engineering where Izin still sat in the same position I'd left him in hours before. "What have you got?"

"There's a highly structured logic behind these numbers, Captain, the like of which I've never seen before. It is far too intricate to have been conceived of by humans."

"Because we're not smart enough to have thought of it?"

"Isn't that what I said?" Izin motioned towards the ghost numbers filling the screens to his right. "It is a complex, cognitive theorem, quite challenging until I was able to reconstruct the core algorithm."

"You mean you reverse engineered Mataron mathematics in your head, in one evening?"

"I had no alternative, Captain. The ship's processing core was unable to assist me."

No wonder the rest of the galaxy kept Izin's species under lock and key. "You'll have to do better next time," I said, although Izin didn't realize I was joking.

"Now that I understand how their logic works, I will be able to solve this kind of problem faster in the future. It was the purpose of the theorem that deceived me."

"What purpose?"

"It's a synthetic intelligence, a mathematical clone

of an actual Mataron."

"I've never heard of mathematical clones."

"Human technology is limited to biological cloning only," Izin said. "This is something considerably more advanced. It is a virtual representation of the consciousness of a real Mataron known as Hazrik a'Gitor."

"Hazrik a'Gitor ?" With my bionetic memory wiped, I had no way of checking if the EIS were aware of this particular Mataron.

"The Antaran Codex spawns the synthetic intelligence into human computer systems. The SI then functions as the actual Mataron agent would, drawing on all his experience and knowledge, making intuitive leaps when needed to carry out his mission, all without being detected. That's why it triggered the core collapse of the base's energy plant. The explosion would have destroyed the Codex, the base's processing core and erased all evidence of the synthetic operative's existence."

"But why destroy itself? It could have hidden, waiting for a chance to complete its mission."

"It did complete its mission, Captain. I said the SI erased *evidence* of its existence. I didn't say it erased itself. You see, the Codex spawned twice. The first time into BBI's processing core, which enabled it to lock down the base and overload the energy plant. That's why the ejection pods couldn't launch until after the *Soberano* destroyed the base's processing core."

"Ah, so Vargis saved the terraformers."

"Yes. The *Soberano* destroyed the first spawning of the Mataron SI when she took off, although they wouldn't have known that at the time. The *Silver Lining* picked up an emergency signal from pod control, telling the *Soberano* the processing core was blocking their launch, asking for help."

I guess it made sense. BBI and Vargis were both Consortium. Even so, Vargis had saved the lives of almost two thousand innocent people!

“So what did this simulated Mataron agent hope to gain by destroying the base?”

“When the energy plant went supercritical,” Izin continued, “the base’s emergency warning system automatically activated, giving the Codex access to every node on the base’s datanet. The ghost numbers you saw were the second spawning, piggybacking on the warning system.”

“But the base is gone. What’s the point of spawning twice?”

“The spaceport was a hub and every ship docked was a node,” Izin explained. “The Mataron synthetic intelligence spawned into the *Soberano* before she took off.”

“What!” So even if Vargis locked the Antaran Codex away in his specially sealed vault, it no longer mattered. The SI had already infiltrated his ship’s systems without him even knowing it! “How long before the *Soberano* breaks down – like the *Heureux*?”

“Marie’s engineer broke the link between the Codex and the *Heureux*’s processing core before the SI finished spawning. That’s why her ship became disabled. The spawning into the *Soberano* is already complete. The Mataron SI will not disable the *Soberano*, it will take command of her.”

So that was it! The Matarons wanted control of the *Soberano*, a virtual battleship equipped with the latest Earth-tech weapons. Even Earth Navy frigates would have trouble taking her on, if they knew where she was headed and if they could catch her.

Izin pointed to a group of numbers on one of the screens. “Those are navigational coordinates showing the *Soberano*’s destination.” Izin called up astrographics, displaying a soft orange star with a glowing red warning ring encircling it. “According to the Tau Ceti charts, it’s a restricted system.”

Restricted systems were off limits to mankind for any number of reasons. If the *Soberano* entered that system, it would count as a minor Access Treaty violation. It wouldn't be enough to cause another embargo, but it would add at least a century to our qualifying period. Another hundred years would hurt, but surely that wouldn't be enough for the Matarons. They wanted to destroy us, not delay us.

"Why there?" I asked warily.

Izin's vocalizer never revealed his emotions, but for once I sensed even my tamph engineer was on edge. "The *Soberano* is going to destroy an entire civilization. That will make mankind as hated in this galaxy as my own species, and you will no doubt suffer the same fate."

At last, I understood. The Antaran Codex was the means by which the Matarons would have their revenge!

* * * *

It was almost midnight local time when I entered the Tree House, Refuge's noise and smoke filled tavern. Jase was engaged in drinking games with five leather-faced survivalists while Marie was line dancing with several dozen inebriated townsfolk. I caught her eye, indicating we were going. She thanked those around her and started for the door while Jase was singing some local song he'd been taught. There was a round of clapping in rhythm, then they gulped down a small cup of dark yellow liquid. A moment later, all the men were coughing and beating their chests as they swallowed the alcoholic poison.

"Skipper!" Jase yelled drunkenly when he saw me arrive. "Sit down! You got to try this stuff. It's made from kelp! It tastes terrible!" He laughed as his drinking friends raced to fill each other's cups.

I put my hand on his shoulder. "Time to go."

"One more round!" Jase yelled, eager to break into another song.

"We really have to go," I said, lifting him out of his chair. Jase's band of new best friends howled in protest, demanding he stay for one more song, inviting me to join them. “We’ll be back,” I promised.

Klasson emerged from the crowd, a large drink in one hand, yet as clear eyed as ever. Obviously, he could hold his liquor better than my extroverted copilot. He stuck out his big calloused hand. “You’re going after them?”

“I have to,” I said as we shook hands.

“Good luck. I’ll be waiting for my guns,” he said with a crooked grin, not really expecting me to bring him any weapons.

“If I’m alive, you’ll get them,” I promised, then supported Jase to the door.

He waved to his drinking companions, who seemed genuinely sorry to see him go, then one pretty young woman stepped in front of us and planted a big kiss on his lips. She gave him an inviting look as she stepped aside, then he reached for her, but I dragged him back.

“No you don’t!” I said, pushing him towards the door where Marie was waiting.

Outside, she asked, “I take it Izin figured out where Vargis has gone?”

“Yeah, and it’s bad.”

Once aboard ship, Marie helped Jase to his stateroom to sleep it off while I went to the flight deck and started on our preflight checklists.

Soon Marie appeared, taking the copilot’s acceleration couch. “He’s sleeping like a baby.”

“Did all the terraformers make it out of the base?” I asked.

“No. There are nearly two hundred missing, probably trapped in the base by the lock down.”

After checking the airspace overhead was clear, we lifted off on low power. Once we were high enough that Refuge wouldn’t feel the down blast from our engines, I throttled up then activated the intercom.

“Izin, how are those autonav safeties coming along?”

“Disabling them now, Captain.”

Marie gave me a wary look. “Sirius, what are you doing?”

Every autonav had built-in safeguards preventing human ships from entering – or even approaching – restricted systems. Overriding those safeties was punishable by death, something even the most cold blooded pirate wouldn’t risk for fear of the navy’s retribution.

“Going after Vargis.”

“Vargis might be a slime ball,” Marie said, “But he’s not suicidal. He wouldn’t disable his autonav safeties.”

“He wouldn’t, but the thing controlling his ship would!”

She was about to argue with me when the neutrino detector began flashing. “There’s a huge energy source beyond the planet,” she said, “two million clicks out.”

“How big?” I asked.

“Big enough not to be one of ours.”

Alien ships were always easy to identify by the immense quantities of energy they generated compared to human ships – except for the Tau Cetins whose ships generated no traces we could identify. It allowed us to spot most alien ships even when they were a long way off.

“Izin,” I called urgently over the intercom, “How long for the autonav?”

“Two minutes, Captain.”

I turned to Marie. “Give me any change in the alien contact’s position.”

Without waiting for her response, I set course to climb up from the system’s ecliptic plane, getting us clear of mass obstructions for a quick getaway.

“It’s closing on us – fast,” Marie said.

“Izin, I need that autonav now.”

“Almost there, Captain.”

I swung the optics towards the neutrino source, finding a stretched and flattened teardrop shaped hull silhouetted against the stars.

"I've never a seen ship like that before," Marie said curiously.

"It's a Mataron armored cruiser, Ortarn class."

"Since when did you become an expert on Mataron warships?"

"I have my secrets," I replied, playing down my knowledge of our reptilian adversary, certain it was the same ship that had stalked us in the Shroud.

Marie gave me a puzzled look. Like all humans, she knew who the Matarons were, why they hated us, but very little else. Most information about them was classified and as there was no trade between our two civilizations, civilians rarely saw their ships. EIS agents, however, were given an Earth Navy familiarization course on the Mataron Fleet, although this was the first time I'd ever seen one of their ships up close.

"They know where the *Soberano*'s headed and what she's going to do when she gets there," I said as the black silhouette grew rapidly in size. "And they know we're going to stop her."

I knew it was useless, but I raised our shield to let them know we saw them coming. If they wanted to destroy us, they'd have to fire on us, which would leave tell tale weapon emissions. A simple collision wouldn't be enough.

When Marie saw me raise our shield, she could scarcely believe her eyes. "You don't seriously think the Matarons are going to attack us!"

An attack would give the TCs hard evidence of their involvement, something I knew the Matarons wouldn't risk, not this close to the *Soberano* committing genocide in humanity's name. "They just want to scare us."

The Mataron ship came in fast, passing so close I thought it was going to ram us. Its black armored hull brushed our shield giving us an up close and personal look at the overlapping scales of their metamorphic armor, the round bulges of their weapons and the sensor and shield ridges that ran the length of their ship. Static electricity from our shield tickled their hull so weakly its armor didn't even activate. A radiation alarm sounded as the *Lining* detected a weak stream of charged particles slice through our shield for a fraction of a second, causing no damage. A moment later, the black hulled ship vanished.

Marie studied the sensor display with growing confusion. "It must have bubbled," she yelled over the radiation alarm.

Suddenly main power failed, immersing the flight deck in an impenetrable, silent blackness. We floated off our acceleration couches in zero gravity, aware that even the sound of air from the life support system was gone. We were adrift, completely dead in space.

"I don't hear any decompression," Marie's voice sounded out of the darkness. "They didn't hole us."

"It was too weak to be a weapon." Whatever it was, they'd fired inside our shield so we'd scatter any residual traces, making detection impossible. It was clever, even for snakeheads!

"If we stay like this, we're as good as dead," she said, always thinking like a spacer.

With our engines silenced, it was only a matter of time before the planet pulled us back down. I was about to push towards the hatch at the rear of the flight deck, to feel my way blindly to engineering, when the lights blinked back on and we tumbled down onto our acceleration couches. A moment later, the wrap around screen and our consoles came back to life.

"My apologies, Captain," Izin's voice sounded through the intercom. "The Mataron ship scanned our processing core. They detected the ghost numbers you recorded and uploaded the SI. I didn't have time to block it, so I killed the power before it could take hold."

"Is it gone?"

"Yes. It needs time and power to take root. That's its weakness."

"Can you stop them doing that to us again?"

"Now that I know what it is and how they use it, I can build a defense."

"Make it a priority," I said, glad Izin was watching over the ship.

"The autonav is ready," Izin said.

"All right, let's get out of here!"

Marie retracted sensors while I passed control to the autonav. It accepted what it would normally regard as a prohibited course and bubbled, rendering us safe for now. Not even the Matarons could intercept us while we were superluminal, although now they knew we'd cracked their little secret.

"Izin, did the Matarons take anything else?"

"No, Captain," Izin replied, "But they may wonder how we recorded the ghost data so accurately." That was Izin's way of telling me he was wondering the same thing and knew I was holding something back.

"Some humans have eidetic memories," I said.

"One in a billion humans, Captain. Do you have an eidetic memory?"

"No, it was a memory trick. I'll teach it to you someday."

"Thank you, Captain, but my species achieved perfect memory several million years before *Homo sapiens* evolved. However, if the Matarons believe you have such a memory, you retain evidence of their involvement in your head. Clearly, no human intellect could have devised such a complex theorem, so if the Matarons are to succeed, they will have to kill you."

For once, stupidity was an undeniable defense. If Izin was right about the complexity of the Mataron synthetic intelligence, the Tau Cetins would know humans couldn't have designed it.

"Cheery thought, Izin. I'll keep it in mind." And keep my gun close.

"Because I solved their theorem," Izin added, "the Matarons will also have to kill me, if they are aware of my presence on this ship."

"Assume they know you're aboard, Izin. Take any precautions necessary to protect yourself."

"I always do, Captain."

His reply was so mild, so unassuming, I almost felt sorry for any snakehead who tried to kill my deadly little tamph engineer. The Matarons might be a xenophobic, aggressive, militaristic race, but they were amateurs compared to Izin's people who'd almost conquered a third of the galaxy more than two thousand years ago.

I switched off the intercom, feeling Marie's eyes upon me.

"So why exactly do the Matarons want to kill you?"

Chapter Six : Vintari System

Restricted System – Sanctuary Class
Vintari System
Outer Cygnus Region
7 planets, Vintari II inhabited
946 light years from Sol
280 Million Indigenous (Non-human) inhabitants

The *Silver Lining* unbubbled outside the Vintari System in the heliopause, that narrow expanse where a star's plasma wind meets the interstellar medium. It was as clear a natural boundary as the coastline of a continent, and had defined the limits of stellar sovereignty since the dawn of interstellar travel. All that lay within the heliopause belonged to the system and its Bronze Age inhabitants, protected by the Access Treaty and closed to mankind.

Moments after our bubble dropped, we extended sensors and began scanning for the *Soberano*, hoping Vargis had found a way to stop his ship from crossing into restricted Vintari space.

"There's only one energy source in the entire system," Jase announced as the *Lining's* sensors identified a neutrino hot spot far inside the hydrogen wall dividing interstellar and interplanetary space. "She's crossing the orbit of the sixth planet, accelerating hard."

The curved view screen flashed to life, revealing Vintari as a distant point of yellow light and the *Soberano* as a very dim blue dot. Jase zoomed the optics towards the blue pinpoint, resolving it into a tightly packed cluster of glowing engines organized into four rows of four.

"That's the *Soberano*'s engine configuration all right," I said.

"Why didn't they bubble all the way to the planet?" Marie wondered.

Unfortunately, we couldn't ask them. At that distance it would have taken over thirty hours to bounce a signal off the *Soberano* – time we didn't have. Instead, I had the autonav extrapolate her course, confirming she was heading for Vintari II.

"Skipper," Jase said. "I'm picking up a transmission, audio only."

"Put it through."

Vargis' voice burst from the comm system with an emotional fervor he'd shown no sign of on Icetop or Deadwood. He must have transmitted the message at least fifteen hours ago for it to be reaching us now. ". . . *the day of the Lord will come like a thief, and then the heavens will pass away with a roar, and the heavenly bodies will be burned up and dissolved, and the earth and the works that are done on it will be exposed!"*

"What the hell's he talking about?" Jase asked.

There was a moment's pause, then Vargis spoke again. *"Immediately after the tribulation of those days the sun will be darkened, and the moon will not give its light, and the stars will fall from heaven, and the powers of the heavens will be shaken!"*

The intercom sounded as Izin, who'd been listening in from engineering, cut in. "He's quoting from a pre-

Unity religious text known as the Christian Bible."

"How can you tell?" I asked.

"I read it once, years ago."

I'd skipped ancient monotheism altogether. "What does it mean?"

"I'm not sure, Captain. I find ancient human religious texts to be rather cryptic. He's quoting from the Books of Peter and Matthew."

I realized the Matarons were using our ancient belief systems against us as Vargis' began chanting another passage: *"And the great dragon was thrown down, that ancient serpent, who is called the devil and Satan, the deceiver of the whole world – he was thrown down to the earth, and his angels were thrown down with him!"*

"That was from Revelations, twelve nine," Izin added.

"They're doomsday quotes!" Marie said.

"He sounds like an end-of-the-universe religious nut," Jase said.

"That's exactly what he's supposed to sound like," I said, motioning for Jase to kill the signal. "Vargis is a lot of things, but he's no zealot. That's the Mataron SI talking, mimicking his voice."

"But there's no one out here to hear it, except us," Marie said doubtfully.

"Not yet there isn't, but those signals will be drifting for centuries. Anyone who wants to hear them just has to fly out ahead of the signal and wait for it to reach them. It's a confession to the future."

The autonav's intercept course indicated we had to bubble in towards the sixth planet followed by a twenty hour stern chase. By the time we caught the *Soberano*, we'd be hurtling along at a small fraction of the speed of light, so fast that we'd have virtually no helm control and little time to board the super transport before we reached Vintari II.

"Pull sensors," I said, "We'll micro-bubble in

behind her."

"You can't go in there," Marie said. "It's Access Treaty restricted."

"I can't let the *Soberano* reach that planet, so unless you've got a better idea . . .?" She opened her mouth to protest, then fell silent.

"We could bubble ahead of them," Jase suggested. "Fire a drone down her throat as she passes."

"She's too big," I said. "Our drones would be pinpricks, and head-on we couldn't hit her critical systems."

"What about that fancy new burster Izin's installed?" Marie asked.

"How about it, Izin?" I asked. He'd been working with his hull crawlers night and day for weeks to get the new cannon installed.

"The *Soberano*'s relative velocity is too high," Izin replied. "She would be in range for only a fraction of a second. That's insufficient time to target and fire our new weapon. There is an alternative solution if you are determined to stop her."

"I'm listening."

"We could bubble ahead of the *Soberano* and place the *Silver Lining* directly in her path."

"Let her hit us?" Jase said incredulously. "That's insane!"

If I thought it would work, I might have tried it. We could have taken to the lifeboat and hoped for a pick up, but I knew it would have been for nothing. "Nice try Izin, but the Mataron SI would see us and raise the *Soberano*'s shield. We'd bounce off her like a bug hitting an elephant."

"Are you sure we need to do this?" Marie asked. "By the time the *Soberano* gets to the planet, she'll be going so fast she won't be in weapons range long enough to do much damage."

"The *Soberano* isn't going to bombard the planet," I said, throwing the autonav extrapolation up onto the screen. "She's going to crash into it." The screen showed the super transport's course leading directly into Vintari II.

"Why go to all this trouble just to destroy the *Soberano*?" Marie said, puzzled.

"The *Soberano* is the weapon," I said, "a kinetic weapon to destroy the entire planet."

"It's a dinosaur killer!" Jase said, shocked.

The *Soberano* was smaller than the comet that hit Earth sixty five million years ago, but her velocity would be more than thirty times greater, making the impact far more destructive.

"Izin," I said, "how bad will it be?"

Silence filled the flight deck as he did the math. "If Vintari II has a structure similar to Earth's, the *Soberano* will crack the planet's crust and eject enough debris into the atmosphere to cause a global winter that will last for decades, collapsing the planet's ecosystem. The impact will generate a shockwave that will pass through Vintari II's interior, rupturing the crust on the far side of the planet and triggering super earthquakes and mega tsunamis that will roll across the surface for days. Complex life will not survive."

Shock appeared on Marie's face. "The Matarons are going to murder two hundred and eighty million people, just to get back at us!"

"It'll look like fanatical humans did it," I said. "The Forum will have no choice but to lock us away for a very long time."

"They'll throw away the key!" Jase said soberly.

"That's why we have to board the *Soberano* and get the Codex." I still had the SI fragment in bionetic storage, but the Mataron's would claim I stole it. What I needed was irrefutable proof we'd been framed, and only the Codex could provide that.

We retracted sensors and blink-bubbled a fifth of the way around the edge of the Vintari System. When we could see again, we found the *Soberano's* faint engine bloom now obscured the star's distant yellow point, confirming we were perfectly aligned astern of the giant Consortium super transport.

We blink-bubbled again, this time in towards the *Soberano*, becoming the second human ship in two days to enter a restricted system, violating the Access Treaty and putting at risk everything I'd sworn to protect.

* * * *

Two hours after the stern chase began, I found Izin in engineering studying our fragment of the Mataron synthetic intelligence that now controlled the *Soberano*.

"It's a pity I don't have more of it to analyze," Izin said. "It's a fascinating logical construct."

"But can you destroy it?"

"Unlikely, assuming it has full control of the *Soberano*."

"Can it fire her weapons?"

"I expect so," Izin said, "which is why we must approach from behind her engines, to prevent her bringing those weapons to bear."

"Let's hope she doesn't have drones." Energy weapons required line of sight, but one drone could fly around and hit us while we were hiding astern.

"The *Soberano*'s weapons are not our problem, Captain. Catching her is. By the time we get alongside, it will be too late to save the planet, the Codex or even ourselves.

"Are all tamphs as optimistic as you?"

"Both ships will be travelling too fast to avoid the planet."

"Then we blow her up."

"Detonating her energy core will simply break her superstructure into several smaller pieces which would result in multiple strikes on the planet, multiplying the damage."

"Can we push her off course?"

"Our engines aren't powerful enough," Izin said, pulling an image of Vintari II up onto one of his displays. It was a brownish, arid world, with fewer but deeper oceans than Earth. Great rivers flowed from snow covered mountain ranges, through vast dry plains to dark blue seas. The rivers formed strips of fertility, bordered by irrigated fields and pockmarked with burgeoning stone and mud brick cities.

"Could we bounce her off the atmosphere or use the planet's gravity to slingshot around Vintari II?"

"Our linear momentum will be too great. We'll have no effective maneuvering ability and no time to avoid a collision."

"You want to think about that some more?"

"I've considered every possibility. No human ship is designed to maneuver at that flat space velocity."

"There's two hundred and eighty million people down there who are going to be dead in twenty four hours if we don't think of something."

"Yes Captain, I know."

If the Local Powers hadn't enforced interstellar law for eons before the rise of *Homo sapiens* on Earth, mankind might never have made it this far. I was damn sure the tiny bronze age riverine civilization of Vintari II would get no less from us.

"Put that oversized brain of yours to work, Izin. Find a way to miss that planet."

"I have considered every logical alternative." Izin's voice was its usual synthesized calmness, but I sensed his helplessness.

"Then find an illogical alternative!"

"Illogical thinking?"

"Yes!"

Izin's bulbous eyes blinked slowly. "I will try to think more like you, Captain."

"That's the spirit!" I patted Izin's shoulder encouragingly. "You've got eighteen hours."

* * * *

The glow of the *Soberano's* engines had been growing steadily on the flight deck's wrap around view screen for hours, giving me time to think. Finally, I made a decision and caught Marie's eye, nodding for her to meet me in the corridor while Jase remained dutifully focused on the ship's systems and sensors.

Once outside the flight deck's airtight hatch, I whispered, "There's something I want you to do."

Marie gave me a seductive look. "Really Sirius? At a time like this?" She shrugged helplessly. "Well, if you insist."

"No, nothing like that."

She looked disappointed. "This might be our last chance."

I was momentarily tempted, then shook my head. "No. I want you to get into the lifeboat and steer away from us – you and Jase."

She sobered. "And watch as you incinerate yourself on Vintari II? I don't think so!"

"Someone has to tell the TCs what happened. Izin's convinced by the time we catch the *Soberano*, it'll be too late to save either ship."

"You're seriously out of your mind if you think I'm leaving!"

"If we save the *Lining*, I'll pick you up later. If not, the TCs will come. They'll find you no matter how far out of the system you've drifted."

"I'm not leaving you here," she whispered.

"Yes, you are. Izin and I can handle this."

"You really think you're going to get Jase off this ship?"

"Not willingly. I'm going to stun him and put him in the lifeboat, then you're going to pilot it away. We're still slow enough for you both to get clear."

"Not going to happen, Sirius!"

"Absolutely not going to happen!" Jase exploded

behind me.

I spun around to see my tall, blonde copilot standing in the hatchway with an angry look on his face. "I don't need either of you onboard for this!" I said.

"The hell you don't!" Jase said. "You can't fly straight without me!"

"You'll be throwing your lives away if you stay."

"We're not throwing anything away, Sirius," Marie said, "because you'll think of something."

"Izin says it's impossible."

"So how are you going to save the Codex?" she asked. "Or are you planning to die with it in your arms?"

"I'm going to replace a drone's warhead with the Codex and fire it into space. The drone's acceleration is much greater than ours. It'll get clear and eventually the Tau Cetins will find it. If you two get off the ship now, you can tell them where to look."

"I've got a better idea," Marie said. "You take the lifeboat and Jase and I will put the Codex in a drone and you can explain it to the TCs."

The thought of watching from the lifeboat as the *Lining* crashed into Vintari II – as she died – flashed into my mind. "I can't do that," I whispered.

She took my hand. "Neither can I, so you better come up with another plan, because I'm not leaving."

I glanced at Jase, who slowly drew one of his pistols and began spinning it in his hand. "Don't mind me, I'm about to mutiny!"

"This is nuts," I said slowly, realizing I wasn't going to get either of them off the ship.

"Now that we've got that sorted," Jase said, "I thought you should know we have company. There's another ship out there."

"Where?" I asked, following Jase back onto the flight deck.

"Six billion clicks above the star," he said as he slid back into his couch. "It's just sitting up there watching us."

A grainy image of the black, stretched teardrop shaped Mataron cruiser filled the fully zoomed view screen.

"It's got the same energy signature as the Mataron ship that's been tailing us," Jase said.

"Why don't they do something?" Marie asked.

"They don't need to," I said. "They know if we keep going, we're dead." If it had been any of the other Local Powers, they'd have already stopped the *Soberano*, but not the Matarons. They were simply going to watch their handiwork play out.

"They might hate us," Marie said angrily, "but the people on Vintari II have done nothing. They're innocent."

"I know, that's why we have to save them."

* * * *

Seventeen hours after we began chasing the *Soberano*, Izin summoned us to engineering.

"I have an idea," he said as he projected a three dimensional representation of the planet into the center of the compartment. "This is Vintari II," he said, then zoomed out until the *Soberano* and the *Silver Lining* could be seen as two tiny points moving in a line towards the orbital path of the planet. "In less than four hours, both ships and all life on Vintari II will be destroyed when we collide with the planet."

A timer appeared beneath the image counting down to the moment of impact. At minus twenty five minutes, the pair of dots representing the two ships became one as the planet's orbit carried it into their path.

"At this point," Izin said, zooming in towards the two dots, "we will dock with the *Soberano*." The dots resolved into images of the two ships, locked together side by side. "Note the relative aspect of the two ships." The *Silver Lining's* stern was facing towards the gigantic *Soberano's* bow.

"How does docking backwards help us?" I asked.

"The *Silver Lining* will apply three percent thrust," Izin said, pointing to the soft glow produced by the *Lining's* two maneuvering engines. "It's the maximum thrust we can use without breaking free of the *Soberano*'s docking system."

The timer counted down as the *Soberano* slowly rotated until it was travelling sideways towards the planet, its engines blazing with light, vainly trying to push it onto a new course.

"You're using the *Silver Lining* like an attitude thruster!" Jase said.

"Yes," Izin replied. "There isn't time to overcome the *Soberano*'s linear momentum, but we can turn her sideways and let her engines do the rest."

I watched the super transport's sixteen large engines blast away for a few seconds, achieving very little. "How far can we move the *Soberano* off its current trajectory?"

"One third of a degree."

"That's not enough!" Jase said.

"It will take time to turn the *Soberano*," Izin said. "That leaves very little time to change course."

"But we'll still hit the planet," Marie said.

"Not according to my calculations," Izin said, zooming back towards Vintari II where a small dark sphere drifted across the face of the planet. A moment later, the *Silver Lining* and the *Soberano* struck the tiny moon, shattering it in a brilliant flash and spraying a cloud of debris over the arid world below. We all jumped, startled by the unexpected explosion. The timer stopped at planetary impact minus zero point zero nine seconds.

"Turning the *Soberano*," Izin explained, "will provide sufficient lateral thrust to redirect both ships into Vintari II's smallest moon. The moon will be vaporized, but it will shield the planet from a direct impact. Granular debris will strike Vintari II and burn up harmlessly in its atmosphere." Izin turned to us, waiting patiently as we absorbed his plan.

"That's not a solution!" Jase declared.

"The Captain asked me to find a way to save the planet. This is the only idea I could come up with."

Jase gave him an exasperated look. "But . . . we're still dead!"

Izin seemed puzzled by Jase's response. "I didn't say it was a good idea."

"We'll do it," I said. If all else failed, at least the planet's population would be saved. "Now I've got another job for you, Izin. I want you to run a simulation for me."

"A simulation, Captain?"

"I want to see how big a curveball we can throw, a spacetime curveball."

Izin and the others listened with rising anxiety as I outlined my plan.

* * * *

The flight deck's view screen filtered down the glow of the *Soberano's* engines as we came up behind her. Keeping to starboard of her engine blast, we glided up to and around the spherical bulge of her stern, bringing the long straight wall formed by her cargo holds into view. The number three starboard cargo door was open, revealing a dark rectangular cavity, although at that extreme angle, not what lay within. If the cargo hold housed a naval gun, we were safely out of its field of fire while we hugged the super transport's stern.

"That's not the same cargo door she fired from on Deadwood," Marie said.

"I'm taking no chances," I said, nudging us up and over the *Soberano*, giving the open cargo door a wide berth.

Once clear of her weapons, we glided above the vast hull towards the smaller elongated sphere at her bow, watching for any sign of the super transport rolling to bring her big guns to bear. She remained rock steady, considering us no threat. No doubt, the Mataron's had calculated at that speed, we couldn't escape the *Soberano*'s fate. Once we reached the bow section, I followed the gentle curve of her hull around to her starboard airlock.

"Their auto-docker isn't responding," Jase announced.

"They're just playing hard to get," I said, switching our docking system from partner to the emergency solo mode. The big screen reset to the view from our port airlock, looking straight across to the *Soberano*. Vertical and horizontal calibration scales appeared over the center of the big freighter's docking ring, guiding me towards a perfect alignment. Even though we were both moving through flat space at a small percentage of the speed of light, with our velocities matched we appeared to be floating motionless, side by side, making docking a simple procedure. We slid up against the *Soberano*, lightly kissed her hull and clamped onto her docking ring.

"She isn't locking onto us from her side," Jase warned.

"Our clamps will be enough." I cut our engines and activated the intercom. "Izin, send a crawler back along the *Soberano*'s hull. Find out what's in that open cargo hold."

"It'll take the crawler a few minutes to get back there," Izin replied.

"How's the drone coming along?"

"I'm removing the warhead now, Captain. I'll have the distress beacon installed by the time you get back."

The beacon would ensure that when the Tau Cetins came to investigate the destruction of Vintari II's smaller moon, they'd find the drone. Izin had calculated if we launched it ninety seconds before impact, its high acceleration would allow it to avoid colliding with the planet's atmosphere. The drone would be going too fast for any human ship to catch, but the TCs would have no trouble running it down. Once they took it apart, the Matarons would have a lot of explaining to do and mankind would be off the hook.

I threw a timer up onto the view screen, counting down from twenty four minutes, the time we had until both ships vaporized Vintari II's smaller moon. Izin needed four minutes to seal the Codex into the drone and then we'd need a minute to prep it for launch. Once the hypervelocity drone was away, I wanted to give it a full two minutes to clear the planet, just to be safe.

"Keep reading the timer out to me," I said. "I want to be back on board with seven minutes to spare."

"You got it," Jase said, glancing at the sandy colored world now beginning to fill the view screen.

"She's all yours," I said as I climbed out of my acceleration couch. "Spin her nice and easy."

We were still facing in the same direction as the *Soberano* because we'd had to keep accelerating until we docked, to stay matched to the larger ship. Now that we were locked together, the super transport was towing us. Jase now had to rotate the *Lining* one hundred and eighty degrees around her port docking ring to point our bow towards the *Soberano's* stern. Only then could he apply a trickle of thrust to pull the super transport around so its sixteen engines could nudge her sideways.

"It'll be the slowest maneuver I ever pulled," Jase said as he tapped his personal console, resetting it to helm control.

Marie followed me to the airlock. When I gave her a puzzled look, she said, "It'll be faster if we do this together."

"The Mataron SI has control of the *Soberano*," I said, not wanting to worry about her while I was searching for the Codex.

"I'll be careful," she said, tapping the twin needle guns holstered at her hips. "The *Soberano*'s a big ship and you don't even know where to look."

She was right. It would be faster with two of us. "OK, but this is a grab and run. No delays no matter what else we find over there."

"Hey, you know I'm a grab and run kind of girl," she said with a beguiling smile, reminding me she'd already successfully stolen the Codex out from under my nose.

We reached the locker compartment adjoining the airlock and quickly changed into our pressure-suits, strapping our guns on over the top.

"Out of all the ways I thought I'd die," Marie said, "crashing into a moon backwards wasn't on the list."

"It was number three on mine," I said, reaching for my transparent pressure helmet.

Marie put her hand on my helmet, stopping me from fitting it, then pulled my head down to hers and kissed me. "In case that's the last time."

"It won't be," I promised, then we secured our helmets and cycled through the airlock into the *Soberano*.

We emerged into a dimly lit metal corridor. "I'm reading atmosphere," I said, surprised the ship was still pressurized.

"Should we remove our helmets?"

"No." There were plenty of chemicals aboard a ship like the *Soberano* that the Mataron SI could use to produce toxic gas. "Assume the air is unbreathable."

"OK. Where to?"

The *Soberano* had one long passageway running the length of the bow section, dotted with ladders and companionways to other levels. The central corridor passed through airtight hatches into a pressurized walkway that ran through the cargo holds all the way back to the twin energy plants in her stern. I figured the vault would be in the forward section, where Vargis could keep his eye on it.

"If you find the vault first and it's locked, call Izin."

"A safe cracking tamph?" she said. "I have to get

one of those."

"You look for Vargis' stateroom, I'll search the bridge."

"Yes sir," she saluted. "And here I was thinking this was going to be fun."

"This is how I have fun," I said, knowing I was giving her orders, but she'd volunteered and time was running out.

We were almost halfway to the ship's spine when Jase's voice sounded in our earpieces. "Twenty minutes, Skipper."

"Understood. How's the spin going?"

"We're at thirty one degrees," Jase replied, "and the crawler's nearly halfway to the open cargo door."

When we reached the central passageway, we split up. Marie went aft towards crew country while I headed towards the bridge. Halfway there, I passed the ship's armory. Its heavy security door was open and several of the gun rack's cradles were empty.

"Marie," I said activating my suit communicator and looking back along the central corridor to where she was searching hatch to hatch. "There are rifles missing from the armory."

"I'll be careful," she said before stepping out of sight into a compartment.

I hurried forward to the bridge. It was spacious compared to the *Lining's* cramped flight deck, and was equipped with an immense view screen and lavish control consoles that would have made a navy survey ship's commander envious. The only light came from the crew consoles and the view screen which displayed the approaching planet and the luminous orb of the Vintari star behind it. In several places, small circles of hissing white static marked where weapon's fire had struck the screen, destroying fragile technology.

Vargis lay dead on the deck with a hole in his chest larger than my fist. The edges of the wound were charred black and the gun he wore was still in its shoulder holster. It was the first time I'd ever seen him carrying a weapon and the fact he wore it on the bridge indicated he knew there was danger aboard. Vargis might have been a Consortium lapdog, but he didn't strike me as the kind of man who'd die without getting at least one shot away – yet that was exactly what had happened.

Four other bridge officers were dead from similar wounds. They'd barely begun to decompose, which in the ship's sterile environment told me they'd been dead at least a week. Whatever had hit them had been so hot, it had vaporized bone and flesh in an instant, cauterizing the interior of the wound and limiting the amount of blood that had spilled onto the deck.

I activated my communicator. "Vargis and his bridge crew are dead."

"There are two more back here," Marie said. "I've never seen wounds like these before."

A female officer lay face down on the navigation station, shot precisely through the spine. The blast had continued across the bridge and struck the main screen where static now hissed. Beneath the drops of blood splattering her console, a collision alert was flashing. The ship should have been ringing with an alarm, but the siren had been disabled. A single bloody smudge marked where someone had disabled the alarm. Whoever had killed the crew had been here recently – after the autonav had become concerned about the ship's collision course with the planet.

A short distance from the navigator's body, another officer lay dead on the deck. A hole had been blasted through his shoulder and another between his eyes. His weapon, lying nearby, had been fired three times, although there was no sign he'd hit whoever had killed him. His wounds, like the navigator's, showed a precision comparable to the best EIS eye-hand modded sharpshooters.

The helm display indicated the autonav was off and the ship was being flown manually, no doubt by the

Mataron synthetic intelligence. Every ship system was on minimum power as all available energy was being fed to the engines. The ship's internal lighting was low, but if everyone was dead, why have any lighting or atmosphere at all?

"Captain," Izin's voice sounded from my earpiece. "My hull crawler has reached the open cargo hold. There's a small craft inside."

"What kind?"

"I don't recognize the hull geometry or the propulsion technology. It's sealed itself to the inside of the cargo hold. It may have cut into the ship."

If Izin didn't recognize the ship in the *Soberano's* cargo hold, it wasn't human, which could mean only one thing.

"Marie, get back to the ship!"

"I've found something!"

"It's too late. The Matarons are aboard. They killed the crew. Get out now!" I waited, but there was no response. "Marie, acknowledge." When she didn't reply, I said, "Jase, are you receiving her?"

He didn't respond either.

WARNING! NON-HUMAN CONTACT! flashed from my threading into my mind.

My sniffer picked up movement behind me. Without looking back, I dived sideways as a flash illuminated the bridge and a wave of heat passed my shoulder. My threaded sensors tried locking onto what was shooting at me, but I already knew it was a Mataron. Unlike the encounter in Sarat's penthouse, this snakehead was using his own weapons because he knew no energy signatures would survive the impact with Vintari II.

I stole a look over a crew console as a tall, slender form in a skin-tight black suit leapt agilely to the left. He had to stoop to prevent his triangular reptilian head striking the ceiling, then he swung his short barreled plasma rifle towards me and fired. I rolled behind a crew station as another flash threw sharp shadows across the bridge and a console exploded in sparks. Coming up on one knee, I fired twice, but the Mataron was moving so fast, my armor piercing slugs crashed harmlessly into the view screen, turning another section into white noise.

The Mataron leapt across the bridge, closing on me fast as we circled each other. Snakeheads were taller, faster and more agile than unmodded *Homo sapiens*, although they had weaknesses we didn't – none of which helped me fighting one of their best at close range in a p-suit. I fired a blind shot as I darted away while my threading finally figured out the contact was a snakehead, then confirmed it wasn't the same Mataron who'd nearly killed me on Icetop.

I knew his alien-tech was tracking me with precision. Fortunately he wasn't carrying the kind of dampening field Sarat had used. It allowed my DNA sniffer and thermal optics to keep me in the fight, revealing his movements when he was wasn't silhouetted by the view screen. We both used the bridge consoles for cover, knowing that to stand still for a moment would be fatal. I fired into the darkness several times at a dim thermal blur, never having time to properly aim. He did the same, narrowly missing with each shot as he continually underestimated my speed. If he'd been fighting an unmodded human, every shot would have been a kill. Thankfully, against my ultra-reflexed agility his timing was off, but he was learning fast.

The Mataron leapt in front of a damaged section of view screen, aiming ahead of me, trying to anticipate my moves, but I darted back the other way a moment before he fired. I sent another armor piercing slug his way through a console, striking the Mataron's leg with a static electric spark – not the crack of shattering bone I'd hoped for. He stumbled, then leapt away unhurt. I fired again rapidly, seeing my slugs flash harmlessly against his skin shield. The AP slugs were like hammer blows, knocking him off balance but doing no real damage. I held fire for a moment, lowering my aim. When the snakehead turned to fire I blasted the plasma rifle out of his hands.

I'd guessed right! He was shielded, but his gun wasn't!

The plasma rifle flashed as it hit the deck, then without hesitating, the Mataron charged, leaping as if to kick me but at the last moment, spinning in the air and whipping his thin flexible reptilian tail at my neck. I rolled away onto the deck as the tail cut the air with enough force to take my head off. The tail-whip would have killed a slower human, but my genetically engineered speed saved me again.

The Mataron landed gracefully and for a moment stood staring at me. I could no more read his expression than I could any non-human's, but I sensed he was wary, confused by my speed.

"We know who you are human!" He said in a deep, synthesized male voice. "E – I – S!"

So much for Lena's impenetrable security! "And you're just another ugly snakehead."

"I am Zatra e'Ktari and I am going to kill you," he said, drawing his quantum blade from the angled chest scabbard in his body armor, the twin of the weapon I'd seen in Sarat's penthouse. "It is a pity I'll not be able to keep your head as a trophy, but I was never here." He raised the Q-blade menacingly. "I will have to be satisfied with the memory of your death."

I fired my P-50 at the quantum weapon, but the armor piercing slug vaporized on contact without even causing the blade to quiver.

"This is not a weapon you can destroy."

"It was worth a try," I said backing away. "Why are you here, on board the *Soberano*? Taking a big risk aren't you?"

"The crew were going to destroy their own ship once they realized what was happening. We could not allow that."

I glanced at the corpses of Vargis and his dead officers with new found respect – and rising anger. Even someone like Vargis would rather sacrifice his life than risk mankind violating the Access Treaty. I remembered they'd been dead a week, and wondered why the Mataron was still aboard?

"The Tau Cetins will figure it out."

"They will find trace elements of two human ships and the ravings of a deluded, fanatic," he said, then leapt forward, sweeping his Q-blade at me.

I jumped back out of reach, putting a crew console between us.

"You are fast for a human," he said.

"You're slow for a snakehead."

"Many times I have killed simulated humans. None move like you."

"Your simulations underestimate us."

"I'll see that is corrected."

The Mataron charged again. When he was almost on me, rather than sweep the Q-blade, he lunged forward, trying to spear me. I took a fast step to the side, turned as the blade passed my chest and grabbed his black gloved hand. Even through his skin shield, I felt hard thin bones and strong sinewy muscle. He shifted his weight, trying to break out of my grip as his free hand lunged at my throat. I dodged, twisting the Mataron's knife arm, locking the joint, then slammed the barrel of my P-50 against his elbow and fired. The armor piercing slug struck his skin-shield, unable to penetrate, but still breaking his elbow joint.

He grunted and tried pulling away. I dropped my P-50 and twisted his wrist with both my hands, turned the quantum blade into his chest. The Q-blade flashed against the Mataron's skin-shield before slicing open a bloody tear in his armor. The tall reptilian staggered backwards, shocked. I slipped my foot behind his ankle, tripping him, then threw my weight on top, driving the deadly weapon into his lungs as we hit the deck. The Mataron grabbed my throat with his free hand, choking me as I forced the quantum blade down through his heavy spine into the deck plating.

The Mataron shuddered, but hung onto my throat, squeezing with all his failing strength. "We will never let you join," he wheezed, spitting blood, then his hand fell away from my throat and his body went limp.

I pried his fingers off the Q-blade and pulled it clear of his chest, finding not a drop of blood adhered to it. After briefly examining the ornate weapon, I switched it off and slid it into my belt.

My threading flashed another proximity alert into my mind. I scooped my P-50 off the floor and turned to fire as Izin appeared in the hatchway. He was holding his shredder pistol level in one hand and carrying a tool kit in the other. The small amphibian approached the Mataron curiously.

"An impressive species," Izin said. Considering Izin's kin were feared across the galaxy, that was quite a compliment. "I'm surprised you could defeat it, Captain."

"Thanks for the vote of confidence," I said, holstering my gun. "What are you doing here?"

"Captain Dulon has located the vault. As you hadn't responded to our communications for several minutes, I came to see what had happened to you." Izin glanced at the dead Mataron. "He must be carrying a signal jammer."

"How long have we got?"

"Sixteen minutes."

"We're cutting it close."

We hurried out of the bridge and ran down the corridor towards the crew's quarters. Even though Izin was only two thirds my height, he had no trouble keeping up. Tamphs could sprint short distances with amazing speed, but they tired quickly. Luckily for Izin, we didn't have far to go.

"Want me to slow down?" I asked.

"Why? Are your long human legs getting tired, Captain?"

If that was tamph defensiveness, Izin's vocalizer gave no hint of inflection. "Just checking."

We jogged past several open cabins glimpsing crewmen murdered in their bunks, then turned into a side corridor where a body lay slumped against a bulkhead. It was Jawbones. He had a charred plasma wound in his chest and a black market neutron rifle on his lap. The charge indicator showed he'd got one shot away before he'd died.

"I've heard of these weapons," Izin said, holstering his little shredder pistol and picking up the rifle, turning it over curiously. It had a slender beam emitter mounted above a cylindrical radiation chamber and was fitted with fore and aft hand grips. Flesh destroying irradiation weapons had been banned since the twenty-ninth century, yet a handful of companies still manufactured them in secret – anything to earn a few extra credits.

"Could it penetrate a Mataron skin-shield?" I asked.

"I don't know enough about their technology to say," Izin said, testing the feel of the short range weapon. Originally designed for close quarters combat in urban environments, it was ideal for enclosed ship corridors because it killed without damaging bulkheads or sensitive ship systems.

We hurried on past Jawbones' body and entered the large cabin where I'd first encountered Vargis back on Hades City. The same chair I'd been restrained in stood in front of his polished desk. At the far end of the room, Marie stood beside the two meter high painting of the ancient sea battle, the *Battle of the Albrolhos*. The painting was affixed to a hidden door which now stood partially open.

"Where is it?" I asked, rushing towards her.

She stood side on, facing the space behind the painting. For a moment I wondered why she didn't turn towards me, then I saw the tension in her face.

"Marie?" I said, stopping short of the painting.

Her eyes gave me a warning look, then the thick barrel of a Mataron plasma rifle appeared from behind the painting, aimed at her head.

"Drop your weapon." It was the same synthesized male voice the Mataron I'd killed on the bridge had used.

I aimed my P-50 at the painting. "Drop yours."

"Your weapon is ineffective against my shield, human, whereas mine is quite deadly. I will not ask again." He lifted the barrel until it touched Marie's forehead.

"Wait! Wait!" I yelled, placing my P-50 on the deck.

Marie gave me a furious look. "What are you doing?"

"I'm unarmed!" I yelled.

The painting and the hidden door it was attached to swung slowly open. A snakehead, the twin of the one I'd killed on the bridge, stood in front of a circular silver metal vault aiming his rifle one handed.

"He's going to kill us both!" she said angrily.

"He wants something, or you'd already be dead," I said, remembering Lena's warning that I had a weakness. She'd read me right. I couldn't let the snakehead kill Marie, even at the cost of the mission.

"Open the vault," the Mataron ordered.

I glanced towards where Izin had been standing, intending to ask him to get to work on the vault door, but he was gone. I'd heard about the instinctive ability of tamphs to camouflage themselves, but I'd never seen Izin do it. He'd vanished so fast, so silently, the Mataron had no idea there was even a tamph – an Intruder! – on the ship.

"What are you waiting for?" the Mataron demanded.

"This ship's about to be destroyed," I said. "Why do

you want it?"

"The vault will shield the Codex from the crash."

I looked past the snakehead to the armored door. Its silver surface was polished to a mirror sheen, giving it an impressively impregnable appearance.

"Why haven't you already opened it?"

"We couldn't find it."

"Why not?" Vargis had said it was shielded, but that shouldn't have stopped the Matarons.

"We lost contact with the Codex as soon as it was brought aboard. That could only happen if the vault was shielded by non-human technology."

If anyone had the resources to obtain alien masking technology, it was the Consortium. No wonder Vargis had been so confident he could move the Codex without it affecting his ship.

"So how'd you find it?"

"I didn't. She did."

I glanced at Marie, who shrugged. "I always was good at finding things that didn't belong to me."

The Mataron stepped away from the vault door, keeping his weapon aimed at Marie's head. He turned towards me, seeing the quantum blade stuck in my holster's belt. "Where did you get that?"

"What, this old thing?" I said, drawing the Q-blade. This Mataron's black body armor lacked a chest scabbard and was less ornate than that worn by Zatra e'Ktari.

The Mataron's hand dropped to his hip, touched a triangular surface, then he uttered several guttural sounds. When there was no response, he said, "Where is the Honored one?"

"You mean the snakehead I disemboweled on the bridge – with this?"

"You killed him? With his own weapon?"

"Drove it right through his spine."

"You lie!" The Mataron swung his plasma rifle towards me, aiming at my head. "The Black Sauria are sworn to let no brother's death go unavenged."

"Now you tell me!"

A blue flash came from behind me as a neutron beam streaked across the room, striking the Mataron's chest. He looked down surprised at the sparkling light flickering harmlessly against his skin shield, then I flicked on the Q-blade and threw it in a single motion with ultra-reflexed precision. The blade buried itself in the reptilian's angular head, stopping only when the hilt struck his translucent faceplate. The Mataron's knees buckled and he crumpled to the deck.

Marie looked down at the dead snakehead, surprised. "You throw knives?"

"You should see what I can do with laser cutters," I said as Izin appeared in the hatchway holding Jawbones' neutron rifle.

"In answer to your earlier question, Captain," Izin said, "the neutron beam is unable to penetrate Mataron skin-shield technology."

"But it sure makes a good distraction."

Izin placed the neutron rifle in his tool box and produced a rod like scanner which he attached to the vault door. His large blue-green eyes watched as the scanner's display quickly drew a schematic of the door's locking system. "It's an infinite probability combination locking system."

"Can you crack it?"

"If I developed an infinitized heuristic solution."

"How long will that take?"

"Seven months," Izin said, removing the scanner from the vault door.

"And we have how long?"

"Nine minutes," Izin said without looking at any time recording device. "We could leave the Codex in there and hope the Mataron was correct, that the vault will protect it."

"He was guessing." I said. "They're worried the Codex will survive and the TCs will find it."

Marie pulled the Q-blade out of the reptilian's skull. "Will this work?"

"Only one way to find out!" I said, taking it from her and plunging it into the vault. The Q-blade sliced effortless through the vault door, generating a fine particle mist as it severed the locking bolts.

Marie glanced down at the dead snakehead at her feet. "How come he doesn't have a knife?"

"He's just a grunt. He doesn't rate one."

"You know that just by looking at him?"

"It's the body armor. If he were an officer, it'd be fancier, and he'd be wearing one of these," I said, nodding towards the Q-blade.

The dead snakehead was Sworn, not Honored like the Mataron I'd killed on the bridge. The Q-blade was a ritual weapon awarded to Honored Assassins of the Black Sauria, a sinister organization part death cult, part secret service, part religious order. The Black Sauria was strictly hierarchical, governed by an inflexible code of obedience and deference that embodied the Mataron's obsession with feuding over even the most innocuous of slights. It was why blood feuds lasted generations and were rarely ever settled until one side or the other was exterminated, and why we could never placate them.

"You seem to know a great deal about Matarons, Captain," Izin observed. "About their ships, their soldiers, their weapons."

"Just enough to stay out of their way," I said as I pulled the Q-blade from the vault door. I deactivated it and returned it to my belt before pulling on the ponderous vault door. The circular armored slab slid silently open, revealing a small compartment. Sitting on a low table in the center of the vault was the Antaran Codex. I moved towards it, then remembered how aggressively it had tried to invade my threading. "Izin, you take it. " Without a word, the diminutive tamph retrieved the alien device while I picked up the Mataron plasma rifle and Izin's tool box. "Now let's get the hell out of here."

We ran back down the corridor towards the airlock as the sound of air whistling through the corridors began to grow.

Once we were outside the range of the Mataron's signal jammer, Jase's voice sounded in our earpieces. "Skipper, are you there?"

"I hear you."

"The Mataron ship in the *Soberano*'s hold just took off like a lightning bolt."

That's what the whistling was! They'd left the airtight hatches open so the hole they'd cut into the ship would decompress the *Soberano*.

"Have you got the *Soberano* turned?"

"Yeah, we're heading for the little moon, just like Izin planned," Jase said unhappily.

We climbed into the airlock, then the inner hatch irised shut, sealing us off from the growing howl of decompression in the corridor.

"Nice trick," Marie said, "Running and leaving us to get sucked into space."

"The Matarons left because we took the Codex out of the vault," Izin said. "Now they believe it will be destroyed, along with us."

"Good, that gives us a chance to surprise them," I said.

We cycled through into the *Lining*, then wary of the Codex's ability to take over the ship, Izin said, "There isn't time to load it into the drone, and I can't take it to engineering."

"Put it in the smuggler compartment. It's the most insulated part of the ship, but keep an eye on it." While Izin went to store the Codex, Marie and I ran to the flight deck. The view screen timer clicked below one hundred seconds as we climbed onto our couches. It was already too late to fire the Codex away in a drone, and even if we did, the Matarons would just grab it.

"I can't release the *Soberano*!" Jase said. "She

locked onto us when you were in the airlock, and won't let go."

The Mataron SI was now intent on dragging us – and the Codex – into Vintari II! Jase could hit the docking controls with a shock-hammer, but it would make no difference. The *Soberano* was never going to release us.

I glanced at the view screen again. The timer was down to eighty five seconds and the sandy orb of Vintari II and the small dark sphere of its moon were both rapidly swelling in size as we hurtled towards them.

"I have the helm!" I announced, taking piloting control. "Retract every second optical sensor and all the non-visuals."

While Jase buttoned up our sensors, I angled the vector nozzles on both engines hard to port, directing our thrust sideways at the *Soberano*, trying to blast our way free. All the non visual readouts vanished from the screen and the image quality dropped noticeably as half our optical sensors retracted.

"Ah, Skipper," Jase said anxiously, pointing to the view screen. "Why is the *Soberano* doing that?"

I looked up to see eight of the super transport's large square cargo doors opening in front of us. A large silver naval gun, mounted on a circular swivel mount, began sliding out of the nearest of *Soberano*'s holds.

"The SI's not going to let us leave with the Codex," I said, activating the intercom. "Izin, is the burster ready?"

The heavy naval gun locked into place. It was almost as big as the *Silver Lining* and right in front of us. Behind it, seven more guns identical to the first were extending towards their firing positions. If they'd been on a navy ship, they'd have been inside armored turrets, but on the *Soberano*, their protection was normally limited to the ship's shield.

"I haven't test fired it, Captain, or calibrated the targeting –"

"Forget targeting. Is it ready to fire?"

"Yes Captain."

I nodded to Jase. "Charge it up, and hang on!"

Jase switched his console to weapons and activated the proton burst cannon as the *Lining's* collision alert sounded, warning Vintari II's moon was now dangerously close. The timer ticked down to forty seconds as I fed more power to the engines. The *Silver Lining* shuddered, but couldn't break free as the big naval gun locked in place.

I kept sliding my finger up the throttle control, pushing through ten percent, but our mated docking rings remained stubbornly locked together. Fifty meters from our bow, the big silver gun began to swivel slowly towards us, the same weapon that had destroyed the BBI base's processing center with one shot.

"Can we survive a hit from that gun?" Marie asked.

"Don't worry, you won't feel a thing," I said, knowing with our shield down, at point blank range and with us a sitting duck locked to the side of *Soberano*, one shot would vaporize everything inside the *Silver Lining's* paintwork, except for the Codex!

"That makes me feel so much better!" Marie said.

I pushed engine power to twelve percent, causing the *Lining* to shudder like crazy, but she couldn't tear free. "I thought we could only apply three percent!"

"For twenty minutes!" Jase said. "Not five seconds!"

I glanced at the screen. The big gun was almost pointed towards us. "Jase, fire!"

He tried, but nothing happened. "It's not charged yet!"

I dumped more power into the engines, wondering if they would tear the hull apart before the docking rings shattered. Status indicators began flashing red on my console and the main screen, warning of an impending catastrophic hull failure.

"You're going to tear the side out of her!" Jase

declared.

"Better we lose half the hull than the whole ship!" I said, pushing the engines past fourteen percent. On the big screen, the body of the nearest naval gun began to glow.

"It's charging!" Marie said.

I wanted to push the engines to full power, but that would have destroyed the ship. Restraining myself, I crept the energy feed to fifteen percent. A piercing metallic shriek reverberated through the ship as the hull began to tear apart under the strain. There were so many warning indicators flashing, I couldn't tell if the engines were about to fly out their housings or the docking ring was failing.

Jase's weapons console flashed a green ready indicator as the cannon reached full power. "About time!" He yelled, slamming his palm onto the firing control.

A ball of brilliant yellow light erupted from the top of our wrap around screen and streaked towards the nearest naval gun. For a moment, a brilliant white flash filled the flight deck, then a shower of metal burst from the where the gun had been and began raining back along the *Soberano's* hull towards the other big guns as the super transport accelerated through the debris.

"Damn!" I said, surprised at the power of the burster cannon's blast.

The *Lining* suddenly tore free, almost throwing us off our acceleration couches. With our engine thrust directed hard to port, we spun uncontrollably away from the *Soberano*, challenging our internal inertial field to offset a flat spin it had never been designed for. A spray of hull plates, airlock doors and docking rings flew out from both ships, some after us, most falling back towards the naval guns arrayed along the *Soberano*'s hull as she continued picking up speed. The second gun exploded as metal fragments crashed into it while the six remaining guns all swiveled after us. First one fired, then another, but we were too close, spinning too fast and the big gun's mounts moved too slowly. Their searing blasts flashed around us, scorching our unshielded hull but missing us as we spun uncontrollably towards the *Soberano's* stern.

I angled the engine's vector nozzles against our spin, fighting to get the *Lining* back under control as the *Soberano's* mountainous stern came racing towards us. The next naval gun in line exploded as the thickening swarm of shrapnel tore it apart, then I fired our bow thrusters, pushing us away, narrowly avoiding a collision with the super transport's stern. For a moment, her hull plating filled our screen, then her sixteen enormous engines blazed like blue stars in front of us as the super transport pulled quickly away from us. Beyond the bulge of her stern, now blocking her gun's firing arc, a ripple of explosions shot out into space as the debris cloud destroyed one exposed gun after another.

I was dizzy and disoriented and the autonav was warning me we were far outside Izin's curveball simulation, but empty black space now lay dead ahead and that was all I needed to know. I killed the bow thrusters and the engines as our spin died.

"Skipper, we're forty degrees off!" Jase yelled as the tiny moon hurtled towards us. We were so close now, the port side of the view screen was filled with craters and dark jagged ridges.

"Too late!"

Every parameter was off, but one – the only one that counted – Vintari II and its moon weren't in front of us! I triggered Izin's curveball maneuver as the moon's surface raced up towards us. A single large crater swallowed the view screen and us with it, then the screen turned to static – except for the impact timer – as the *Lining's* bubble fried half our optics.

It was a low power bubble, barely half the speed of light, but stable. If I'd tried the same maneuver at a thousand times the speed of light, the bubble would have collapsed and torn the ship apart. After just a few seconds, the sublight bubble dropped and we were back hurtling through flat space on our original course.

"Get the sensors out!" I yelled.

Jase quickly deployed our eyes and ears, bringing the view screen back to life. It was a little grainier than usual now that half the optics had melted, but at least we could see where we were.

Vintari II was to starboard and from our relative motion, I realized we were heading backwards across the planet's orbit. A mini nova of brilliant white was expanding beside the planet where its small moon had been obliterated by the *Soberano*. As we raced away, the planet slowly eclipsed the expanding fireball behind it while molten droplets showered the planet's upper atmosphere in a rain of fire. The fine particles quickly burned away, illuminating the planet's dark side sky with an eerie orange light that was already triggering religious awe from the planet's primitive inhabitants. The night the gods turned the sky orange and one of the two mythical sky travelers disappeared would mark a global turning point in their bronze age civilization that would influence their belief systems for thousands of years to come.

Marie gave me a wry smile, relieved we'd avoided the planet. "Only you would blind micro bubble inside a crater!" She leaned forward and kissed me on the cheek. "I knew you'd think of something."

I turned the *Lining's* bow in the direction our flat space momentum was carrying us, watching Vintari II and its mini nova roll across the view screen to the port side. The dazzling golden orb of the Vintari star appeared on the starboard side and followed the planet across the view screen until it was in the center of the screen, dead ahead of us.

"Don't thank me yet!" I didn't need the autonav to plot this course. Izin's simulation had planned to take us far enough away to clear the star, but we'd been way off course when I'd bubbled. "We need to blink again, right now! Jase, pull the sensors and let's get out of here!"

I instructed the autonav to plot our next sublight micro-bubble, one that would take us safely away from the star, then nosed the *Lining* around so we were facing out into empty space. When the surviving sensors were safely stowed inside the hull, I gave the autonav control. The sixty distorters started gently curving spacetime around us, then inexplicably, they all lost power simultaneously.

"That's impossible!" Jase exclaimed when he saw the energy readings fall to zero.

"Oh ho," I said warily as I reset the autonav to try again. For a second time, the distorters began to charge, then just before they could form a bubble, they were drained of power again.

"What is it?" Marie asked.

"It's no system failure!" I said, nodding to Jase to push the sensors back out.

When the view screen came to life, the Vintari star filled one side of the screen, and empty space the rest.

Jase took one look at his display and scowled. "They're behind us!" He sent the optical feed from our stern sensors to the view screen, revealing the Mataron ship floating off our port quarter.

"They're jamming us," I said, "letting the star do their dirty work for them. There's no weapons for the TCs to detect, just our own energy signature!"

"How long have we got?" Marie asked.

I glanced at the autonav. "We'll hit the chromosphere in forty minutes."

"They caught us fast!" Jase said, remembering the Mataron ship had been stationary high above the ecliptic plane only minutes ago. Now they were perfectly matched with us.

"Captain," Izin's voice sounded from the intercom. "Our processing core was just scanned. The ghost numbers are gone."

This time, the *Lining's* safety system hadn't detected their attack. Had they learnt how to sneak past our radiation sensors since they'd loaded the SI into us over Deadwood, or was this something different?

"Lock a comm beam on them." When Jase opened the channel, I said, "Mataron vessel, release my ship."

The flight deck's comm system came to life almost immediately. "Surrender the Codex and I will let you leave."

I was tempted to say 'what Codex', but the Earth-tech jamming field we had hiding the *Lining's* smuggler compartment would be no obstacle for them. For a moment, I wondered if our new burster could hurt them, then shelved the idea. Any weapon we had would be ineffective against their ship, while firing first would give them the right to return fire.

I nodded for Jase to close the channel. "Izin, have you removed the warhead from our drone?"

"Sirius!" Marie exclaimed, "You can't give it to them!"

We certainly couldn't fight a Mataron armored cruiser and if I refused to give them the Codex, they'd simply ride us down until the star burned us to a cinder. "They sure as hell aren't going to let us keep it!"

"I have yet to remove the payload," Izin said.

"Get started. I'll meet you there," I said, motioning for Marie to follow me.

When we reached the smuggler compartment hidden amidships, I removed the hatch cover, then wary of the SI lurking inside the Codex, turned to Marie. "Can you remove it?"

She gave me a confused look.

"It's a long story and we don't have time."

Marie shrugged, then retrieved the Codex and offered it to me.

"No." I backed away, refusing to touch it. "This way," I said, leading her to the cramped bow compartment housing the drone launcher. Izin had removed the anti-ship drone's nose plate and was releasing the restraints holding the penetrator warhead in place. I motioned to the deck. "Put it there, please."

"Please?" she said surprised, then placed the Codex on the deck while my mind raced.

The Matarons were cleaning up, removing any trace of their involvement. The *Soberano* was gone and so was the synthetic agent that had taken control of her. Now they'd wiped our processing core, eliminating Izin's work on the ghost numbers. All they wanted was the Codex, which told me they didn't realize how easily Izin had reverse engineered their simulated agent. They must have thought our processing core had cracked it, so either they didn't understand what a tamph was capable of, or they really didn't know he was aboard. The trouble was, it didn't matter what Izin knew, no one would ever believe a tamph – especially not the Tau Cetins.

The Matarons also hadn't demanded me as prisoner, proving they didn't know I still carried the raw ghost numbers in my bionetic memory. Even so, a fragment wasn't enough. I needed a full copy of their synthetic agent for the Tau Cetins to take apart. That would get mankind off the hook and might well end the Mataron Supremacy as an interstellar civilization.

"This is a mistake," Marie said, thinking this was about handing over the Codex. "What's to stop them blasting us to pieces as soon as you give it to them?"

"Fear of the Tau Cetins," I said, turning to her and holding her arms. "There's a woman called Lena Voss in Hades City. If something happens to me, I want you to deliver my body to her." Lena's people could tap my threading's bionetic memory and extract everything recorded there.

"What are you talking about?" Marie demanded, shocked.

"Alien technology. It's a bitch! Now promise me. You'll make sure I'm delivered to Lena if I can't make it myself."

"Now you're scaring me, Sirius!"

"Promise me!" It was no longer a request, but an order, the only real order I'd ever given her – ever would give her.

"I . . . OK," she said, sensing a change in me she'd never seen before. "I promise."

"You might cheat me every chance you get, but I trust you more than anyone I've ever known," I said, then took her in my arms and kissed her – a goodbye kiss.

When I pulled back, there was fear on her face. "Sirius, what's going on?"

"I'd like to tell you, but we're out of time."

I turned and knelt beside the Codex. "You know what to do, Izin. Load it, fire it, then save the ship. Save yourselves."

"Yes, Captain," Izin said as he lifted the meter long penetrator out of the drone.

DISABLE AUTO-PURGE, I thought, ensuring my threading would not delete my bionetic memory, even if my life signs failed. I rubbed my hands together slowly, preparing myself. "All right, let's see what you're made of," I whispered, then placed my palms on the Codex.

An alien presence immediately surged through the bionetic threads in my hands. It tingled at first, then the dominating clone consciousness entered the biological threads woven through my bone structure. It explored every organic filament, every nerve junction, every memory sequence, searching for an anchor. Behind it came the genuine touch of the Antaran Codex itself, automatically reaching out to my biological network, unaware of the monster using it as a way to strike down its enemy.

The benign aspect of the Codex measured my capacity, determined my fit and allowed the data to flow. The sheer magnitude of it distracted me from the beast prowling through my body, searching for a home. In an instant, eons of exploration – the collective work of countless civilizations who'd collaborated on mapping entire galaxies – was visible to me. Planets, stars, nebulas, all manner of celestial objects and the invisible dark matter drifting among them, all flashed through my mind. Woven through this vast cosmic tapestry were the precise, constantly changing pathways used by billions of ships across millions of years to traverse dozens of galaxies. It was far more than I could ever hope to recall, instantly translated into the language I understood by the genius of the Antaran Codex.

It happened so fast, for a moment I forgot the beast within, then it reared its head as it fought to take control of a system it had never seen before and did not understand. It found itself, not the master of the kind of complex electromechanical device it had been designed for, but trapped in a bioelectric creation of unexpected simplicity. Try as it might, it could find no way to imprint itself into a biologically based memory. Finally, it swarmed towards what it perceived to be the central processing unit, hoping to rewrite the base logic of what was to it, a strangely alien system.

Desperate to survive, the synthetic intelligence revealed itself as the disembodied reflection of Hazrik a'Gitor – his life, his character, his knowledge. It thought the way he did, it plotted and schemed as he did. It was as ruthless as he was. Suddenly I knew him as well as myself: Hazrik a'Gitor, Exalted Blademaster of the Black Sauria, holder of the highest and rarest rank and a force within the shadowy world of Mataron politics. As his synthetic consciousness began to overwhelm me, I saw the universe through his eyes, through Mataron eyes.

For an instant, I was Mataron!

I realized how afraid they were! Of all the others. Of us!

My head throbbed as the essence of the Mataron master assassin tried to write itself over my identity. I was sweating, shaking, crying in agony as it clawed its way into my mind.

"Sirius, what is it?" Marie yelled as her hands tore at my arms. "Izin help me," she screamed.

I knew I had to let go of the Codex, but I couldn't break free. Hazrik a'Gitor wouldn't release me!

The Mataron synthetic intelligence moved to its last strategy, to force a complete system shutdown and reinitialize its new conquest.

I screamed as lightning bolts of pain exploded inside my head, then a heavy metallic object crashed against my skull.

* * * *

I awoke, blinking spots from my eyes. Marie knelt over me with a concerned look. A blood splattered molecular spanner lay beside her.

"You hit me?" I slurred, touching my forehead, finding a small pressure pad in place over the wound.

"Only in the head," Marie said sweetly, "where it'd do no damage."

"Can you turn off that siren," I said, "Or is that just the ringing in my ears?"

Marie smiled and stroked my hair gently. "You know what they say, Sirius – love hurts."

"It was the only way to get you away from the Codex," Izin explained. "The effect it has on you is most surprising, considering the rest of us are immune to its influence. Why is that, Captain?"

Izin was too smart for his own good, always asking questions I couldn't answer. "Maybe it knows I'm the captain, and wants to control the ship through me."

Izin blinked slowly, but said nothing. I'm sure he didn't believe me, but he couldn't prove it wasn't true.

I took a deep breath, trying to calm the throbbing inside my head, and searched for any trace of the Mataron synthetic intelligence. It had vanished, but the memory of Hazrik a'Gitor remained in my mind, my real mind, not my bionetic data store. Once the connection with the Codex had been severed, the SI had lost contact with its progenitor. Having found no way to embed itself into my biological system, it had ceased to exist.

"Where's the Codex?" I asked.

Izin pointed at the fully re-assembled drone. "In there. As we are approaching the Vintari star, now would be a good time to launch it."

"How long was I out for?" I said sitting up warily.

"Not long," Marie said.

"The battle shield's up," Izin said, activating the intercom. "Jase, what's our shield's status?"

"Bleeding star heat like crazy. It's starting to saturate. How's the Skipper?"

"He's alive and conscious," Izin said. "His head is remarkably durable for a human."

"And the Matarons?" I asked.

"Still on our tail," Jase said, "riding us all the way down."

I climbed to my feet unsteadily, giving Marie a pained look. "Did you have to hit me so hard?"

"You can thank me for saving your life later," Marie said.

"I'll thank you now, in case we're all dead later."

"You're really going to give them the Codex?" she asked.

"I'm going to see how badly they want it." I gave her a mischievous grin. "Izin, keep the shield up, no matter what."

"Very well, Captain."

While Izin went to engineering to tweak the ship's energy supply, Marie and I hurried to the flight deck.

Jase glanced at the patch on my head curiously as I climbed onto my acceleration couch. "The shield's at a hundred and forty percent. It's red lining across the board."

Shield regeneration, stability and heat dissipation were all failing simultaneously, something I'd never seen before. If we didn't put some distance between us and Vintari soon, we'd be cooked.

The star's boiling orange orb filled one side of the screen, smeared by the red glow of our rapidly suffocating shield. In the center of the screen was black space, while the other side was filled with the Mataron armored cruiser, now encased in a soft glowing egg-shaped field. Clearly, they were having an easier time of it than we were.

Jase followed my eyes to the screen. "Our thermal sensor has their shield as the coldest thing out there."

"Figures," I said, taking helm control, turning the *Lining* towards the star.

"I had us angled away," Jase said, "so we could get out of here fast, if they let us go."

"Change of plan." I fed power to the engines, accelerating the *Silver Lining* towards the star.

Jase eyes widened. "Are you feeling all right, Skipper?"

"Ten G's should do it."

"Do what?"

Marie leaned forward. "Sirius, maybe you should let Jase pilot the ship, until you're feeling better."

"I feel fine! I'm just sick of those God damned snakeheads playing games with me!"

"Diving us into a star isn't going to make any difference to the Matarons," Marie said.

"It might!" I said as a now familiar synthesized voice blared from the comm system.

"Why are you accelerating towards the star?" the Mataron Commander demanded. "Give us the Codex and we will release your ship."

I nodded to Jase to open the channel. "If I do that, I've got nothing for the Tau Cetins. On the other hand, if I crash into that star, they'll retrieve the Codex and show it to *all* their friends." Now that I knew how Matarons thought, I knew how to spook them. Their extreme xenophobia was their weakness.

"You are throwing your lives away for nothing. Not even the Tau Cetins could recover the Codex from the surface of a star."

"I know different!" Thanks to Hazrik a'Gitor's memories, I now knew the Matarons were completely baffled by Tau Cetin technology, giving me a perfect opportunity to lie through my teeth.

"What do you know?"

"I know once the Tau Cetins retrieve the Codex, you're going to have to explain to the Forum, to *thousands* of other species, why you tried to exterminate a bronze age people because you don't like humans. And from what I know of the Forum, you don't have many friends." I motioned for Jase to cut communications.

"Skipper, that's a terrible plan!" Jase said.

"Can the Tau Cetins really do that?" Marie asked incredulously.

I shrugged. "Who the hell knows what they can do. The Matarons sure don't and that's all that matters."

"They're hailing us again," Jase said.

I relaxed into my acceleration couch, ignoring their hail, studying the plating in the ceiling absently. "We really need to get the atmo scrubbers replaced. Remind me next time we're in Hades City."

"Are you going to answer them?" Marie asked anxiously as the star loomed before us.

"Yeah, but not the way they want," I said, switching my console to weapons. I winked at Jase, then opened the outer doors and fired the drone at the star. A point of brilliant white light accelerated away from the ship at over two hundred gravities. The drone's shielding, designed to withstand short range defensive fire as it approached its target, would get closer to the surface of the star than the *Lining* ever could. "OK, let's hear what the snakeheads have to say now."

The flight deck's comm system erupted with the Mataron Commander's synthesized voice. "What have you done, human?"

"If you want the Codex, go get it. It's got a homing beacon on it to make it easy to find. Easy for you, easier for the Tau Cetins. I'm done talking." I motioned to Jase to terminate the link, then spun the *Lining* to face away from the star. The big Mataron cruiser rolled out from behind us and dived after the drone.

Jase and Marie both gave me astonished looks.

"Will they catch it?" Jase asked.

"Who cares! I just hope for their sake that fancy ass shield can handle the heat down there." The spacetime distorters began charging, indicating the Matarons had stopped jamming us. "Now let's get the hell out of here while we can still fly!"

I caught one last glimpse of the Mataron ship streaking down through the chromosphere's superheated orange plasma clouds then our screen went blank.

"Punch it," Jase said, confirming our surviving sensors were all safely tucked away.

I ordered the autonav to execute another micro-bubble, then for several seconds, we crawled away from the star at sublight velocity. When the bubble dropped and we could see again, we found Vintari no longer lay ahead of us, but floated like a great seething wall of gas to port.

"Any sign of the snakeheads?" I asked.

"No," Jase replied, studying his sensors. "The star's masking them."

"You know," Marie said, leaning forward, "technically, they're only distantly related to snakes."

"Yeah, but snakehead says it all."

I rolled the ship and began decelerating. We might have got away with a couple of sublight blinks, but we couldn't cruise safely until Izin's hull crawlers repaired some of the damage we'd taken breaking away from the *Soberano*. While Izin patched the hull, we'd kill our flat space velocity so there'd be no surprises when we unbubbled next time.

I rubbed my throbbing head, realizing I was tired and hungry. "So, what's for lunch?"

* * * *

Two hours later we were all in engineering watching one of Izin's crawlers tip toeing around the ragged hole in the hull where the port side airlock had once been. Almost ten percent of the *Lining's* pressurized interior volume was now exposed to vacuum, although the flight critical sections were undamaged.

"Lucky those blinks didn't tear us apart!" Jase said.

"We didn't bubble long enough, or travel anywhere near fast enough, for the quantum forces to build up," Izin said. "A catastrophic failure would have required several seconds of superluminal flight."

"How long before we can get out of here?" I asked.

"It will take several days to install replacements for the two distorters we lost near the airlock and –" Izin suddenly froze.

We watched him for a few seconds before I stepped toward him and looked curiously into his unblinking eyes. "Izin, are you OK?"

"The ship's engines have stopped." He motioned meaningfully to the biosonar lobe bulging from his forehead. It gave him a sensitivity to the ship's vibration *Homo sapiens* could never fully comprehend.

I glanced at the energy and propulsion displays. They indicated everything was functioning normally. If there'd been a mechanical failure, a warning alarm would have sounded. "Looks OK to me."

"I assure you, Captain, we are no longer decelerating." Izin glanced at the other data displays. "In fact, we're in a stable orbit."

I didn't doubt his judgment, but it should have been fifteen hours before we were slow enough to enter any kind of orbit.

"Around what?" Marie asked.

Izin listened for a moment longer, studying screens filled with engineering numbers. "Ambient spacetime curvature indicates a planet, and that could only be possible if we were no longer in control of the ship."

"It's the Matarons!" Marie exclaimed. "They've come back."

While Izin began wading through engineering diagnostics, we ran to the flight deck. I expected to see the Mataron cruiser floating alongside us, preparing to exact retribution for my stunt with the drone, but when we entered the flight deck the view screen was filled with the image of long, sleek silver dart. Its glistening hull reflected starlight with mirror-like efficiency and a ghost-like shimmer enveloped it from bow to stern.

"That's not Mataron!" Jase said as we climbed into our acceleration couches, "Is it?"

"No, it isn't," I said, activating the intercom. "Izin, forget your diagnostics. You won't find anything."

"I agree, Captain," Izin replied. "None of our monitoring systems are giving correct readings."

"There's nothing wrong with the ship," I said, gazing at the view screen. To my knowledge, the EIS had exactly four images of such ships. All had been taken by the Earth Ambassador who'd been transported halfway across the galaxy in one about four hundred and fifty years ago to the Forum meeting that had ratified ending the Embargo.

"You know what it is?" Marie asked.

"It's a Tau Ceti Arbiter." Few humans had ever seen such ships because when the Tau Cetins came to Earth, they did so in small, deliberately unimposing diplomatic craft so as not to unsettle us. "It's the most powerful warship in this part of the galaxy." One like it had stopped the entire Mataron Fleet from destroying Earth two thousand years ago without firing a shot.

"They sure got here fast!" Jase said.

Somehow, the Tau Cetins had discovered one of Vintari II's moons had been destroyed and sent an

Arbiter to investigate in just a few hours. The odds of such a ship being near the this system were small, which meant it had come a long way, very fast.

Vintari II was visible below the Arbiter. Its upper atmosphere glowed with orange light as vaporized rock from the destroyed moon continued to burn up in its atmosphere. Dirty gray clouds were forming close to the surface and beginning to spread across the planet.

"I'm getting nothing from the Arbiter," Jase said as he tried to detect energy readings from the Tau Ceti ship, "but there's a big reading behind us. Guess who!"

He reoriented the optical feed to reveal the Mataron cruiser floating ten clicks away. Its hull was scored black as if a giant plasma torch had blasted it. The edges of the ridges running along its hull from bow to stern had melted and its weapon blisters now looked like burnt out craters laced with melted metal.

"They don't look so good," I said with some satisfaction. Clearly, their shield wasn't quite as resistant to star heat as it at first appeared.

"I wonder if they got the Codex back?" Marie said.

The image of the Mataron ship vanished as the Tau Cetins took control of our view screen. A pale skinned, vaguely humanoid face appeared. The Tau Cetin's eyes were green, horizontal almonds set lower than a human's on a face half again as wide. A shallow central ridge of a nose divided the face above a small mouth and a weak, slightly pointed chin. The TC had no hair of any kind, although his skin was slightly dappled, a natural camouflage inherited from the shadowy forests his species had evolved in hundreds of millions of years ago. He wore a dark green jacket that lacked a collar and was decorated with vertical silver insignia running down the center of his chest. Tau Cetins were bipedal and almost as tall as humans, although they weren't mammals. Earth xenobiologists classified them as *oviparous ratites*, a fancy way of calling them large flightless, egg laying birds, but such analogies scarcely made sense for such an advanced species.

The Tau Cetin's tiny mouth made small, rapid movements, which came through into the flight deck perfectly translated. "I am Siyarn. I speak for the Forum to preserve order."

My diplomatic training was limited, but I knew that was a formal introduction telling me he was an Observer, responsible for maintaining the rule of law throughout the Galaxy. That made him the Big Cheese in the Orion Arm.

"My name is Sirius Kade. I'm captain of this ship."

I could have claimed to be an Earth Ambassador, knowing the EIS would confirm it later, but that would have made my actions authorized acts, increasing any penalty against Earth. If Siyarn's judgment went against us, I'd already decided to declare myself a renegade, hoping to reduce whatever punitive measures were to be imposed against mankind.

"The Mataron Commander claims your entry into this restricted system is a violation of the Access Treaty."

"About that," I said. "We can explain-"

"As the authorized Observer for this Protectorate, I am required to conduct an investigation. If I find you have committed a treaty violation, because your species has only probationary status, a Forum Inquisitorial will be conducted at which time your explanation will be heard."

"An inquisitorial? Where would that be?"

"The next Forum Session will be held at Anrak Orn in ten days."

I was afraid of that. I'd never heard of Anrak Orn. "And where is that?"

"Sixty one thousand light years from here."

"That's kind of a problem for us. It would take," I did a quick calculation in my head, "forty five years for us to get there." That's if I knew where it was!

"If an Inquisitorial is convened, we will transport all

those required to provide evidence to the Session."

The image of the Tau Ceti Observer was replaced by our own sensor feed of the damaged Mataron cruiser.

"Those lying freaks over there are framing us." Jase declared. "We should lodge a complaint. We can do that, right?"

"Yeah." I pointed to the screen. "With him. He's the guy."

"Oh," Jase said, deflated.

I reoriented the view screen so the TC Arbiter and the Mataron armored cruiser were both visible above Vintari II. The planet was now suffering the most extreme upper atmosphere event it had experienced in several billion years, although fortunately there was no impact on the surface.

"We are in a restricted system," Marie said ominously. "Technically, we broke the rules."

A stream of tiny brilliant red points of light emerged from the Arbiter and streaked out across the Vintari System. Some dropped towards the planet, others found the trajectory the *Silver Lining* had followed, some moved off into the more remote corners of the system while a few passed outside the Vintari System altogether.

"I guess we're going to find out how advanced the TCs really are," I said. I'd never seen their technology before, but they were obviously piecing together what had happened. Several of the TC snoopers skimmed the Mataron ship's hull while a couple gave us the once over.

"If they decide we screwed up," Jase said, "Will they shut us down, like before?"

"That's the Mataron plan," I said.

"But we saved the damned planet!" Jase exploded.

"And destroyed its moon." Marie added soberly. "And probably scared two hundred and eighty million people half to death!"

Presently, the red points of light came streaming

back to the Arbiter.

"Now what are they doing?" Jase demanded.

I tapped my console impatiently. "Working out who's guilty."

Marie leaned forward. "They're supposed to be fair."

"They don't do favors," I said, "and they don't have much evidence to go on. The Matarons saw to that."

Siyarn appeared on the left side of our view screen and an image of the Mataron Commander appeared on the right. The Mataron seemed identical to the two snake heads we'd encountered on the *Soberano*. He wore an ornate black uniform with a chest scabbard containing a Q-blade and a thin black circlet around the top of his head marking him as a high ranking member of the Black Sauria.

"I demand you execute the Violation Provisions!" The Mataron Commander declared. "The law is clear!"

"Indeed it is," Siyarn agreed, "however there are discrepancies between our analysis and your explanation."

My hopes began to rise.

"What discrepancies? A human ship deliberately destroyed one of the moons of Vintari II, affecting the primitives on the planet. It is a clear violation of the rights of the Vintari II civilization. Under the First Principle, the humans must be held responsible."

"They will be judged responsible for their actions," Siyarn agreed. "As will you."

"Me?" The Mataron Commander baulked. "There is nothing preventing us from being here."

"That is true."

"We are conducting long range, non invasive cultural studies of the primitives on Vintari II, as is our right."

"Does the Mataron Supremacy typically conduct these cultural studies from within the photosphere of a star?" Siyarn asked.

Jase burst out laughing, then I silenced him with a look.

"We had engine trouble," the Mataron said.

"Is that why your ship remained inactive while the two human ships approached the planet?"

"We didn't know they were here. Our sensors were affected by the star's plasma wind."

"Your level of technology is resistant to such interference. Even if your sensors were disrupted, we have detected the presence of a small Mataron craft interacting with the human ships. Why did you send such a craft?"

"We ordered the humans to withdraw. They ignored us!"

"How did you know to issue such an instruction, when your malfunctioning sensors could not detect the human ships?"

"We didn't know what we were detecting. It was only after our reconnaissance ship identified them that we ordered them to withdraw."

Siyarn listened impassively. Like all aliens, if he had facial expressions, I couldn't read them. "Once you identified the two human ships, you still did not act to protect Vintari II."

"We tried, but the humans killed two of my crew! They are murderers and fanatics. We detected their transmissions. Listen to them yourself. They prove the human intentions."

"We detected the transmissions, however, irregularities in the signal indicate a synthetic rather than a biological source."

The Mataron ignored Siyarn's observation. "The very fact the humans are here proves their guilt!"

"That is one interpretation."

"The human ships attacked Vintari II! There is no other interpretation."

"There is the Ninth Principle."

"That does not apply!"

"It applies!" I said, daring to interrupt for the first time.

"Do not listen to that murderer!" The Mataron Commander demanded.

Siyarn paused a moment, perhaps receiving advice or data. "The human ship known as the *Silver Lining* may have entered this system to preserve life. The Preservation Principle always permits an action to save life, irrespective of other Treaty restrictions – even for probationary signatories."

"That is not what happened!"

"Yes it is!" I said. "We tried to save the planet from them!"

The Mataron gestured emphatically with his hands, but no sound came through.

"What's happening?" Marie whispered.

"Siyarn just pulled the plug on the snakeheads," I said.

When the Mataron stopped talking, Siyarn said, "I find discrepancies between the physical evidence we have gathered and the testimony offered by the Mataron Supremacy. While I reserve my right to Summation for a later date, all parties should understand that if we proceed to an Inquisitorial Session, the evidence I would present to the Forum will be conclusive."

He knows! He wouldn't say what he had, but he'd figured it out! I wanted to leap out of my couch and demand a hearing, but the risks of the decision still going against us made me hesitate.

The Mataron Commander stiffened, sensing a veiled threat, but said nothing.

"Our preliminary analysis indicates," Siyarn continued, "the humans of Earth would be justified in invoking the Preservation Principle, nullifying other Access Treaty conditions which may have been technically violated. Does the Mataron Supremacy wish to challenge my initial findings and have me present a Summation to the Forum Session on Anrak Orn?"

The Mataron hesitated. He had no idea what physical evidence the Tau Cetins had found. Could it possibly implicate the Matarons in a plot to destroy a helpless bronze age civilization?

"I request that the Tau Ceti evidence be presented at Anrak Orn," I cut in, "along with additional evidence in my possession."

"He cannot make such a request!" The reptillian Commander snapped. "Humans have no standing in the Forum."

"That is true, for now," Siyarn conceded. "However, should an Inquisitorial be convened, I will fully and impartially examine any evidence Captain Kade possesses and if I find it relevant, I will present it as part of *my* Summation."

Anything Siyarn presented would have overwhelming weight behind it, the weight of an Observer counseling the Galactic Forum.

"I'm totally happy with that!" I said. "We're prepared to give you everything we have, right now. I'll be right over!" I had nothing to give, but the Mataron didn't know that and this TC Observer was clearly hanging him out to dry.

The Mataron Commander murmured something that didn't translate. It sounded almost like a growl, then he said, "I remember you, human."

I shrugged. "You snakeheads all look alike to me."

"I should have killed you on Icetop."

So, it was that Mataron, the one Jase had winged in Sarat's penthouse.

"How's the shoulder? A bit stiff?" I summoned the DNA profile my sniffer had made of the drop of blood I'd found on the ledge outside Sarat's penthouse and DNA locked it for future reference. If this Mataron ever came near me, I'd know it was him.

He fixed his gaze upon me, speaking in a low voice. "I am Hazrik a'Gitor and you human, slew my brothers-in-arms this day."

"You're Hazrik a'Gitor?" He was the Exalted Blademaster the synthetic intelligence had been modeled on. I knew him almost as well as I knew myself. I had his memories, knew his training, could see his family. "You shouldn't spread yourself around so much, people will talk."

The Mataron ignored me. His hand settled on the hilt of his Q-blade. Even though his voice was synthesized, his words were rhythmic and ritualistic. "A blood-debt now stands between us, a debt that only death will resolve. Yours or mine! So let it be known!"

I'd had death threats before, but never from a Mataron Exalted Blademaster. I wondered how he could possibly realize his threat, but if I understood what he was telling me, one day, one of us was going to die.

I held up the Q-blade I'd souvenired off the Mataron Honored Assassin I'd killed on the *Soberano's* bridge. "Does that mean I get to keep this?"

"I gave that sacred weapon to the one you killed. One day, I shall take it back."

"But I have it now and you'll have to explain that to . . . *Akti*."

"What?" Even through his synthesized voice and alien demeanor, his surprise was unmistakable.

"Akti a'Gitor. Your daughter . . . his widow."

"How do you know this?"

"I know all about you Hazrik a'Gitor, Exalted Blademaster of the Black Sauria." I tapped my head. "It's all in here and you put it there."

The reptilian commander fell silent, wondering what I was talking about, then he spoke to Siyarn. "The Mataron Supremacy we will not press its claim!"

The image of Hazrik a'Gitor vanished from the screen, replaced by our own optical feed of the damaged Mataron cruiser. It made a quarter turn, then bubbled and streaked away.

I turned to Siyarn. "You figured it out."

"I have my suspicions."

"You said you had evidence."

"I gave the Matarons a choice and let their conscience decide. The most persuasive evidence was their decision not to press for an Inquisitorial."

"You bluffed them!" The Tau Cetins had us all convinced their technology was so superior we could hide nothing from them, but in reality they were running a giant confidence trick!

"My people are among the most ancient and revered in the galaxy," Siyarn said. "We do not bluff!"

"Remind me never to play poker with you guys."

Siyarn made a gesture, a quick tilt of the head, then said, "We did not get to where we are, because we are stupid."

"I can see that." The TCs might be the most advanced civilization in the Orion Arm, but they had a hidden streak of larceny in their DNA.

"We will remember what you did here today, Captain Kade. It stands well for your people, and their aspirations."

"Thanks."

"Remember," Siyarn said, "we are always watching."

The image of the TC Observer was replaced by a view of the sleek, Arbiter class super battleship. Without any indication it was preparing to move, it simply vanished.

"We kicked their lizard asses," Jase said defiantly, then gave me a sideways look. "Matarons have asses don't they?"

"They must," I chuckled, "because we just kicked them!"

"Did you have to show him the knife?" Marie said. "It's bad enough he swore to kill you, but did you have to make him mad?"

I thought about it a moment and nodded. "Yeah, I really did."

Laughter filled the flight deck, then I stared at the

view screen, realizing we were now the only ship left in the Vintari System. We floated above an arid little world that now had only one moon. The glow in its sky was beginning to fade as the debris burning up in its atmosphere thinned. On the surface, several hundred million bronze age primitives stared in wonder at a phenomenon they didn't understand and would never see again, unaware how close their world had come to ending.

Perhaps in ten thousand years, we'd tell them what really happened.

Chapter Seven : Hevelius Base

Dwarf Planet
Argolis System
Outer Cygnus Region
0.677 Earth Normal Gravity
982 light years from Sol
6,200 Crew + transients

It took several weeks to nurse the Lining to Hevelius Base, named for the seventeenth century creator of the Vulpecula Constellation. Hades City had better facilities, but was much further away and Izin was so obsessed with the hole in our side, he barely slept. Hevelius was a free base, a joint venture initially established by a group of agricultural companies specializing in pressurized greenhouse farming. Their bioengineered produce flourished in the dwarf planet's low gravity and the red giant's starlight, turning the otherwise desolate planet into a regional food production center. The docking space was limited and the hull repair costs inflated, but with Izin watching every move the repair bots made, we'd be able to bubble at full power long enough to get to Hades City for a proper overhaul.

Hevelius was partially built into a mountain, honeycombed with rough hewn tunnels filled with aging machinery and vast produce storage facilities. Its supply of bars and brothels was sparse compared to mining bases, but there were enough to lure Jase off the ship soon after berthing. By day, Marie would sneak off in search of trade contacts among the farmers, always refusing to give me any hint as to what deals she'd struck, while by night we made the most of our time together, knowing she'd soon be back aboard the *Heureux*. Neither of us were in a hurry for the repair work to be completed, although Izin badgered the maintenance engineers constantly as if we had somewhere else to be.

When the repairs were well advanced, the ENS *Nassau* appeared over Hevelius. She didn't dock, preferring to float above the dwarf planet's wispy atmosphere tinted red by the distant star, and shuttle her crew down to the base for rest and recreation. According to the locals, no Earth Navy ship had visited Hevelius Base in fifteen years, so I knew they weren't here just for R&R. I assumed Earth Intelligence Service agents had reported our arrival as a matter of routine, unaware how eager the regional EIS Commander was to meet with me.

Within hours of the *Nassau's* crew coming ashore, a cryptic invitation arrived for my eyes only. I waited until Marie was out drumming up business and Jake was chasing tail with a drink in each hand, then packed one of my *Soberano* souvenirs in a bag and headed for the base's excuse for a red light district. The handful of bars and houses of ill repute were full of navy sailors letting off steam, and occasionally exchanging punches with contract farmers who objected to the competition for female attention.

It didn't take long before my threading warned I was being followed. I stopped and locked eyes on my shadow, who showed no surprise that I'd spotted him so fast. He simply nodded for me to follow him. Since I'd wiped my contact list, I couldn't validate him, but he moved like an EIS field agent; unhurried, smiling to the hookers, occasionally chatting with the stim dealers as if he belonged. Perhaps he'd been the one who'd reported my arrival, as a grubby little outpost like Hevelius didn't rate more than a couple of EIS residents.

My guide led me through several dark and dusty tunnels to a shadowy saloon called the Free Fall Bar. It was modeled on a twenty sixth century dream-den, with stim vending machines through the center of the saloon and scantily clad, perfectly sculpted body-jobs serving drinks. Sitting alone and in pairs was an uninspiring selection of working girls wearing just enough to leave nothing to the imagination. Clearly, they'd ended up on Hevelius as the last stop before unemployment.

The far wall was a floor to ceiling pressure window looking out towards distant, jagged mountains, while floating ten clicks away above the misty surface was the gray hulled ENS *Nassau.* Sitting alone beside the window was a striking black woman smoking a long fume-stick that would have made Sarat envious. Her overcoat was thrown back over the chair, revealing long stockinged legs, crossed provocatively. Her pose was relaxed, as if she belonged, but her looks and bearing put her well above the competition. An intoxicated agritech approached her and asked how much. She smiled, told him she was on a break and to ask again later. He leaned forward drunkenly, with rising anger.

"Ain't I good 'nough for ya?" he shouted at her. "I got money, lots of money!"

She didn't say a word. Her eyes focused on him as if she was drilling into his soul, then he staggered back, shocked. He turned and hurried away, glancing back once with a frightened look on his face.

My guide stepped back into the shadows as I approached the table and took the spare seat opposite the woman. Before I could speak, a waitress approached. I swiped her reader with fifty credits and told her not to come back.

“Moonlighting?” I asked.

“No,” Lena Voss replied, “but I may have chosen the wrong career. He’s the sixth potential customer I’ve refused since I got here.”

“At least you’re popular, although that breaker trick you pulled on the drunk is bad for business.”

“I told you, I’m no breaker.”

“I’d believe you, except you’re the only person here not armed, and the only one I’m afraid of.”

She smiled, pleased she intimidated me, then femininely tapped the fume-stick on an ash tray. “Is it over?”

“For now.”

She nodded slowly. “My people went over Sarat’s penthouse on Icetop. There was no trace of the Matarons.”

“They used our weapons.”

She nodded, having already been briefed by her forensic team. “Did you get the merchandise?”

“I had it. It’s either destroyed or the Matarons got it back, or maybe the TCs confiscated it for evidence.”

“What made it so valuable?”

“Complete astrographics of every galaxy in the Local Group.”

She looked surprised. “Hmm, perfect bait for us.”

“I linked with it.”

“Really?” She said, intrigued. “How much did you get?”

“As much as I could store.”

She looked up, hanging on my words.

“I got everything out to six thousand light years.” It was sitting in my bionetic memory, packed so tight I couldn’t even store a vault-key number. “Billions of star systems, planets, resources, civilizations and every gram of energized dark matter out there. Five percent of the entire galaxy!” Mapped Space just got a whole lot bigger.

She smiled. "And the Matarons don't know?"

"No one knows. Not even the TCs."

"How did you manage it?"

"It wasn't me. The Codex saw what I could store, found Earth was my homeworld and used that as the reference point. I didn't even know what it was doing until later. I was kind of busy at the time."

"Technically, it's not a violation of the Access Treaty," she said thoughtfully. "Any unclaimed novarium deposits?"

It was the one thing we lacked, our own source of the mineral that powered starship energy plants. No matter how far we'd come, we were still dependant on the TCs' generosity and trade with other civilizations. They helped us because keeping us in the game promoted stability for the existing interstellar order, one in which they were a leading player. Not to help us would force us to compete with them and even though we could never catch them, they wanted collaborators and partners, not competitors. So they made sure we never ran short of novarium, but we never forgot we were living on handouts. It was the problem with being last to a very old game – the main players already had all the chips. Almost.

"There's a rogue planetoid adrift in deep space. It's not part of any star system."

Her eyes widened with interest. "How far out?"

"Twenty seven hundred light years from Sol. Four thousand six hundred metric tons of the stuff."

"Tons?" Her eyes widened in surprise.

We'd been trading a king's ransom for a few kilograms. It was enough to power every starship we could build for millennia to come. "The density is low. We'll have to do lots of digging, but that's what mining bots are for."

"And there are no prior claims? You're sure?"

"All we have to do is go plant a flag on it and it's all ours."

"They'd see us. They'd wonder how we got out so far."

The TC charts gave us safe navigation out to almost twelve hundred light years from Earth, much further than the Tau Cetins – or anyone else – thought we'd get with our technology in such a short time. It was a safe little sphere in which to contain the youngest, most energetic interstellar civilization in the galaxy, at least until we were off our training wheels.

"Send out a hundred probes," I said. "A thousand. Let most of them crash into dark matter or end up in dead end systems. So what if one gets lucky?"

"Do the TCs believe in luck?"

"I don't know what they believe in, but there are no laws against prospecting in unrestricted space, and if they realize we got something out of the Codex, they won't hold it against us."

"You don't know that."

"I don't think the TCs like the Matarons much."

"Why?"

"They stayed neutral during the Intruder War, when the Tau Cetin's own homeworld was attacked. Even people as enlightened as the TCs wouldn't forget something like that." I leaned forward. "And I swear, the Observer I met enjoyed making the Matarons back down. They won't take sides, they can't, but I think they'd be amused at seeing the Matarons discover they let us out. The TCs don't care what we do, providing we play by the rules. If we do that, we can do anything we damn well want."

Lena tapped her fume-stick over the ash tray thoughtfully. "You've done well, Sirius, better than we'd hoped for."

"So how do you want it?" I asked.

"Like this," she said, extending her fingers sensually towards me as if this was the first step in me hiring her services. Soon, she turned her palm upwards, inviting my touch.

I took her hand, wondering how I would explain holding hands with Lena to Marie, if she saw us. There was a tingling sensation in my palm, then our two biological networks connected and perfect, detailed mappings of five percent of the galaxy flowed from me to her. I didn't know if she'd wiped everything she had or if her capacity was greater than mine, but it took almost a minute to complete the transfer. We pretended to look into each other's eyes, implying the offer and acceptance of sexual favors to come – although I suspected Lena was probing me. When the data transfer was complete, Lena held my hand a moment longer. Before I knew what had happened, everything the Codex had given me was gone.

"You didn't have to wipe it."

"I'm sorry, Sirius, but I can't let you keep any of it." She'd done it to protect our newest and most precious secret. I couldn't blame her, although as a trader, the charts would have been useful. She released my hand and sat back with a satisfied look, as if we'd agreed a price and time.

"What will you do with it?" I asked.

"Hide it. We won't send it to Earth, that would be too visible, too many eyes watching us there. We'll find a remote system, pretend to study amoeba or rock slime while we find out what is most useful for us. And we'll only ever store it bionetically, never in hard technology. Very few people will ever know we have it, just in case the TCs or the Matarons or someone else decides we're not entitled to it. We'll use your probe idea, only we'll launch millions of them, and every year Earth Navy Survey will issue an update, pushing the boundaries of Mapped Space out a little further."

"The Matarons will have a fit! It took other civilizations hundreds of thousands of years to do that mapping."

"I know. And thanks to you, Sirius, we got it all in just a few minutes." She looked thoughtful, adding,

"And now we know about their synthetic agents as well."

"They knew I was EIS. That means they're on Earth – inside the EIS!"

Lena nodded. "Yes. They must have infiltrated every secure system we have. It explains a lot."

"You'll have to wipe them all down to raw metal, rebuild everything from the ground up."

She gave me a deliciously scheming look. "That's the one thing we won't do. Now that we know what to look for, we'll find them and we'll let them stay – and we'll tell the Matarons exactly what we want them to know. We'll use their own technology against them, do to them what they've been doing to us for a very long time. That knowledge alone is worth more to our security than everything you took from the Antaran Codex." Her eyes narrowed as she focused on me. "What about the quantum blade? Can we have it?"

I hadn't mentioned the Mataron weapon in my report. "You took my memories as well, while we held hands?"

"You have no secrets from me, Sirius." She put the fume-stick to her lips, then slowly exhaled gray smoke. "We could study that blade. Its technology is–"

"Yeah I know, seven hundred thousand years ahead of ours," I said cutting her off. "Which means even if you could reverse engineer it – which I doubt – you couldn't make another."

"True," she said wistfully.

"I'm keeping it. Considering the Black Sauria have sworn to kill me, I may need it."

"A lot of people have sworn to kill you, Sirius. I'm sure the Matarons will find out just how difficult that is to achieve."

"My chances will be a whole lot better if I had ammo that could punch through their skin shields."

"We're working on it. If we come up with something, you'll be the first to know." She took another draw on her fume-stick. "What about the neutron rifle? I really should make you hand it over. It'll get you life in prison and your ship confiscated, if you're caught with it."

"I know, but Izin really likes it. It would break his heart if I took it away from him." I put the souvenir bag on the table in front of her. "You can have this instead. One used Mataron plasma rifle. The owner doesn't need it any more on account of his being . . . dead and all." We could never copy such an advanced weapon, but understanding what damage it did might help develop a defense against it.

"I love it when you bring me gifts, Sirius." She pulled the bag towards her, opened it just enough to see inside, then with an approving look, placed it below the table out of sight – deal made. She smiled, slowly shaking her head in disbelief. "A tamph with a neutron rifle! Now that really would scare some people, but he did well. Very well . . . Maybe it's time we brought a few tamphs into the Service. I could create a special department for them, dedicated to reverse engineering whatever the Matarons are using against us."

"Good luck with that," I said, knowing the opposition she'd face on Earth.

"Bringing the tamphs in will scare a lot of people, but we need them and they're ready to play a part. Izin proved that." She gave me a knowing look. "And anyone who really opposes it . . ." she shrugged helplessly.

"Will be subverted by you or others like you?"

"For the greater good, Sirius. I'll call it . . . Team Izin."

"He'd like that, not that he'll ever know."

"Only the males though," Lena added. "No females. Even I don't trust them."

"I trust Izin, but he's the only one. You'll find the males are honorable. If they give you their word and you keep the females away from them, you could work with them. Earth is their home too, don't forget that."

She nodded slowly. "So how much do you want? This was a contract and you have a crew to pay. Shall we say 5 million credits?"

My eyes bulged. "I could buy a new ship for that!"

"You've earned it."

"It's too much. I couldn't explain it to my crew. Izin's already suspicious."

"They don't need to know. Think of it as your personal retirement fund."

I gave her a bemused look, realizing that even though she was a prober, she really didn't understand me at all. "The repairs will cost thirty five thousand. Add shares for Jase and Izin, and Marie's cut . . . " I did a few quick sums. "Make it a hundred thousand. Small profit for everyone. Not too conspicuous. I'll tell them Jie Kang Li always pays his debts and I would have got a lot more if I'd delivered the Codex."

"It's believable."

"I also want you to put the survivalist community on Deadwood back into the navy's astrographics catalogue."

"That's a little sentimental, Sirius, even for you."

"It's the deal I made. They help us save mankind's right to the stars, we save their planet from the Consortium. It's a small price to pay."

"OK, the navy will make sure they have prior claim."

"And I want a thousand SN6 sniper rifles, a hundred thousand rounds of smart ammo – various types – and fifty orbital cannons."

She gave me a wide-eyed look. "Are you serious?"

"This mission would have failed without Klasson. We owe him. You owe him. Or you could give me the five million and I'll buy them on the black market, but I'd rather not have the navy catch me smuggling weapons. I want it legal. Consider it a fitting punishment for the Consortium consorting with the enemy."

"Unknowingly consorting," she corrected.

“Come to think of it, I really don’t like the Consortium. I want an orbital gunship as well. Klasson wrecked the piece of junk he was flying saving my ass. It’s the least I can do.”

Lena grinned. “Any particular model?”

“No, just something with a big gun, a comfortable acceleration couch and a case of genuine Earth-distilled Kentucky bourbon, for the pilot.” When she gave me a puzzled look, I shrugged. “What can I say? I like Klasson.” He probably couldn’t stop the Consortium from terraforming Deadwood, but a little leverage might let him save his corner of it. I leaned towards her. “I gave him my word. You’re not going to make me break my word are you?”

She sighed. “OK, I have no love of the Consortium either. You can pick up your weapons from Armin’s in thirty days and the navy will look the other way, although, you might have to wait a few years for the bourbon.”

“It’s always a pleasure doing business with you, Lena.”

She gazed at me, seemingly perplexed, or maybe she was doing her spooky prober thing on me again. Eventually, she said, “If you really don’t care about money, Sirius, why did you leave the service?”

“I like the freedom, and my brother’s out there somewhere.”

“Forget about him, Sirius. You know what he’s become.”

“People can change. Sometimes, all they need is the right encouragement.”

“What about Marie? She almost cost you your life on the *Soberano*. You shouldn’t have dropped your weapon to save her, you know that. You should have killed the Mataron with the Q-blade, while his gun was pointed at her head. That was the smart option.”

And Marie would certainly be dead. Fortunately, I’m not that smart. “That’s another reason why I left the

Service. I don't make decisions like that."

"Marie Dulon is your blind spot, Sirius. While she's around, you will make mistakes."

"Yeah, but what mistakes!"

"She'll get you killed one day."

"Maybe, but not today." I offered Lena my hand. "I guess it's time you switched me off." The mission was over and my threading was still active.

Lena looked at my hand thoughtfully, then slowly shook her head. "You may not realize it, Sirius, but you're the best agent we have out here. I told you on the *Nassau*, we consider you a freelance asset. Judging by what's happened, we were right. You keep doing whatever it is you do and when we need you again, we'll be in touch. And if you find something that needs doing, you take care of it."

"I don't even know how to contact you." Since my threading's emergency purge on Icetop, I'd lost the keys to the kingdom: all the authentications and recognition codes were gone.

"Don't worry," she said. "All it takes is a handshake to bring you back up to speed."

"Goodbye, Lena," I said standing, certain she was never going to let me go, but now that it was on my terms, it might be a good deal for both of us.

Perhaps I'd always been a freelance asset without ever realizing it. For now, I had another week with Marie before the *Lining* was repaired. A week with no cares, no Mataron's, no responsibilities, just one headstrong, tantalizing woman to keep the nights long and the days stimulating.

It would be a week to remember.

Visit the author's webpage at:

www.StephenRenneberg.com

If you enjoyed this book, please post a recommendation and rating on the site where you purchased your copy.

The Mothership
by
Stephen Renneberg

A blockbuster science fiction thriller
– Kirkus Reviews

A massive alien ship crashes into one of the most remote places on Earth – cutting all contact with the region.

Within hours, Major Robert Beckman and his specially equipped Contact Team are hurriedly dispatched from Area 51 to investigate. Is it a forced landing, or the beginning of an invasion - a technological treasure trove, or an extraterrestrial Pandora's box that spells disaster for life on Earth?

Infiltrating the vast tropical wilderness of northern Australia, Beckman's team encounter strange machines, alien structures and a handful of human survivors struggling to evade capture.

When Beckman's team penetrates to the heart of the Mothership, they discover an answer they never expected and a universe far larger than they had ever imagined.

ISBN: 978-0-9874347-3-9

The Mothersea
by
Stephen Renneberg

Everything a great sci-fi novel should be: visionary, immersive, and thematically profound.
– Kirkus Reviews

Ten years after *The Mothership* crashed on Earth, an alien probe from 65,000 light years away splashes down in the Pacific, seeking to solve a cosmic riddle.

A trawler inexplicably vanishes at sea and a body washes up on a deserted beach with a single extra-terrestrial clue that reaches all the way to Area 51.

Colonel Beckman and two of his team are dispatched to unravel the mystery. They board an oceanographic vessel which carries them to one of the most remote places on Earth, where an elusive alien presence is preparing to challenge the dominance of the human race.

It is there, in the baking tropical heat of *The Mothersea*, they learn a terrible truth – that one world cannot have two masters.

ISBN: 978-0-9941840-3-0

In Earth's Service
by
Stephen Renneberg

Utterly Satisfying. A sci-fi novel that offers a relentlessly paced, action-packed, and undeniably epic in scope adventure.
– *Kirkus Reviews*

An alien colony world, a routine deep cover mission gone wrong, a chance encounter with a mercenary hit squad and the murder of an Earth Intelligence Service agent combine to launch Sirius Kade on a desperate mission to the distant reaches of Mapped Space.

He finds himself embroiled in a complex web of alien technologies, pirates, gun running and stellar intrigue, where ancient galactic enemies and new ambitions vie for supremacy.

While Sirius seeks to unravel a conspiracy threatening to shatter Human Civilization, he discovers Mankind may soon find itself caught in a gathering whirlwind building far beyond the limits of Mapped Space.

As an interstellar minnow among galactic giants, it is a cosmic storm humanity – the youngest space faring civilization in the galaxy – may struggle to survive.

ISBN: 978-0-9941840-0-9

The Riven Stars
by
Stephen Renneberg

**Blistering action. Arresting characters.
A densely plotted epic.
Renneberg aptly portrays strikingly different worlds ... (in) an exhilarating espionage tale involving the threat of galactic war.**
– *Kirkus Reviews*

Earth Intelligence Service agent Sirius Kade is sent to intercept a mysterious visitor to the Orion Arm from the remote Cygnus Rim. He must discover why an alien race humanity has never before encountered conspires against Earth and its far flung colonies.

While civil war ravages mankind, Sirius discovers old and new enemies entwined in a sinister scheme of cosmic proportions. His mission takes him to barbaric human and oppressive alien worlds before a final reckoning in the ancient halls of galactic power.

Deceived and betrayed, Sirius is forced to choose between love and duty as the fate of galactic civilization is decided.

ISBN: 978-0-9941840-5-4

The Siren Project
by
Stephen Renneberg

A fast-paced political thriller that is a page-turner from beginning to end ... a strong five out of five stars."
– *Manhattan Book Review*

When a top secret 'black' project turns rogue, a shadowy organization entraps disgraced former Secret Service Agent John Mitchell into tracking down the missing scientist behind the project. What he uncovers is an insidious conspiracy reaching to the highest levels of the military and the government. The discovery makes him the most hunted man on earth, pursued by a ruthless enemy armed with a sinister new technology.

Aided by a woman with extraordinary abilities, and an enigmatic defector from deep within the conspiracy itself, Mitchell challenges the greatest technological undertaking since the creation of the atomic bomb. To his horror, he finds that rather than destroy entire cities, the monolithic Siren Project threatens to destroy the free will of Mankind itself.

ISBN: 978-0-9874347-2-2

The Kremlin Phoenix
by
Stephen Renneberg

Renneberg delivers a typically exciting thriller, with plenty of sharp turns, heavy weapons and touches of science fiction
– *Kirkus Reviews*

Craig Balard, a young New York lawyer, is caught in a conspiracy threatening to trigger the fall of the West and the rise of a new totalitarian world order.

Hunted by a ruthless assassin, Craig encounters a mysterious woman who knows his every step *before* he makes it, and who intervenes to keep him alive for her own purposes.

He soon discovers she represents the survivors of a cataclysmic 23rd century war seeking to use him to change their past and save mankind's future.

Under her guidance, Craig becomes the fulcrum of time, where his every move triggers changes in the timeline that will either save humanity or guarantee its extinction.

ISBN: 978-0-9874347-7-7

78239278R00190

Made in the USA
Middletown, DE
30 June 2018